Frank 'n' Stan's Bucket List #4

Bride of Frank 'n' Stan

J C Williams

Copyright © 2019 J C Williams

All rights reserved. No part of this book may be reproduced in any manner without written permission except in the case of brief quotations included in critical articles and reviews. For information, please contact the author.

All characters appearing in this work are fictitious. Any resemblance to real persons, living or dead, is purely coincidental.

ISBN: 9781707846474

First printing December 2019

Cover artwork by Paul Nugent

Proofreading, editing, and interior formatting & design provided by Dave Scott and Cupboardy Wordsmithing

Chapter
ONE

A mop-haired young man with questionable hygiene hovered, poised and ready to strike, like a king cobra. His aquamarine-coloured velvet suit with generous lapels could well have been stolen from his grandad's wardrobe or possibly from a corpse. Spotting a potential victim approaching, he moved forward a pace, eager to engage, but unfortunately the musty smell of his attire arrived before him, causing the mature lady that was his target to smile politely before she stepped around him, giving him a wide berth. He lowered his head, returning to his hole, so to speak, like a homesick mole now, as opposed to a striking serpent. Back at his starting point, he brushed the fabric on his trousers before flicking back his greasy black fringe, resetting, as it were, to lie in wait for his next mark. Sadly, however, those people making their way towards him — and then sailing right on past — were most adept at finding something of interest to stare at in the opposite direction, or finding something to rummage for in their pockets which absolutely couldn't wait a single moment longer, drawing their attention effectively away in either case.

Then, a new, more-promising quarry presented itself before him — a plump middle-aged woman with jam-jar glasses, smiling vacantly. She was clearly residing in some sort of happy place of her own devising, there in her own head, lost in thought. As such, and unlike the others, she was in no rush to move on past. She dawdled, as it should happen, appearing to be in no hurry at all, and lingering within easy striking distance. And the young fellow in the very old clothes, poised in cobra mode once again, and sensing the moment was ripe, seized the wireless microphone that was resting on top of the stool sat next to him, gathering the implement up in his hand and clicking the 'on' button, readying it for action.

"Hello, madam," he offered, revealing his yellow teeth with a half-grin.

Before the unsuspecting woman had chance to employ any evasive manoeuvres like so many of those prior, the young gentleman then produced a red rose that appeared to have been watered more with vinegar than with actual water, placing it into her somewhat less than receptive hand. Then, the hapless woman's attention having thus been captured, he leaned over, pressing buttons on an oversized stereo on the table beside him, maintaining eye contact with his victim as he did so. "I'm Dwayne Lovestruck," he said, deepening his voice for effect.

The woman glanced over her shoulder uneasily — perhaps for assistance — but, alas, she was in the thick of it now and it was too late for her to break free.

Young Mr Lovestruck missed his intro as the stereo kicked into play, stuttering to catch up with the instrumental accompaniment now playing. "I-I–" he began to sing, catching the attention of further passers-by, curious as to the source of the sudden racket. "I... I..." he continued, getting into the rhythm. He gripped his microphone like it was an ice cream cone, though half-closing his eyes in an attempt to appear soulful and moody.

Eventually, the impassioned entertainer caught up with the beat of the music. "I just called to say, I love you. I just called to say how much I care, I do," he crooned, but with his youthful voice undulating on the *do*, and resulting in something sounding rather more like a yodel than the intended soulful quaver. Undeterred, Dwayne moved in close — yes, *too* close, as far as the woman was concerned, thank-you-very-much — grinding up and down. He was in danger of dry humping the poor lady, so intimate were his thrusting gyrations to her person, and with this serving only to produce a bit of sick up into her mouth by the looks of things.

CHAPTER ONE

Dwayne butchered the beloved Stevie Wonder classic with his own painful rendition of several of the verses. He was just about to launch into yet another verse when he opened his eyes back up, in order to see how much the recipient of his warbling was enjoying the sweet serenade...

But the woman was no longer stood where she'd been stood. Rather, she was, as it turned out, in the process of making good her escape. Dwayne quickly thrust a business card in her direction, but it was no use as, by this point, Dwayne could only see the back of her. She was making haste, her figure rapidly receding into the distance, and his business card was thus not received. It fluttered down through the air, falling to the floor like a dead autumn leaf.

Still, not allowing himself to be entirely dejected — after all, he'd almost snagged himself a customer — he cleared his throat, returned to his stool, and set about scouring the throngs for his next victim. It'd been a long morning, however, and the heat from the bodies in attendance was stifling — and even more so, perhaps, for someone dressed in a velvet suit. So Young Mr Lovestruck sat, perspiring, and struggling to raise a smile for the conveyor belt of people passing by.

"Do some magic!" petitioned, suddenly, a wet-nosed kid, the underside of the child's nostrils impressively slick with snot. It was a new, unexpected arrival, and one Dwayne hadn't noticed at first, as he'd been scanning the crowd at a somewhat higher elevation relative to the boy's low-lying head. The boy's mum now joined her son as well, with both stood before Dwayne and patiently waiting for the magic show to begin.

Dwayne — with the sweat of his underarms fortunately hidden by his velvet coat — shook his head from side to side. "I don't do magic," he replied, holding out his arms. "Look. Nothing up my sleeves," he said.

But it was an unfortunate choice of words. "Nothing up my sleeves" had been meant to show onlookers that there was nothing hidden there, no magic-related props lying in wait. But it was also precisely the sort of thing a magician might very well say at the start of a performance. And so the crowd watched on expectantly

— as did the young boy with the leaky nose — waiting for the magic to begin...

Though none did.

The boy tugged on his mother's hand impatiently. "Make him do some magic, Mummy!" he said, with an impertinent stamp of the foot to punctuate his demand.

Dwayne shuffled in place, shifting his weight from one foot to the other uneasily, as additional people stopped and waited for whatever performance that was about to begin to indeed begin. The singing had certainly been rubbish, was the general consensus of the onlookers, but a magic show was something else again. The promise of a rabbit appearing from a hat, or perhaps something even more remarkable, was a welcome change of pace.

"Look, I don't do magic," Dwayne reiterated — although, taking into consideration the speed at which the crowd had favourably evolved, he almost regretted that this was not the case, as magic seemed at present a preferable option for him.

"Why are you wearing that dumb suit, then?" asked the boy.

The boy's mother — apparently well-versed by now in heeding the whimsical demands of her brat — scowled at Dwayne. "It's not the done thing to get the boy's hopes up with the promise of a magic show, only to disappoint in the end," she added, and then shaking her head and tut-tutting in disapproval.

This was followed by similarly disillusioned expressions of displeasure from the crowd. A *"tsk-tsk"* could be heard, as well as a *"shame on you,"* and a *"worst magic show ever,"* and the like.

With no magic show to be had — save for the disappearing act of any potential customers — Dwayne watched on as the crowd dissipated and the woman dragged junior onwards with promises of cake or something similarly sweet and sugary. "I'm a wedding singer!" he shouted out, jumping to attention with business cards at the ready. But the crowd had now evaporated — unlike the sweat patch that had formed, quite helpfully, on the back of his shirt. Had it been visible to Dwayne or to anyone else present, it would have been noted as appearing similar in shape, very curiously, to a map of Australia.

CHAPTER ONE

Dwayne Lovestruck (this was of course his stage name, with his actual name being a less impressive but perhaps more accurate Dwayne *Loveless*) could take a kick in the balls with the best of them. But as he saw the ill-mannered, magic-loving little lout turn round right then — to offer up a lovely gesture, just before the child disappeared from view — throwing up a middle finger, and coupled with a tongue extended as well, Dwayne was starting to question his career choices. All the other stalls were packed, so what he was doing wrong, he couldn't imagine. He considered packing up and pissing off, but the stall had cost him forty quid. Also, his mum wasn't due to pick him up until five. So, what that meant was, if he did decide to pack it in, all he'd have ended up doing was sitting *outside* looking miserable rather than sitting *inside* looking miserable.

"Ed Sheeran," Dwayne muttered, attempting to pull himself together. "Right. Bloody Ed Sheeran always gets 'em going, dunnit it, now?" he went on, fiddling with his stereo in order to queue up the appropriate music. "Come on, Dwayne... you've *got* this, lad," he told himself, rallying the troops, as it were, in a rousing statement of intent. He gripped his microphone once more, readying himself for action. He paced back and forth as he waited for the first notes to come out over the stereo's speakers, strutting around the allocated section of the auditorium that was his stall, though being careful not to encroach upon the confines of the overly-friendly male florist's assigned space beside his. Earlier, the fellow had commented admiringly on the snugness of Dwayne's trousers. This, in itself, was perfectly understandable, of course. After all, the effect of Dwayne Lovestruck's animal magnetism spanned the genders, such was its intensity. Still, Dwayne thought better of repeating his earlier mistake for fear of encouraging the poor man. Instead, spotting something that looked promising, he locked onto his next victim...

He pressed the microphone to his lips, teasing out a breathy, whispery-voiced tribute to Ed Sheeran once the music kicked in, offering a cheeky wink should there be any onlookers, which, he was certain there would be — after all, who wouldn't be completely mesmerised by his amazing rendition of Sheeran's "Shape of You"?

He sidled up towards the woman he was presently targeting, who stood with her back to his stand, arms crossed, and with her attention currently taken by the wedding tattooist peddling his services in the stall sat opposite to his own. Dwayne continued crooning, and to be fair a few people turned, which served to see his confidence growing and with his voice increasing in volume commensurately as it did so.

As he took up position behind her, and now he was closer, it was apparent that she was twice, possibly three times his size, and so far doing a wonderful job of ignoring him, though he was certain this would soon change — that is, he felt certain she wouldn't be ignoring him for very much longer, while her size, meanwhile, would of course likely remain the same.

Dwayne, now faced with a brief lull in the song between verses, took the opportunity to remove the microphone from about his lips, placing it tenderly on the oversized woman's shoulder, before tapping it several times in quick succession as he readied himself for the next verse. As he did this, he offered those few inquisitive onlookers a bob of the head and a crafty smile.

The woman unfurled her arms, and she turned, very slowly, like an oil tanker on the water. Or, perhaps, more like a garbage scow. In either case, the expression on her face was such that it caused Dwayne to falter, prompting him to slaughter a note, and then another still. Her lower lip dropped in contempt as she examined the man stood before her, the man foolish enough to touch her without invitation. The paper of her hand-rolled cigarette stuck fast to her lip, going along for the ride as her jaw lowered like a drawbridge as she contemplated what might shortly be issuing forth from it.

"The *fuck* you think you're doing?" she growled, once she'd settled upon a suitable response, and this while dusting her shoulder off where contact upon her person had been so unwisely made.

Dwayne — by virtue of those assembled at the event sensing trouble, perhaps, and gathering 'round to view the outcome of said trouble — now had the biggest crowd he'd managed to attract all day. But the cheeky smile he offered them did not appear to sit well with the generously-sized woman, once she'd caught sight of it,

CHAPTER ONE

and with it only adding to her displeasure. "I'm... *erm*... a wedding singer...?" spluttered Dwayne by way of explanation, and in hopes of defusing the situation.

"You won't be singing when I rip out your oesophagus and use it for a skipping rope!" the large woman replied, reaching into her handbag.

"She's got a knuckle duster!" shouted a panicked onlooker. It was unclear just yet what, exactly, the woman had in her bag, actually, but by the looks of her this was a fair enough guess. "Call security!"

This was a statement that Dwayne took as his invitation to get the right hell out of there. The woman, however, continued to rummage through her handbag, causing Dwayne to trip over the flared ends of his bell-bottomed trousers when he spun 'round on his heels to escape in panic, as he could only assume she was reaching for more weaponry with which to potentially assault him. "I only want to entertain!" he pleaded, before falling, face-first, onto the linoleum floor. "I'm an entertainer!" he explained desperately, his voice slightly muffled now, his face pressed to the floor as it was.

Taking advantage of Dwayne's prone position, the plus-sized woman placed her foot on the small of his back, effectively holding him in place, and affording her the opportunity to furiously rifle through her bag still further, in an effort to locate and procure whatever it was she was attempting to locate and procure. She was like a tramp foraging in a bin, with several items flowing over the sides of her handbag and dropping to the floor.

"It's a cosh!" declared the florist from the nearby stall, in reference to one of the items. This produced a gasp from the crowd. But then the florist screwed up his face, getting a better look at the item in question. "No, wait," he added. "I think... I think it's a dildo...?" he said, correcting himself, and with the mixture of fear and concern etched on his face changing to include a bit of tentative arousal as well.

At this point, a bronzed figure appeared, moving through the growing crowd at pace. Assuming him to be someone from security come forth to address the present kerfuffle, people parted like the Red Sea, allowing the man safe passage. Except this wasn't Moses, or, for that matter, security.

"Stella!" the fellow shouted, touching her on the shoulder, once he'd reached her, as Dwayne had made the mistake of doing. Stella tensed up, preparing herself for an attack. But, on seeing that it was just an exasperated Stan, she lowered her defences somewhat.

"We've got a dress fitting in fifteen minutes," Stan advised, taking her gently by the arm. "And we leave you alone for two bloody minutes, and all hell breaks loose!" he chided her in frustration, though at the same time grinning for the benefit of the concerned onlookers. "Don't worry, folks, everything's under control!" declared Stan reassuringly, even though it really wasn't, as, when it came to Stella, things were never entirely under control. With her arm in his, Stan attempted to direct Stella away and guide her along. But Stella was going nowhere fast. Like a donkey or a mule, Stella was not someone who could be moved when she didn't want to be moved, and cooperated only by means of and according to her own immutable and ineffable form of internal logic. "Stella, we need to get out of here," said Stan, showing his pearly whites to those still observing to offer an air of calm.

Stella swivelled her shoulders, cracking the vertebrae in her upper back, between her shoulder blades. "Happens to me. A lot," she offered, pointing a chubby finger from her free hand in the direction of Dwayne. She was no longer atop him. She had moved away, but only a short distance, and now she just stood there, pausing in reflection.

Stan gave a further tug on Stella's arm, but could see it was useless. Stella was going nowhere she didn't want to go. He sighed and reluctantly acquiesced, letting go the arm. "What does, Stella?" he asked, tapping his watch to impress upon her the urgency of the situation, even while knowing such a gesture was useless. He scanned the ceiling for cameras, worried that actual security might well show up at any minute.

"Men," replied Stella, with a sage-like, world-weary expression emerging from beneath the depths of her trowelled-on makeup. She grasped the rear gusset of her thin black leggings, pulling great swathes of the elastic material that had disappeared up the

CHAPTER ONE

crevice of her arse during the course of her struggle with the wedding singer. Her first attempt was not successful, resulting in further exploration and correction of her undergarments, this time plunging her hands down inside of her leggings for maximum purchase. She arched her neck, releasing a contented smile, as the fabric was returned to its intended resting place.

Stella hadn't broken eye contact with Stan throughout the process of sorting out her leggings, and brought matters to a close by pressing the palm of her extracted hand to her nose, taking in a lungful of air, and, content that it was relatively clean enough of contaminants, returned to the topic of conversation. "They do funny things around me," she said. "Like that scrawny muttonhead over there," she added, in reference to Dwayne, who was back to working the crowd — or attempting to, at least — in hopes of generating business. "Can't help themselves, I expect," she went on. "They see a voluptuous, desirable woman like me, and they just go and revert to their caveman urges. I kind of feel sorry for them, actually. Because, you know, come to think of it, if our positions were reversed, I imagine I'd do exactly the same." She shook her head sadly, gave her hand another quick sniff, and then, using the same hand, indicated for Stan to lead the way now that she'd said what she wanted to say and there was no longer any reason to hang about.

It would be fair to assert that Stella wasn't entirely embracing the role of the blushing bride-to-be. Indeed, Stan and Susie would be considered the driving force in the day's arrangements. Stan had a little business to attend to back home in Liverpool, where they now were, so it was the perfect opportunity to tie in a visit to the wedding fayre held there. Frank was not so eager, choosing to remain in the Isle of Man where he was currently embroiled in making plans for his own wedding — which largely consisted of smiling at every suggestion Jessie should offer up, and producing encouraging noises accordingly at appropriately-timed intervals. Meanwhile, Stan was in his element, however, being involved in the organisation of two weddings. And presently surrounded at the fair by the abject gaiety of all things celebratory in nature, he was quite enjoying himself and his role.

"Just there, you've got a dress fitting very shortly," said Stan, nodding in the direction of a particular pop-up shop a certain distance away. "And then..." he said, retrieving a notebook from his blazer pocket to review their itinerary. "And then..." he repeated, glancing back up from his notebook, but subsequently not finishing what he'd meant to say. He looked at Stella, and then took a step back to assess the state of her. He found himself staring at Stella's head, in particular, though trying not to be too obvious about it. Still, he saw fit to ask...

"Stella, have you, *ehm*... that is, have you thought about what you're going to do with your hair?" He smiled inanely as he said this, knowing he was venturing into dangerous, fisticuff-related, potentially tooth-disordering territory by daring to broach the subject. He stood there, right eye twitching— though, to be fair, that could simply have been as a result of a recent Botox injection he'd had.

"My hair?" asked Stella, with a shrug of her broad shoulders. "What about it? And for what?"

"For the wedding, of course," said Stan. And, with that, Stan made a viewfinder with his fingers, placing Stella directly in the middle, like a film director. "You're going to look beautiful, Stella!" he assured her.

Stan felt a paternal duty towards Stella, eager to have her looking radiant on her wedding day. It was a tricky thing to imagine right at present, though, what with her unflattering skin-tight leggings complemented by hobnail boots and a well-worn t-shirt with the inviting words *I DIDN'T FART, MY ARSE BLEW YOU A KISS* smartly emblazoned across the front of it. Still, Stan knew things such as these were easily fixed. Her hair, on the other hand, was a different matter entirely. Previous hairdressers had in fact described Stella's hair in polite terms as "problematic" — so much so that Stan had even once brought Stella to his own stylist who was particularly expensive, and with his stylist, in slightly less polite terms, then suggesting Stella's hair as being the resultant lovechild of an overused tennis ball and a wire dish-scouring pad.

"I dunno," said Stella, in answer to Stan's question, "Probably wear a baseball cap...?"

CHAPTER ONE

"Well, we can worry about your hair later," he said, catching sight of Susie, who was waiting for them over by the wedding dress pop-up shop.

Stan and Stella made their way over. "Apologies for the delay. Sorry to keep you waiting," Stan said to Susie once they were there. "It was her," he added, leaning in to whisper so that Stella couldn't hear, and in reference to the recently occurred commotion.

"Ah," said Susie, whispering back. "I suspected as much."

Susie led the charge in marvelling over the array of lace, satin, and silk on display. "They're absolutely lovely," remarked Susie. "Stella, aren't they lovely?" she asked. Stan's opinion was readily evident, and mirrored Susie's own, as he was drooling like a famished mongrel, but from Stella no response was immediately offered.

Stan took Stella's hand, patting the back of it tenderly. "Now don't you worry yourself about the cost of the dress, okay?" he told her. "Frank and I have got this covered."

"Can I help you?" asked a severe-looking woman with greying hair pulled back into a tight bun and secured with a pencil, like a stern headmistress. She crossed her arms, giving Stella a quick and dismissive once-over and frowning in disapproval.

Susie reached for an appointment card from her purse. "We're here for a dress fitting," she explained cheerily, and before she'd even snapped her purse shut, Susie had a tape measure thrust against her thigh. "Ooh," she giggled, moving back.

The dour woman advanced further, poised with the tape in her outstretched arms for another effort. "Stand still!" the woman commanded, clicking her heels together like a World War II prison camp commandant.

"No, no, it's not me who's getting married," explained Susie, stepping to one side to afford the woman a better view of Stella. But Stella was no longer there. Somehow, in the span of only a few moments, she'd managed to reposition herself over by a nearby fire exit, and was appearing, at present, somewhat disinterested. "Stella! Over here!" said Susie, waving Stella back over.

"*Her?*" the woman asked, disbelieving. "*She* is the one getting married?" she said, unwilling or unable to hide her contempt.

Susie wasn't one for aggression, but a few years working with Stella had certainly toughened her up. *"Yes,"* she said curtly, leaving the grim-faced woman with no doubt at all as to who indeed was getting married. "And we're here to buy her a *dress*," Susie went on. "And if I were you, I'd lose the attitude, as Stella is one of the most amazing women you should ever happen to meet."

"She certainly is... remarkable," the woman could only agree.

Once Stella had rejoined the group, she took up position on a comfortable suede chair, providing her a view of the many dresses on offer.

"Hi! My name is Libby, and can I offer you a glass of prosecco?" asked a bubbly assistant, who was, Susie and Stella were happy to see, the complete opposite in demeanour to the miserable cow from just prior.

"Hmm, don't mind if I do," replied Stella, reaching out and snatching up the proffered glass with very little hesitation.

"You must be so excited!" said the new girl, and it was clear her effervescent manner wasn't the least bit forced.

"For the free drink?" asked Stella, innocently.

"I adore your boots!" the assistant added, handing a glass off to Susie and Stan, as well, as she did so.

Stella wasn't often the recipient of a compliment, and eyed the girl suspiciously. But the girl was so genuine that Stella could tell quick enough that she was being sincere. So she just shrugged, drained the contents of her glass in one gulp, and said, "Thanks. I'll have another," and swooped her hand in for a second glass, plucking it up off the decorative tray the girl was holding before the assistant could even respond one way or the other. "Keep them coming," Stella assured the girl, "And we'll get along just fine."

And it wasn't long before Stella was both half-pissed and showing signs that she was actually enjoying the dress-shopping experience — even allowing her foot to tap along to the ABBA soundtrack emanating from the changing room area they were now in. Libby had lined up a group of shortlisted dresses on a rolling rack positioned outside the dressing room where Susie, ever patient and now also three sheets to the wind, was on standby to help Stella into each outfit should the need arise.

CHAPTER ONE

"I could murder a ciggy right about now," said Stella, now stood behind the dressing room curtain in nothing but a leopardskin-patterned thong.

Susie fanned through the selection of gowns, picking out the first outfit for Stella to try on. "We'll get you one as soon as we've tried these on, Stella," said Susie through the curtain, clutching the first dress to her own chest and twirling around like Cinderella or some other Disney princess. "These are simply beautiful," she gushed. "Stella, you're going to look so elegant. A proper lady," she said, easing the curtain open and handing the dress over.

Seeing Stella all but naked wasn't new for Susie, given Stella would strip off at a moment's notice and think nothing of it. In fact, she had often found Stella on the roof of the taxi service building during the summer months, topless, and enjoying the warming rays of the sun on her exposed body. It had been Susie's job to provide additional applications of sunscreen spread over areas of Stella's body she couldn't herself reach — that is, until the various complaints from the office block which overlooked them shut the whole sunbathing affair down.

Still, though Susie tried her best to avoid it, her eyes were drawn like magnets to Stella's bikini line, where the vision of overspilling hair there gave the impression that she was smuggling a collection of seaweed or kelp in her knickers. The overly lush growth didn't stop there, either, as her thighs had a generous application of hair to an extent that Susie could have leaned over and formed it into plaits, she was certain.

"You know, Stella," said Susie, stepping behind the curtain to join her friend and co-worker. "We should have a girlies weekend before the wedding," she suggested. "You know, spa, makeup, hair, and... *oh!* ..." she went on, playing off like she'd just been struck with a completely incidental afterthought... "We could get waxed as well, Stella! Legs and foo-foo!" she said.

But Stella wasn't really paying much attention to what Susie was saying, appearing more interested in when the next shipment of prosecco might arrive than listening to grooming tips.

"Well, I've, *ehm*, got a suit fitting..." said Stan, speaking to the fabric curtain of the dressing room. With both the women inside, there wasn't much for him to do except stand there like an idiot. So, without waiting for a response, he decided buggering off smartly and leaving the girls to it would be the best course of action. And he genuinely did have his own fitting to attend to, tasked with procuring suits for both himself and Frank. As Stan routinely gave such ardent attention to his appearance, and Frank therefore deferring in such matters to Stan's expertise, Frank had agreed to empower Stan to order outfits for the pair of them— though with one caveat, Stan being under strict instruction that nothing should be too ostentatious. Famous last words.

As for Susie and Stella, the first three of the selected dresses were slipped on and then swiftly rejected. They weren't revealing enough as far as Stella was concerned, with not enough of her boobs showing, she insisted. Stella had impressive cleavage and wasn't about to cover it up for anybody, and so who was Susie to argue? And, anyway, arguing with Stella would have been an exercise in futility even should Susie have been so inclined.

In a brief recess before trying on the next round of choices, Susie helped Stella by clearing away the sweat from her back, as one might wipe down a racehorse, or a boxer, after a particularly gruelling competition — though the sweat, in Stella's case, was more the result of an overly warm dressing room and too many proseccos rather than the result of any real physical exertion. Still, Susie attended to the task with cheery aplomb, whistling along to the tune of the current ABBA selection playing over the speakers, "Knowing Me, Knowing You," as she did so.

"Make sure you don't miss any spots," instructed Stella.

"What a year this is turning into. You and Lee getting married at the same time as Frank and Jessie! And you're going to look wonderful!" replied Susie, dreamily.

Stella raised up her right hand, indicating that the current perspiration mop-up exercise be placed on hold momentarily. There was something on her mind. "I need to ask you something, Susie. Something serious," said Stella.

"I'd love to!" replied Susie, excitedly giving her answer to Stella's question before it was even asked.

CHAPTER ONE

Stella turned, lifting one eyebrow. "What? What are you on about, exactly?" she said. "All I was going to ask is if you'd be a dear and pop out to the car to get my lighter."

Susie lowered her head, taking a rather sudden interest in her shoes, it would seem. "Oh. Right. Okay," she replied glumly. "It's just... well, it's just, I thought you were going to ask me... ask me to be your..." she said, but trailing off at the end, not wishing to embarrass herself further by saying out loud what she'd been thinking.

"I'm joking, you soppy sod!" cackled Stella, after a suitably long pause. Still topless, she took Susie's head and thrust it into her ample bosom. She rubbed the back of Susie's neck affectionately, kneading it like she was a wad of bread dough. "Susie, would you be my maid of honour?" she asked.

"I-I'd be honoured," Susie spluttered, which was impressive given the reduced flow of oxygen owing to her mouth presently being obstructed by quite a large amount of boob.

Stella gave a contented grin, releasing Susie from her wrestling hold and allowing Susie to breathe again. "It might be the wine talking," said Stella. "Or the lack of nicotine doing my head in. But you're my best friend, Susie," she said, in an exceptionally rare glimmer of emotion.

"Me too, Stella," replied Susie, picking up a tissue to wipe Stella's boob sweat from her face. "Me too."

The other, previously empty, dressing rooms were now occupied, and, unable to remember which was which, Stan was poking about in search of the one particular room that held his two travelling companions. He was like a game show contestant, eager to see what might be revealed behind each mystery curtain — though the occupants were not overly impressed by having Stan's head appearing around their fabric partition.

"Awfully sorry!" said Stan, playfully placing his hands over his eyes. "Don't worry, I'm gay!" he said to another lady, after copping

FRANK 'N' STAN'S BUCKET LIST #4 – BRIDE OF FRANK 'N' STAN

a serious eyeful. "Susie, where are you??" he shouted, for fear of having security called on him.

"Oh! You're back!" remarked Susie, poking her head out to reveal in which room, in fact, she and Stella were residing. "Hang on. I thought Frank said you weren't getting kilts...?"

"Well, not exactly," replied Stan. "He said nothing too ostentatious. But he's not here to decide what's ostentatious and what's not, now is he?" he told her, tapping the tip of Susie's nose playfully, seeing as how it was presenting itself to him. "Now. Where is the most beautiful bride that..." he began to say, but then the curtain was parted, revealing Stella in all her glory.

"Just there," said a smiling Susie.

"I think... I think I'm going to cry," said Stan, fanning his face theatrically.

"I thought your tear ducts didn't work on account of all the collagen treatments...?" Stella teased.

But Stan was too engrossed in admiring the vision of loveliness stood before him to bite. Libby & co had worked miracles on what had to be one of their more challenging projects, taking a big lump of clay and moulding it into something radiant. The ivory white fabric of the dress gave Stella a warm glow, and the shimmering pearls around the plunging neckline brought a warmth to her ordinarily impassive eyes.

"You can still see enough of my tits?" asked Stella, lowering her chin to get a look at herself.

"Your tits are simply magnificent, Stella! And they aren't laid hidden, no," Stan assured her. "So. How do you like my *own* dress?" he asked, giving a twirl of his kilt.

"Ostentatious?" Stella offered.

Stan laughed. "You might be right," he said. "Anyway. Your grandmother would be very proud of how you've turned out," he said, leaning in for a gentle kiss on her cheek. "I wish Frank was here to see you now because I know he'd be just as happy as I am."

"Whatever," said Stella, noncommittally. She wasn't about to go all soft on him. But a slight grin emanating from one side of her mouth betrayed her emotions, telling Stan that she did indeed appreciate the comment.

CHAPTER ONE

"Right. Well. Now that's sorted," said Stan, eyes still feasting, nevertheless, on the vision before him, "I might need your help in telling Frank something, Stella. He's a bit intimidated by you, so it might be more effective coming from you rather than from me."

"Oh?" asked Stella, narrowing her eyes. "What's this?"

Stan threw his thumb over his shoulder. "Well, you know that dopey-looking lad you had an altercation with earlier?" he asked. "The one in the velvet suit?" he added, as if Stella could well have had several altercations and require clarification as to which one he might be referring to. "Well, as I passed by, I saw him talking to security."

"And?" said Stella, not really arsed.

"They were on their way to review CCTV footage, as it turns out. Looks like charges were going to be pressed, Stella. I had to *do* something," said Stan, arms outstretched, palms raised.

"And...?" repeated Stella, slightly more arsed this time.

Stan flashed his expensive smile. "So. I'd like you, Stella, to tell Frank that I've managed to book him a wedding singer for his wedding. For *your* wedding," he added with a wink, in reference to the upcoming double wedding ceremony. "You can tell Frank that one Dwayne Lovestruck is all booked up and ready for a visit to the Isle of Man to perform at the wedding of the year."

"And there'll be no charges, then?" she asked, receiving a nod from Stan in confirmation, indicating that she understood the arrangement. Stella patted his arm. "Good work, Stanley. Don't worry about Frank. I'll sort it," she said. "Oh, and Stan?" she added.

"Yes?" he asked.

"Stop looking at my tits, you dirty old get," she told him. Though the truth of it was, she really didn't mind so much, as the more attention her tits got the better, as far as she was concerned.

Stan removed his eyeballs from the location of Stella's cleavage, as instructed. "You do look lovely, Stella," he said by way of explanation, adjusting his kilt's sporran nervously. Stan lowered his head for a moment, wiping a tear with the back of his hand.

"Are you thinking about how much this dress is costing you and Frank?" cackled Stella.

FRANK 'N' STAN'S BUCKET LIST #4 – BRIDE OF FRANK 'N' STAN

Stan's voice wobbled for a moment. "You look beautiful, Stella. I'm thinking about me and Frank walking you down the aisle, and you know what, you'll make two stupid old buggers the proudest men on earth. Your grandmother would be very proud to see you right now. You know that, don't you?"

"Oh, bugger off," replied Stella, with just the slightest hint of her hairy lip trembling.

"Oh, fiddlesticks," said Susie, attending to her own watering eyes. "Now you've got me going," she said. "Stella, you're going to be a beautiful bride and Lee is very lucky to have you in his life."

"Come on, you two," said Stan. "We'll finish up in here and I'll take you two lovely ladies for a bite of something, as well as a drink of something, the fizzier the better!"

Chapter
TWO

Dave cupped his hands together, blowing gently into them, capturing breath, then poking his nose in for a good sniff. He repeated the process, but the results were proving inconclusive. "Oi! Smell my breath, will you?" he asked, reaching out and pulling a reluctant Monty in close like they were ballroom dancing partners.

"Not a chance, mate!" said Monty, tilting his head back and away, and avoiding the area of Dave's mouth at all costs.

"Come on, Monty. I've done worse for you, yeah?" Dave wheedled. "Do I need to remind you about the time I extracted that Lego piece for you from where it'd somehow ended up, and not once did I question how it got up into that particular part of your anatomy in the first place? And it took days for me to get the smell off of my fingers!"

"I told you! I was hanging curtains in the nude, and I fell back on it!" Monty protested.

"Like the other time, with the potato?" asked a sceptical Dave.

"Exactly!" replied Monty.

"Well, regardless of how the Lego piece got there—" Dave started to say.

"It wasn't just a piece. It was a whole Imperial Stormtrooper I'd made," Monty quickly corrected him.

"It was in pieces by the time I took it out!" Dave told him.

"Hmm, fair point," Monty conceded. "Anyway—"

"ANYWAY," said Dave, cutting back in. "You asked me to sort it, Monty, and I did, didn't I? And you know why?" he asked, staring lovingly into Monty's roving eye. "Because you're my best friend, Monty. *That's* why," he declared, answering his own question.

"Oh, bloody come here, then!" replied Monty in defeat. Monty stopped struggling in Dave's grip and leaned in for what could almost have been a tender smooch. "Right, then. Breathe on me," he instructed. But what should have been a gentle breath was in fact delivered with the force of a sudden sea squall, blowing Monty's fringe back from the very strength of it.

"Well...?" enquired Dave

Monty wiped off two or three globules of spit that'd landed on his chin. "Have you been eating onions?" he asked in response, having assessed Dave's breath and come to a tentative conclusion.

"Dammit! I knew I shouldn't have eaten those several packets of Pickled Onion Monster Munch earlier," moaned Dave. "This is all your bloody fault, Monty!"

"Oh, so it's *my* fault you stole my crisps I was saving for later, is that it, Dave??" Monty chided his friend, casting an evil eye in Dave's direction. He was only able to cast the one evil eye, of course, as his eyes rarely worked in tandem. But it served to relay the message well enough.

"Well I have to blame *someone*, don't I?" Dave reasoned.

Monty couldn't argue with that kind of perfect logic. And, breath aside, Monty fussed over Dave like a proud father seeing his son out the door on prom night. Monty stepped back, running his eyes over Dave like an artist with a freshly painted canvas. "Here. We need to fix your collar," he said, fiddling with his friend's blazer.

Since Dave and Monty had started working full time at the TT Farm, the scent of used motor oil that was their normal eau de cologne was now enhanced with the smell of the farmyard — described by some as pungent, and by Frank as smelling like horse manure left in a solarium over the course of an especially hot day. But Dave scrubbed up not too badly for an ordinarily grease-covered oaf, and his brown shoes had been polished, and with the blue blazer over a crisp white shirt, he had a rare sophistication about him of sorts.

CHAPTER TWO

"I'd say you look presentable," offered Monty.

But Dave was now pacing around the kitchen at the TT Farm like he was awaiting results from the VD clinic. "Breathe, Dave," he was saying to himself, shaking his head to clear his senses, but his level of agitation wasn't decreasing when he couldn't find what he was looking for. "Where's those flowers I bought?" he asked, for some reason now pulling kitchen drawers open as if the flowers could have somehow made their way in there.

Monty smiled a reassuring smile. "Relax, Dave. I've got it all under control," he said. "I went and put them in water for you. See? Just there. In that vase," he explained, pointing out the kitchen window to a table outside.

"*Aww, nooo*," moaned Dave, staring desperately at the now-ruined bouquet. "That's not a vase, you pillock, it's an old chutney jar! And it's not water in it, it's turpentine! Did the paintbrush sat in there not give you a clue that it wasn't a vase with water in it?"

"Oh. I *wondered* what that paintbrush was doing in that flower vase," said Monty, mystery now solved. "It *did* seem rather odd to me, come to think of it."

Dave rushed outside, gathering up what remained of the flowers, freeing them from their poisonous bath. But it was useless, as they'd already gone on to the Great Beyond and were well past saving.

"They look like they've been exposed to nuclear fallout," said Dave glumly, coming back in the kitchen empty-handed. He wiped his solvent-covered hand on the upper sleeve of his jacket, without realising what he was doing.

"Hmm, I *wondered* why they'd gotten a little droopy," remarked Monty, this additional mystery now solved as well.

"Oh, bloody hell, look what I've gone and done!" wailed Dave in despair, noticing he'd violated his blazer jacket. "Now I smell of onions *and* turps!" he cried. "And she's going to be here any minute!" He drew his hand into a fist and shook it to the heavens. But, alas, there was no assistance forthcoming from that direction.

"You can gather up another bunch of flowers?" Monty suggested. "Or I can do it for you? There's loads of them in the meadow, I think?" he said. "No, wait, it's December, isn't it? So maybe not," he added, reconsidering. "Anyway, keep your pecker up, mate!" he told Dave, trying his best to raise his friend's flagging spirits.

Dave clenched his teeth, and possibly his buttocks, releasing a high-pitched whine that sounded like a motorbike slipping out of gear with the throttle held wide open. He fell into a chair at the kitchen table, and then proceeded to bang his forehead onto the tabletop repeatedly.

"It's fine. It'll be fine," Monty assured him, patting Dave's back encouragingly. "Just go out without the jacket, right? That's a very smart-looking shirt you've got on, yeah? You'll be fine, mate," he went on, providing additional pats to Dave's back for good measure.

Dave was all but sobbing. "*Nooo! I can't!*" he keened.

"What?" said Monty, not understanding Dave's meaning. "Have you forgotten how? Sometimes I forget how," he told Dave. "But it's dead easy. Here. All you've got to do is take one of your arms, right? And then, all you do is—"

"It's not that!" cried Dave, pulling off his blazer, and doing it without any trouble at all. "Look! See?" he said, pointing towards his back.

"How peculiar," remarked Monty. "Dave, you've got a triangular-shaped dark spot on the back of your shirt, right in the middle," he observed. "Dave, do you know you've got a triangular-shaped—?"

"Yes, I bloody *know* I've got a triangular-shaped dark spot on the back of my shirt, right there in the middle, Monty!" Dave told him, interrupting. "*That's* what I'm bloody on about!" he shouted, slamming his sledgehammer of a fist down onto the table.

"Here now, shouting's not going to help matters any, Dave," Monty admonished him. "I'm only trying to help, mate!"

Dave sighed. Steam having been expelled, he explained, more calmly now, "When I was ironing my shirt," he said, "I was trying to remember the last time I'd actually ironed something. Kind of daydreaming, I suppose. And the next thing you know, I've gone and burned my shirt so that it now looks like—"

"A triangular-shaped dark spot on the back," Monty finished for him, helpfully.

"Bastard!" Dave shouted, but then immediately looked guilty. "Sorry, Monty, I wasn't calling *you* a bastard. I meant bastard just in general. Because, my options, right now, are to go out with either the remnants of oil paint wiped all over my jacket sleeve... or a burnt-on ironing mark showing, and, one way or the other, it's looking pretty grim."

Monty paused, looking up and to the left, as one does when lost in thought — or at least one of his eyes looked that way. He nodded his head, bobbing it along as he motioned his finger in the air like he was working on some sort of intricate calculation, and moving pieces around on an imaginary abacus. "I've got it!" he exclaimed, finally, a broad smile spreading across his face in triumph.

"Yes?" asked Dave, a tide of relief washing over him, his troubles swept away in an instant. "Let's hear it, mate," he said, looking up expectantly, eager to hear whatever solution it was that Monty had come up with.

Monty didn't immediately speak. His lips moved silently, rehearsing the words he was about to say. He wanted to be sure he'd worked it all out correctly before revealing his thoughts, not wanting to let Dave down as this was important.

"*Yeeesss...?*" said Dave, impatiently.

"Right," said Monty, satisfied. "Right, it was when we turned up to the wrong christening. Remember?" he went on. "You said it was at the one church, and I said it was at the other, and we ended up at the wrong one," he concluded, looking very pleased with himself for such obvious cleverness in relaying this information.

"What the actual hell are you talking about, Monty? You're making not the least bit of sense," said an exasperated Dave.

"*Duh,*" replied Monty, tapping the side of his head to indicate that this was a thinking man's game. "The last time you *ironed something*," he informed Dave. "I clearly remember you ironing your jeans before we went to the wrong church."

"Fucksake, Monty. I thought you were going to tell me what to do about tonight and my current clothing predicament??" Dave related somewhat pointedly.

"Oh, that," replied Monty, shrugging his shoulders. "Ah. Well. No. No, I've got nothing on that, I'm afraid. Sorry, old chum. Why don't you just take one of Frank's t-shirts?" he said. "He's got a couple laying about in his office 'round here. They may or may not be clean, you never can tell. But you could always sniff the armpits to see if they're safe to wear, that's what I do when I nick one... *ehm*, I mean borrow one."

Dave didn't answer. He just sighed, allowing his head, on the deep exhale, to drop once again, hitting the kitchen tabletop with a resounding thump.

A cheerful, lively Italian maître d' worked the room like an artiste — effortlessly handling, in animated fashion, the topping-up of wine glasses, the dispensing of freshly grated Parmigiano-Reggiano upon demand, juggling armloads of plates to and from the kitchen like a circus act, and lingering occasionally with flattering words to charm and titillate adoring women drawn to both his golden olive skin and to a melodious accent that could snap knicker elastic from across a room.

"You wan-na I bring-a dessert-ta menu?" he asked, stopping at Dave and Becks' table, and speaking in the drawn-out, more-syllables-than-necessary way that he did. "A beautiful la-a-dy," he observed, in his typical sing-song lilt of a voice. "Deserves to be-ya hyp-o-no-tised by a my-ya tiramisu!" he said. "It's-sa... *bellissimo!*" he added, punctuating this proclamation with a loud smacking of the lips against the tips of his fingers for extra added effect. This performance was enough to elicit a murmur of tittles and giggles from the various women occupying nearby tables, their attention on the spirited maître d' still rapt.

Dave grinned a pained grin. He was immune to the charms of Giuseppe, having watched the fellow's act throughout the course of the evening, as well as during two previous occasions where he'd brought Monty along to the same restaurant when they'd been in the mood for some good Italian. Firstly, Dave — through no fault of his own — liked women well enough, and so Giuseppe's vocal stylings had little effect upon him, and did not especially tickle his fancy. Secondly, the way Giuseppe spoke was so exaggerated and over-the-top that Dave found it difficult to believe it was genuine. He suspected that 'Giuseppe' was more likely Italian in ancestry

CHAPTER TWO

only — given his olive skin — but actually a Brummie called Warren, or what have you, and using the Italian lingo and affectation to attract *le signore* to his restaurant in particular and perhaps women in general.

Whatever Giuseppe may or may not have been, his restaurant's food was indeed exquisite, and the ladies lapped up both it and his act. And not only the ladies, either. After a previous visit, as a matter of fact, Monty — his defences against Giuseppe's charms being somewhat weaker than Dave's — had gone through an unfortunate Italian phase in admiring imitation, slicking back his hair, and spouting lines gleaned from repeated viewings of his *Godfather* boxset on VHS that he'd pulled out and dusted off... until Dave had to tell him enough was enough.

On this particular visit, with Becks, Dave had opted to leave his jacket on, taking a chance with the faint smudges of the painted handprints smeared across his sleeve rather than having the much more obvious burnt-on iron mark on his shirt showing. His hope was that, in the dim romantic lighting of the Italian restaurant, his jacket-related mishap might remain hidden to an extent. Presently, he was staring across their cosy little table at Becks. A solitary candle placed in the centre of the table setting illuminated her face, and the flickering light of the flame danced across her visage. Dave was captivated. He held his head in his hand, and looked at her, smiling. Becks was busy telling him an anecdote about something or other, but he wasn't really listening to the content of her story. It wasn't out of rudeness, though. Rather, it was more the case that he was simply mesmerised watching the dimple on her chin and how she covered her mouth whenever she laughed.

Becks was sincere and passionate, and just the decentest sort of person you'd ever care to meet, without a malicious bone in her body. She exuded positivity, with those around her becoming better people merely by being in her presence. She'd arrived at the TT Farm with her son, initially, merely to escape her past and in need of a safe haven. But in very short order, she had become an integral part of their community, adding to the general soul of the place to such an extent that they couldn't imagine it without her.

In fact, with Christmas a few short weeks away, she'd taken it upon herself to make sure the place looked particularly festive. It was a simple enough gesture on her part, but typical Becks, and a perfect example of her generous nature and desire to make the world a nicer place for those around her.

"I need to powder my nose," said Becks, at the conclusion of her anecdote, and effectively snapping Dave out of his daydream.

"What?" said Dave, his head still a little foggy, trying to get his bearings.

"My nose," Becks repeated, tapping her nose to illustrate to Dave what she was referring to when she'd said *'my nose.'* She rose up out of her chair. "You'll excuse me?" she asked politely, "While I go for a powder...?"

"Oh. Oh! Of course. I'm sorry. Yes, have at it, then," Dave told her, standing up to attention himself, instinctively.

Dave had never done that before, standing up for a lady as he'd just done. Not once. *Ever.* But with Becks, it had just come naturally.

Once Becks was off, Dave sat himself back down, a little self-conscious. The couple at the table next to theirs was giving him funny looks. Maybe it was because he'd said, *"have at it, then,"* to Becks. Like an idiot. Or it could have been they'd spotted the vague outline of painted handprints that were there, all over his jacket sleeve, because, again, he was an idiot.

Dave picked up a menu from the table and pretended to read it, ignoring the odd looks. But, on the subject of his jacket, he mused, Becks, very graciously, hadn't said a word about it, he realised. She was so good-natured, he considered, that she didn't even judge the handprints on the outerwear at all, probably assuming them to be part of some sort of nouveau design, perhaps. A *shit* design, to be sure, Dave laughed to himself hopelessly. But, still. She didn't judge. And bless her for that.

He took the brief interlude, in Becks' absence, to wonder if women really did go powder their noses, as they said, or if it was simply a polite euphemism they used instead of, say, "Oi, I need to go have a p–"

But that thought was mercifully cut short as Dave felt his phone buzz in his pocket. In fact it had buzzed several times

CHAPTER TWO

earlier as well, and Dave figured now was as good a time as any to check his messages...

Text from Frank:

> Take her to that Italian place... Giovanni's or something it's called. I'll check with Stan.

Text from Stan:

> Frank said you're looking for a nice restaurant. Giuseppe's it's called. Don't listen to Frank.

Text from Frank:

> Ignore me it's not Giovanni's it's... Shit, I've forgotten what Stan said.

Text from Stan:

> Make sure you stand up when she leaves the table. It's manners. Listen to me.

Text from Frank:

> Stan, that dozy bugger has gone out on a date with painted handprints all over his jacket and a burnt iron mark on his shirt.

Text from Frank:

> Ignore last message. It was for Stan. Sodding phone.

Text from Stan:

> Tell me you've not gone out covered in paint!!!!! You're coming clothes shopping with me. Make sure you stand up when she leaves the table and sits down. It's manners.

Text from Monty:

> Them two are doing my bloody head in. Stan said you have to do a handstand or something and he's taking you shopping. I accidentally told him about the paint. Don't forget to use plenty of breath mints as your breath stinks.

Exhausted after reading this exchange, Dave took a mouthful of wine before reaching for his breath mints. He was grateful for Monty's reminder there, at least. Then, at Becks' return, he stood to greet her and welcome her back to the table. The lads needn't have worried in that respect, thought Dave, as he'd already had the standing bit covered. He may have been an idiot, but he was not, after all, a *blithering* idiot, he told himself. "Right. All sorted?" he asked. "You know. With the, *ehm*... the thing? I mean, that is, the *erm*... the thingy? That you, *em*..." he said, waving his hand around the general area of his nose, and then dipping it down and circling his hand around the area of his crotch, as well, in order to cover all possibilities.

Well so much for not being a blithering idiot, Dave thought to himself despairingly. But, fortunately, Becks seemed a little distracted for some reason, and she likely hadn't heard him anyway. "Becks? Everything okay?" he asked.

Becks chewed her lip, looking back on the route she'd just travelled. "There's a man sat at the table around the corner, near to the toilet. I'm sure I recognise him," she said, taking her seat, her mind clearly preoccupied. She screwed up her hazel eyes, looking to the ceiling for inspiration. "You know him. I'm certain you do," she said, looking back down. "Yes. I'm certain you do," she added, satisfied that she was correct in her recollection. "I can't work out his name just yet, but I know you know him. And I'm fairly certain you think he's a nincompoop."

"Nincompoop?" replied Dave, laughing merrily at the suggestion, while at the same time admiring Becks' good-natured innocence for using such a word. "I don't think I've ever met someone I'd refer to as a *nincompoop*, necessarily," he told her. "At least not put like that. I might say something along the lines of, maybe, a complete and utter cun–"

"Tea or coffee?" asked Giuseppe, appearing unexpectedly, and saving the day as well, lest Dave allow some unnecessarily salty language to slip past his lips. He might have to thank Giuseppe for it later, thought Dave. Or was it Giovanni? Dave couldn't be sure at this point, as reading the flurry of text messages just earlier had scrambled his brain in that regard.

"Tea, please," said Becks, though nodding her head slowly at Dave as she said it, as she was still trying to remember the thing that she was trying her best to remember.

Dave ordered himself an Irish coffee, with *'extra Irish.'* Becks waited until the headwaiter — and *only* waiter, it would seem, as Giuseppe was everywhere at once — had moved on, before continuing. "I've got it. Or part of it, anyway," she said. *"You don't like him,"* she declared, throwing speculative inferences around like a clever TV detective.

"Who? Giuseppe, or Giovanni, or whatever his name is?" asked Dave. "No, it's not that I don't like him, exactly," he explained. "It's more that I just don't think that accent of his is really—"

"No, silly. The fellow I saw at the other table," Becks corrected him.

"Oh, you're still thinking about that one?" said Dave. "Yeah, you already said I thought he was a nincompoop. Though I'd never use a word like—"

"No, listen, I remembered something," Becks told him. "It's that annoying bloke you said you wanted to put your foot nine inches up his bum."

Dave laughed a jolly laugh. This narrowed things down a bit, but not really all that much. "My milkman?" he asked, followed shortly by, "Wait, hang on. Is it the bloke who owns that kebab stall? Jason Donnervan?" And then this was followed immediately by, "No, no, it's got to be... is it my dentist?" he asked, as if Becks would have the faintest of clues about his dentist, or any of the others for that matter, and what his issue with any of them could possibly have been.

"That's a fair-sized list of people you want to insert your shoe into to come up with at a moment's notice, Dave, and quite scary how quickly you conjured it up," Becks replied with a chuckle, not entirely confident she should be amused or if instead she should be concerned.

Dave tucked into his tiramisu, offering a shrug of his shoulders. "You can't get to this stage in life without wanting to smack a few people about. And, also, it's not good for the blood pressure to keep those feelings all bottled up," he declared sagely, by way of explanation, in so thoughtful and reflective a manner as might make Confucius proud.

"No, but there's something else," Becks went on, thinking now to bring up a detail that might well be pertinent. "It's the chap with the annoying nasally voice. You remember the one?"

But Dave repeated his shrug. His mind was on little else but pudding right at that particular moment.

"You know him, Dave," Becks reiterated. "He wears that thing around his neck," she said, wagging her finger in front of her mouth, as if to coax the proper word from her tongue. "It's a, *em, you know*... one of those..." she said, furiously close. "Ah! A cravat!" she said, finally victorious. "He wears a cravat."

Dave lowered his spoon before pudding had been completed for the first time in his life, a look on his face like he'd just stood in a pile of freshly laid dog doody. "Rodney Franks...?" he said, gravely.

"Yes, that's the one," replied Becks, happy that was sorted, but concerned by the expression on Dave's face.

Dave pushed his plate away, the mere mention of the name *Rodney Franks* enough to destroy what was ordinarily a relentlessly hearty appetite. He turned, angling his neck for an attempted

CHAPTER TWO

visual confirmation, but he couldn't see around to the table in question from where he and Becks were sitting. He did, however, receive auditory confirmation shortly thereafter when he heard the particular brash, nasally voice he knew and loathed so well. It was strident and arrogant, and deliberately spoken too loudly, so as to draw attention, such was the sense of self-importance of the man. How Dave hadn't noticed it before, he couldn't say.

"What's that insufferable twit doing on the Island?" asked Dave, bristling. Now that he'd unfortunately focussed in on the sound of Franks' voice, he was finding himself unable to tune it back out. Restless and agitated, he moved his chair back, got up, and edged around the table.

"Where are you going?" asked Becks.

"I want to see what he's doing here," Dave answered her.

"At the restaurant?" said Becks.

"No, I mean here on the Island. Back on the Island," explained Dave. "Because, every time he's on the scene, something happens. And the thing that happens is never good."

"Don't go," Becks told him, placing her hand over her mouth in worry. "You might get hurt, Dave."

Dave laughed at this — though not in an unkind manner, but because he thought she must have been joking. "Oh. You're being serious," he replied, when he could see from her eyes that she was being sincere. "Don't worry, I'll be fine," he said, giving her a wink. "The guy's about seven stone wet through, and wears a cravat. I should be okay, but thanks," he said to her, and he meant it and appreciated her concern.

"But won't he recognise you?" Becks asked, now whispering. "We don't want to cause any trouble...?" she suggested.

"I don't think so," Dave reassured her. "The only time he's ever seen me is when I've been with my helmet. So I think it'll be okay."

"That's not a nice thing to call Monty," observed Becks. "Isn't he your best mate?"

"Brilliant!" replied Dave, laughing again, until realising that, for a second time, Becks hadn't been joking. "No, no," he told her, chuckling gently at her mistake. "Monty *is* my best mate. And he's not as daft as he sometimes appears, so I wasn't... Well, maybe, to be fair, he *is* as daft as he sometimes appears... Though I'm not sure I've been really able to work that out, actually, one way or the..."

Becks looked confused.

"Ah. Sorry. I'm babbling," Dave apologised. "I just mean that I wasn't calling Monty a helmet. That's not what I meant. I was referring to my actual helmet," he said, pointing helpfully to his head. "The only time Rodney Franks has really seen me in the past is around the racetrack, in my racing gear, and probably with my helmet on as well. So I doubt he'll recognise me outside the track, and in my civvies, so to speak," he told her. "Right. So don't worry. Back in a moment," he said. Dave chuckled to himself as he set about navigating his way through the restaurant. Becks' mistake aside, calling Monty a helmet was still jolly good fun as far as Dave was concerned.

Generally speaking, Dave had the grace of a lame elephant. Presently, the three large glasses of wine he'd quaffed, plus the Irish coffee with extra Irish, were doing him no favours, either. But he tried his best to remain inconspicuous as he made his way to the rear of the restaurant. How fitting that the waitstaff had seated Rodney by the loos, he thought.

Dave made like he was going to the gents', but then he stopped outside the door and hung back, pressing himself against the wall, trying to blend in like wallpaper, and casting his eyes around the room in search of his intended target. And sure enough, there was Rodney Franks. Though the lighting was dim, his form was unmistakable, it having been burned into Dave's memory via the sheer revulsion he felt for the man. On a lighter note, Dave had often wondered if Franks wore a toupée, and now seemed like an opportune moment to test out that theory. Just one quick tug would have done it, while Franks wasn't looking... But, no. No, best not, thought Dave. He didn't want to have to try and explain to Monty how he'd been pulling Rodney Franks off in a fancy Italian restaurant.

The man sat opposite to Franks had a more refined appearance as compared to Rodney, with a very smart-looking pinstriped suit and thin-rimmed glasses, and appeared to be controlling the conversation. Dave turned his ear toward them, but the ambient

CHAPTER TWO

music made it near impossible to make out clearly what they were saying, especially since Rodney, uncharacteristically, was speaking more quietly now. Frustrated, Dave edged closer, and then closer still, until he was hunched over, two tables away, next to an elderly couple who were celebrating an anniversary judging by the big balloon tied to the back of the white-haired lady's chair. Dave smiled politely at the couple, with the old dear looking up at him expectantly.

"Oh, Harold, you old romantic," said the pensioner, taking her husband's hand. She waited patiently, flicking her eyes between Harold and Dave, and then back again. "Is he going to sing or play something?" she asked finally, after several long moments of nothing at all happening. "Why's he not doing anything?" she asked of her husband.

Through a brief lull in the music filtering through the speakers, and taking a step or two closer, Dave was able to tune his ear into Rodney's conversation. But, lumbering ox that he was, Dave wasn't particularly efficient at blending into the wallpaper, despite his best efforts, as intended. And so he was unable to shake the attentions of the waiting pensioner, who was fully expecting some sort of personal serenade to commence at any given moment, courtesy of and performed by Dave...

"Harold? Why's he not singing, Harold?" demanded the old dear in consternation, reiterating her previously stated concern, and lowering her napkin in disapproval.

But Dave was now perfectly placed to eavesdrop, and was listening intently to Rodney and the other fellow at Franks' table. It wasn't long before Dave had heard enough, and found himself clenching his fist tightly. His fist, in fact, very much wanted to rabbit-punch Rodney in the side of the head, and it took Dave every ounce of willpower to keep it at bay.

"Ah, jolly good," said Harold, quite unsure what was going on, but now also assuming Dave to be some form of entertainment the management had kindly arranged. "You, sir," he went on, now addressing Dave. "The lady wants a song. And what my Mildred wants, she gets. So... *rapido*," he instructed, giving his hands a quick, sharp clap to indicate to Dave that he should commence with the commencing.

Dave was still in digesting mode — both his half-eaten tiramisu and the information he'd just overheard from Rodney's table — and so was a little distracted. "Eh... no," said Dave, turning to the anniversary couple once again. "I'm not a singer, I'm the... I'm the waiter," he told them. It was the only thing he could think to say at a moment's notice. Dave was preparing to shuffle off, back to whence he'd come, but Rodney had other plans for him, it would seem, evidently overhearing Dave's false claim about being a waiter.

"You! Waiter!" shouted Rodney, twisting his scrawny neck to look in Dave's direction, and snapping his fingers.

Dave walked over, initially only with thoughts of perpetrating physical violence upon Rodney's person, perhaps buffeting him about the temples with a flurry of fist-strikes. But, spotting the business papers laid out on Rodney's table, he thought better of it. Instead, he decided to use his fortuitous proximity to peer down surreptitiously at the paperwork at hand in order to glean more information from it. He was impressed with his spying prowess, and he took a mental note to tell Monty, who'd likely be equally as impressed. And so he took up his role as waiter, and...

"What can I get you, good sir?" he asked. "And, if I may be so bold, I should like to compliment you on your cravat, sir? Very masculine, and in impeccable taste," said Dave, in a manner with only the slightest of hints that he was, as it were, taking the piss.

"We've been waiting twenty bloody minutes to order our food!" complained Rodney bluntly, ignoring Dave's question. He looked Dave up and down disapprovingly, not bothering to make eye contact. "And looking at the size of you, I'm guessing that's because you've already *eaten* most of it," he said boorishly, and to the clear embarrassment of his dining companion. Rodney ran his finger up and down the menu. Despite having twenty minutes to decide what he wanted, he still hadn't decided what he wanted. He deferred to his dinner guest, indicating for the other fellow to order before him, though this was not done out of graciousness, courtesy, or good manners. Rather, it was, again, simply because Rodney hadn't yet decided what the hell to order.

CHAPTER TWO

Dave nodded along politely as the rather more respectable-looking pinstripe-suited man read out his order, though Dave was of course more interested in scouring the paperwork down in front of him with his eyes for clues. Then, it was Rodney's turn to order, and *finally* he'd decided what he wanted...

"Smoked *stracciatella di bufala* for starters," he said, whistling from his nose as he spoke, like a clarinet with a slightly defective reed. Expecting some kind of verbal confirmation, he looked up at Dave when no response was in fact received. "You're not writing this down, you cretin!"

"I've a wonderful memory, sir," replied Dave, offering a salute for some reason even he didn't know. It just seemed like the thing to do.

"What did I just order, then?" asked Rodney, lowering his menu.

Dave glanced at the palm of his hand. "Chicken pizza," he replied with a wink. "Extra anchovies, sir. See? I never forget."

Rodney's face screwed up. "Are you stupid?" he asked, and then turned to his companion for a second, confirmatory opinion. "Is he stupid?" he asked. And, then, back to Dave, "Smoked *stracciatella* for starters, and *crudo di branzino* for mains. Have you got that? Do you want me to write that down for you in crayon?"

Dave was about to reply, but Franks wasn't finished. "In fact, in view of how long it's taken to receive service, I'll pay for this now so we're not hanging about even longer when we're done," he said.

"Jolly good," said Dave, a twinkle in his eye.

Rodney opened up his wallet, which was stuffed thick with fifty-pound notes. He pulled out the wad of bills, fanning through them and making a show of counting them out, so that those around had ample opportunity to see just how much cash he was carrying around with him. "Take this," Franks ordered curtly to Dave, handing over three crisp fifty-pound notes, and as Dave turned to move, added, "And I'll be expecting change as well. Now, you're not going to muck our order up?"

"No, sir," Dave assured him. "I've got it this time. I was getting confused with a previous order just before, but I've got it now right enough, you fuckwit." Dave mumbled the *'you fuckwit'* part, of course, so that Rodney couldn't catch it clearly.

"Excuse me?" said Rodney, rearing up.

"I asked if the table wanted garlic bread, sir?" said Dave cheerily, taking Rodney's money.

Rodney glared back at him. "No," he barked. "And hurry up with our orders, we've got another engagement after this," he added, staring at Dave with an odd look on his face. It may have been that Dave looked vaguely familiar to him. Or, it may have been that Rodney was noticing the unique design on Dave's jacket sleeve. Or, then again, it may well have been that the stupid look on Rodney's face was simply the result of it just naturally looking stupid.

"Right away, sir. Very good, sir," replied Dave, giving a short bow. He was really enjoying his roleplay as newly employed waiter.

As Dave was making his exit, deciding not to press his luck any further, he couldn't help but notice his previous acquaintances, Mildred and Harold, who still appeared to sport a glimmer of hope that a song or melody might somehow be coming their way. And so he made it a point to take a slight detour back in their direction. "Sorry, folks, but the singer is off tonight," he said, leaning over and speaking to them softly, as he reached their table.

This news was met with a sort of sad disappointment. But then Dave had an idea. "It's your anniversary?" he asked, nodding at the celebratory balloon.

"Fifty years," announced Mildred, taking her husband's hand once more, a tender expression emerging from her timeworn face.

"Splendid," said Dave. "That's lovely," he added, and he truly meant it. He smiled at the couple warmly, acknowledging the importance of the occasion and the significance it held for them. "I do apologise for the earlier misunderstanding," he told them sincerely. "I wish I *were* a singer, so that I could serenade your dear one properly," he said, addressing the husband directly. "But all I know are rather salty sea shanties, and rude drinking songs and such," he said, giving Mildred a wink as he did so, the sort of wink that said, '*sorry about that, luv.*'

Mildred had a thoughtful look on her face, as if a vulgar sea shanty just might actually do, in fact.

"Harold?" said Dave, turning to Harold again, lest he be called upon to indeed belt out an embarrassing version of "Little Sally

CHAPTER TWO

Racket" or the like. "With your permission, sir, to make up for the misunderstanding, and as a token of my affection for you both, I'd like to contribute this towards your evening," offered Dave. And with that, Dave took the pile of notes given to him by Rodney some moments earlier and placed them into the hand of a slightly confused, yet grateful, Harold. "Here's to many more years," said Dave. "And, my treat, I'll have another waiter bring you a second bottle of something nice and bubbly to celebrate, as my, *erm*, shift is now ending," he added. "Cheers, folks," he said, as he bid them *addio*.

As he was heading away, Dave crossed the path of a *real* waiter heading in the direction of Rodney's table in order to, Dave had to assume, take Rodney and the other man's *actual* order. Dave managed to intercept the fellow, pointing discreetly over to the table in question. "I was asked to pass along a message?" Dave said innocently. "The bloke with the cravat? Just there? He's still looking at the menu, and said he'd be another twenty minutes or so deciding... so if you could leave him be for a while? Right. He said he'd appreciate it, so thanks for that."

"Ah. *Grazie*," said the waiter, happy for the assist, and dropping an Italian word into his reply. Dave could only imagine the poor fellow was instructed to do this at every possible occasion by head waiter Giuseppe.

"Oh, and drop a bottle of something fizzy on the old couple's table, if you'd be so kind?" Dave added, pressing the appropriate amount of dosh into the fellow's palm, and indicating which table he was now referring to.

"Jolly good," said the waiter obligingly, slipping out of character and forgetting to speak in a faux Italian accent and such.

Shortly thereafter, Dave collapsed back into his seat, taking a slug of his drink. "How was pudding?" he asked.

"I thought he'd attacked you or something, or you'd attacked him, or... well, you'd been gone so long, is all," said Becks, showing genuine concern.

"No, no, nothing like that," Dave told her, assuaging her fears. "Things took a little longer than expected, sorry about that. Met a lovely older couple in the process, though," he said, smiling at the thought of Mildred and Harold. "Almost had to sing them a song."

Becks looked confused by this last bit. That was because she was confused by this last bit. But she decided to forego seeking an explanation for it for now, sallying forth in regard to the matter of Dave's original interest, or goal, instead. "So what does this Rodney Franks fellow want?" she asked.

Dave pushed out his plump lower lip. "I dunno... monkfish, it might have been? Or pasta... Yes, pasta, I think?" he said. "Either way, he's going to be waiting an awfully long time for it. It's a shame we likely won't be here by the time he realises he's been had, with us already having eaten our meal," he added, letting out a contented sigh, and allowing himself a satisfied grin. Annoying Rodney Franks was something that made Dave very happy.

"No, silly," Becks chided him. "It was him, then?"

Dave wolfed down what was left of his pudding, enjoying his tiramisu now that ruining Rodney's evening had raised his spirits again to previous, optimum levels. "Oh, yes, that's Rodney Franks, alright," he said in answer to Beck's question, taking a moment to nod. "Charming fellow, he is," he remarked dryly.

"You know why he's on the Island?" asked Becks.

Dave was about to answer her, but the sound of a champagne cork popping diverted his attention momentarily. "Rodney Franks has just made an old couples' night with his generosity, but he doesn't even know it," he told Becks, by way of explanation, as she must have been wondering about the broad grin he could feel suddenly spreading across his face.

"*Ehm...* okay...?" replied Becks.

"Sorry. I'll explain everything later," Dave told her. "But, listen. I just want to say, Becks, that I've had one of the loveliest nights I've ever had. And that's all because of you," he said. "Don't tell Monty I said that, though, okay? He does get awfully jealous," Dave added with a chuckle.

Becks smiled. "No, I did sense that," she said in reply. "You seem to come as a pair, the two of you, rather like—"

"Tits...?" suggested Dave, helpfully.

CHAPTER TWO

"What?" asked Becks. "No, of course not *tits!*" she protested. "I was going to say Tom and Jerry, Morecambe and Wise. That sort of thing," she told him, laughing.

"Come on, Becks. There's always a few taxis waiting outside, so I'll get you home before you turn into a pumpkin." Dave stood — as instructed, several times, by Stan — holding out his hand to Becks. "We should definitely go," pressed Dave, fearing a genuine waiter would be soon heading in the direction of Rodney Franks' table to actually take the order that Rodney believed to already have been taken. "And on the subject of tits, that's the biggest one you'll ever come across. I think I'll call him Pamela Anderson from now on."

"You've got tits on the brain tonight, Dave?" remarked Becks.

Dave tilted his head back a couple of inches, eyebrows raised, pondering that thought for a moment. "Come on, then," he said eventually, just on cue for Rodney's oafish voice rising above the level of the ambient music. "Do you mind if we stop by Frank and Stan's on the way home?"

"Sure," said Becks, starting to place her arms into the coat that Dave presented to her. "Wait, this isn't my coat, Dave."

"It's not?" he asked.

"It's a different colour. Where did you even get this? It's as if your mind is on something else," she teased. "What is it? That fellow Rodney?" she asked, but she was being charitable, as she knew it was more likely the subject of tits from a moment earlier that was still occupying most of Dave's thoughts.

She escorted Dave to the coat stand, pointing out the correct one. "Is it not a little late to be calling around their house?"

"It'll be fine, and to be honest, what I need to tell them probably can't wait to the morning," said Dave.

Before they left, Dave pressed his head around the corner of the restaurant to sneak a view at Rodney's table, and witnessed the pinstripe-suited man sat with his head in his hands, mortified, by all appearances, to be in the company he was presently in. Dave smiled a happy smile. "Night, Harold! Night, Mildred!" he called out to his earlier, much more charming pair of acquaintances. "Here's to many more anniversaries!" he said, with a friendly wink.

Chapter

THREE

Stan grinned from ear to ear — providing a stern test to the collagen injections visited upon various portions of his face. There was a warm twinkle in his eye as he took hold of the tightly woven fabric keeping hidden the object of his most dearest affection. He grasped the covering between his fingers and pulled it back, only just a bit, and ever so gently — almost reverently, even — while letting out a contented groan.

"Well...? You *like*...?" said Stan provocatively. The fondness and pride he felt were evident in his voice, and, with the object now partially revealed, Stan couldn't help looking down at it himself, stealing an admiring glance.

Frank's chin laid rested on his splayed thumb and forefinger, perched there in observation, and he made agreeable clucking noises with his tongue for Stan's benefit. "You know, you really are a crackpot at times, Stan," volunteered Frank, when eventually he spoke. "What even made you think of this?"

"Ah. Well, I'll tell you, it's something I've always wanted for myself," replied Stan, happy to explain, and not appearing the least bit embarrassed about it, either, it seemed to Frank. "Ever since I was a teenager, I think, I've wanted it, in fact," Stan told him. "I'd see other men with theirs, you know? Showing them off. Flaunting them. And then of course I'd compare, yeah? I mean, how could I not? It's only natural, after all, and I couldn't help but hold mine up against theirs, right?" said Stan. "As one does."

"As one does," repeated Frank automatically, not really agreeing one way or the other, as he was still looking hard at the thing that Stan was showing him.

"And whatever I had, you see, in comparison to theirs..." Stan went on... "Well, it always put mine to shame, know what I mean? You know what I'm saying, right, Frank?"

"Not really...?" said Frank playfully, not taking the bait quite so easily. Plus, he was still a little distracted at the moment.

"You're staring, Frank," laughed Stan. "Frank, you can have a closer look if you like," he added, encouragingly. "Have a go at it, even, feel how smooth it is," he teased, reaching down and giving it a stroke to show his friend how it was done. "*Feeelll iiiit*, Frank. You *know* you want to!"

Frank lowered his hand, freeing his chin, and eased himself forward, allowing himself to be fully reeled in now. "I've often thought about it, Stan, if I'm being completely honest," he said, slightly giddily now he'd let his reservations go and his inhibitions slip away. "But, being a little bit older now, I just didn't know what people might think...?"

"Feels nice, Frank, doesn't it?" asked Stan, now that Frank was actually giving it a proper rub. "Don't be shy, you can't hurt it," Stan cooed reassuringly. "There you go. Yes. *Yeeesss...*"

"Stan, I think you might be enjoying this just a bit too much, mate...?" said Frank with a giggle.

"Nonsense!" replied Stan. "Frank, can you imagine if you got one as well, just like this? Let's just say that Jessie would likely be the happiest woman ever. Over the moon, in fact!"

"*Hmm*," replied Frank, chewing the idea over.

"In fact, Frank, if you want to ask Jessie if she'd like to come 'round and have a look at mine...? If it's something you decide you want for yourself, that is? I mean, if so, then she's certainly welcome to pop by and give mine a spin? Try it out for size? Any time, of course. No trouble at all."

"I'd want mine a little different, maybe...?" mused Frank. "No offence. I just think mine shouldn't be exactly the same...?" he said, ruminating aloud.

"Of course, of course," Stan assured him. "Good thinking."

CHAPTER THREE

"I agree that's not a bad idea, though, Stan," Frank continued. "Her having a good look at yours and trying it out, I mean. It *would* put a smile on her face, I expect. And with the age mine is, I have to admit, it *is* starting to look a mite tired and shabby. And, so, yeah, I'd say I could do with a bit of improvement in that regard. Do you... would you mind terribly if I got a better look at yours?"

"Oh! Of course," said Stan. "Sorry about that. I'd been so worried about properly building up the surprise that I forgot you hadn't the opportunity to see the whole thing yet! Here you are, then," replied Stan, pulling the remaining fabric covering away, and affording Frank a complete view.

Frank took several steps back, first standing in one position here, another position there, and then moving to another position yet again, admiring the entirety of the thing from every possible angle now that he was able. After a few moments of pondering, he asked, "Can I... Stan, do you mind if I touch it once more...?"

"Absolutely. Have at it, my friend!" answered Stan accommodatingly, eager to please. "It's well polished, isn't it?" he remarked. "Have you noticed?"

"It most certainly is!" exclaimed Frank, in full agreement. "I can almost see my reflection in the end of it!" he marvelled, moving in for a closer look once again, his face only inches away this time. "Yes, I'd say it's definitely obvious someone has given this baby here a fair amount of loving attention," he added, pursing his lips and nodding in approval.

"Cheers, mate," replied Stan, well chuffed and pleased as punch.

Frank stood, addressing Stan at eye level. He looked at him up and down, the whole of him, and he cocked his head quizzically.

"What is it?" asked Stan.

"It's just..." Frank began to say, tilting his head to the other side now.

"Well? Spit it out, man," Stan told him. "Out with it!"

"It's just that I know you're not afraid of the cosmetic surgeon's knife, Stanley," replied Frank, a crooked grin forming as he spoke.

"And...?" said Stan.

"I know you're not afraid of going under the cosmetic surgeon's knife, Stanley. But I never thought you'd go for what amounts to a penis extension?" said Frank, completing his observation.

"*Amounts* to? Cheeky bugger! I'll have you know, this *is* a penis extension!" answered Stan. "And a damned fine one at that!"

Frank laughed, but then right after that he sighed, taking another long admiring glance at Stan's pride. "It *is* a magnificent beast, isn't it?" he declared.

Stan looked down, admiring the splendid animal in all its glory. And then he sighed a long, satisfied sigh as well. "Nineteen sixty-five Austin-Healey 3000 Mark III BJ8," he said, finally.

"Yep," said Frank.

"A magnificent beast," said Stan.

"I already said that," Frank reminded Stan.

"I'm just agreeing!" said Stan.

"She's a thing of beauty, Stan, I'll give you that," said Frank, absorbing every classic automotive line and curve.

"I knew you'd come 'round to my way of thinking," Stan sniffed.

"As far as penis enhancements go, however, this is a rather expensive one, isn't it?" Frank asked of his chum. "Dare I ask how much it cost?"

"*Hmm*," replied Stan, pondering this question for a moment or two before giving Frank an answer. "I suppose it cost a fair bit of dosh," he conceded, eventually. "With the money I spent, I guess I could have gotten that nose job I've been thinking for a while now of getting, plus a few other minor procedures done as well, and still had change left at the end. But..."

"But?" asked Frank.

"Penis extension, it was!" declared Stan, thrusting a finger up into the air in triumph.

Frank rolled his eyes, but he wasn't disagreeing, really, nor faulting Stan for his choice.

"Hey, you can't take it with you, right?" said Stan, as if more persuading was in order, even though it wasn't, necessarily. "No offence," he went on, "But what with your ongoing health issues in mind, and plus my own flirtation with mortality only a few short months ago, I thought, *You know what, sod it*, and—"

CHAPTER THREE

"Wait, hang on now!" Frank interrupted him. "Are you referring here to your *kidney stone incident* as a 'flirtation with mortality,' as you put it??" he asked, eyes wide in comical disbelief.

"You can laugh all you want, Frank, but those little bastards are like squeezing your head through a garden hosepipe!" protested Stan. "They hurt! They hurt *loads!*"

"All right, all right, fair enough," conceded Frank, deciding it wasn't worth the fight.

"Right. I should say so," answered Stan, starting to sulk now the painfulness of his pain should be brought into question.

"Anyway," replied Frank, deftly changing the subject. "Are you going to take me to this wedding venue, as you promised?"

"Oh, yes. I almost forgot!" said Stan, his mood brightening.

"So... shall we be taking your new vehicle, Stirling Moss?" asked Frank, in reference, of course, to Stan's newly purchased Austin-Healey. "Will I actually get to take a ride in this thing, or was the great unveiling purely for show?"

"No!" replied Stan. "I mean yes!" he corrected himself. "I mean, no, it wasn't just for show. And, yes, we're taking my new car!" he clarified, and his spirits now effectively buoyed beyond doubt.

"Excellent," said Frank.

"Can I keep the top down?" enquired Stan.

"Stan, it's December, and I'm not a well man!" Frank had to remind him.

"*Pfft*. When you've passed a bowling ball through your urethra, as I have, *then* you can talk to me about pain," declared Stan.

Wedding plans had been in full swing and whilst Frank was overjoyed to have met and been marrying his soulmate, it's fair to say the finer details had been delegated to Jessie and Stan. What with Stan's camp flair and attention to detail, especially, he and Jessie were the perfect match to put in place the plans for the veritable Wedding of the Year. Lee and Stella were in a similar boat, in that Lee was busy running the charity in the UK and Stella, well, if it were up to Stella, they'd likely be getting married at a twenty-four-hour Tesco or a chip shop — and so, for them, leaving the planning for the double wedding to Stan and Jessie worked out just fine.

Also, the date had been brought forward to the back end of March, ostensibly due to the short notice of the wedding and the minimal number of venues on the Isle of Man. Frank didn't delve into the reasoning further, but he suspected his questionable health, as well, was a consideration in holding the wedding sooner rather than later. They could, of course, have arranged to have the wedding over in the UK, affording them greater flexibility. But the consensus was to have it on the Island, which was the place that Frank and Stan now called home. Stella, for her part, found the Isle of Man location agreeable enough, especially as she didn't want to get married in Liverpool, stating, in her own inimitable fashion, that *"You don't shit on your own doorstep."* Quite what that meant in this context, nobody was particularly clear on, so they just went with it, happy that Stella was happy.

Presently...

"What's it called?" asked Frank, shouting loudly in order to make himself heard over the turbulence he was experiencing from the brisk breeze assaulting him in the face.

Stan eased his new toy along Douglas Promenade, and perhaps, in his mind, he was driving down Route 66 or perhaps to a casino in Monaco rather than in the throes of winter on an island in the middle of the Irish Sea.

"What...?" replied Stan, wiping the salty wash of the misty sea breeze from his face.

"The name of this place where we're going to view this wedding venue!" replied Frank, but his voice was simply carried away by the wind. Frank's wispy greying hair was being blown this way and that, whereas Stan's, by contrast, remained steadfast, cemented with product to an extent it could withstand a hurricane.

"You'll need to pull over and put the roof up, Stanley!" Frank shouted. "I can't feel my lips anymore!"

Stan jabbed his finger into the rush of briny air, pointing in the direction of the Isle of Man Sea Terminal car park. "It's no use!" he

CHAPTER THREE

shouted back, looking across the seat to Frank, "I can't hear a word you're saying, so I'll pull over and put the roof up!"

"That's a wonderful idea!" said Frank, with an enthusiastic yet hypothermia-ravaged thumb raised in agreement.

Stan manoeuvred through the car park, offering a cordial wave to a young lady pulling out of her parking space, giving Stan a lingering stare, to which Stan replied with a generous smile.

"Did you see the number of people looking at us coming along the Promenade, Frank?" Stan asked, once he'd pulled safely into his own parking space. "We're quite the eye candy, it would seem, riding in this car of mine," he offered with a wry smile.

Frank appeared rather dubious as he stepped out of the car. "Eye candy?" he replied. "They were probably just staring at the two daft old plonkers freezing their bollocks off!" He rubbed his hands together, then swung his arms around in windmill fashion, like Pete Townsend playing the guitar, in order to restore blood flow to his fingertips. "You put the roof back on, and I'll pop into the ferry terminal and pick us up a couple of coffees, yeah?" suggested Frank, after his extremities were once again in suitable working order.

Stan walked around his car, admiring the elegant lines, taking a moment to run his hand along the bodywork. A car like this definitely deserved to be driven with the roof down, he thought. But, with the vehicle being new — at least to him — and the threat of rainfall from angry clouds overhead, Stan was eager to keep his new loved one protected. The only problem was...

While the roof had retracted without fuss earlier in the day, reinstating it did not appear to be as easy a proposition. Try as he might, Stan was having a difficult time of it. He recalled the car salesman showing him how it was performed, and even seeking confirmation that Stan had indeed understood — to which Stan had nodded in assent. But the truth was, even as he'd been nodding along, he was imagining himself posing in his new toy, behind the wheel, driving along the motorway... and so not really paying much attention to what the man had been saying.

"Shit," he said, as a solitary raindrop landed on the back of his neck. He gently tugged at the folded-up roof, fiddling with it this way and that, trying to coax whatever mechanism it was that held it in place into action. He wondered if it was an electric-powered roof, until he remembered the car was nearly as old as he was. "Bugger," he added, leaning over the rear wheel arch in search of an improved grip.

The roof was jiggling in response to Stan's ministrations, but that's all it was doing, and his pristine leather seats were in danger of being drenched on their first outing under his stewardship if he didn't sort this out, and soon. He reached in further, stretching fully now, into the rear compartment where the retracted roof lay continuing to resist his efforts. He balanced on the side of the car precariously, his feet lifted from the floor of the car park and wiggling and pumping in the air like he was riding an invisible bicycle.

But the roof remained resolute in its refusal to cooperate. And the more Stan struggled, with his upper half swallowed into the depths of the roof compartment, his arse skyward, and his lower half thrashing about, the more it looked like he was in very real danger of being eaten by his own car.

"Nice bum!" shouted a voice from across the park, followed by a hearty laugh.

"If you help me fix this soddin' roof, then I'll let you have a squeeze!" yelled Stan, though his voice was muffled. He struggled to retain his balance, with his feet, still aloft in the air, now looking like he was performing some sort of drunken tap dance. Conscious of how much this vehicle had just cost him, it was a balancing act in more ways than one: he was anxious to provide as much force as possible to persuade the mechanism into motion, but at the same time he worked very gingerly for fear of breaking it.

"Oi!" shouted Stan, with his head still buried in the darkened recess at the rear of the car, like a gynaecologist... or a proctologist. "Get yourself over here and help me pull this off!" he said, the pitch in his voice increasing in direct correlation to the intensity of the raindrops. "I've been tugging on this thing for ages, but nothing's happening! I think I'm getting blisters on my fingers!"

A welcome hand soon arrived, easing itself under Stan's armpit and onto the fastened leather strap, as it should happen, preventing

CHAPTER THREE

the roof being set free from its retracted state. The two of their bodies pressed tightly together as Stan's saviour weaved his arm through the available space, leaning over against Stan to gain purchase on the offending leather clasp. Even in Stan's agitated, distressed state, he couldn't help but notice the glorious aroma emanating from the body held against him, and he took in a lungful, inhaling the scent deeply. "Frank, have you put new aftershave on or something? Because, suddenly, you smell rather amazing?" he asked, puzzled but slightly intoxicated.

As far as the roof was concerned, where Stan had been fumbling at the mechanism like a teenage boy on his debut introduction to a bra hook, this other hand released it like a seasoned lothario, sorting the problem out quickly and efficiently.

"Frank, I could kiss you!" shouted Stan, struggling to reorient himself.

"Allow me," insisted a courteous, elegant voice — a voice that clearly didn't belong to Frank, as Stan had expected — in response to Stan's flailing. And in short order, Stan was soon set right, properly oriented, and with feet firmly planted once again upon solid ground.

"Oh. You're not Frank," observed Stan, stating the obvious now that he was face-to-face with his saviour, and also acutely aware that his mysterious benefactor still had the palm of his hand on Stan's rump from where it'd directed him from the car. Stan blushed — which was somewhat impressive, given the layers of tanning agent on his face.

"I'm Edgar," the fellow said, finally removing — to Stan's great regret — his hand from the region of Stan's posterior.

"Oh," Stan repeated. "You're not Frank," he said again, blinking like his eyes were overcome by very bright sunshine even though the sky was grim.

"Edgar Seaforce," said the fellow by way of proper introduction.

"Oh," said Stan, still a little dazed.

"If I may…?" said Edgar Seaforce, reaching in Stan's direction.

"Yes, of course!" Stan answered, more than happy to submit to anything Edgar might have had in mind. But then it occurred to Stan that Edgar was likely just offering his hand for a handshake, and so Stan stuck out his own hand in response, belatedly, holding it out for Edgar to take up.

But Edgar sailed right past him, at least for the moment, attending to the car instead. "You just need to ease that strap, as I showed you, and…" he said, with a confident, pleasant grin.

Stan looked on as Edgar worked his magic.

"And… there it is," said Edgar, the mechanism released and the roof easing very smartly into the closed position in a smooth, fluid motion, and just as the rain began to hammer down.

"And there it is," agreed Stan, smiling happily despite the rain.

"Let's get out of this!" Edgar encouraged, ushering Stan over to the safety of the roof overhang outside the sea terminal building. Stan didn't need asking twice, and allowed himself to be escorted quite willingly.

Edgar wasn't dressed for a downpour any more than Stan was, and the bright pink blazer he wore was peppered with dark rain spots, as were his white linen trousers, along with the portions of his emerald green shirt not covered by the bright blazer. Edgar also sported Italian loafers in lovely Jaffa orange. For a dull, overcast day, Stan thought, this fellow Edgar's vibrant, somewhat eccentric dress sense certainly introduced a welcome smattering of delightful brilliance to the afternoon. The collection of colours gave the appearance he'd perhaps gotten dressed in the dark, but somehow it all worked in the end. He made Michael Portillo appear dour, considered Stan, and almost like a funeral director by comparison.

"Seems as though we both got caught with our trousers down," remarked Edgar.

"I'm sorry…?" said Stan.

"The rain," explained Edgar. "Neither of us has brought an umbrella with us today, it would appear."

"Ah," said Stan. "Ah," he said again, and then proceeded to shake the rain off of him, like a dog just out of the bath. "Oh! I'm so sorry!" he said quickly, realising what he'd just done.

"It's all right, I'm already well lubricated," replied Edgar with a jolly laugh.

"I'm sorry…??" said Stan once more.

CHAPTER THREE

"The rain," explained Edgar for a second time. "I'm already fairly wet," he added. "Now about this car of yours," he went on. "You've got the hang of how the roof works now?"

"Yes! And thanks for that!" Stan answered him. "I've just bought it, you see, and, well..."

"Did the salesman not explain to you how it operated?" asked Edgar, showing genuine concern.

"No, no, he did," said Stan. "It's just, *ehm*, well..." fumbled Stan, trying to think of an answer that might seem reasonable and not make himself appear a complete idiot.

"Let me guess, you didn't listen to any of the instruction given, because you were too busy admiring the bodywork?" asked Edgar, smiling widely.

"Definitely admiring the bodywork," replied Stan. "Definitely busy admiring the bodywork," he reiterated, and he meant it in more ways than one.

"I'm chairman of the Isle of Man Classic Car Club," said Edgar, retrieving a business card from inside his bright, flamingo-pink jacket and handing it to Stan. "That's why I'm so experienced with this sort of thing," he explained.

"I'm not experienced at all," replied Stan, a little too quickly. "I mean I have some experience, of course," he added. "Just not as much experience as I'd like."

"Ah," said Edgar, but it was a non-judgemental sort of *ah*.

"I'm pretty hopeless with classic cars, I'm afraid," Stan clarified, lest Edgar should get the wrong idea. "I'm Stan, by the way," said Stan. "Stan Sidcup."

"Pleased to meet you, Stanley," replied Edgar, extending a hand cordially, which Stan readily took up. "I'm sorry I didn't shake your hand earlier. Wasn't trying to be rude. Just wanted to get that roof sorted for you."

"Not a problem," Stan assured him, pumping Edgar's extended hand vigorously.

"Who's Frank?" Edgar asked Stan abruptly, looking him directly in the eye.

"Pardon me?" replied Stan. Edgar's manner was gentle, but the suddenness of his question had taken Stan off guard.

"Frank. You called me Frank. Something about kissing him, as I recall?" Edgar answered.

"Ah. A friend. Just a friend," Stan immediately replied, seeming very eager indeed to distance himself from whoever this fellow named Frank was.

Both men stared at each other, grinning politely, unsure what to say, or do, next. Stan let go of Edgar's hand, now that he was done having his way with it, and shuffled awkwardly in place, taking a sudden great interest in his feet, from all appearances.

"Well, then," said Edgar, after a few moments. "Now that you're watertight and raring to go, I suppose I should leave you to it...?" he proposed.

"You should come for a drive!" suggested Stan, clutching an imaginary steering wheel in front of him, and making engine noises, like a three-year-old. He lowered his hands when he realised what he was doing, afraid he was indeed making a fool of himself. And yet...

"Why not?" replied Edgar agreeably. "I'm free now, and I'd be daft to turn down a drive with something so wonderfully put together," he told Stan, patting Stan's shoulder and giving him a wink. "So I'd say I'm all yours," he said.

Stan was about to lead the way when he remembered Frank, who he'd completely forgotten, somehow, in just the few moments since he'd mentioned him. How he could have suddenly entirely forgotten about his oldest and dearest friend in the whole world, he didn't know. Well... he *did* know, actually, as he'd found himself pleasantly distracted.

"Oh, dear. Another time, perhaps?" said Stan. "Only I've just recalled that I have Frank with me, who'll be back shortly, and the car only holds two, unfortunately, it being a, *ehm*, two-seater, and *erm*, sorry..."

Stan worried it might sound like he'd changed his mind and was making excuses, even though he most assuredly wasn't.

"Of course," replied Edgar, looking out from under the shelter of their perch and up to the heavens, to see if the rain was showing any signs of abating. It wasn't. And so he pulled the collar of his

CHAPTER THREE

jacket up over his head, and set off. "I meant it, by the way!" he called out over his shoulder.

"What's that?" Stan shouted back.

"About you having a nice bum!" Edgar called out, looking back, before trotting off to the rear of the car park, and offering a friendly wave before he did so.

Stan waved in return, with only the tips of his fingers, like a young child, though Edgar couldn't see him by this point. "Bye," Stan mouthed into the rain. Had Edgar told him he had a nice bum? He *had*, hadn't he? thought Stan. He was so overcome by his Brief Encounter-type encounter that he'd almost forgotten!

"What are you doing stood over here, instead of sat in your car?" asked Frank, appearing onto the concourse beside him, with two coffees and a small bag in hand. "I bought you a doughnut as well," Frank said amiably, handing one of the coffees over to a rather vacant Stan.

Stan accepted the coffee without looking, and didn't respond.

"Are you okay?" asked Frank, as ordinarily the offer of a free doughnut was met with a more favourable, enthusiastic response.

"What? Oh yes, very good," said Stan automatically, still not really paying attention.

"I asked them to put an extra helping of strychnine into your coffee," continued Frank, testing out Stan's precise level of awareness.

"Just how I like it," murmured Stan, watching as Edgar's compact sports car eased out of the car park onto the exit road which ran in front of where he and Frank stood sheltered from the rain. His eyes widened as the car slowed to a crawl out in front of them. Edgar peered over the empty passenger seat through the half-opened window, and, once parallel with Frank and Stan, he shouted over the growl of the finely tuned engine.

"Nice to meet you, Frank!" Edgar said cheerily. "And you, Stanley Sidcup!" he yelled. "Stan, you've got my card if you should like to get hold of me! Oh, and if you ever need any help getting it up again, as well!" he added.

Frank watched on, rather bemused, as the car pulled away. "Friend of yours?" he asked Stan.

"He was talking about the roof," replied Stan, keeping one eye on Edgar's car as it sped off and faded from view. "You know. When he mentioned about getting it up," he clarified.

Frank smirked. "Are you blushing, Stanley Sidcup?" he asked, moving in for a closer inspection. "You are as well!" he observed cheekily. "Something you want to tell me?"

Stan smiled broadly. "Just someone I met in the car park," he said dreamily, like a schoolgirl fawning over the captain of the football team.

"Is he, eh, *you* know...?" asked Frank, quite unsure how he should go about asking these things, or how to phrase such questions.

"I should say so," confirmed Stan. "He was dressed smartly, but the colours told me all I needed to know."

"Doesn't mean he's, you know..." began Frank.

"He also said I had a nice bum," added Stan.

"Ah. That'll do it," said Frank, handing over the doughnut. "It's not bad, I suppose," he remarked, peering at Stan's bum. "Not as good as mine, though," he added matter-of-factly, extending his buttocks for Stan's closer inspection.

Even on a miserable overcast winter's day, the natural beauty of the Isle of Man was obvious. Stan still took great delight in any opportunity to explore this emerald in the middle of the Irish Sea, and what better way to enjoy the quaint delight than in a two-seater sports car. His new toy purred like a kitten, competently navigating the hallowed tarmac of the TT course through twisting country roads — although at a rather more sedate speed than the racers would have been used to. Their destination was the historic Milntown Estate, an idyllic country house a short hop from Ramsey, in the north of the Island. Set in fifteen acres of sumptuous gardens, it was the perfect wedding venue and one that Jessie had fallen in love with immediately upon her initial inspection with Stan.

It was ingenious, really, this trip, as far as Stan was concerned. Stan didn't want Jessie or Frank to be overly influenced by each

CHAPTER THREE

other with regard to the prospective wedding venue, so bringing them separately was inspired. It also meant that Stan was able to sample the venue's culinary hospitality on two separate occasions, which was not at all an unhappy prospect. Lee was happy to go with the majority opinion, as far as deciding on the venue went, and Stella, well, Stella didn't give a shit either way — so long as she could *go outside for a fag*, she was relatively happy.

Once arrived, Frank and Stan eventually found themselves on a quiet corner of the sprawling grounds underneath an impressive oak tree that, judging by its size and girth, would have surveyed this land for centuries. Caught out by the rain once again, the pair had sought shelter from the elements, although a tree without leaves was rather like an umbrella with a hole in it.

"Best place to be if this weather gets thundery," remarked Stan, slapping the tree trunk with an assured hand. He peered up through the bare branches as dollops of water bounced off his forehead.

Frank smiled, taking in the spectacle of the wonderful gardens. He'd always enjoyed being outside in the rain, listening to the drops. It soothed him. "Wait... what?" he laughed, when Stan's words had sunk in. "Shelter under a tree when it's thundery?"

But Frank could see his chum was not joking. Rather than correct him, however, Frank reasoned that Stan had reached this period in life without being hit by a lightning bolt, so who was he to say Stan's theory was in fact incorrect? On the other hand, perhaps Stan *had* been struck by lightning at some point... which would possibly explain quite a lot.

"What's all this, then? You look like you've the weight of the world on your shoulders," remarked Frank, noticing Stan's suddenly pensive demeanour. Frank flicked the excess rain on his hand in Stan's direction playfully.

"I've been thinking about that arsehole," replied Stan, shaking his fist for extra effect.

This pronouncement brought a raised eyebrow from Frank.

"No, I don't mean like *that*, you dirty old bugger," protested Stan. "I mean what Dave was telling us about that Rodney Franks."

Frank dismissed this with a wave of the hand. "It's fine, he can't do anything to us now," Frank reassured his friend. "I spoke to Henk earlier, and his legal team went over everything when we took control of the farm. There's nothing that can be done at this point to muck things up by that cravat-wearing..." he said, raising his eyes to the heavens in search of just the right word...

"*Cockwomble*," Frank eventually continued, finding the appropriate nomenclature, and raising his finger in admiration of his own insult-related brilliance.

"Nice," replied Stan, in perfect agreement of Frank's choice of words. He turned into Frank like a long-lost lover, gripping the fabric on Frank's jacket. "Life's good, Frank, what with the farm and everything," he said, letting go Frank's lapels now and turning to place both hands on the tree, and moving in like he was about to offer it a tender kiss. "I just don't want that... that..." he went on, still addressing the tree, "I just don't want that cravat-wearing *cockwomble* to screw up all of the good work we've done."

"Henk said there's nothing to worry about," Frank told him. "The farm is ours, Stan, signed, sealed, and delivered, and there's nothing that Rodney can do, so don't worry."

Stan shrugged his shoulders, seemingly appeased by Frank's reassurances.

"Now I think we need to get you out of this rain, yes?" suggested Frank. "Before you create a chemical spill?"

Stan shrugged again, inspecting his sleeve, wondering what Frank was wittering on about.

Frank rotated his hand around Stan's face like he was turning the steering wheel of a car. "Something or other is running down your face," he observed. "Dye from your hair, perhaps?" he posited, extending an investigative finger towards the area in question. "I think there's an orange substance in there, as well?" he added, peering closer. "And what could possibly be mascara, also? How odd, I've never known you to wear mascara. But whatever it is, all of this, it's like a rainbow is melting down your..." he concluded, trailing off, and turning the steering wheel, once more, to finish illustrating his point.

CHAPTER THREE

Stan eased his hand down the side of his face, taking a lingering look into the palm once finished. "Cheeky bugger," he said, when it was clear the palm of his hand was, well, perfectly clear. "So what do you think about this place?" asked Stan, changing subject. "It's a wonderful location for the wedding. And, also, the great thing is, they can accommodate at short notice," he told Frank. "I mean, *ehm*, that is..." he faltered... "Well, what I meant to say was, ah... as I'd told you before... they just happened to have an opening, *erm*, sooner, rather than later, as it turns out, which we could totally take advantage of, for, *em*, no reason at all other than it's an opening which had just..." he said, coughing... "Happened to have, *erm*, opened up," he continued, *"And no other reason at all."*

Frank let Stan stammer on, allowing him to finish up before offering a conciliatory smile. "It's fine," he said in an assured tone, in response to Stan's rambling. "I appreciated the whole cock-and-bull story that you, Molly, and Jessie came up with previously."

Stan displayed his feigned shock with a sudden intake of air. "What are you on about?" he asked innocently, blinking several times in quick succession.

"It's fine," said Frank, with a half-smile. "I understand I'm not exactly endowed with good health, and you all wanted to get the wedding booked sooner rather than later. I'm fine with that."

"I can tell you about health issues!" Stan exclaimed, harping on about his favourite subject again, pointing to his crotch. "When you've pissed a—"

"Yes, yes, yes. A bowling ball straight through your urethra," Frank finished for him. "Or was it a watermelon?"

They both fell silent for a bit, lost in their own thoughts, and listening to the raindrops landing on the sodden ground.

"Thank you," said Frank, after a time.

Stan lowered his head, taking a deep breath. "Come on, then, you old bugger," he said, his voice betraying a tinge of emotion. "Should we go and see about paying the deposit on this place?"

But, to Stan's surprise, Frank held his arm out, delaying Stan's progress. "I don't think so, actually, mate, to be honest," he said gently, taking a lingering look around him.

Stan screwed up his face— as best a man with thousands' worth of filler could, at least. "You don't like it?" asked Stan, his face now dropping like a child watching its new balloon disappearing on the breeze.

"No... I mean, yes. Yes, of course I do," said Frank. He was eager to stress the point that he *did* certainly like the place well enough, for he knew the effort Stan had spent on this. Granted, Stan had been well fed in the process, what with two taster meals now happily under his belt, and all. But, still, Frank appreciated his friend's efforts. "Don't get me wrong, it's completely beautiful, Stan," Frank told him, twirling like a ballerina, and fanning his hand out and around as he spoke, to indicate the surroundings. "Beyond amazing, in fact. But..." he said, racking his brain for a way to put it politely... "It's just not what I want."

Stan's career as a wedding planner was evaporating before his eyes. "Oh," he began, shoulders drooping. "Oh. Well. Never mind, then," he said, the wind taken from his sails. "We'll just have a look for another venue..."

"No, Stan, there's no need. I think I already know where I'd like to use as the venue," Frank answered. "I know you and Jessie loved this place, and I can absolutely understand why. I just think, though, that I'd like to have the ceremony... at the TT Farm...?" he suggested, offering Stan a moment or two, allowing the idea to filter through his friend's brain.

"Hmm, I like it!" said Stan, bouncing back, his role as fledgling wedding planner now restored, and the gears in his head turning. Stan circled Frank like a matador 'round a bull. "We can do it on the bottom field," he began, with a knowing finger raised. "It's got a wonderful view over the hills!" he went on excitedly. He continued circling, stroking his chin for inspiration. "We'll need to hire a marquee, something to accommodate all the guests, as they won't fit in the farmhouse, of course..." he continued, thinking aloud.

Frank shook his head. "We don't need anything too big, as there really won't be that many people to invite," he entered in.

"Nonsense!" declared Stan, with a sharp clap of the hands, like a schoolmarm getting a sleepy student's attention. "There's your family, Lee's... Stella's... Jessie's..."

CHAPTER THREE

Frank laughed, but not in an unkind way. "Stan, I don't want the world and his dog there. My family — my family that really matters, that is — is small, just Molly and a few close relatives. Other family members I haven't seen for ten years or more, and they know I've not been well, and yet how many of them have gotten in touch?"

Frank didn't need to elaborate on this last point, as Stan took his meaning.

"*We're* Stella's family," Frank went on. "And Jessie is like me in regard to family, in that she's only close to a few. So, perhaps a half-dozen or so guests to invite altogether, I'm thinking?"

"But, hang on, you're not taking Lee into account?" countered Stan, though not especially convincingly.

"Stan, remember where we first met Lee?" replied Frank. "He was a tramp, if you recall. A tramp living in a wheelie bin. His car was a shopping trolley. And so I'm not sure too many of his family will be wanting to come to the wedding, judging by the fact that they had no use for him then, when he needed them the most."

"Fair point," conceded Stan, his shoulders starting to droop again, his dreams of the grand affair he'd envisioned fading.

"All I'm saying, Stan, is that those that're close to me are around me. I've got a small circle of family and friends, and I'm good with that. In fact, scrap that— I love it. I've got the best family and friends that I could possibly wish for, as far as I'm concerned, and I want to spend my special day with those people that I love. Not pretending to like people I've not seen for who-knows-how-many years. Do you know what I mean, mate?" Frank placed his hands on Stan's cheeks, before leaning in to place an affectionate kiss on the side of this face. "So please don't think I'm being ungrateful, all right?"

"I get it, Frank. I do," replied Stan. "And it makes perfect sense. The TT Farm is a wonderful venue," he said, warming up to the idea. "Do you reckon Jessie will be okay with it?" he asked.

Frank sucked his teeth. "I don't know, buddy. You let me know what she says after you've told her, will you? After all, you're the wedding planner!"

Stan laughed. "So it's decided, then," he proclaimed, the old oak tree stood overhead bearing witness. "The TT Farm is going to play host to the wedding of the year!" he said.

But the look of enthusiasm on Stan's face faltered somewhat as he took his phone from his pocket and looked at the screen.

"Everything okay?" asked Frank.

Stan stared down at the screen with what appeared to be terror, perhaps, etched on his face. It was a peculiar sort of expression, and it was difficult for Frank to tell what exactly it was, precisely.

"Stan, is everything okay?" repeated Frank. "What's the matter?" he added, starting to panic now that Stan wasn't answering him. "Is it bad news? What *is* it, mate?"

Stan eventually lifted his head, his lower jaw dangling down, his visage haunted in appearance. He glanced back down again at his phone, as if having to confirm the words he'd just read were indeed the words he'd just read. "What, *ehm*... no," he replied, his attention taken by whatever it was he was seeing. "It's just..."

"Just *what?*" demanded Frank, anxiously.

Stan pulled up his jaw like a drawbridge, allowing, once it was set back in place, a crooked smile to slowly emerge. "I think... that is... it would seem, well... that I've got a date," he announced, his voice tremulous, and sounding very much like it emanated from someone much younger and of the opposite gender, such was his nervous giddiness.

"What?" replied Frank with a chuckle, pleased that it wasn't, as it should happen, anything terribly serious. "Who with?"

"Edgar Seaforce," said Stan, clutching the phone to his chest in delight.

Frank laughed at the sight of his happy friend. The only thing missing, to complete the picture properly, he thought, was a dainty pirouette on Stan's part, followed by a small bluebird landing on his shoulder.

"I sent him a text to thank him for helping me get it up earlier," Stan elaborated. "Getting the roof up, I mean," he quickly clarified.

Frank felt rather like a proud father at this moment in time. "Looking at the smile on your face, Stanley, I'd say it's a fair bet

CHAPTER THREE

that roof of yours isn't the only thing this Edgar Seaforce fellow has successfully brought up today," he proclaimed merrily.

Stan didn't necessarily disagree. "You know what this means, don't you, Frank?" he asked.

"That your trousers have suddenly gotten much tighter?" Frank ventured.

"No!" replied Stan, almost drunk with delight. "I mean besides that!" he chided his friend. "It means that I might just even have a date for the Isle of Man's wedding of the year!" he said, grinning from ear to ear.

Chapter
FOUR

The TT Farm sat nestled in the idyllic Manx countryside, with panoramic views over the rolling hills that'd surely bring a smile to the face of even the grumpiest of buggers. But if that wasn't enough, the generous space the farm afforded allowed Frank to indulge in something that he'd hankered after for years but had always kept putting off. In truth, he didn't need too much cajoling, and the latest addition to the farm — funded from his own pocket — was a bubbling box of luxury.

The idea of a hot tub at first sounded like an indulgent excess, with Dave and Monty both claiming they could get the same result from farting vigorously in the bath, and suggesting further that only a dopey old plonker would part that much dosh on what they viewed as nothing more than a glorified washing machine for geriatrics. Ironic, then, that since it was installed Frank had found it necessary to surgically remove the two of them from it on multiple occasions, such was the pair's adoration for this new indulgence. And not only that, but with no cover overhead to obscure an upward view from the hot tub, and with minimal light pollution, the stars on a winter night were like, quote, *diamonds shimmering in the endless abyss,* according to Dave — with Dave's poetic musings offering a rarely seen glimpse of the more sensitive side of him.

There had been a few early teething-type problems, so to speak, regarding the new indulgence, it has to be said, which largely centred around Dave and Monty failing to grasp the concept of remaining at least *partially* clothed in order to use it. But, after a smart reprimand, along with a good bleach cleaning to the affected device, the hot tub was restored to fully-sterilised, clean working order. Unfortunately, however, with one issue having thus been sorted, another soon arose to take its place from the murky depths, as the boys now liked nothing more than jumping in after a hard, dirt-encrusted day spent tending to the various chores required to maintain an industrial rural retreat. The concept of showering before entering was, again, rather lost on them, with Dave boldly stating, "What's the bloody point in getting clean in order to jump straight into water?" With the water soon resembling, and smelling, as a direct result, like a herd of dinosaur had dropped their guts into it, action had to be taken yet again. This time, it came via Frank in the form of threats of castration, which eventually produced the desired outcome. Whether the boys had genuinely learned the error of their ways, or if they were simply cowed into submission, Frank didn't care, as it was the end result that mattered most, and showering before entering was now part of their routine.

Presently...

"Come *on*," urged Monty, rattling his fingers on the computer mouse impatiently. He'd deliberately left Dave soaking his weary muscles in the tub so that he could return to the laptop in the office, but his IT skills were very much like his current clothing — virtually non-existent. Stan certainly wouldn't thank him for defiling his sumptuous leather chair, what with being sat only in his dingy, sodden Y-fronts. A generous grin emerged as the desired website finally appeared onscreen about the same time as his tongue ran along his upper lip in anticipation.

"*Yes*," Monty whispered, patting the mouse that was now his friend again. He moved his head closer to the screen, taking a moment to ensure the door behind him remained in the closed position with a cursory glance. He bit his bottom lip, hammering away on the keyboard, appearing to forget, such was his concentration level, that he needed to actually *breathe* once in a while. "Oh, *yes*," he said, satisfied, placing his hands behind his head now and collapsing back into the chair, his protruding belly obscuring the

CHAPTER FOUR

view of his shabby underpants. Monty held one eye on the screen, while the other was held, well, somewhere else... possibly on the coat stand next to the window. While he didn't have a computer of his own at home, he had to admit, in that precise moment, he was starting to see the definite virtues in owning one. He removed one hand from behind his head, reaching for a tissue from the box placed neatly on Stan's desk, taking care not to move anything because Stan, being Stan, would know. He feasted on the vision before him, and he held the tissue patiently, waiting to dab at himself once the need should arise.

"Whaddaya doing!" screamed Dave, a sentence which spanned his journey from outside the door, straight through to his opening of it and arrival inside the room — all complete in milliseconds.

Monty screeched like a schoolgirl, with an expression like his face had melted like the Nazi bloke from the Indiana Jones film, pushing his chair away from Dave in abject terror, and throwing his tissue in Dave's general direction in what appeared to be some form of pathetic defence manoeuvre.

Dave had barged in covered in nothing but his underpants and a towel draped over his shoulder. "You're a mucky little bugger!" he continued yelling, shaking his fist like a craps dealer, outlining visually his suspicion as to the mischief and self-abuse to which he felt convinced Monty must surely be engaged. "I knew you were up to something when you left our hot tub session earlier, you filthy rotter!" he went on. "And you missed a shooting star," he added, solemnly now, disappointed, and pointing skyward. "So what is it, then?" he said. "Did my naked torso get you all hot and bothered, Monty, is that it?" he asked, lowering his towel from his shoulder to present a full view of the goods on offer. "It's okay, I'm not upset anymore," he added, his face softening. "I knew you likely couldn't help yourself."

Monty leapt to his feet, possibly to put some distance between himself and the computer, or perhaps to demonstrate, as well, that Little Monty had remained safely tucked away in his cage. "What? Don't be daft!" he protested. "And give me that tissue back!" he added. "I'm sweating from the hot water, that's why I had it, so get your mind out of the gutter!"

"Oh, aye," remarked Dave, with an exaggerated rolling of the eyes, and clearly not believing in Monty's excuses.

The pair of them facing off, with the both of them being plus-sized individuals and both of them in only their undies, it almost looked like a sumo match was about to kick off.

"How did you know I was in here?" asked Monty, scouring the ceiling for hidden cameras.

"There were wet footprints through the kitchen, then through the hall, and then..." Dave answered him, arching his thumb and pointing to the door he'd just recently burst through. "So I don't exactly need to be Sherlock Bloody Holmes, now do I?" he asked rhetorically.

Monty only grunted in response.

"You'd best hope Stan doesn't see that carpet, and god only knows what he'll say when he knows what you've been doing in his chair," Dave went on. And, having said that, the horrors of the tissue he'd caught only moments earlier mid-air as it had come wafting ever so gently down following Monty's furious assault, and was still held firmly in Dave's grasp, suddenly dawned on him. He threw it to the floor, and then wiped his hand on his towel, several times, in order to clean off any possible residue. "I'm not surprised, Monty. Truly I'm not," he said reasonably. "Disappointed, perhaps. But not surprised. I have this effect on a lot of people, so you needn't be ashamed."

"Shut up for a moment, dickhead!" Monty told him. "Here. *Look*," he said, grabbing the excess skin at the rear of one of Dave's chubby arms and steering him towards the desk. "Look for yourself," he advised.

Monty removed his hand from about Dave's person, leaving several red finger marks behind, which Dave nursed with a gentle rub. Dave approached the laptop cautiously, eyeing Monty with suspicion. "You needn't have been so rough," he complained. "Now my arm hurts," he pouted.

"JUST LOOK," Monty demanded, pointing to the laptop computer.

Dave stared down at the screen, and the expression on his face changed instantly. "Oh, yes, Monty," he said, rubbing his thumb and forefinger together approvingly, happy now at having been

CHAPTER FOUR

provided the introduction to what he was now happily viewing. He looked on for a moment longer, his eyes scanning the page, taking it all in, savouring it, and nodding along as if to an imaginary tune in his head. "Oh, *yes*, Monty, my son," Dave reiterated, turning back to Monty with a look of wide-eyed wonderment, exclaiming, "It's the most beautiful thing I've ever seen, Monty, me old mucker!"

"It's pretty special, isn't it? Really gets you tingling inside," Monty offered.

"Tingling," said Dave, repeating Monty's observation in perfect agreement. "In fact, I probably shouldn't be stood this close to you in my undies, as Little Dave may be about to turn up."

"Cold outside?" asked Monty, glancing down.

"Freezing," confirmed Dave most agreeably, lest things get a bit weirder than they were presently. "Now, you're sure you want to do this?" he asked.

Dave gave up his seat so that Monty could sit down once again, with Monty taking his place, finger hovering expectantly over the mouse. "More than anything else, Dave. More than anything else," he said. "And once I hit this button, there's no going back..."

"Do it, big boy. *Do* it," Dave encouraged, now rubbing his friend's weary shoulders in support, giving a little squeeze of reassurance.

Monty patted the hand tenderly rubbing his shoulder, looking back with a soft expression. "Dave and Monty back at the TT races," he said dreamily, returning his attention to the Isle of Man TT website — a portal for those would-be heroes of the tarmac to fulfil their destiny. They were only one click away from fulfilling their destiny once more, one single click away from submitting their entry, once again, to the greatest sporting event on earth, and nothing was going to stop them now, nothing except...

"Bollocks!" shouted Monty, smashing the mouse down on the desktop. "The bloody entries don't open until next month, and I've just spent the last twenty minutes in my undies filling this in for nothing!" he wailed.

"Not for nothing, Monty. Not for nothing," said Dave, leaning in. "Come on, Monty, bring it in," he encouraged, and the two very-nearly-naked sumo wrestlers embraced in a generous, enthusiastic cuddle. "We're going to do the TT again," Dave whispered into Monty's ear, snuggling his chin into Monty's neck.

And then...

"What the actual fuck are you two doing, and which idiot has left a trail of watery footprints throughout the bloody farmhouse?" shouted Stan, slamming the door behind him. "Honestly, since we got that hot tub installed, this place is like a soddin' Turkish baths!" he complained. "And that'll stain the bloody carpet if you've brought dirt in with you, now won't it?" he added admonishingly, pointing here and there to illustrate the soggy areas of concern.

Dave didn't lift his head from Monty's neck. "We're doing the TT again," said Dave, though his voice was muffled by the thick layer of Monty's neck blubber.

In an instant, Stan's anger was gone. "Yes!" he yelled. "Come here, you two big, dozy doughnuts!" he said, pressing forward to place his head on Monty's spare shoulder. "That's made my day, boys. Truly it has."

Several minutes of lingering flesh-pressing was followed by a satisfied sigh as Stan broke away and stood back up, as did Dave. "Hang on. Are you two wearing matching underpants?" asked Stan.

"Eyes up north, you dirty old get!" said Dave, tut-tutting.

"Hey," said Stan. "You know who else will be over the moon by this news?"

"The postman!" replied Monty immediately.

"Yes, the... what? No, not the postman," replied Stan, confused.

"Terry, the postman, is a big fan," explained Dave.

"Tel," added Monty. "It's Tel to his friends."

Stan's eyes were still, God help him, drawn to their matching underpants. "No, I'm not talking about Terry," he said.

"Tel, to his friends," Monty reminded him.

"Terry. Tel. *Whatever*," snapped Stan, although instantly softening his tone at the same time he — mercifully — adjusted his eyeline. "Sorry. I'm talking about Frank. I meant Frank. He's been a little bit down these last few days."

"He's lost weight, even," observed Dave.

CHAPTER FOUR

"I know he has. I need to speak to him about it," said Stan. "And this will help, I think. He needs a little bit of good news, and with this being his last—"

"Don't you say that," Dave cut in firmly. "Don't you even say that."

"Fit as a fiddle, that man," added Monty, as if saying it could make it true.

Stan was not for arguing the point, and the assurances, overly optimistic as they might have been, gave him a much-needed lift under the circumstance nevertheless.

Monty tilted his head. "You seem a bit down yourself, Stan."

Stan offered a forced smile, and for someone ordinarily so upbeat, it was obvious he was in danger of heading squarely into the doldrums. "It's just... thinking about Frank, you know? It hurts. It really hurts," he told them. "I just don't want to even think about... about..." he said, trailing off, voice breaking.

"Come here," said Dave, opening his arms like a flasher pulling apart his trenchcoat.

"And me," offered Monty, standing up to join the two of them, and repeating Dave's pose.

Stan didn't even have a chance to move before, in seconds, he was enveloped within about thirty stones or more worth of warm, hot tub-moistened man flesh — and at that particular moment in Stan's life, there was precisely nowhere on earth he'd rather be. "I love you two crazy loons," he said, from somewhere below Dave's right armpit, and with his face pressed somewhere above Monty's breast. "Though, bloody hell, this is like playing a game of Twister with the wrong instructions," he added, gasping to take a breath, unsure when the opportunity for the next might be available. "Can we tell him tonight?"

"Who, Frank?" asked Dave. "Sure, of course," he replied, cradling and caressing the back of Stan's head.

"He's going to be on cloud nine when he knows Team Frank-and-Stan are back in action at the TT races," remarked Stan happily. But, then, not quite so happily... "*Erm*, Dave?" he asked. "Something's prodding into my thigh, and ordinarily I wouldn't complain, but, you know..."

"Monty's still got the mouse in his hand?" suggested Dave. "At least I bloody hope he has...?"

But Monty didn't answer, just sighing a contented sigh.

Chapter
FIVE

Life had been somewhat challenging for old Eric Fryer of late. While his establishment, Fryer's Café, was doing a roaring trade on account of the new prison being built a stone's throw away and the accompanying steady stream of construction workmen coming in, the sweet sound of his till ringing had been drowned out by the heavy burden of unrequited love. Since Eric had found out about Stella's engagement, he was beside himself. He was off his food, so upset was he, even though its preparation was his very business (and even if the food wasn't off him, judging by the colour of his soiled work apron that an abattoir veteran would've been ashamed to be seen in).

Despite his obvious faults — of which there were admittedly many — Eric Fryer wasn't going to bow down without a fight. To that end, he began his campaign by peppering the taxi office where Stella worked with flowers for three days solid. They weren't the freshest of flowers, it had to be said, and Susie in the taxi office knew for a fact that Eric's sister worked as a nurse on the coronary care unit at the hospital, so the flowery tributes were likely, at best, to be second-hand.

With his floral warfare proving unsuccessful, Eric then upped his game by hiring a mariachi band. He knew Stella liked Mexican food, and he assumed, through his own unique line of reasoning, that her musical tastes would thus translate over to Mexican music also. He even bought himself a sombrero for the occasion in order to lead the romantic charge, entering the taxi office with his

FRANK 'N' STAN'S BUCKET LIST #4 – BRIDE OF FRANK 'N' STAN

musicians in dynamic tow, and with a solitary red rose clenched between his teeth. Unfortunately for Eric, however, the timing of their arrival was somewhat less than perfect as Stella had — as evidenced by the bellowing coming through the toilet door of the taxi office — gone for her morning shit. They waited for about twenty minutes, but the band had a limited repertoire to last beyond ten minutes and they also had another booking in Skelmersdale that they had to get to.

There were other efforts as well and eventually Stella, although she'd been relatively patient with the whole situation, had to tell Eric to *"back the fuck off."* And, to his credit, Eric did in fact back the fuck off. Which was good, because Stella, for her part, didn't want to have to resort to physical violence just yet, as she was rather partial to her daily sausage, black pudding, mushroom, and egg sandwich from Fryer's Café and didn't want to make things awkward enough between them to necessitate an interruption in this regular sandwich-to-mouth supply.

And so, with the flower deliveries having dried up and it having been several days, at least, since Eric had phoned the office in tears, Susie could be forgiven for her surprise in suddenly seeing him with his nose pressed up against the window. "Oh my," said Susie, putting her hand up to her mouth.

Eric peeled his face off the cold glass, leaving a greasy imprint behind. He raised his hand like a salute, deflecting the winter sun so he could see inside. Then, he stretched his arm out so he could open the door whilst leaving the maximum portion of his body out in the street, should the need for a quick getaway arise. "Hi, Susie," he ventured. "Is it safe to come in?" he said in a whisper.

Sensing no danger, Susie released her grip on the wooden cricket bat that Stella had installed behind the counter.

Regarding the bat, most workers in an office environment were expected to undergo fire safety drills, and perhaps first aid training and the like. But not at Frank & Stan's Taxis. At Frank & Stan's Taxis — because of the drunken clientele such a business might reasonably anticipate encountering at all hours, plus as a result of a previous armed robbery — Susie was expected to perform a weekly drill which included resisting a chokehold,

CHAPTER FIVE

placing pressure on a windpipe with the flat edge of a teaspoon or other handy implement, and unleashing at a moment's notice a cricket bat that Stella had secured in place with Velcro under the reception counter. The training appeared to be working, with Susie, by this point, handling the cricket bat with practised ease and without even having to look down — rather like a cowboy gunslinger seamlessly liberating their Colt Peacemaker from its leather holster mooring.

"You're fine," Susie assured Eric, adopting a friendly smile. "Come on in."

"Is she in there?" he asked, glancing over to the loo, flaring his nostrils like a trained English springer spaniel smelling out a truffle.

"No, she's gone shopping for special wedding underwear," Susie answered. But as soon as the words left her mouth, she knew she'd said too much. Eric's shoulders drooped, followed shortly thereafter by his head as well. He sighed, taking the dirty nail on his left thumb to scratch off some dried-in egg from his at-one-time-white cooking apron.

"You, eh, just come from the café?" asked Susie for no apparent reason, because the fact he was stood in his chef's uniform was an obvious indication where he'd just appeared from. And if any further confirmation were required, the distinctive smell of frying grease that filled the air of the taxi office waiting room would have provided it. No, it was more that Susie was asking it by way of distraction. Because, despite being crestfallen only a moment ago, he now appeared to be having lustful thoughts judging by his dilated pupils and his palms rubbing manically on his trousers. Susie could only imagine it was the result of her having mentioned "Stella" and "underwear" in the same sentence.

Eric shook his head like a horse tossing its mane to shoo away flies, successfully clearing his mind — it seemed to Susie, based on Eric's pupils returning to normal — of thoughts of Stella in her lingerie, at least for the moment. "I could do with speaking to her," Eric said, softly.

"I'm sorry, my love. She's not here at the moment, as I said," Susie answered him, nodding her head to appear sympathetic to his apparent pain.

Eric didn't move, speak, or blink, so to avoid the slow death, Susie felt the need to fill the silent void somehow. "So. *Em...* Stella said you'd gotten a tattoo...?" asked Susie, grimacing slightly. She didn't really *want* to ask, necessarily. It was more a case of simply making conversation. Even so, this prompted Eric to cast off his apron in less than an instant and to roll his t-shirt up over his bulging stomach and tuck the bunched-up fabric into his armpits, without need of further invitation.

"Next to my heart," said Eric, his voice tinged with a sort of sad melancholy. "A fat lot of use it done for me, though," he added, cupping his left breast for Susie's closer inspection, even though this was something she neither asked for nor in any way, shape or form desired.

Susie resisted the very strong urge to avert her gaze or be a little sick in her mouth. She tilted her head, squinting her eyes like she was trying to solve an optical illusion, or one of those pictures where you have to look at it in a certain particular way in order for the image to properly come into view. Now, Susie had a lovely disposition, generally, and kicking a man when he was down was the last thing on her mind, but she had to ask...

"I... *ehm...* Eric, I'm sorry, but I don't know what that is...?" she said, moving her head from side to side in little *no-no-no*-type shakes.

"It's Stella," replied Eric confidently, pressing his thumb into his flabby chest. "See?" he added, highlighting the outline of the tattoo by running his finger around the edge of it. "It's a silhouette of her," he explained, momentarily drifting off to a happy place, a happy place where he was the one holding up prospective wedding underwear for her approval.

"You sure?" asked Susie, but not unkindly. "It's like... it's like..." she stammered, buying time, as inspiration was presently eluding her. She chewed her lip, tapping her nails on the wooden surface of the countertop, and then said, "Okay, you know when you buy a balloon and the image distorts a few days later as the helium

CHAPTER FIVE

escapes? It's like that." She added, "Or, well, in your case, maybe after more helium has been pumped in and it's expanded," in reference to Eric's extra-plump tit, though fortunately Eric was too oblivious to take this as an insult. But then Susie tilted her head to one side again, continuing to gnaw on her lip. "Oh, wait, that's it!" she said after a moment, very pleased with herself now, and raising her finger in triumph. "It looks like one of those Rorschach inkblot things!" With the image being difficult to make out what it was exactly, and it being a solid black amorphous blob, and so open to interpretation to a great degree, Susie felt this was a brilliant observation.

Eric was somewhat less impressed with the analogy. "I have no idea what that is that you just said," he replied. Eric pressed out his jaw, lowering his head to peer down at his tit, with several new chins forming in the process. "But *this*," he said, pointing to his breast, "*This* is Stella's hair. A thing of beauty it is, too," he declared. "And this..." he said, and then blathered on from there, continuing to identify what the different aspects of the tattoo were.

It wasn't too long at all before Susie had seen enough, flapping her hand to encourage the restoration of Eric's clothing. "It's a nice gesture, the tattoo," she offered rather magnanimously. "I'm still not sure I can see the likeness, mind. But it's a nice gesture all the same," she added with finality, eager to close this particular line of conversation.

"He's a master," Eric went on, appearing not quite as ready to let go the subject, either figuratively or literally, as he continued to squeeze out his breast in order to afford both himself and Susie a fuller view of tattoo-Stella.

"Who is?" asked Susie, reluctantly.

"Filthy Barry," Eric replied, lowering his breast, to Susie's relief. "He did the tattoo of my lost love. The One That Got Away," he sighed, and finally pulling his shirt back down over his generous stomach — also to Susie's great relief — before adding, "He was the go-to person if you wanted ink at Belmarsh prison. Well, he was up until he got out last year, that is. But I'd say their loss was definitely my gain."

"Filthy Barry? Why on earth is he the...?" Susie began. "Actually, never mind," she said, immediately correcting herself and in no way wanting to know the answer. She glanced around, hoping for any form of distraction to present itself, anything at all. It was ironic, she thought, and unfortunate as well, that the office phone ordinarily rang incessantly but was right now choosing to remain quiet. It was as if it were listening in to the conversation and didn't want to interrupt.

"The reason I'm here..." said Eric eventually, and to Susie's great delight, as she was happy there was some sort of reason that might not involve Eric pining relentlessly over Stella and/or removing articles of clothing. Eric fastened his apron around himself again, and then appeared to forget he was about to say something.

"Yes...?" replied Susie, waving her hand in a circular motion, like a buoy bobbing gently on ocean waves, encouraging Eric along.

"Weeelll," said Eric, drawing the word out as he took a moment or two to get his train of thought back on track. "Some bloke has been in the café asking after you lot. Scruffy-looking bloke, with a cheap, scruffy suit, and scruffy hair."

"So... he was scruffy, is what you're saying?" asked Susie.

"Yes, exactly!" Eric answered, Susie's mildly sarcastic tone again going completely unnoticed. "He made me feel a bit unclean, to be honest," Eric added, removing the tip of his little finger from inside his ear canal, where it'd been placed a few seconds earlier. He examined the finger's nail for earwax, checking the yield, before continuing, "You know, the kind of bloke that makes you feel a bit... uneasy?"

"Yes," replied Susie instantly. "Yes, I do," she said, the irony in her comment washing straight over Eric's head.

"Asking all sorts of questions, he was," said Eric.

"About who? Stella?" asked Susie.

Eric reached into his other ear, delving further, continuing on with his exploratory earwax expedition. "He was asking about Stella, yes," he confirmed. "But also Frank, Stan, everyone. Basically everyone."

"Even me?" Susie asked.

Eric thought a moment. "No, not you."

CHAPTER FIVE

"Right, so not everyone, then," Susie replied. "Perhaps he was wanting to know about the charity? A journalist, maybe?" she suggested.

Eric shrugged his shoulders. "I guess," he said, but the odd expression on his face suggested he possibly remained not entirely convinced. Or, it could have been that his burrowing fingertip had broken straight through to his brain compartment. Whatever the case, he went on, "There was just something about him, you know? Something not quite right. I can't place my finger on what, exactly," he said, wiggling the tip of his pinkie around in his ear for deeper purchase. "And I probably shouldn't have said anything to him. It's just..."

"Just what?" asked Susie, suddenly losing the will to live.

"Well, I didn't realise it at first," he answered her. "But he was definitely digging around for something. And then, when he started asking about my Stella, and her relationship to Frank and Stan, well, that's just when I had to put my foot down!" he said, exclaiming at this last point, and actually stamping his own foot down like an angry bull to punctuate it. At the same time as he did this, he pulled his finger from his ear as well, finally, resulting in a loud popping noise.

"I see," said Susie, nodding her head along, humouring him, but secretly hoping he'd go away soon.

"Nobody meddles in my Stella's personal business apart from me!" Eric clarified, in some sort of perverse version of chivalry. "Anyway, I thought I should let you know that this scruffy weirdo has been asking about you all around the neighbourhood, yeah?" he said, adding, "*Ehm*, when I say *you*, I mean you in general. Not *you*, you."

"I understand," Susie assured him, wondering when this was all going to end. She picked up her office telephone, tapping the switchhook button on the handset cradle repeatedly to get a dial tone and to make sure the thing was still operational. She set the phone back down and sighed. "Anything else?" she asked.

"You'll be sure to tell Stella that I've got her back?" Eric said, starting towards the door.

"I will indeed, Eric," Susie said, eager to see him on his way. "I'll let her know straight away, just as soon as she comes back in," she promised him.

With Eric's limited detective skills, the last ten minutes would have made for the worst episode of *Midsomer Murders* ever. Still, he puffed out his chest as he made his way out the exit, proud at having defended Stella's honour, and proud of performing his civic duty at relating to Susie that he'd done so. And, now, with that duty fulfilled, he was off to tend to the congested arteries of his loyal patrons once more.

Susie gratefully watched him leave, offering a friendly wave as he looked over his shoulder from the street outside. "Bye, now," she mouthed to him through the glass...

... Just as she was interrupted by the phone. "Oh, of course, *now* you bloody well ring!" she said, offering the inanimate object the most indignant frown she could muster.

The afternoon pressed on, leaving Susie with an anxious knot in her stomach on account of there being no Stella to speak of. Susie had sent several worried messages but had received nothing in response. Ordinarily, there would be no cause for concern, as Stella could look after herself quite well. But, taking into account what Eric had mentioned earlier, Susie was starting to panic. The next line of enquiry would be with Lee, but Susie was reluctant to involve him at this stage, not wishing to get him worried as well, at least until she knew there might actually be something worth worrying about.

After a bit, Susie glanced at her mobile once more. "Where *are* you, Stella?" she wondered aloud, twisting her hair around her pen with her free hand. "Right, then," she said, setting down her pen, readying herself to call Lee. But her dialling finger came to an abrupt halt as a looming figure, its back to Susie, collapsed against the entrance door. Instinctively, Susie undid the Velcro strap, unleashing the cricket bat from its station under the counter, and pushed her chair back several inches in readiness, bracing herself

CHAPTER FIVE

for action. "I'm armed!" she shouted, holding the handle of the bat firmly in both hands.

The figure eased away from the door, just slightly, and then turned around.

"Oh, Stella!" shouted Susie, now that she could see clearly who it actually was, and that it wasn't some knife-wielding maniac. She lowered her weapon and ran over to the door, fussing as she went. "Are you okay?" she asked. "Are you okay, Stella?" she asked again, once she'd reached the door, pulling it open. "Are you all right??"

"Hmm? Yeah, sure. Why wouldn't I be all right?" Stella asked casually, then sucking the life from her fag in hand and exhaling in Susie's direction so Susie could enjoy the cigarette smoke as well. Stella was considerate like that.

"I was worried!" Susie told her. "The way you were slumping against the door like that!"

"What in the hell are you on about?" asked Stella, thoroughly perplexed by, what seemed to her, Susie's bizarre overreaction. "And I wasn't slumping. My feet are killing me, that's all," she explained. "All this bloody clothes shopping!" she went on. "I don't know how people do it on the regular. Anybody gets any enjoyment from shopping must be mental!"

"I told you I was happy to come with you to help," said Susie, checking Stella over for visible signs of damage, of which there appeared to be none, or at least nothing new.

Stella snubbed her ciggy out on the back of her hand. "Grab them bags, Susie," she instructed, pointing to the several bags she'd set down on the doorstep. "I'm bloody knackered, and I need to go to the bog for an intimate wash!" she announced, with no effort to lower her voice in case anyone should be about that might possibly overhear.

"So did you find something... sexy, then?" asked Susie by way of conversation, pronouncing the word *sexy* in possibly the most unsexy manner imaginable. She received only a grunt in response, and then Stella was off, making a beeline to the toilet.

Susie returned, bags in hand, to her side of the counter, smiling, impressed that Stella had been out shopping like a proper lady. She sat down, peering inside one of the bags at what appeared very much like a folded parachute. "I'll just leave them in here," she said to herself, the realisation of what they actually were — a very, *very* large pair of cream knickers — dawning on her, and patting the bag gently once closed over.

Susie figured her friend would be in need of a cup of tea and a nice biscuit, and so got up and busied herself in doing exactly that. A boiling kettle, as it should happen, was also useful in drowning out the groaning noises emanating from behind the closed door of the loo.

"I was sweating my tits off in those shops!" announced Stella, reappearing once her intimate wash, or whatever it was she was doing, had been concluded. She collapsed into her chair, running her fingers over her tight natural perm.

"Did you find what you were looking for, at least?" enquired Susie, with an expectant smile.

"What, in the bog?" asked Stella. "Oh," she said. "Oh, you mean at the shops. I'm not built for shopping," declared Stella, not really answering Susie's question directly. "I must have tried on thirty pairs of knickers, and it's not comfortable at all doing that when they've got the bloody heating turned up so high in those changing rooms!"

Susie tittered, fully expecting Stella to crack a smile... But, no, no smile was forthcoming, as it turned out. "Stella, I don't mean to pry or anything, but what do you mean exactly when you say you tried knickers on?" she asked.

Stella narrowed her eyes. "I mean I tried them on. What *else* would I mean?" she said. "How the hell are you supposed to know if they fit you unless you try them on?" She looked at Susie like Susie was incredibly daft.

Susie's grin evaporated. "So, you actually wore the knickers?" she asked, incredulous. "And put the ones back that didn't fit? Even though, especially, you were warm and sweaty as you said? You put them back on the shelf?" she added, just to clarify the journey of all the various knickers that didn't pass the grade and end up in Stella's shopping bags.

"What else am I meant to do with them?" scoffed Stella. "Have you been on the gin again?"

CHAPTER FIVE

Susie had a moment's silence, in reflection of the poor lady of a certain size who'd soon have the misfortune of buying the knickers that Stella had returned, soiled, back to the sale rack.

"I was worried about you," offered Susie eventually. "You were much later than I thought," she said. "And what do you mean, *on the gin again?*" she added.

But Stella was rummaging through her shopping bags. "Hmm? Oh, I was getting my lip waxed," she said. "It took them longer than they thought."

"Oh, I didn't notice," said Susie. "Does Lee like it?"

"Why would Lee like getting his lip waxed? You're not making any sense," replied Stella, removing her head from the plastic bag and wiping specks of dirt off a partially eaten egg & cress sandwich she'd recovered. "I thought I'd lost you!" she said, holding her new snack aloft, and addressing the snack.

"No, I meant—" Susie started to say.

"Lee likes a bit of facial hair, I must confess," said Stella, cutting in. "He says it tickles his balls," she told Susie, without breaking her adoring stare at the remains of her lunch. "He'll get used to it like this," she said, throwing what was left of the sandwich into her cavernous mouth and masticating enthusiastically.

Quite unsure where to go with the unnecessary and unsavoury titbit of information regarding Lee's tickled testicles, Susie opted for a change of subject instead. "Eric Fryer was in earlier," she said.

"Dirty get," replied Stella, her face instantly etched with disgust, and offering no further explanation.

"He showed me his tattoo," Susie went on. "It's... well, it's lovely," she offered.

"Lovely, my arse!" Stella shot back, rearing up. "It looks like the outline of a tree! Are you saying I look like a tree, Susie?"

"What? No. No, of course not," Susie answered. She went quiet for a moment. "It was... poetic, maybe?" she suggested, eventually. "What with it being a silhouette and all?"

"It looked like it was in the shape of a bloody toilet brush to me," said Stella. "Or a... a..." she added, searching for the right word.

"A Rorschach inkblot?" offered Susie bravely.

Rather than offering up a slap with the back of her hand, as Susie was afraid she might, Stella started to chuckle. This was a great relief to Susie, but also a little unnerving as it wasn't what one might consider a normal reaction. But Stella was something of an enigma in that regard, and where most would take offence, Stella was now sniggering away merrily to herself. "I don't know what that thing is you just said. But it reminded me, my teacher used to always call me Inkblot Head at school," Stella said wistfully, patting her hand over the wire scouring pad that was her hair. It was a fond, nostalgic memory Stella was recalling, judging by the temporary laughter lines forming around her eyes, such laughter wrinkles rarely revealing themselves. "Inkblot Head," she repeated, chuckling to herself, and then letting out a contented sigh.

"Anyway..." said Susie, interrupting Stella's trip down memory lane. "I was saying about Eric?"

Stella snapped back to the present. "If he thinks he's getting that torque wrench back, he can sod right off! He bought me that fair and square!" she said, returning to form.

"No," said Susie. She had no idea what a torque wrench even was, much less why Stella's mind would suddenly jump to the subject of torque wrenches. "He said to mention to you that some scruffy chap — *very* scruffy-looking, in fact, if Eric is to be believed — has been around the café asking questions about you, about your relationship with Frank and Stan, and also about the charity," she explained. "Oh, and that he defended your honour," she added in. "He wanted me to be especially sure I told you the part about him defending your honour."

"It's my torque wrench!" continued Stella, wanting to make certain her point about this was clear. "Wait, what are you talking about, Susie? Who's been asking questions about me?" she said, the rest of what Susie was saying finally filtering in. "If someone's been poking their nose into my business, they'll end up with that torque wrench embedded in their skull!"

"Have you noticed any suspicious behaviour around you lately? Anyone acting weirdly, of late?" asked an obviously concerned Susie earnestly, but receiving only a frosty stare in return.

"Including you, or excluding you?" asked Stella.

CHAPTER FIVE

"No. Leaving me to one side for a moment," Susie told her. Stella now had her thumb hooked under her chin and was stroking with her finger the reddened area above her top lip where the hair of her lady-moustache had been extirpated. Susie tried not to stare, as the association between it and Lee's bollocks was now upsetting.

"Hmm, well there was that one bloke acting a bit odd," Stella considered, still stroking her upper lip.

"Oh? What bloke is this?" asked Susie, but Stella had taken to looking into her bag again.

"Have you seen my receipt?" asked Stella, scouring the floor and offering no further explanation as to the odd-acting chap.

"Stella, what about the bloke acting oddly?" pressed Susie.

"It's nothing," said Stella flatly. "I thought it was the bloke from the downstairs flat trying to look at me in the shower again."

"What...?" asked a horrified Susie. "Did you call the police??"

Stella broke away from looking for her receipt. "Police? Just for looking at me in the shower? Don't be bloody stupid, why would I do that?" she asked incredulously. "You don't call the police for something so trivial as that," she said. "Besides, it wasn't him anyway, now was it?" she added, as if Susie should know this. "It was someone rummaging through the bins."

"Rummaging through the bins?" asked Susie.

"Yes. I thought maybe it was Lee," said Stella.

"You thought Lee was rummaging through the bins?" asked a confused Susie.

"*Yes.* Aren't you listening to what I'm saying?" replied Stella, on the verge of becoming cross. "I didn't pay it too much attention, at that point. I mean, old habits die hard, right? And what with his former life living on the streets and all..." she explained. "Anyway. This other bloke saw me and buggered off, quick smart."

"Wait, are you talking about the fellow rummaging through the bins now? Or the bloke who saw you in the shower, previously?" asked Susie, trying to make sense of everything Stella was saying. "He saw you in the shower, and then he ran away...?"

"No, the man scavenging in the bins!" barked Stella. "If it was the bloke watching me in the shower, why would he turn and run?

Think, Susie. I mean, if he was getting a proper eyeful of yours truly *au naturel*, then why in hell would he run away?? Don't be daft!"

"I wasn't implying…" Susie started to say, but then thought better of it, as she didn't want Stella working herself into a lather over it. "Anyway, I think we should tell Frank and Stan," ventured Susie. "What with this fellow poking around in your bins, and now this fellow down at Eric's café, it all seems a bit odd to me," she said. "And I can't imagine it's a coincidence."

"Ah!" exclaimed Stella happily. "I've found the receipt!" she said, reaching into the bag to recover it. "Good, good. Because I'm going to have to return these pair of knickers as there's a stain on them already."

"A stain? Oh, that's awful," said Susie supportively, peering over Stella's shoulder and into the bag. "Which ones?"

"These," said Stella, holding a lemon-coloured thong up high. "I wore them on the way home to break them in, but when I went for my little wash, I noticed a stain. So they'll have to go back."

Susie shuddered. There were days, like most people, when one's work duties proved to be a little trying. Draining, even. But at that moment, Susie felt nothing but compassion, and the deepest of sympathy, for the unfortunate shop assistant who was going to have to handle Stella returning her stained underwear, with Stella fully expectant of a refund.

"*Soooo*, anyway," said Susie, changing tack and gently sailing the conversation back to the subject she felt was of far greater concern. "I'm going to give Stan a quick ring and let him know that we've got us a mystery stalker or two on our hands. At this point, we don't know if it's one fellow or two. It could be the same person." She paused, considering this. "Stella. The man going through your bins. Was he scruffy-looking, by any chance…?" Susie asked tentatively.

"Dunno. Didn't get that good of a look at him," Stella replied. "Though anybody going through bins is bound to be fairly scruffy-looking, I expect," she told Susie. She said this distractedly, like she was only half-listening.

"Well, either way, we should be on our guard, I think," Susie cautioned. "This person, or persons, could be someone dangerous, right? You just never know. I mean, there are some really disturbed

CHAPTER FIVE

individuals out there, am I right, Stella?" The fear in Susie's voice was evident. Or at least it would have been if Stella was hearing it.

"Stella?"

But Stella's eyes had glazed over. She wasn't listening at all now. She had something else on her mind, presently, and was still thinking about something from earlier.

"Stella...?" asked Susie again, gingerly trying to coax a response out of her friend.

"There's no way that bloody idiot's getting his torque wrench back!" Stella blurted out, very suddenly, like a demented Tourette's sufferer.

Susie sighed, and then picked up the phone.

Chapter SIX

Mistletoe sprigs, twinkling lights, and a plethora of brash gewgaws hung from every available square inch of fabric, including one that let out a high-energy version of the seasonal classic "Let It Snow! Let It Snow! Let It Snow!" every time the protruding carrot nose of a decorative snowman was pressed. It was festive campness in overload, but Stan wouldn't have had his Christmas outfit any other way. It was difficult to discern, but underneath the various and sundry adornments, his green suit was also covered with felt Christmas pudding patches from collar to trouser cuff. He really had put an excellent shift in with the effort that'd gone into his suit.

What else was deeply impressive, aside from Stan's outfit, was the progress that'd been made on the TT Farm, as the boys had officially named it. Dave, Monty, and the rest of the building team had worked tirelessly since Frank and Stan had secured the farm earlier in the year, and whilst there was still a great deal of work to be done in order to finish off their master plan for the place, the guest accommodation quarters were coming along just fine. The only permanent residents, for now, were Becks and her son Tyler, at least until the remaining rooms in the guest wing were renovated and due to welcome their first guests in the spring, subject, of course, to the building works finishing to plan. Although, it could be argued, as well, that Dave was at least a semi-permanent resident, due to the amount of time he was spending with Becks.

FRANK 'N' STAN'S BUCKET LIST #4 – BRIDE OF FRANK 'N' STAN

Becks had prewarned everyone on her arrival to the TT Farm that Christmas was 'her thing,' and that if nobody objected she'd love the opportunity to get the place looking particularly festive. Of course, nobody objected, with Frank and Stan offering her free rein as far as decorating duties, even digging deeply into their wallets and providing a generous budget to buy plenty of lights, decorations, and a splendid tree to place in the courtyard that was tall enough to pose a hazard to passing aircraft — and with Frank suggesting that the lights on the tree, once decorated, would drain the national grid the first time they were switched on.

The collection of blinking lights fastened up to every available outer wall brought a warm sense of nostalgia to Christmases long ago, and a fondness for simpler times. Adding to the Christmas-card-scene look of the place were the various animals of the farm wandering at will and coming in from the field to see what all the fuss was about. With the animals about, and Frank dressed up as a shepherd for his Christmas outfit come Christmas day, the TT Farm was very much resembling a nativity scene. It truly was the most wonderful setting to host friends and family for a Christmas day feast lovingly prepared by Frank.

A turkey large enough to feed a small town hadn't gone to waste, and the barn they'd converted to use as the education centre once the farm was completely up and running provided a wonderful venue for the day. Frank sat at the head of the table with his hand wrapped around his wooden shepherd's crook, clearly embracing his character for the day's proceedings. He smiled simply, running his eyes around the dinner table. The barn had been derelict for decades, yet here it was now, playing host to laughter and kindness, a venue to truly embrace the spirit of Christmas. Frank took a sip from his wine glass, peering over the rim to Stan sat on the opposite side of the table from him, close enough to engage in conversation but far enough away to tune out if he so desired. Stan, for his part, was midway through a brilliantly theatrical singing performance of the Christmas favourite "The Twelve Days of Christmas." To enhance his performance, he was utilising his acting skills to animate the rendition, flapping his arms when birds were mentioned, and jumping to his feet to

CHAPTER SIX

illustrate when the lords had started a-leaping, for instance. His rendition — at least on the occasion of a certain young observer being present — necessitated the removal of the rather bawdily-demonstrated action of maids a-milking, a bit he ordinarily would have been keen to act out on such recitations on Christmases past. Tyler, who sat glued to his mum's arm, watched on in wonderment and squealed in delight as Stan went through each successive verse, replete with exuberant hand gestures and a performance worthy of the stage.

Monty's chair, next to Tyler, was empty. After eating one Christmas meal with his dear friends, he was off to spend time with his family, threatening to polish off yet another turkey dinner with all the trimmings. Lee was next to the empty chair with Stella sat directly opposite to him. She screwed up her eyes, concentrating on the paper in her grasp. Such was her attention to the matter at hand that she looked like she could have been in pain — or wracked with post-turkey wind — eventually looking across the table to Lee, opposite. Without warning, she started howling with laughter, much to Lee's delight, while reading the slip of paper extracted from the larger portion of the cracker she'd retained in the struggle with Lee a few moments earlier.

"Tell me what it says?" asked Lee, but Stella was still roaring with laughter.

At that moment, seeing Stella happy, with a man who loved her for who she was, Frank had the urge to walk over and give her a cuddle. He resisted the impulse, as she wasn't done with the joke she was reading, but also because creeping up on Stella — and especially initiating physical contact with her unannounced — was potentially dangerous.

Stella wiped her eyes with the back of her hand, leaving great smears of mascara — and looking like a heavy metal singer in the process as a result — as she lowered the paper.

"Tell me!" Lee said again, slapping his hand on the table in mock protest.

Stella struggled for breath. "W-what do you get if you c-cross a snowman with... with a vampire?" she stammered, struggling to get the words out and gasping for air.

Frank noticed Lee mouth the answer to himself as Stella recited the line — with Lee evidently having been familiar with this joke from some Christmas prior — but noticed, also, that Lee very graciously still let her go on, not wanting to ruin the punchline.

"I don't know. What *do* you get if you cross a snowman with a vampire?" asked Lee, repeating her words back and feigning innocence like it was the first time he'd heard them.

"Frostbite!" bellowed Stella, erupting in laughter once more as she delivered the punchline with comic precision. "Oh, bugger, I think I'm going to piss myself!" she cried mirthfully, much to the amusement of Lee, smiling on with kind eyes, and with Stella now screaming for air.

Tyler glanced over — taking a short intermission from Stan's musical performance — with a flicker of apprehension at the volume emanating from the 'big scary lady' (as he'd referenced her to his mum previously). His nerves were mended when those around her erupted in laughter, however, and he briefly sidled over, eager to hear the joke repeated, but with his mum's arms dragging him back so as not to leave Stan without an audience.

Sat either side of Frank, and engaged in their own conversation — although briefly interrupted by Stella's joke also — were Jessie and Molly, sat opposite each other across the table, and talking at a rate, pitch, and intensity that made it difficult for the male of the species to possibly keep up with. It was for this reason that Frank was allowing his attention to wander across the table — though he was half-listening in to them, at least, as the two ladies in his life were discussing wedding-related matters and so allowing his attention to wander too far would be perilous. "Sure, totally agree," he'd chime in with periodically, making encouraging noises as required, with the occasional bob of the head for good measure.

Of course the two girls knew full well Frank wasn't entirely paying attention, but they let this slide. It was, after all, the season of goodwill.

Frank continued to watch Lee and Stella. With Stella having settled down, Lee was now employing his acting skills, appearing to be performing from something written on a scrap of paper he'd stolen a glance at. Charades, thought Frank. Frank liked charades,

CHAPTER SIX

and was eager to get in on the action but also fearful of leaving the wedding conversation he was pretending to be involved in. Stella, meanwhile, watched Lee's flailing, gesticulating limbs but to no avail, the clues evading her. Frank watched on as, eager to help his beloved, Lee mouthed a clue, possibly giving away more than he should.

"Everything okay, Frank?" asked Jessie, leaning over to top up his glass of red.

Frank offered a benevolent smile, further accented by a twinkle in his eye. "I'm more than okay," replied Frank, and, once his glass was replenished, took Jessie's hand before reaching over to take Molly's as well. "In fact, I'm wonderful," he added, placing a gentle kiss on the back of each of their hands. "Good food, good wine, and good company? What more could I possibly want?"

"Hard cock!" screamed Stella. This was shouted out just as there was a lull in the conversation, which served only to bring Stella's proclamation into further, stark relief.

Becks immediately placed her hands over Tyler's ears, even though it was too late to do any good. And, Tyler, for his part, was now giggling, and with a snot bubble in danger of forming from his nose.

"No, no, hang on!" added Stella, correcting herself, working out the solution. "Don't tell me, don't tell me! It's... it's... *Hard Rock Café!*" she squealed.

"Correct!" announced Lee, turning over his cracker gift to reveal the phrase she'd just screamed out. "I don't know where the hell you got Hard... you-know-what... from?" he said, whispering the *you-know-what* part, for fear of Tyler's eager ears tuning in once more in curiosity.

"If you find out more about that subject, will you let me know?" asked Stan, who then immediately mouthed an apology. "It must be the vino," he offered by way of an excuse.

Later...

It was completely past Tyler's bedtime, but nobody was saying anything about that and so neither was Tyler. He'd moved away from the stuffy adults, for the most part, and was now making good use of the radio-controlled monster truck that Dave and

Monty had bought for him. Monty, bless his heart, had spent hours over the course of the previous week diligently applying a new paint job to the toy so that its colour scheme precisely resembled that of his and Dave's big-boiled-sweet sidecar. He'd even bastardised a couple of Lego figures so that they bore a passing resemblance to himself and Dave, and then placed them in the driver's cab. And Dave had taken great delight in lending his own personal touch by adding with permanent marker, onto the face of Monty's figure, one eye looking at the steering wheel and one glancing simultaneously over to the wing mirror.

As to the adults, the crisp vibration produced by a knife gently tapping a fine crystal wine glass had little impact on interrupting the enthusiastic chatter around the room. With the first volley on the glass having little impact, Frank took to his feet to offer another salvo, this time accompanied by a purposeful clearing of the throat.

"Oh, blimey, a bloody speech!" said Stan in protest. But this was accompanied by a good-natured smile.

"Cheeky bugger!" remarked Frank, lowering his glass — giving Molly the opportunity to top it up for him lest it should run dry, but also in preparation for the toast.

Frank took a moment to clear his thoughts, to think about what it was he wanted to say, and to simply soak in and enjoy the scene and occasion. "Oh. I almost forgot I was dressed as a shepherd," he said, glancing down at his tunic and adjusting the sleeve of his wine-bearing hand. "Anyway," he went on, "I just wanted to take a couple of minutes to, well, you know, say a few words. And I promise you all that I won't keep you from the drinks cabinet for too terribly long."

"Hear, hear!" shouted Dave, in happy reference to the drinks cabinet.

"Anyway, it's been quite a year, hasn't it," Frank announced as a statement, pressing onward. "I reflected on all of this as I watched the lot of you enjoying yourselves. We've got ourselves a TT winner here, for instance, sat over there," he said, motioning over to Dave, who gave a little bow. "Who I'm delighted to confirm is going to race at next year's TT races, along with our Monty, once again,"

CHAPTER SIX

Frank went on, a pronouncement resulting in Dave, in Monty's absence, lifting his beer can up in acknowledgement in a sort of malty salute. "Also, we've got my beautiful daughter, Molly," said Frank, continuing on, and turning to her now. "She's found herself a wonderful career she's really enjoying, that—"

"Doesn't involve me getting my tits out!" interjected Molly, gyrating her chest for effect, and also to show off her surgically enhanced dual assets.

"I was going to say, *that has wonderful prospects*, young lady," Frank replied, to a round of laughter.

"Tits!" Dave called out merrily, for no apparent reason other than that he really, really liked tits. And of course this set Tyler, from the other room, to giggling again.

Frank waited until everyone had settled down before carrying on. Then, he looked over to Stella, though Stella's attention was elsewhere, rummaging through a group of discarded crackers, likely in search of another joke that got missed the first time around, by the looks of things. "And then there's our Stella," said Frank, attempting to draw her notice. "We've got our wonderful Stella, who's now management in the taxi business..."

"Senior management!" she shouted back without looking up.

"*Senior* management," Frank repeated for her benefit, and with proper emphasis. "And I'm sure Molly won't mind me saying this, but you, Stella, you're like another daughter to me. Well, you're like a daughter to both Stan and myself, I should say, rather. And the two of us, Stan and me, have watched you grow from a rather formidable, menacing young lady into a... into a..." he said, pausing to reflect for a moment.

Stella shot him a furtive glance, half looking up from her pile of crackers to see what kind of rubbish Frank was about to spout.

"Well, pretty much the same thing, actually, only a bit older," Frank went on, garnering a round of chuckles. "But you're a caring, compassionate member of this family, and one who's turned out to be a successful businesswoman, at that. I mean, who *else* can keep a load of hairy-arsed taxi drivers in check, as well as making sure Stan and I don't get ourselves into too much mischief?" Frank stopped to take a sip of his wine glass before blowing Stella a kiss, a kiss that was promptly ignored, although he did catch a glimmer of a smile across her face before she turned her attention back to her collection of crackers once again.

"Stan, Stan, Stanley. Thank you for being you," Frank carried on. "You've been the most loyal friend, companion, and business partner a man could ever wish for. If it wasn't for you, old pal, I wouldn't be the man I am today. For that, I'm honoured to call you a friend."

Stan tapped his fist next to his heart in appreciation — setting the singing snowman decoration on his suit into action in the process. "You, too, Frank. You too," he said, desperately fiddling with the frosty, foolish device to try and get it to shut up, squeezing it here, there, and everywhere. Eventually, he just gave up and with a resigned, comical shrug, let it sing its happy song. This started a cheerful, lively, impromptu sing-along, which Frank was more than willing to let interrupt his speech.

Once the unexpected musical interlude had come to its eventual conclusion, Frank then turned his sights to Lee. "Lee?" he said. "Lee, you're an inspiration to me. To *all* of us. You've overcome adversity to head up our charity efforts across the UK. We've now got hostels across the country helping those who're homeless and those just in need of a little help at a difficult time of their lives. Additionally, we've now got food shelters in nearly every major city in the UK, with more being added on the regular," said Frank, beaming with pride. "How many have we got now, at present? Do you know, by chance?" he asked of Lee.

Lee held his hand up, fingers extended, lowering each one in turn and counting along as he did so. He chewed his cheek, jigging his head as he counted out the numbers in his head. When he was done, he did this all over again, going through his fingers, and counting them out in his head, multiple times. "Hang on," he said, still working on it. "Still counting…"

"It's a lot, let's just say," Frank entered in, saving poor Lee from getting carpal tunnel syndrome as a result of all the repeated counting motions he was having to perform.

"That it is," Lee agreed happily. He shared a laugh with Frank before Frank continued…

CHAPTER SIX

"The work that Lee has done — with the support of a good lady in his life — is remarkable. And speaking of the charity, that brings me 'round to the subject of this place..." Frank said, running his admiring eyes around the room, and setting down his wine glass to offer those present a playful round of applause as he did so, like each and every one of them had gone up on stage to win an Oscar. "It's truly amazing what's been done with this place so far, and continues to be done. And as if that weren't enough in itself, the plan is to get several more places, similar to this one right here, across the UK, as well, over the next couple of years!" Frank turned back to Lee, addressing him directly, saying, "Who'd have thought, from that night we met you in that shop doorway, that—"

"That you'd just come from the strip club...?" Lee interjected happily.

"Well, yes. I mean, technically, yes. But that's not what I was..." Frank began to say, but he was drowned out by the sound of Dave's laughter.

Dave eventually settled down, the result of the stern look Frank cast him, though Frank couldn't help grinning a little himself.

"Oh, bugger," said Lee, worrying he was spoiling the moment, and looking over to Molly and Jessie apologetically. "I'm really sorry, I didn't mean to say..." he offered, trailing off.

Stan couldn't resist chipping in at this point. "You don't need to apologise to Molly!" suggested Stan, throwing Molly a mirthful smile. "After all, we'd just left her inside the club, now didn't we?"

"You brought Molly to a strip club??" asked Becks, giving Stan an incredulous glare.

Stan shook his head no, but it was Frank who answered Becks' question for him. "*Bring* her there? Of course not! What kind of father do you think I am? No, Molly was *working* there!"

"She was," Stan duly confirmed to a sceptical-looking Becks. "It's true, she really was," he said with a jolly laugh.

"It was right after I'd got my boobs done!" said Molly, pointing to her boobs just in case there was any confusion as to where they were — although, alternately, one would have been well-served to simply follow Dave's eyeline, as his eyes were presently homed in on that direct location. "Dad told me I needed a job," Molly went on. "And so..." she said, not bothering to finish the thought out loud, since she felt the decision for getting a job as a stripper after having a boob job was entirely logical and eminently self-evident.

"You should have seen your dad's face, Molly, when he not only spotted you there, but realised you were *working* there. Priceless!" Stan told her, grinning. "And this was shortly after Frank had just been accused of stealing Ivanka's knickers, if I recall, resulting in us being asked to leave," he added, sighing contentedly in fond, nostalgic recollection — despite the small matter that he was in fact reminiscing about them being ejected from a seedy strip club up a grubby back street.

"Her name was *Ivana*," protested Frank. "And I didn't steal her knickers, they were caught on my belt," he added, as if this in some possible way made things sound any better. "Besides. That stripper had stolen my hat," said Frank, looking to a surprisingly amused Jessie. "Anyway," he went on, with a dismissive sweep of the hand, like a rubbish magician's poor attempt at misdirection, "That was some time ago, and besides, Stan dragged me along — kicking and screaming, I might add! — and I wouldn't do anything even *remotely* disreputable like that now. Not anymore," insisted Frank, taking Jessie's hand into his own. "Not since I met *you*, my love," he said to her adoringly, laying it on extra thick, blinking innocently, eyelashes fluttering.

"Wait, *hang* on," said Dave, feeling the need to jump in at this point. "You'd never do anything even remotely disreputable now, is that what I heard you just say?? Do I need to remind you about that time, not so long ago at all, that you were spotted with my mum, in her car, out on some remote country lane, doing *god-only-knows-what?* I distinctly remember this, mind you, because you nearly got me arrested for dogging when the police recognised the car when I was unfortunate enough to be out driving it soon after and they thought they'd finally caught up with a certain perverted perpetrator of most decidedly disreputable things!"

"*Aaaannnyway...*" said Frank, hoisting up his wine glass again, and tapping it with his engagement ring in a *lets-bloody-move-on*, sharpish kind of way. "What I was trying to say, Lee, is that Stan and I are exceptionally proud of the way you've turned your life

CHAPTER SIX

around, and the fine character that you've become. I know that, under your stewardship, the charity will only go from strength to strength. And so, given all that, I have to say I couldn't be any more pleased that you've agreed to take our Stella to be your wife."

Lee nodded in appreciation, allowing Frank to continue.

"And speaking of impending weddings, that moves me on to this wonderful lady to my right, Jessie," said Frank. He turned, looking her straight in the eyes, and shifted his wine glass to his other hand so that he could take hers up with his right. "Jessie, I have to pinch myself to remind me that meeting you was not a dream," he told her. "You make me smile, you make me laugh, and above all, you make my life..." he said, pausing, his voice wobbling. He took a deep breath. "Jessie," he said, soldiering on, "You make my life complete, and I cannot wait until I get to call you Jessie Cryer— Jessie Cryer, my wife." And with that, he leaned in to place a tender kiss on her cheek.

"Don't you think I've forgotten about Ivanka," she said, feigning displeasure.

"Ivana!" shouted Stan, helpfully. "It was..." he began, but then trailing off when all eyes turned to him. "Ivana," he said again, rather more sheepishly this time.

"What's a stripper?" asked Tyler, wandering back over to the adults at the table in order to retrieve his monster truck. The toy had driven under the table, and was now caught up, bumping against chair legs in search of an exit. Tyler was turning the joystick on his remote control this way and that, but the truck wasn't coming free.

Dave leaned over to retrieve the vehicle from the bars of its chair-leg prison. "A stripper?" said Dave, handing the toy truck back to the boy. "Ah. Well. A stripper, you see, is someone that takes wallpaper off the walls," he said authoritatively. "Like a painter and decorator, for instance," explained Dave, offering a wink back in Becks' direction as he did so.

"Oh. Okay," said Tyler, appearing happy enough with Dave's explanation. "So Aunty Molly is a painter and decorator?" he asked, innocently.

"Something like that, yes," Dave answered, and then watched on as Tyler guided his new toy back into the adjoining room with a precision application on his controller. "They don't miss a bloody trick, do they?" said Dave, once Tyler was out of earshot.

"May I...?" asked Becks of Frank, easing her chair back tentatively.

It looked like she wanted to get up and say something, and Frank was delighted to oblige. "Please, go right ahead," said Frank, inviting her to continue, as he himself took a seat to accommodate her.

Becks wasn't an introvert, by any means, but she did appear somewhat modest and shy at that moment as she prepared to address those sat around the table. Frank offered her a sincere smile of encouragement.

Becks checked over her shoulder to make sure her little ankle-biter hadn't reappeared, so that she wouldn't embarrass him with what she was about to say. Then, she began. "I was outside today, putting up some additional fairy lights," she said, pointing to the window. "Tyler was fussing around the Christmas tree out in the courtyard, putting up those glittery baubles you bought, Stan. A bit like the ones on your suit," she said, in reference to Stan's charmingly garish attire. "I couldn't stop watching Tyler as he moved around the tree, placing each ball carefully in place on the lower branches he could reach," she went on. "He finished up, and then wandered over to the stables, and although I couldn't hear every word he was saying, he was explaining to some of the animals, as near as I could tell, about why the Christmas tree was there and what it meant, in case they might be confused about it."

"*Awwwww*," came the collective reply, to which Becks grinned appreciatively.

"Anyway, to be completely honest," Becks said, continuing on, "I wasn't entirely sure where the Isle of Man actually was — I think maybe I thought it was where the Isle of Wight was? — so, when I had the chance to come over here, I didn't really know what to expect. But I have to tell you, my time spent here has been the best I can remember experiencing for a long, long time, for both of us, both me and my son. And, in fact, I've spent the last few days

CHAPTER SIX

wondering how I can possibly thank you all for welcoming me here."

Becks lowered her head for a moment, as she was getting a little choked up. Dave patted her hand. "It's our pleasure," he told her reassuringly. Becks smiled and, composing herself, continued...

"To hear the passionate way you all speak about the charity, and to hear Frank speak about it just now, has me overcome with emotion. And as a direct recipient of the charity's work, I couldn't even begin to tell you what it means to Tyler and me. To think that you all are going to be able to help several more families here on the farm, and more across the UK as well, in similar fashion, is simply wonderful. I know that, for myself, this time last year I had no hope, no future, no money, and no real desire to carry on. If it wasn't for Tyler, well..."

Becks dabbed at her eyes, before resuming...

"It's no secret that I was in an abusive relationship, and that I simply had nowhere to go. We had nowhere to go, me and Tyler. Last year, I was in a damp flat with no heating and next to no food. Our Christmas dinner was a small bowl of cornflakes apiece, and the only thing I had to give Tyler for Christmas was an action-man figure the chap in our corner shop was kind enough to give me out of pity. But not once did that little boy complain about what he received. And, now, here we are. And look at us now, and the world of difference you've all made in our lives," she said, looking around the table.

And this time it was everyone else sat at the table dabbing at their eyes.

"I know you all know you're a part of something special," Becks carried on. "But I just wanted to say that from the very bottom of my heart, you've turned our lives around. And for that, I'll be eternally grateful," she told them all. "Oh my," she added, fanning her face with her free hand, "I'm impressed I managed to get to the end of that!" She raised her glass. "So, apologies to Frank, the toastmaster. But, if I may, can I propose a toast to Frank and Stan's Charity, and to you all, who do so much to make people's lives that little bit nicer?"

"To Frank and Stan's Charity!" came the enthusiastic response, followed by the reverberating, chinking sound made from a bevy of glasses being clinked together.

Once the glasses were lowered, there was a hushed silence, with those present perhaps reflecting on their own good fortune, or perhaps just caught up in a moment of being surrounded by good friends and loved ones.

"Hard cock!" exclaimed Stella, punctuating the moment, and chuckling to herself. It may have been the wrong answer she'd given earlier, but it still remained the best answer as far as she was concerned.

Chapter
SEVEN

It's often suggested that people can, on occasion, look like their pets. One thing that has probably never been suggested is that someone could possibly resemble their office. But, that's exactly what Rodney Franks had achieved with his HQ on the outskirts of London: out-of-date, old-fashioned, stuffy, and in desperate need of a complete makeover. Tacky green wallpaper with golden flecks running through it was greeted on the floor by ostentatious chocolate-brown carpet of which the shag pile must easily have been two inches deep. If you dropped your keys on this carpet, you'd likely need a metal detector to find them again. To walk inside this throwback of a room was like stepping back in time to an early 1980's episode of the TV classic *Dallas*, but instead of finding J R Ewing behind an imposing oak desk — the top covered generously in green leather — it was a smug little man with his feet placed up on the desktop, easing back in his chair, caressing the silk fabric on his cravat like an extra in a low-budget porno film.

"Oh, what the hell do you know about money, Lachlan?" sneered Rodney to the man sat opposite to him.

Lachlan shifted uncomfortably on the seat of his orange velvet high-backed chair, but it wasn't as a result of nerves. Rather, it was more a case of every fibre of his being presently resisting the overriding, overwhelming urge to leap over the desktop and clutch Rodney by the larynx.

"What do I know about money? Did you honestly just ask me that?" said Lachlan, trying his best to remain calm, but not entirely succeeding. "I'm only your bloody accountant, Rodney. It's what I do for a living, remember? And this accountant is paid by you to tell you when you're being stupid. That's my job. And, Rodney, you're being stupid. In fact, you're so far past stupid that you're verging on the nonsensical."

"You're treading on thin ice, Lachlan. You may have worked for me for an inordinate amount of time, but do remember your place, my dear boy. I've got plenty of money, so, what exactly is the problem?" Rodney asked with a dismissive rolling of his eyes.

"Yes, you've got money, Rodney. You've got plenty of money, but the crucial factor is that you *can*, and *should*, have even *more* money. This ridiculous feud you've had with that big German fellow—"

"Dutch," said Rodney. "He's Dutch."

"Fine! Dutch, then!" snapped Lachlan. But then he softened his demeanour somewhat, leaning forward in his chair, and pressing down on a pile of papers he'd presented to Rodney a few minutes earlier and sliding the papers forward in the hopes that Rodney might actually take a look at them. "Rodney, you're a wealthy man," he said. "But the problem for you," he explained, "is that you're rich in terms of assets, but you're rather poor when it comes to actual available cash. Your business interests are generally lucrative in nature, mind you, but this obsession you seem to have for revenge is insatiable, especially where matters of money are concerned, and it's having a worryingly detrimental effect on the state of your overall finances."

"I simply don't like losing, Lachlan. Never have, and never will," Rodney declared. "This big oaf Henk, along with his friends, have made a fool of me a little too often of late. And I don't like being taken for a fool."

"Nevertheless, it only takes an economic downturn in the area of your business interests before cash-flow becomes a serious issue for you," Lachlan continued. "Look, Rodney, I'd be remiss in my duties to not point this out to you. It's what you pay me for, after all, and it's my responsibility to handle these affairs. All I ask is that you check in with me first before you go out and make very large purchases so that I can free up the cash from your assets, all right?"

CHAPTER SEVEN

"What purchases?" asked Rodney, casually picking under his thumbnail with a silver envelope opener as if the question were entirely unimportant.

Lachlan stared at his boss, incredulous. He reached inside his jacket, removing his glasses, which he then hurriedly placed onto his nose. "These," he said, as he flicked through the papers on the desk. "Here, for instance. Right here," he said, pulling one particular paper, a handwritten ledger, to the top of the pile and turning it around again so that Rodney could see it. "You bought a racetrack, of all things, in someplace called... Jurby," he said, tapping his fingertip on the appropriate line of the ledger to indicate the purchase in question. "Jurby? I don't even know where in God's name that is, and I thought you'd been scammed until I saw your actual signature on the contract."

"It's in the Isle of Man, Lachlan," Rodney replied coldly, as if Lachlan were the idiot and not the reverse.

"My point exactly," said Lachlan. "I mean, why would you even want to buy a racetrack that you're never going to use? The upkeep alone on something like that will be astronomical. Now, as to the Isle of Man, I suppose I can certainly understand the association with the TT races and motorsport in general. This at least makes a modicum of sense, I'll admit, and is aligned with one of your core businesses, that of selling motorsport accessories. But what is this ludicrous obsession of yours with building a hotel?"

"First of all, you know full well where Jurby is if you've looked through the paperwork. And secondly, you're talking to me like I'm stupid, Lachlan," said Rodney, through clenched teeth. "And I don't like people talking to me like I'm stupid."

Lachlan took to his feet, moving to the window and looking outside. "I'm sorry, Mr Franks," he said after a moment, without turning back around. He never called Rodney *Mr Franks*, such was their relationship. "I'm just looking out for your interests, Rodney, surely you can see that. Why do you even want a hotel?" he asked, still looking out the window.

"I don't," Rodney replied simply.

"What, I... What? Well then why have you spent hundreds of thousands of pounds in legal fees, architect fees, engineers' fees, and heaven-only-knows-what-other fees that haven't yet been posted to you?" said Lachlan, facing Rodney again. "That doesn't sound like a man who *doesn't* want to buy a hotel."

Rodney didn't answer. He just sat there stroking his cravat.

Lachlan began pacing around the office like a crazed bear. He tapped his chin with his index finger as he went, before finally raising it and wagging it furiously as the pieces of the puzzle came together and the solution clicked into place, clear in his mind. "I know exactly why you've spent so much trying to secure this land — and this TT Farm, as it's now called, that sits on it — for your hotel," he declared confidently.

Rodney removed his feet from his desk and placed them back down onto his overly plush carpet. He moved his chair forward, propping his elbows up onto his desktop now and pressing his hands together like he was praying. "Oh? Yes?" he replied. "Well. Let's hear it, then." And he said this like he was genuinely interested in what Lachlan might have to say, even though the underlying smarminess in his tone carried through just fine.

"It's because you're like a spoilt brat who's had his wickle toy rattle taken by a bigger boy, *that's* why," said Lachlan, brazenly sarcastic now and not holding back. "That's it, Rodney, isn't it? That Dutchman and his friends in the Isle of Man took from you what you wanted so badly, and now you'll stop at nothing until you have it back in possession for yourself, am I right? And that would certainly explain the thousands you've just spent in legal fees having lawyers checking and then re-checking old contracts, now wouldn't it?" he said, accusingly.

Rodney slammed his fist down onto the surface of his desk. "I don't like being beaten!" he screamed, expelling several globules of spit in Lachlan's direction in the process. "That big windmill-and-tulip-loving, wooden clog-wearing oaf and his idiot friends have made a fool of me, and I want what is rightfully mine!"

"*Aww*, so you *do* want your rattle back, *Wodney?*" mocked Lachlan, appearing none too concerned about the state of his current employment. "Did the big mean bullies take something from you, and now you're going to be so completely blinkered that you're going to throw good money after bad?" he asked. But before a

CHAPTER SEVEN

fuming Rodney had an opportunity to reply, he went on, "Rodney, seriously now, you need to listen to me and just let this go, okay? Sure, carry on with your motorsport exploits. But forget about reclaiming this TT Farm property, and as to that absurd decision to buy a racetrack, for the love of God, please consult me in the future when you have one of these demented urges? And as for the money you've spent to date on your more fruitless endeavours, accept it as a loss and move on. Please, listen to reason," Lachlan advised, to a not too terribly receptive Rodney. "Oh, and that shabby-looking simpleton sat outside, who says he's a private investigator?" added Lachlan, glancing in the direction of the reception area, and loosening his tie now and wrestling with his top button. "Let me guess," he said, moving over to the pile of documents on Rodney's desk once again. He sorted through the paperwork with the solid precision of an experienced accountant, which in point of fact he was. "That PI outside," he went on, once he'd found what he was looking for. "That would be these charges here, yes?" he asked, flapping the paper in the air.

"I can't see what you're indicating, Lachlan, because *you're* holding the damn paper, and I'm not," replied an annoyed Rodney, and sounding very much like he wasn't all that interested in actually seeing it anyway.

"Well I'll tell you what it says," answered Lachlan, waving the paper around. "What it shows are listings for over a dozen invoices from one 'Ridley & Company,' paid for what's described here as 'Miscellaneous Services.' Rodney, you've given this outfit over a hundred and fifty thousand pounds! How is it even possible to spend that much??" Lachlan slapped the papers back down. "I'll bet you've paid them to find dirt on the nasty men who took your rattle, is that it? Am I right?" he asked, but the absence of a response told him all he needed to know. "I know exactly how your mind works by now," said Lachland. "It's Small Man Syndrome, Rodney. You've been like this your entire life, and I'm telling you, it'll end up costing you all you've got."

"I appreciate your concern, Lachlan, I really do," replied Rodney. He sighed, and appeared almost, but not quite, regretful. "I'd like to say that this pains me, Lachlan. But it doesn't..."

"What? What are you on about now?" asked Lachlan. "*What pains you?*"

"Me firing you," said Rodney in answer. He was calm now as he said this, his anger having faded away. Or at least, if he was still angry, he wasn't showing it. "Lachlan, you're fired," he said simply, with the same sort of mild, dismissive indifference he'd use to, say, reschedule a meeting, as opposed to uttering the words that would destroy a man's career.

"Ha!" laughed Lachlan, stomping towards the exit. He threw the office door open, looking back over his shoulder to Rodney. His eyes were drawn northwards, up the wall slightly, towards the large gold-framed portrait above Rodney's head. He couldn't help but think it looked particularly ridiculous now. "I've always meant to say this, Rodney, but what sort of prat has a portrait painted of himself riding a horse when he's never actually ridden a horse? Also, did you pay the artist to make you look much taller than you actually are, you vertically challenged, cravat-wearing pillock??" He smiled, pleased to have finally said what was on his mind, and lowered his voice for a moment, adding, "And you cannot fire me, Rodney, because you're my brother, and also because you need me more than I need you." And then, "STOP SPENDING MONEY!" he screamed. "You're starting to look like the bad guy in a Scooby-Doo cartoon!"

Lachlan then moved into the reception area, addressing the unkempt man in a rumpled suit who was sat there waiting patiently. "Mr Franks will see you now!" he snapped, looking the shabby fellow up and down with disdain. "And for goodness sake, make sure you wipe that chair down before you leave!"

Rather than take offence, the seated chap picked up his faded carrier bag, offered a courteous nod, and slowly eased his tired carcass out of the chair. "Much obliged," he said to Lachlan, though Lachlan was already out the door and halfway to the car park by this point. The rumpled, shabby fellow then carefully made his way through the door and into Rodney Franks' office. "Mr Franks, sir," the fellow said, presenting himself in front of Rodney's desk. "Terry Scupper," he announced, holding out an excessively grubby hand in Rodney's direction.

CHAPTER SEVEN

Rodney leaned back in his chair, horrified that such a filthy-looking hand should be presented to him. Terry must have been used to this type of reaction, however, as his hand was soon sheathed in his pocket without complaint.

"You want me to take my shoes off?" asked Terry.

"What? Of course not!" replied Rodney. "Why on earth would I want you to take your shoes off?"

"It's just that this is some really nice carpet, and I'm not sure if I stood in something outside, in the car park?" offered Terry, looking down now, and shuffling the sole of his right shoe back and forth against the shag pile, in exploratory fashion, to see what might possibly be worked free from the shoe. He looked back up, shrugging, when this produced no noticeable results. "Anyway. It's nice to finally meet you at last, sir, face to face," he said.

"What have you got for me?" asked Rodney, clearly not the slightest bit interested in entertaining small talk. "And *don't* sit down," he added quickly.

"Well, sir," began Terry, sitting down anyway, and making himself comfortable. "Truth be told, not a great deal." He held up his carrier bag which, apparently, doubled up as his briefcase as well, in a vague effort to demonstrate his industrious efforts to date, and then placed it down on his lap, patting it affectionately.

Rodney rattled his fingers on the desktop. "Not a great deal, Terry? You know how much money I've spent with your company for *'not a great deal'*? You can understand how those words don't exactly fill me with comfort, Terry, can't you?"

Terry shrugged his shoulders, as if he didn't really understand at all.

"You *are* a private investigator, are you not, Terry?" asked Rodney.

"Yessir," Terry replied, offering, for no required reason, a smart salute.

"And, are you a good private investigator, Terry?" said Rodney, tapping his desktop with his pen. "Only your company has been employed for weeks, full-time. And, as there doesn't appear to be much at all held inside that dodgy-looking shopping bag you're holding—"

"I use it to blend in!" said Terry cheerfully.

"I'm sorry?" replied Rodney.

"The shopping bag! I use it to blend in!" Terry happily explained. "That way, no one suspects I'm a private investigator!"

"I see," said a decidedly unimpressed Rodney, wholly unconvinced that this was a case of cleverness on Terry's part. "Well, regardless, there doesn't appear to be much at all held inside this shopping bag of yours, Terry," Rodney went on. "And so I'm starting to ask myself whether this has all been money well spent, you see. So, again, you are a *good* private investigator?"

"Sure!" Terry proclaimed proudly. "You remember that phone-hacking scandal a few years back?" he asked, taking a careful look over his shoulder as if anyone might well be interested in what he was about to reveal and possibly attempting to listen in right that very minute. "Partly down to me," he said, beaming. "That should show you, Mr Franks, sir, how far I'm willing to go to get the job done." He concluded this with yet another smart salute, even though none was called for nor necessary.

"All right then, Terry, amaze me," said Rodney coolly. "Show me just how good of a PI you are." Rodney then leaned back in his chair, raising his hands up against his chest and steepling his fingers in anticipation, although he wasn't anticipating all that much, really, from this rather unimpressive man before him. "Go on. Dazzle me," he said, raising one eyebrow expectantly, though with a sort of guarded scepticism.

Terry made a show of rummaging through his carrier bag — even though its contents were few — before finally removing a tattered ring binder. Even though it looked like it'd been chucked in a bin by a seven-year-old school pupil once they'd used it up, Terry held it aloft for a moment like it was a sacred text, as if it was some long-forgotten, lost gospel of Jesus. Once the imaginary angels in his head had stopped singing, he set the book down on his lap and started flicking through the pages, darting out his tongue periodically to wet his thumb in a vulgar display that made Rodney fear he might vomit.

When eventually Terry had found the page he was looking for — which, oddly, was back on the very first page — he said, "Okay, so you asked me to look into this fellow Hank?" and then looking

CHAPTER SEVEN

up for confirmation. "I'm sorry, make that *Henk*," he said, glancing back down to where his finger was holding his place. "A one Henk van der Berg, to be precise?" Terry put forth, looking back up. It was a rhetorical question, but he paused dramatically, as if he were waiting for some kind of eager, appreciative response.

"Yes?" Rodney replied impatiently. *"And?"*

"Ah. Well. Nothing, actually," said Terry. He pored over several or more lines of his notes, tracing along with his finger as he went, just in case something might magically appear. "Yes. Nothing," he verified cheerfully, as if this was good news rather than bad.

"Nothing at all?" asked Rodney unhappily.

"Nope! Nothing!" confirmed Terry. "For a guy with as many business interests as he's involved in... nothing," he added, pressing his bottom lip out. "I couldn't even find an unpaid parking ticket for this chap, unfortunately. Clean as a whistle, he is."

"That is most unfortunate," replied Rodney. "I had hoped—"

"Oh, wait, I do have one note here on this Henk person," Terry interrupted, after finding something he'd overlooked.

"Ah! Splendid. Let's hear it, then," said Rodney hopefully.

"Well, see, I had a difficult time finding anything out about this fellow at first when I asked after him using his surname," Terry answered him. "Turns out everyone just refers to him as 'Dutch Henk,' although I haven't really quite worked out why just yet."

"Maybe because — and taking a stab in the dark here — but maybe because... he's *Dutch*...?" offered Rodney sarcastically. His patience was wearing thin, and he held his head in his hand in disbelief.

"Oh, is he?" asked Terry. "Well now, that explains much, then. Mystery solved!" he said cheerfully, and scribbled a note into his binder that said: *Henk called Dutch Henk because Dutch.*

Rodney was ready to throttle PI extraordinaire Terry Scupper at this point. The only thing that was stopping him was that he didn't want, in the quite literal sense, to get his hands dirty in the process.

An oblivious Terry licked his thumb and turned to the next page of his notes. "Frank Cryer and Stanley Sidcup," he announced meaningfully, and moistening his lips with his tongue as if

FRANK 'N' STAN'S BUCKET LIST #4 – BRIDE OF FRANK 'N' STAN

something of great import was about to immediately issue forth from those lips.

"Yes...?" asked Rodney, his ears perking up in anticipation, hope returning that all was perhaps not lost.

Terry ran his eyes up and down the page. "Nothing," he said, after what was, to Rodney, an interminably and agonisingly long delay.

"*Nothing?*" asked an exasperated Rodney.

"Nothing of merit on either of them, I'm afraid!" confirmed Terry buoyantly, despite the distinct lack of actionable information.

Rodney was about to voice his continued displeasure, but then Terry continued on.

"They do own the largest taxi firm in Liverpool, however, but I'm not sure if that's of any help to you, necessarily," Terry told him. "Oh, and the Frank Cryer fellow paid for his daughter's tits to get enlarged," he added. "Nice they are, too," he confided, waggling his eyebrows, and darting his obscene tongue out to lick his lips again in a manner so lascivious that it made even Rodney — who was hardly, himself, a paragon of virtue — shudder with revulsion. "Anyhow, so this Frank character seemingly has some sort of serious underlying medical condition, I'd say, judging by the amount of time he spends at various doctor's offices," Terry said, plunging onward. "So, not sure how that helps you either...?"

"Wait. A taxi firm?" said Rodney. "Hmm, I didn't know about that. That could be interesting."

"I've also looked into this charity of theirs, Frank and Stan's Food Stamps, in detail," Terry went on cheerily, encouraged by the positive feedback. "And also their additional charitable initiatives across the UK, and of course the TT Farm in the Isle of Man as well."

"Yes?" said Rodney, hoping there'd finally be some meat there for him to chew on.

"Nothing, nish, nada, zippo!" said Terry brightly.

"So, for a master private investigator you've brought me the grand total of... bugger-all?" asked a clearly disappointed Rodney. "Is that what you're saying, Terry?"

CHAPTER SEVEN

"Well there was one more thing," Terry replied. "There's this one chap, see. Name of Lee Watson." He ran his hand through his very greasy hair as he said this, and then he casually placed the oil-slicked hand down onto Rodney's expensive office chair's armrest, much to Rodney's chagrin.

Rodney responded with an irritated *who-the-fuck-is-that* sort of expression painted on his chops, waving one hand impatiently for Terry to elaborate but fully expecting very little of value to be revealed.

"This Lee chap heads up their charitable efforts, by all accounts. Apparently, Frank and Stan recruited him from the streets," Terry told Rodney.

"*The Streets?* What's this? Some other company, you mean?" asked Rodney. "They headhunted him, you're saying?"

"No. I mean the streets as in, literally, the streets," explained Terry. "A tramp, by all accounts."

Rodney sighed. "This does nothing for me, Terry. And you're seriously boring me now," he said. "Shall I throw you out of my office right now? Is that what you'd like? Because you're telling me nothing. Nothing useful. How does this help me?"

Terry, for the first time, felt like he might possibly be losing his current audience. "No, no, listen," he said, setting his stall out. "This Lee is due to get married to some fat bird called..." He looked down at his notes again. "Stella," he said, finding what he was looking for. "Yes. Stella. No last name. Just Stella."

It was unclear if Terry had not discovered this Stella's last name, or if she didn't have one. Rodney didn't bother to ask.

"And that Lee deserves a medal, I'll tell you, because she's a big old unit. You wouldn't want to run into her in a dark alley, is what I'm saying," Terry went on. "Right. Anyway. So word on the street is that our Lee was a bit of a naughty boy in the past, see? So the way I figure it, if you're looking to get Frank and Stan to pay attention, then this Lee fellow is the key. Because this Stella bird that he's marrying? See, she's like a daughter to the pair of them. They brought her up from when she was a young child, so they're bound to be very, very protective of her."

Rodney perked up at this. "Yes?" he said, suddenly satisfied that Terry was perhaps worthy of sharing his oxygen after all. "Do carry on," he said, leaning forward in his chair with interest.

Terry leaned forward as well, wriggling his bum as he did so and nestling it deep into the seat of his chair like a cat making itself comfortable on a plump pillow. "This Lee got his big break when he was credited for tackling a group of armed robbers a few years back. It was in all the papers," he said animatedly, continuing on. "So the way I see it, is that this Lee chap has built his present life on a lie, right? Because, get this, Lee was all set to rob this cash-in-transit van himself, but then ended up inadvertently becoming a hero when another mob turned up to rob it also!"

"Holy shit," said Rodney, his attention rapt.

"Yep. A whistle-blower put me onto it," proclaimed Terry proudly. "Some greasy bloke who owns a café and holds a grudge, name of Eric Fryer. Poor chap was nearly in tears talking about his lost love. Turns out he totally fancies Stella as well, if you can believe it!"

Rodney didn't bother pointing out the irony in Terry calling someone *else* greasy. Rodney didn't want to interrupt the flow of information, which was just getting juicy. "Hmm. But this is just hearsay, then? From a biased source?" he asked, of course liking the information just fine, yet wondering about its reliability.

"Ah! Well!" said Terry. "I've managed to get hold of another camera angle of the incident, with CCTV footage showing this Lee fellow sprinting over, ill intent written all over his face, at least twenty seconds before he could possibly have known that another armed gang were about to barge onto the scene and rob the van! And not only that, but this greasy chap, Eric Fryer, is happy to stand as witness. Apparently, Lee confided all one night when they were drunk down the pub! This was before the rivalry over the Stella bird emerged and Eric's grudge began, mind."

"I see, I see," said Rodney, nodding along.

"So our Lee Watson here is no choirboy, as it turns out. If it wasn't for fate intervening, he'd have likely either succeeded in his robbery efforts or got caught in the attempt," Terry continued. "And it's only by virtue of a completely unforeseen, unexpected

CHAPTER SEVEN

turn of events that he isn't spending time in prison right this minute."

"Now who's this Eric Fryer?" enquired Rodney, wanting to make certain he understood everything, and how each player fit into the picture.

"Owns the local café near the taxi office. Does a good full English breakfast, actually, if you're ever up in Liverpool?" suggested Terry, giving his hearty endorsement by rubbing his belly affectionately.

"I see, I see," said Rodney again, still nodding along.

"So, in summary, Mr Franks, even though the charity itself is squeaky clean, the *head* of that charity is not at all what he seems to be. And if he were to get himself locked up, well, his oversized bride-to-be is going to be stood up at the altar, isn't she? And I'm sure your good friends Frank and Stan won't want that to happen, and will do anything to avoid that, fond of her as they are."

"Yes!" yelled Rodney, in a rarely witnessed display of pleasure. "Even if this Lee character didn't actually end up doing anything, the fear of a possible prison sentence will do wonders to motivate him, and may prove very useful indeed," he added. He closed his eyes for a moment, visualizing the wonderful prospect of revenge forming in his mind — revenge being Rodney's very happiest of places — a broad, contented grin spreading over his face.

Terry was getting extra comfortable now, leaning back in his chair and pressing his shoulders into the plush upholstery. If Rodney Franks was happy, Terry Scupper, his sleuthing skills thus validated, was happy as well. "Sure, and don't forget that even the *sniff* of a criminal background tainting Lee's reputation will send all of the charity benefactors running for the hills, and that's when things go... KABOOM," Terry said, illustrating the *kaboom* by way of exploding fingers. "And to only make matters worse, the charity commission will then be all over them like flies on honey, going over their books and previous projects with a fine-toothed comb looking for even a *hint* of anything untoward."

"And there's no way we can somehow implicate the big Dutch dunderhead in this as well?" asked Rodney, ever hopeful.

"Henk van der Berg? Sadly, no. I tried, but I couldn't dig up anything negative on him," replied Terry. "Though I could maybe fabricate something...?" he offered. "You know, I really like this chair," he added, by way of nothing. "It's quite comfortable."

Rodney made a mental note regarding the chair. He'd need to mention something to Marlene, his receptionist and secretary. But, for now, he grinned a toothy grin. "I like you, Terry," said Rodney. "I admit, I had my reservations at first. But I like you. Now, granted, you could definitely do with smartening yourself up a bit and taking a shower. But you're a devious little shit, I have to say, and I like that in a person."

"Thank you, Mr Franks," replied a rather well-chuffed Terry, apparently oblivious to the obvious insult included part and parcel along with Rodney's praise.

"You can go now," said Rodney, dismissing the PI now that he had what he wanted for the moment. "And next time, cut to the interesting bit so that I don't have to sit through all the boring bits, okay?" he advised.

"Very good, Mr Franks. Very good, sir," said Terry. And, with that, Terry dispatched himself, quick-smart.

Rodney sat at his desk grinning inanely. "Lee Watson, indeed. You little monkey," he said with an undertone of menace to his voice. Well, as menacing as a man who wears heel supports to look taller and a silk cravat is *able* to sound — which wasn't particularly menacing at all, actually, despite Rodney's best efforts. "You could be just the missing piece of the puzzle needed in order to solve my little issue in recouping all of the money I've invested," he said aloud to himself, laughing calmly at first, but then increasing in pitch and intensity as he rolled along, like a steam train on the tracks. He also took the opportunity to steeple his hands together again, this time tapping his fingertips together repeatedly in a kind of wicked delight. That was the exact moment he understood his brother's reference to a Scooby-Doo villain, in fact. But was he bothered? Not in the slightest.

"Marlene," he said, pressing the button of an oak-covered box on his desktop.

"Yes, Mr Franks," replied a polite voice through the speaker.

"Marlene, can you run around the office with the air freshener, please, because I simply cannot get the fetid odour of that repulsively filthy investigator out of my nostrils. He smelt very much like he'd been diving into rubbish bins," Rodney told her. "Oh, and when you're done with that, hire someone to come in and give the carpet and furniture a good scrubbing, yes? Everywhere he may have touched, I want cleaned thoroughly," Rodney instructed.

"*Ehm...* yes sir, Mr Franks," replied Marlene nervously. "*Erm*, Mr Franks? Mr Scupper is still here, sir. He's, *em*, standing right in front of me?"

"Right, that's fine, Marlene," Rodney answered her, showing not the slightest bit of concern, and adding, "Best wait until he leaves first, and *then* run around with the air freshener. No point in doing it twice, after all."

"Very good, Mr Franks," replied a still polite, yet weary, Marlene.

Chapter
EIGHT

The challenging journey for a racer to the start line at the Isle of Man TT races is one that would have begun months, if not years, earlier. Road racing was an all-consuming passion that emptied bank account balances, strained relationships, and kept folk tinkering in their workshop to many an ungodly hour. They were a special breed, these people. And it wasn't just the racers, either, that were special — it was every man, woman, and child supporting their loved ones in fulfilling this ambition.

Those riders who were fortunate enough to be presently racing in a factory-sponsored team were a little more immune to the expense involved (although were likely to have felt it at one point in their careers), but, for those privateers who were self-funded, the constant financial worry was ever-present and accompanied by many sacrifices made to fund the obsession. To secure the elusive Mountain Course license that would permit you to race the iconic course, for instance, wasn't just a case of submitting an application and then turning up at the start line. No, to be eligible, you'd have to demonstrate to the organisers, each year, that you were a competitor of sufficient competence to tackle one of the most challenging races on the planet. All applicants must have competed in at least six qualifying Road Race days in a defined period, with at least some of the results obtained needing to meet specific qualifying timing criteria. These qualifying races were often referred to as 'signatures' and, essentially, you needed your racing passport stamped at these races in order to even have a shot at securing your Mountain Course license. Securing these signatures would entail having to drive all over the UK in order to attend qualifying racing events, and, unfortunately, the cost to facilitate this was considerable — and this was especially so for our Dave and Monty, who had the extra expense of sailing off the Isle of Man for each of these.

With their commitment of sponsorship, Frank and Stan had definitely been a game-changer for our boys. Even so, the list of recurring expenses was considerable, and so Dave and Monty would still need to dip into their own pockets frequently in order to supplement what their generous benefactors were providing. The problem, amongst other things for them, was that they had precisely no savings to speak of, and their jobs on the farm, while certainly spiritually rewarding, were somewhat less rewarding financially. The lads had always muddled through somehow and made ends meet, and if they were being completely honest the hustle and strain of pulling it all together was actually part of the allure of the TT in some perverse way.

With Dave now a TT winner, having won the previous year's sidecar race, this did aid matters a bit as far as expenses were concerned. Dave's positive notoriety helped entice additional sponsors, eager to support the cause in exchange for a sticker on the sidecar's fairing or for a PR shoot featuring local celebrity Dave, or even, inexplicably, a naked massage from Monty as reward. Dave had offered himself up for massage services as well, of course, but sadly there were as yet no takers.

Even with the financial assistance they were receiving, the lads were realistic, however, in that they knew a place on the podium was unlikely for them given their sidecar (as compared to better-funded machines), and, as well, with Monty onboard as the passenger on that sidecar (Monty, sadly, not being quite in the same league as the big boys, and not to mention his corpulent frame). This was a fact Monty was acutely aware of, but also one that Dave was perfectly at peace with. After all, he had nothing further to prove, or even a strong desire to. No, a top-twenty finish, splendid in its own right, would suit them both just fine. And so

CHAPTER EIGHT

they were happy to just put the best team together that they could, one that was reliable enough to get them 'round the course.

But getting a respectable crew together wasn't exactly cheap, sponsorships or not, and so the boys had committed themselves to several fundraising efforts in the run-up to the TT races. And the first of these efforts, as it should happen, was taking place on a murky-skied Saturday at the end of January, in the Island's capital of Douglas...

"My arse is on fire, Dave!" said Monty, pursing his lips and then exhaling in agony. "I feel like a hot poker has been rammed up my hoop!" he added, to the abject disgust of a frail pensioner easing past on her mobility scooter. "How long have I been going?" he asked Dave, holding his arm out to signal he wasn't wearing his own watch.

"Seffen mimmutes!" replied Dave, spitting crumbs from the partially demolished steak pie he was eating out from his mouth as he spoke. "You've only been going for just under seven minutes, Monty," he said, speaking more clearly now that he'd chewed and swallowed. "You need to man up, mate!"

"A steak pie could help, possibly...?" suggested Monty, wiping a trickle of drool from his chin.

Dave shook his head in the negative. "Monty, you've only just had your breakfast. We're supposed to be athletes, the two of us, and you're falling apart in less than seven minutes!"

But Monty wasn't for listening. He was like a family dog that pestered you at teatime and wouldn't bugger off until you threw it a table scrap.

"Fine. Here," said Dave, relenting. He held the steak pie aloft, out in the general direction of Monty's lips, to which Monty's jaws immediately, instinctively responded, rapidly creating a half-moon bite with the frenzied aggression of a great white shark attacking a seal.

"Better?" asked Dave.

"*Mmm*," said Monty, and then, "No, *argh*, no. I mean, yes, ta, thanks for that. But, no, not entirely better. It's my bloody arse, Dave! It still hurts loads, and it feels like I'm passing molten lava!"

"Hang on, your bum is actually bleeding, Monty, or—?" enquired a squeamish yet concerned Dave.

"I didn't mean literally," Monty cut in. "But it could very well be!" he cried. "Anyway, so how long's that been?" he whimpered.

"How long's *what* been?" asked Dave. "Since your arse started bleeding? How should I know!"

"*Noooo*," said Monty. "I mean how long on the bike!"

"How long on the...? Mate, it's only been fifteen seconds since the last time you asked!" replied an exasperated Dave. "Anyway, did you not bring your salve? For your bum?"

"It's in my bag," said Monty, lifting his hand off the handlebars to point out where he'd stowed his bag. "Will you pass it over?" he asked. "I'll go and put some on when my first stint is over."

Dave held the remainder of his pie between his lips, bending down to unzip Monty's backpack. He rummaged around through its contents, pushing aside a towel, a sports bra, underpants (that Dave prayed to Christ were clean), and several snacks, until finally he grabbed hold of a well-used tube. He held it up for Monty's inspection. "This it?" he asked.

The tube looked to be empty, or very nearly empty, and apparently such was Monty's desire on previous occasions to extract every last dollop of the soothing ointment that he'd rolled it up from the bottom, and rolled it up so tightly the crinkled metal casing perforated at the seams, serving, in the process, only to ruin any usable portion of the tube's contents that may have been left as the remnants now formed a hardened crust over the exterior. Dave unrolled the thing to see if anything could be salvaged, but it was useless, and all he succeeded in doing was making a mess all over his hands.

"This thing is no more, Monty," Dave informed him. "It's gone on to a better place, I think. A better place than this, I hope," he said, looking at the sticky, slimy gunk on his hands in disgust. "Aww, fucksake, Monty," cried Dave. "I've just realised that you use this tube when your haemorrhoids are playing up, so that means your chubby little fingers have been all over the tube when your fingers have all *also* been rammed straight *up there*," he noted despairingly, pointing illustratively over to Monty's arse — an arse

CHAPTER EIGHT

which was, at present, now perched above the stationary bike's seat tentatively in order to avoid any further pressure on Monty's swollen, prolapsed, and embattled blood vessels.

"I told you a sponsored bike ride was a right stupid idea, Dave! Especially with my bum the way it's been of late!" Monty whinged. "There's a chemist over there, Dave. Just there," he said, motioning with his chin. "You'll need to go and get me some more ointment, yeah? *Pleeease?*" he pleaded.

Dave wiped his hands on his bicycle shorts furiously, hoping to get rid of any lingering unsavoury essence of Monty. "I suppose you'll want me to apply it and rub it in for you as well...??" he said, grumbling, before turning to head over in the direction of the chemist, as instructed.

Despite Dave's obvious implied sarcasm, Monty didn't seem as loath to that suggestion as perhaps he should have been. "Oi! Get me a pie if you're passing the bakery, Dave?" he called after him cheerfully. "This is a tough job I'm doing right here, and I need all the energy I can muster, mister!"

Such was the scale of their ambition in regard to the farm that Frank and Stan could envisage a time in the not-too-distant future when an additional employee would be required to coordinate their efforts there. Stan had mooted the suggestion to Frank over a glass of whiskey that Becks could well turn out to be the ideal candidate.

Also discussed during this whiskey-drinking session were ways in which word could be spread about the farm. As such, and with the kind permission of the town council, Team Frank & Stan had secured the use of a small section of the main shopping street off the side of the road in Douglas to herald the work of the TT Farm. With the farm due to open officially in the next few weeks, this would be an ideal opportunity to raise awareness about their endeavours and future plans. They were eager to showcase all that the farm would have to offer in addition to their residential accommodation, which included education sessions, traditional crafting, a petting zoo, flower arranging classes, farming skills programmes, and a multitude of other opportunities that the community could get involved with and participate in.

In addition to the day promoting all the farm had to offer, Frank had suggested that Dave and Monty could also use the opportunity to bolster the funds in their TT campaign. And so it was that the idea of a fundraising bicycle ride on a stationary exercise bike was brought to fruition, with Dave and Monty taking it in turns, in one-hour shifts throughout the course of the day, gathering sponsorship for how many miles they could complete on the bike. To link their efforts into the TT, the boys were equating miles completed on the bike to laps of the actual TT course, and with their ultimate goal being the equivalent of five complete TT laps managed. This was a noble goal, especially when taking into consideration that one full lap of the official TT course was just under thirty-eight miles in length, and also coupled with the fact that the two of them were fat bastards who'd done zero exercise all winter, and so this was quite the undertaking, and quite the spectacle.

Tyler was doing a brilliant job with his fundraising bucket in his *Top Gear* Stig-inspired outfit the lads had cooked up for him, with passers-by giving generously, and happy to support Dave and Monty's TT ambitions. Meanwhile, Frank, Stan, and Becks were manning a penned-off area nearby, eagerly handing out literature about the farm, and having brought along a host of cute, fluffy, or feathered animals that were, by all appearances, eager to breach the confines of their plastic pen and explore this strange new world they'd suddenly found themselves in. It was very much the TT Farm family day out, and the weather, at least for now, was cooperating and playing its part also.

The day continued to pan out nicely, with the goats, chickens, sheep, rabbits, and other assorted creatures in Frank and Stan's menagerie having the desired effect, and soon a steady stream of visitors to their display were being particularly generous with Frank and Stan's own collection bucket and eager to hear more about the TT Farm. It had been a bit of a pipedream for all involved,

CHAPTER EIGHT

at the very start, the farm, so to hear all the positive feedback from the public was a welcome validation of their efforts.

Mercifully, at least as far as Monty was concerned, his first hour-long shift had finally reached its painful conclusion, and with him telling anybody who would listen that it was like someone had sprinkled broken glass in his underpants.

"Make sure you wash your hands afterwards," instructed Dave, handing over the tube of soothing liniment he'd fetched for Monty, as requested. "I was tempted to get a tube of Deep Heat and swap the sticker… but, we're comrades, Monty. In this together, till the bitter end!"

"Har-har, that would've been loads of laughs, Dave," said Monty, unimpressed.

"But the point is, I *didn't* do it!" proclaimed Dave happily, as if this should rightly allay any misgivings Monty might have and highlight Dave as the clear hero in this situation.

Monty didn't answer. He just gingerly climbed down from his seated position on the stationary bike, grabbed his precious salve, and dispatched himself to the public toilets, moving through the shopping thoroughfare bow-legged, like a cowboy who'd spent far too much time out on the dusty trail, leaving Dave to climb aboard the bike for his own turn once he'd inspected and wiped down the saddle. In fact, he wiped down the saddle several times.

"It's not so bad, this," said Dave, who'd opted for the casual shorts and t-shirt approach rather than head-to-foot Lycra that Monty had chosen. "I *said*, it's not so *bad*, this," he repeated, a little louder this time, for the benefit of his colleagues in the petting zoo close by, now that he was picking up the pace and proper verbal encouragement from the others for his vigour was not immediately forthcoming.

"Yes, yes, that's some fine work there, Dave!" Stan called over reassuringly. Then Stan nudged Frank with his elbow. "Check out that soppy bugger," he whispered, giggling. "Watch his stomach every time Becks turns around."

Frank placed the bunny rabbit he was holding into the grateful arms of a small girl who was visiting their petting zoo. "What do you mean?" he asked Stan, but then, after witnessing it for himself, replied, "Ah, yes. I remember those days well, sucking in my gut whenever the ladies walked by. He must really like her."

"It won't last," suggested Stan. "I mean, yes, he'll still like her. But it'll be farting in bed and peeing on the toilet seat in no time at all."

"Speaking from experience, old buddy?" laughed Frank.

Sure enough, every time Dave felt Becks' adoring eyes venturing in his direction, his pedalling efforts doubled, and his midriff halved in diameter like a well-used set of bagpipes. He was sucking in more air than a Dyson vacuum, and in danger of passing out from asphyxia.

Someone else who wasn't entirely impressed with Dave's efforts, a little later on, was a gangly-looking boy of about eleven or so, stood directly in front of the exercise bike with his finger wedged firmly up his nose, gawping at Dave. "My mate said you're a sidecar TT winner!" he shouted at Dave.

Dave went to speak, but as it was nearing the end of his first hour there wasn't too much energy left in the tank to expend on verbal communication. He merely nodded his head, raising his hand slightly to extend a thumb in the upwards direction by way of confirmation.

The lad wasn't for convincing, though, and the river of sweat running off Dave and forming into a shallow puddle on either side of the bike under the pedals probably didn't do much to convince him that he was looking at a TT-winning legend either.

"I said to my mate that you're too fat to fit into a sidecar!" said the lad, arching his neck one way and then the other in order to get the full measure of Dave... and, to be fair, there was quite a lot of measuring involved. "Were you changing the tyres, maybe? Or putting the petrol in, perhaps?" the boy asked, nudging his equally dopey-looking friend to provoke a laugh from him.

"No... I'm... the... driver," said Dave, through a series of laboured breaths.

CHAPTER EIGHT

But the lad couldn't hear what Dave was saying on account of the stereo next to Dave pumping out motivational music, in addition to the various farmyard calls from the nearby menagerie, and plus the further noise of Dave sounding like a dying swan to boot.

The lad pulled his finger from his nose, cupping his ear now instead. "What's that? I didn't hear you, chubs!" he shouted back. "Anyway, you're too fat to be a sidecar racer!" he added, and along with this declaration he threw one of his sweets, catching Dave just above the left eye. If it was Monty that'd thrown it, Dave would likely have congratulated him on the aim. Instead…

"I wasn't too fat for your mum last week, you cheeky little bastard! Put some money in the bucket and piss off, you gormless little shit! And take your stupid-looking mate with you!"

Dave said this smiling, and though he was shouting, he wasn't shouting too terribly loudly, knowing — or at least hoping — that the music and such would serve to drown him out. He also hoped that, to the other people stood watching a little further away, it would only look like he was engaging in general friendly banter with the lad. It wasn't much, but it did make Dave feel a little better, at least.

The lad wasn't bright enough to realise he was being insulted, and was too busy joking around with his friend to pay too much attention to the dumb grown-up besides. It wasn't long before he tired of the fat man on the bicycle, threw a sweet wrapper in the bucket, and ambled off with his stupid-looking mate.

"David Quirk!" Becks called to him, grinning. "If Tyler hadn't popped over to the sweet shop next door, he'd have heard that entire conversation!" she admonished him. Unlike the ill-mannered boy, she'd been paying more careful attention from her nearby position, and she'd caught just enough of what Dave was saying to get the gist of it. "And what's this about another woman??"

Dave sucked in his gut once more. "Well, when you're a famous racer, it comes with the territory!" he joked, bravely gambling that Becks would know he was doing exactly that. But it was when he turned to address Becks that Dave noticed Monty, gazing lovingly into the eyes of a little piglet, completely enamoured. "Oi! Monty!"

he called. "Quit faffing about over there! It's your turn, you lazy bugger!" he shouted over, eagerly dismounting. "Right! That's an hour and five minutes I've done! You owe me five minutes, mate!"

Monty said his goodbyes to his new special friend and moved towards the bike like a prizefighter entering the ring, playing up to the crowd with a series of deep lunges along the way. Well, to say *crowd* was perhaps being generous, but there were four ladies of a certain age — all looking rather distinguished with their blue-rinse hairstyles — looking on at this point quizzically.

"That arse balm did the trick, then?" asked Dave, in reference to Monty's contented expression and fluid motion.

"It was like putting a fire out!" announced Monty happily, full of piss and vinegar, and climbing aboard the bike.

"Those old dears okay?" asked Dave, with a discreet nod towards their elderly fan club, who appeared to be getting a little restless. "Only they don't look too impressed."

"How should I know? I just got here," said Monty, presenting an errant eye in their direction.

"The reason I ask is that they seem to have arrived about the same time as you got back here," observed Dave.

"Did they?" said Monty. "Well I don't know about that. But... your shorts weren't too loose, were they? So that they could see Little Dave sneaking out?" he suggested. "I *told* you that you should have worn Lycra like me, Dave. Lycra makes you look like you're riding in the Tour de France!"

"Firstly..." Dave started to say, but then checked his shorts, just in case. Upon ruling out anything out of order down there, he went on, "Okay, firstly, if Little Dave was appearing, then the women would be queuing up and down the street, now wouldn't they? And as for that skintight... *outfit*... you're wearing, Monty, if you can call it that, the only thing you should be on is a bloody register. Now get going, my old son, we've got money to make and the old girls look like they're getting impatient for you to impress them!"

But, instead of really tucking in with his cycling efforts, Monty's errant eye soon dropped, as did his pace on the bike. He offered a cordial smile to the old folk waiting expectantly, before then leaning in Dave's direction. "Come here," he called to him over the

CHAPTER EIGHT

motivational music. "Dave!" he shouted a little louder, and then continuing, once Dave had lent him his ear, told him, "We might have a small problem."

"Oh?" said Dave.

Monty leaned over, as close as he could without toppling off the bike. "I didn't recognise those old birds at first. All those blue-hairs look alike sometimes, you know?" he said.

"What are you on about?" asked Dave.

"I... I, well, see, I was in the women's toilets earlier..." Monty began hesitantly, relating an incident in the same sort of manner of commencement with which many of 'the accused' at their local police station might similarly start their tales.

Dave, knowing Monty for as long as he did, didn't appear overly concerned, folding his arms and settling in for what would be the rest of this story. "Yes, do carry on," he advised, like a psychiatrist encouraging his patient on the couch.

"I went to the toilets in the multi-story car park, see, and as the gents were all occupied, I went into the ladies," Monty began.

"As you do," remarked Dave with eyebrow raised.

"My arse was on fire, and there was nobody in the ladies at the time. It was an emergency!" explained Monty, though no further explanation was really needed as Dave had already accepted this. "Anyway, by the time I came out of the cubicle there were two or three old ladies waiting," Monty went on. "And I think, now, if I'm not mistaken, that those very same ladies are amongst those stood looking at us this very minute, actually," he whispered, through gritted teeth.

"So just why are the blue-rinse brigade staring intently at us, Monty, and why exactly have they followed you here?" asked Dave, certain there must be more to the story. "Because four old ladies have now just become six, and I can't help but notice there are a couple more milling about on the other side of the shopping street loitering with apparent intent."

"Well, as near as I can figure..." said Monty, trying to work it out in his head at the same time as he was relating it to Dave. "Okay, so I'm in the toilets, right? And one of the old dears suggested I resembled someone who was due to be shot out of a cannon —

what with my Lycra cycling outfit and helmet on, I guess? — and she asked me if I was in a circus. I took it as a compliment, if I'm being honest."

"Why were you wearing your helmet? It's an exercise bike, Monty, it's not exactly dangerous," Dave told him. "Actually, you know what, never mind," said Dave with a sigh. He didn't want to go down the rabbit hole of why Monty felt the need to wear a helmet. "Get to the point, yeah? *Why* are this lot here, Monty? They look like they're waiting for something to happen, and I'm guessing that it's not to see two fat lads on an exercise bike. They thought you were in the circus, but that's obviously not the case, so...?"

"Well, when I came out of the cubicle," explained Monty. "You know, there in the women's toilet, and—"

"Yes, I *know* where you were, Monty," Dave interrupted. "You don't have to keep telling me you were in the women's—"

"Toilet. Right. In the women's toilet, yes," said Monty in happy confirmation, missing Dave's point entirely. "And I came out of the cubicle dressed like this, and nobody was screaming. Which was surprising, really, but definitely the way I wanted to keep it, right?"

"Yes...?" said Dave, arms still crossed.

"So I may have, *erm*, accidentally, *ehm*, sort of... told them that, yes, I was part of a circus act performing today," revealed Monty. "For one day only, I said!" he quickly added, as if this was somehow some sort of mitigating factor. "I thought they knew I was joking," he continued. "But as they still appeared a little sombre, I followed that up with an invitation to come along for tea and cake, knowing how all of the oldies love tea and cake, figuring that would cheer them up a bit."

Dave was about to explain to Monty the faulty logic involved in thinking that, on the one hand, the collection of elderly women should know that he was only joking about being in a circus, and then, on the other hand, offering them free tea and cake at this imaginary circus that he just said they should know was only a joke. Instead, Dave merely sighed again and said, "Yes...?"

"But I didn't think they'd actually come!" Monty exclaimed. "Half of them were that blind they couldn't see down the length of

CHAPTER EIGHT

their nose, so I didn't think they'd find me!" he went on. "I dunno, it must be the animals that gave us away, maybe?" he wondered aloud.

"Not sure about that. They're not exactly lions and elephants?" ventured Dave, glancing over to the petting zoo. "And we didn't bring any of the horses, either. So not much of a circus...?"

"Anyway, the point is," said Monty, "I expect they're all either waiting for me to pop out of a canon or they're waiting for tea and cake. Possibly both. Or, rather, probably both."

"Well either way, we're going to have to do something, Monty," advised Dave. "Word seems to be spreading, somehow or another, and they're multiplying! There's so many of them now gathered here that they're blocking the way and nobody can get to the bloody collection bucket!"

"Juggle or something, and make them think it really *is* a circus?" suggested Monty. "I mean, a pretty shite circus it would be, sure, but a circus nonetheless?" proposed Monty. "Jayzus, do I have to do *all* the thinking around here?" he added distractedly, concerning himself now more with the milometer reading on the bike than with Dave's bleating.

"I didn't realise you'd been doing any of the thinking in the first place," Dave mumbled to himself.

"What's that, Dave? I didn't hear you," Monty answered, but then, lifting his head back up from the bike and noticing the swelling ranks in front of him, remarked, "You know, you have to be impressed by their powers of communication, the old folk. Not one mobile phone between them, and yet their numbers here have increased dramatically in only minutes. They must be able to sense the free cake."

"But there isn't any free cake!" replied Dave excitedly. And then, repeating wisely in a rather more hushed manner this time, for fear of creating a riot, "There *is* no soddin' cake, Monty," he said. "You're going to have to take them to the café or something in order to placate them."

"But I'm on the bike, Dave," Monty answered. "Unless... you want to do another shift...?" he asked tentatively, and with the possible opportunity for cake presenting itself, lifting his cheeks off of the seat in anticipation.

"Another shift? You're joking, right?" said Dave. "You've got another thing coming, mate, if you imagine I'm going to hop on that bike again after having just put in my time!"

"All right, all right, it was just a suggestion," Monty moped. "No need to get excited."

"I'll take care of this lot, don't you worry," said Dave. "Although you'll be paying me back at some point for the money I'm about to bloody spend on your behalf, believe you me," he made clear. "And by the time I get back, I want to see more money in *there*..." said Dave, pointing to the bucket... "And considerably more miles on *there*," he said, pointing to the electronic readout on the bike.

With that, Dave addressed, pacified, and then ushered away his flock of old birds, where the appeal of cake quickly overcame the disappointment of there being no circus to speak of. He was like the Pied Piper of Hamelin, except the children were replaced by old folk, and instead of ushering them to their doom, he simply led them to cake and tea.

"Bring back cake!" shouted Monty, offering an enthusiastic thumbs-up.

By the time Dave eventually returned, exactly one hour and five minutes later, Monty's head was all but resting on the handlebars, and with his legs turning slower than a windmill on a very still summer's day.

"Monty's been asking for you, Dave," said Becks, prewarning Dave before he approached the exercise bike and before Monty clapped eyes on him. "Well, when I say *asking*, I actually mean pleading, begging, and I think, at one point, even crying. Still, the crowds, as such, could see what state he was in and have been filling the bucket with sympathy money, so I guess it's not all bad," she informed him. "Are you going to take over now?" she asked, offering a concerned glance over in Monty's general direction. "The poor fella looks like he's about to fall off," she said sympathetically.

CHAPTER EIGHT

"Wait, hang on. What are you smiling at?" asked Becks, in reference to Dave's broad grin. "Don't you care about poor Monty?"

"No, no, it's not that," Dave assured her. "It's those oldies that I've just taken for a cuppa and some cake. Honestly, what a laugh I've had with them, I could have sat and listened to them all day! Real salt-of-the-earth characters. They're in some club that's been set up on the Island called the Lonely Heart Attack Club."

"Oh? That's interesting," said Becks. "Wait... *heart attack?*"

"The name is tongue-in-cheek, don't worry!" said Dave. "At least I assume it is, since none of them were dropping dead in front of me. Anyway, it's some sort of social club for the elderly which gives them a chance to get out and about and meet other people. The mob that I took out for a cuppa are the more extreme of the bunch, I think. They're not the pipe-and-slippers brigade, so to speak, they're proper adrenalin junkies. They're off to play paintball this afternoon, believe it or not! Not one good set of eyes between the lot of them, so that should be interesting. One of them even asked if I'd take her out for a spin on the sidecar, and I think she meant it as well! Anyhow, I need to tell Monty that they didn't take him seriously about the whole circus thing. They were deadly serious about expecting cake, though. They *do* like their cake, and they take offers of cake *very* seriously," he informed Becks. "Ah! And that reminds me!" Dave added, noticing the flyers in Becks' hand. "I've signed up a few of them to come along to the classes at the TT farm. A couple of them even offered to teach, as well! Things like basket weaving, crochet, and knitting."

"That's great!" said Becks, smiling warmly. "It's cute the way you are right now, by the way."

Dave punched her arm in a playful manner — but not too hard, of course — before following it up with a quick peck on her cheek.

"You're turning into a big, gentle softie, David Quirk," Becks told him.

"I know. I don't know what's going on," Dave replied cheekily, before shouting over to Frank and Stan, "Oi! I've got a few more volunteers for the farm, and possibly a new passenger for the TT!"

"Okay, Dave," said Becks, "I think you really need to go and rescue Monty now. I think he's starting to melt, and his head looks like it's going to explode."

It was looking likely that Dave and Monty — or at least Monty — would be struggling to walk for the next several days, but their donation bucket was filling nicely and spurring them on regardless. They were also going to fall considerably short regarding their early aspirations of completing five TT laps' worth of miles on the exercise bike, that goal being overly optimistic, but their efforts had been heroic nonetheless. The local newspaper had been down to interview Frank and Stan about the farm, and promised to include a snippet about the boys' TT-related fundraising efforts as well. And the flow of people eager to learn more about the farm in general had been constant, and even the four-legged guests of honour in the petting zoo had performed admirably, playing the perfect host to a steady stream of enthusiastic children. So it was all turning out quite nicely.

"What a completely wonderful day," said Stan, dropping into one of the camping chairs they'd brought along for moments of occasional rest. "Here," he said, handing Frank one of the coffees he'd poured from his oversized thermos flask for the gang. "He's still going strong," remarked Stan, pointing his wooden stirrer at a thoroughly knackered-looking Monty who was presently digging in for the final ten minutes of the final shift of the day. Stan popped the plastic lid off his cup, setting the steam loose on this brisk Isle of Man afternoon. "We've come a long way since we climbed aboard that ferry on our first Isle of Man TT adventure," suggested Stan thoughtfully. He ripped open a brown sachet of sugar, pouring the contents and then patiently stirring them in. He stared inside the cup contemplatively, watching the swirling liquid go 'round.

"Mmm-hmm," said Frank.

Becks dashed over for her drink, and grabbed a towel from her bag as well, while she was at it. "I think we'll need us a mop and a

CHAPTER EIGHT

bucket for them two!" she remarked cheerfully, in reference to the pool of moisture encircling the lads' exercise bike like a mediaeval moat, and then she was off again, along with Tyler, to cheer Monty on for the final hurdle.

Stan offered an admiring glance in Monty and Dave's direction, before turning his attention back to his cup. Then he looked over to Frank, sat on the camping chair next to him, and attempted to speak. But the words didn't come. Instead, he chewed his lip with pained anguish. Eventually, he soldiered on...

"Do you remember, Frank...?" said Stan tentatively, searching for the appropriate words... "Do you remember when you promised me that you wouldn't hide anything from me about, you know, this illness of yours? You remember that...?" he said.

Stan bowed his head, with the two old chums now, for a time, as quiet as church mice.

Frank placed his left hand on Stan's knee, giving it a gentle little squeeze. "This is like that time you found me down by the waterfront after I'd first been to the doctor's, Stan," he said eventually. "The coffee is a little better this time, though, don't you think?" he asked gamely, offering a half-smile.

"What is it, Frank?" Stan asked, almost afraid of the answer.

Frank gave Stan's knee another little squeeze, wiggled it around like he was putting a car's manual stick into neutral, and then patted it. "Nothing gets past you, Stan, does it?" he said kindly. "As it happens, I had a letter from the doc..." he went on, but his voice gave way, and he couldn't immediately finish. He took a sip of coffee, and then another, and then several breaths. "The letter only came this morning, Stan. I would have told you, but you were so excited about today, as we all were. I should have known you'd work out something was wrong, though. You know me too well." Frank rubbed his forehead with thumb and forefinger, kneading the flesh together.

"It's okay, mate, I'm here for you. I'm always here for you," said Stan.

"Everything was going so well, Stan," said Frank, beginning to lose the battle against his emotions. "Finding those crazy goons Dave and Monty over there, the farm, meeting Jessie, Stella and

Lee getting married. Everything was going so well. And now..." he said. But he was having great difficulty continuing. He clenched his hand into a fist, in a rare display of anger and frustration at his current situation. "How do I... how do I tell Molly and Jessie...?" he said, his eyes welling up.

"What did the letter say? They might just want you for a check-up, yeah? It could be nothing?" Stan ventured hopefully. "You don't know that it's anything to worry about, Frank, necessarily...?"

"It said they wanted to see me urgently. On Monday," Frank replied. "Trust me, Stan. I've had enough of these types of letters from them to know when it's not a simple check-up they're after," he told him. "I just bloody wish they hadn't sent the damned letter to arrive on a Saturday morning so I'd have all weekend to bloody worry about it!"

"Not very considerate of them at all," Stan commiserated. "Not the least little bit."

The church mice-like silence reappeared at this point, with the two old friends sat comfortably in each other's presence, taking solace in each other's company, and with Stan dabbing with his handkerchief, at regular intervals, at the smattering of moisture appearing under his eyes.

"Do you know one of the things that's been playing on my mind the most?" asked Frank, turning to Stan again after a bit of time had passed. "I-I didn't want to leave you on your own, Stan," he said, choking with emotion. "I want you to find someone special in your life, Stan, so that when I'm gone, you're not alone."

"Don't you worry about me," said Stan. "You focus your energy on yourself," he told Frank. "Don't you worry about me," he said again. "Besides," he said, trying his best to lift Frank's spirits, "I've got the charity to keep me busy, yeah? And I don't think life is *ever* going to be too quiet with Dave and Monty and bloody Stella and company in it!"

"And your new friend, Edwin Seabreeze?" asked Frank.

"Edgar Seaforce!" corrected Stan with a titter. "*Edwin Seabreeze,*" he repeated back, shaking his head softly. "Honestly, now," he said, laughing gently.

CHAPTER EIGHT

"Promise me you'll be okay without me around, Stan?" Frank asked earnestly. "I know you don't want to think about it, mate. But promise me...?"

Stan stared his friend directly in the eye. "That's a promise I cannot make, as I'll *never* be okay without you, Frank," Stan said in answer. "But I *will* continue. I *will* carry on, my friend, as one must."

"You'll look out for Jessie, Stella, and Molly?" enquired Frank.

"That's a question you never need to ask me, Frank, but a promise I will most certainly keep," Stan assured him.

Not a moment later, as if on cue to lighten the mood, Monty staggered over, arm-in-arm with Dave, grinning like an idiot. Their faces were puce, their hair dishevelled, and the two of them were walking like they'd been violated by King Kong himself. The two cyclists gripped each other for dear life, as holding onto each other appeared to be the only way they were keeping themselves upright. "Did you see us?" asked Monty, like a child who'd jumped off the diving board at the pool for the first time. Monty stared at Frank and Stan, full of anticipation. "Did you *see* us...?" he repeated, wide-eyed like a puppy expecting a friendly pat or a tummy rub.

Frank set his coffee down on the ground beside him, taking the opportunity to discreetly wipe his cheek of a remaining tear as he did so. "We saw you both," he said, nudging his friend to join him in bestowing praise. "You're not exactly natural athletes, the two of you, so the fact you turned up and kept going for over eight hours is inspiring, boys. Well done, lads. Well done, indeed. We're both very proud of you today!" he said like a doting parent, and with Stan nodding along in agreement and encouragement lest Monty feel neglected.

Monty puffed out his chest, and the pain in his limbs washed away in an instant by the paternal words of pride. He slapped Dave's arm in an 'aww-shucks' manner, his eyes twinkling.

"Oh, come on, then," said Frank, ushering the two of them in for an impromptu hug-fest. "You, too, Becks and Tyler, come on and get some of this!"

And with that, Frank scooped them all into his arms, holding onto them tightly, and then grabbing hold of Stan and bringing him into the fold as well.

FRANK 'N' STAN'S BUCKET LIST #4 – BRIDE OF FRANK 'N' STAN

"You're a special bunch," said Frank. "A genuinely wonderful bunch of people, you lot, and you've brought quite a bit of joy into this old bugger's existence. Never, ever forget that."

They held this position, each of them pressed into the other, with small farmyard animals nuzzling into their ankles, and with the occasional rattle to be heard of coins being thrown into their bucket by appreciative passers-by.

"Hey, Frank?" said Monty eventually, his face pressed up against Stan's chest in the scrum, and the silence driving him mad.

"Yes, Monty?" replied Frank.

"I'm not exactly sure what's going on?" Monty answered. "But... seeing as how you're in such a good mood just now... do you think we can maybe get an ice cream on the way home?"

"Yes, Monty," Frank told him. "Yes, we can."

Chapter
NINE

A generous application of winter's sun gradually won its battle against the remaining overnight frost. Striking blue sky framed the captivating Manx countryside surrounding the TT Farm in every direction, and for as far as the eye could see. And yet despite Mother Nature's gift on this beautiful morning, a proverbial grey cloud cloaked those fortunate enough to know, and love, Frank Cryer.

Meanwhile, in the renovated stable area, Dave made short work of a large carrot, packing it away in record time. He sidled up to a fence post, using it to relieve an itch in his hard-to-reach rump, and, once satisfied, flared his nostrils, snorted, and looked about in hopes of spotting another delicious carrot. In his subsequent journey across the paddock, however, he came across Monty. Monty was quite enjoying himself, having discovered a bale of hay left there in the field and deciding, apparently, that kicking up the hay would be a worthwhile endeavour in service of whiling away the hours. Aggrieved at Dave's impertinent interruption of said hay-related pursuits, Monty stamped a leg down onto the earthen floor in protest. Monty exposed his prominent teeth at Dave, but Dave simply went 'round him, carrying on in his current quest for carrots undaunted. Monty, noticing Dave's determination, and now curious as to where Dave might be headed, abandoned his frolic in the hay and decided to follow. Granted, the options were limited considering they were in an enclosed area and so couldn't go too terribly far. Still, if Dave found something to be of interest, then Monty found it interesting as well. Dave, for his part, appeared entirely unconcerned at Monty's aggressive display of gnashers only a moment ago. In fact, Dave stopped, waiting for Monty to catch up. And not only that, but in an apparent effort to appease any current tension that might yet remain, he offered his bum to Monty for inspection. This was an offer Monty gratefully took up, this being, after all, what friends generally did for each other. Still, Monty approached cautiously, for he knew Dave well. Indeed, he was right to trust his suspicions, because as soon as he got close enough, his snout near to Dave's rump, Dave's tail lurched skyward, giving Monty no time at all to escape Dave summarily evacuating his bowels... all over poor Monty's face.

Observing this kerfuffle from their position leaning over the fence a safe distance away were, curiously enough, Monty and Dave.

"You know... in hindsight," said Dave, "I'm not entirely sure it was a good idea to let Tyler name the new donkeys...?"

"Pretty funny, though, you have to admit," Monty offered, staring affectionately at their latest charges and four-legged namesakes who, some might well say, had a better general aroma than their human counterparts. "Cheeky little bugger," he chuckled.

"Cheeky indeed," agreed Dave.

"You know, I think I'm starting to really embrace this outdoor lifestyle, and in particular the animals," Monty reflected. "I think I'm turning into that, whutsisname, Dr Dolittle bloke."

"You *Dolittle* 'round here," quipped Dave, but it wasn't his finest comedic effort, failing even to rouse a raised eyebrow from Monty in acknowledgement.

"Anyway," said Monty, skirting around it like a pro, "I'm loving these new donkeys, though. Proper characters, they are."

"That's why the nickname Shrek works so well," replied Dave. *Donkey*," he said, in his finest Mike Myers Scottish swamp-dweller impersonation.

But Monty's face remained impassive.

"You *do* know why I've been calling you Shrek all week?" asked Dave, in response to not even the faintest glimmer of recognition from Monty at Dave's film reference.

CHAPTER NINE

"Sure," said Monty, but then immediately added, "No, actually. I just thought you were being mean."

Monty sighed, and almost on cue his four-legged namesake wandered over to him offering an inquisitive nudge of the nose, almost as if he could feel his two-legged equivalent's anguish.

"Aww, mate," said Dave, turning to his chum. "I wasn't being mean," he said sincerely. "In Shrek, his best friend is a donkey. That's why I was calling you Shrek. Not to be mean or anything."

Monty scoured Dave's face for a hint of sarcasm, or perhaps a follow-up line though none was forthcoming. "Ah. Okay, then," he replied. "I've not seen it, but this Shrek fellow must have good taste in friends," Monty conceded, but even then, he didn't entirely brighten up. "Although I'm not sure I understand, really, if we're *both* donkeys?" he asked, looking at Monty the Donkey and Dave the Donkey. "Anyway, it doesn't matter," he said glumly. "Sorry, I'm not really with it today, Dave, I'll be honest with you, on account of, well, you know..."

"I know, buddy, I know," replied Dave, looping his arm around Monty's shoulder. "He's something special, old Frank," he said, saying out loud what they were both thinking about. "And I don't think I've ever seen my mum so happy as she is with him. And you know what? At this point, I can't even imagine not having either Frank or Stan in my life. It's as if I've known them both for years."

Monty pressed both thumbs into his tear ducts, letting out a gentle sob, which was met with a tighter cuddle from Dave. "He's been like a father to us both," said Monty. "Just the thought of... the thought of... well..."

"I know, buddy," said Dave. "Here. They should be back soon enough," he added, glancing at his watch, before reaching over to say hello to Dave the Donkey, who had decided to join them also. "We just need to be positive and take our minds off it all."

"Hmm. Well, we *could* paint stripes on the donkeys, I suppose," suggested Monty, brainstorming for ideas.

"W-what?" Dave spluttered. "What on earth are you on about?" he replied, grinning. "Why the hell would we go and do that, you silly sod?"

"I dunno," shrugged Monty. "It'd take our minds off the whole Frank situation? And, besides, it'd make people visiting the farm think we had zebras," he reasoned. "All exotic and such," he added, sweeping a hand out across his imagined vision of the majestic Isle of Man Serengeti.

"Yeah, probably best not to, actually," remarked Dave. "But if you're after something to paint, Monty, I suppose you could give this paddock fence a going-over?" he offered. "Although, I don't know, I think it looks good as it is, unpainted and weathered. It looks nice and rustic this way."

"Rustic," repeated Monty, for no particular reason except that he liked the sound of it.

"Besides, we might get into trouble for painting the donkeys," Dave judiciously advised.

"You're probably right," Monty replied, before snapping his head smartly in the direction of the farmhouse. "Wait, do you hear a car? I think I hear a car coming up the drive," he said, gripping Dave's hand in both anticipation and worry.

"Sounds like they're back," said Dave. "Come on, let's go meet them."

The two of them made their way across the courtyard and to the rear of the farmhouse where the drive came to an end, waiting patiently for the car that, from the sound of it, would arrive there very shortly. Dave patted the back of Monty's hand. "Whatever the next five minutes bring, Monty, we're in this together, old chum," he told him. "I'm here for you, and you're here for me, and we're both here for everyone else, yeah?"

They both watched on, anxiously, as Jessie's pink Nissan Micra bunny-hopped across the driveway before coming to an aggressive halt, kicking up stone chippings in the process, and with Jessie over-revving the engine.

"Oh my goodness! Something's wrong!" cried Monty.

"No, no, not necessarily," Dave remarked. "That's the way my mum always drives."

"Ah. Woman driver?" said Monty.

"Don't you dare, Monty. That's offensive!" Dave said in response.

CHAPTER NINE

"What? Oh, sorry," replied Monty, knowing he'd gotten it wrong somehow, though not sure precisely how.

"Her being a lousy driver has nothing to do with being a woman. She's just a lousy driver, full stop," explained Dave.

"Ah," said Monty.

Jessie unclipped her seatbelt, leaning over to the passenger seat, where she placed a kiss on Frank's cheek. There was a moment of panic for Monty and Dave when Jessie placed her head on the steering wheel, overcome with emotion by all appearances, and with Dave giving a distraught Monty a few more consoling pats on the hand. It turned out Jessie was actually reaching into the passenger footwell for her handbag, however, so there was slight relief there, though she may well have been overcome by emotion, also, just the same. It was difficult for Dave and Monty to tell from their vantage point. Jessie then climbed out, clutching her bag with one hand, and offering a tentative wave in their direction with the other.

"Aww, no," said Dave, his worst fears seeming to be confirmed. "Bloody hell, she's been crying," he went on, in reference to his mum's displaced eyeliner. "So's Stan," he added, in reference to Stan's displaced eyeliner, as well, as Stan got out of the car.

"I don't like this, Dave," said Monty. "Not one bit."

The two of them walked over to the car, adopting the bravest pair of faces they could muster under the circumstances.

"All right?" said Dave, hand raised up in a friendly wave, and overly and inexplicably cheery considering the potential of the situation. Perhaps it was the nerves. He soon set himself right by adopting a rather more sombre demeanour. "Be strong," he told himself softly out of the corner of his mouth, attempting to brace himself for what was certain to be bad news.

"I'll try," Monty whispered back, thinking Dave was talking to him. Dave just nodded at him encouragingly and sympathetically, feeling no need to correct him.

Now that Jessie, Frank, and Stan were clear of the car and in full view, the reddened and puffy eyes on each of them made it well evident, if there had been any doubt at all remaining, that it had been an emotionally charged morning for the three of them. Frank, for his part, paused, stretching his arms skyward and taking a lungful of the bracing Manx air. He appeared to Dave and Monty completely relaxed, which was both confusing and slightly disconcerting.

Dave and Monty bobbed their heads up and down and side to side, looking like inquisitive barn owls. They ran their eyes over every contour of Frank's face, searching for something, anything, any kind of clue as to what might be going on inside Frank's head.

"Well?" asked Monty, his voice quavering, when he could finally take it no more. "Tell us!"

Frank stepped over to them, pulling Monty and Dave up close so each of them were both leaning over with their heads resting on either side of his breast. He kissed each of them on the top of the head, and said, "I thought that was it, boys." And then he sighed. But it wasn't a sigh of despair. Rather, it was a happy, relieved sort of sigh.

"Wait. *It's not...*?" asked Dave and Monty in unison.

"Not today, lads," Frank told them. He released his grip on the boys, inhaling deeply and absorbing the sumptuous countryside around them, a grin forming on his face and increasing gradually.

"I don't understand...?" Dave replied. But Frank was too busy simply breathing in the air to answer directly, so Dave looked over to the others. "Stan? Mum?" he asked.

Dave's mum stepped forward, attempting to answer. "Frank's been..." she began, but immediately pressed her hands over her face, and couldn't continue.

"She's been doing this all the way here," offered Stan. "And in her state, she maybe shouldn't have been driving, to be completely honest. Though I suppose it may explain the excessive revving of the engine?"

"No, that's just the way my mum always drives," whispered Dave to Stan.

"Ah," said Stan. Then, Stan took up the story from a still-sobbing Jessie. "Apparently, this tough old bugger has been responding well to the treatment they put him on," he said, looking at his pal with admiration and pride. "He's not out of the woods yet, mind. It's still very serious. But with his prospects not entirely grim, and there being some hope there, the doctor put him forward for a trial

CHAPTER NINE

drug which they think might improve his situation even further," Stan explained. "I forget what it was called, this new drug. Was it OxyOrange...?" he said, flapping his hand, struggling to recall.

"Is that not a cleaning product?" Frank asked, coming back into the conversation, laughing.

"It could be my fake tan brand?" considered Stan, thinking hard on it, but then giving up with a shrug. "Anyway. Some new drug or other," he said. "So, the point being, we may just be stuck with this stubborn old sod for a little while longer," he concluded, patting Frank's back affectionately.

"So you're not going to die?" asked Monty of Frank. "I mean, not this week or anything?"

Frank shook his head in the negative, but gave Monty a cheeky grin. "I can't make any firm promises, Monty. I could get hit by a bus, after all!"

"Or run over by Mum's driving," suggested a smirking Dave.

"Or run over by your mum, yes," agreed Frank happily, before turning serious for a moment. "It's a long journey, guys, buuut..." he said, drawing out the *but*. "There's no promises, and it'll just be a case of multiple visits to the hospital, and I may lose some energy. But I'll damn well keep fighting."

Frank looked them all over. "With your support," he told his merry band of cohorts, "I can get through this. Or at the least keep the illness at bay, for now."

"Brilliant!" said Dave, speaking for all of them.

"Delightful!" added Monty.

"Come on, let's go inside," Jessie directed to Frank. "You'll need to ring Molly back and give her the rest of the details, and it's a bit cold out here. Maybe we should get you a blanket? Are you hungry?" she asked, fussing over him now, and dusting him down for no apparent reason.

"I'm fine," Frank assured her, though appreciative enough of the attention. "You're right about Molly, though. We should maybe see if she wants to fly over for the weekend? It'd be good to see her."

Monty paced in place, kicking his knees up like he was marching and gripping one hand tightly with the other, like a schoolboy waiting to ask permission to pee. "*Staaan*," he said, as soon as an

143

opportunity presented itself to chime in. "Can I tell him, now? Can I tell him, please?" he asked impatiently, glancing over to Frank, and then back to Stan. "I mean, it's safe to tell him now, right? Now he's not dying and everything?"

"What?" asked Stan, not quite sure what Monty was on about at first, but then, "Oh. Oh, yes. That. I'd completely forgotten about that. Yes, yes, go on," he said, inviting Monty to continue.

Monty swelled up, pleased as punch. "Frank, so you know how you're getting married soon?" he asked.

"*Ehm*, yes?" Frank replied, with some degree of apprehension. But the apprehension was not in regard to the marriage. No, it was more in relation to what Monty was about to say as one never could tell, where Monty was concerned, what that might possibly be. "I seem to recall something or other to that effect, yes...?" said Frank, in relation, again, to the upcoming nuptials.

"Well, what with you getting married, and, well, tradition and all..." Monty went on, not really getting to the point.

"Yes, out with it, then," pressed Frank. "I haven't got that much time left that I can afford to waste it, yes?"

"*Weeelll*," said Monty, drawing it out a moment longer. "Now you're not dying immediately... I've booked your *stag do*," he said, jazz hands working overdrive.

"And Lee's," added Dave, lest the matter of Lee marrying Stella also should somehow be forgotten.

"A stag do?" said Frank, raising a sceptical eyebrow. "I don't know, boys, I think I'm a bit old for a weekend in Benidorm being sick on myself from drinking into oblivion."

Monty screwed up his face. "Please! We're classier than that!" he insisted.

"We are?" asked a surprised Dave, in reference to the 'classy' bit, as this was news to him. "Oh, I mean, yes. Quite," he added, quickly correcting himself. "Classy! That's us!"

"So where are you lads thinking, then?" asked Frank, attention piqued, quizzical eyebrow rising slightly higher.

"It's a surprise!" replied Monty. "Now, I really must get on the phone," he said dismissively. "Because I'd told a few people that you might not be making it, so I'll need to check and see if everything

CHAPTER NINE

is still available," he pointed out, as if the former prospect of Frank's possible imminent demise had been a terrible inconvenience as far as questions of plan-making went. "Hopefully they'll still be able to accommodate us," Monty added, throwing his arms across his chest and eying Frank in mock disdain.

"Sorry to be so much trouble?" offered Frank. "Didn't mean for my poor health to throw a spanner in the works?"

"Yes. Well. *Hmph*," replied Monty.

"Do I need to pack my speedos?" enquired Frank, pulling at the waistband of his trousers, but Jessie's face told him all he needed to know in that regard.

"Anyway. Enough about that. We need to celebrate tonight, yes?" said Stan. "We're all going out for a nice meal, on me. And I'm buying the most expensive bottle of fizzing liquid that I can get my hands on!" he said, punching the air for good measure.

As they casually strolled to the farmhouse, it was like a weight had been lifted from the lot of them. The proverbial grey cloud that hung over the TT Farm these past couple of days was lifted in a glorious instant and now replaced with an overwhelming sense of joy. It was days like this that made you truly realise and embrace how lucky you were to be alive — and, not to mention, in a location drenched in such natural beauty.

"Frank," said Monty, trailing several paces behind and staring intently at his phone screen. "Frank, there's a couple of things I need to know in advance of our little stag-do trip, just to be on the safe side. Right. So. You wouldn't be allergic to latex, by chance?" he asked. And then, raising his finger to stress the point, "And also, are you up to date with inoculations, including both malaria and dengue fever?"

Frank turned, expecting Monty to have cracked a smile, but the expression Monty held on his face was deadpan.

"And," said Monty, now on a roll. "You do have my permission to bring your speedos, because, what goes on tour stays on tour."

Chapter
TEN

Stan was a morning person. Always had been. It could be mildly irksome at times, particularly if you yourself were still a bit sluggish and he was skipping around full of gusto like the Energizer Bunny. But even by his own standards Stan was feeling particularly giddy this day, and even the hint of a little hangover after their celebratory meal the evening before wasn't dampening his spirits any. After all, his best friend had received a stay of execution, as it were, the sun was shining, and according to the electronic readout he was looking at he'd lost three pounds this week. He stepped off the weighing scales, flashed his pearly whites in delight, and blew a sincere kiss to the machine that told him he was possibly even more fabulous than the week before. He waltzed into the living room after a brief detour to retrieve his cup of tea from the kitchen, whistling a happy melody that was partially in tune and partially not; he didn't really care either way. He blew gently on the contents of his cup and then placed the cup onto the writing bureau nestled in the bay window, concluding the tea to be not quite at optimum drinking temperature just yet. He took the opportunity to burst into a series of energetic star jumps, and with the occasional lunge as well, spurred on by the occasion of his reduction in BMI and anxious for further progress in that regard.

"Ahem," said Frank from the kitchen, having come down the stairs and arriving there shortly after Stan had exited. "I thought we had a conversation previously about you wandering about in your underpants?"

FRANK 'N' STAN'S BUCKET LIST #4 – BRIDE OF FRANK 'N' STAN

"Morning, Frank," replied Stan, snapping the elastic waistband on his white Y-fronts rather smartly. "I've been doing my morning Pilates," he said, as explanation for him presently only wearing white Y-fronts. "Three pounds I've lost, lately," he added, patting his tummy like an expectant mum. "You should join me, Frank?"

"Let me walk before I can run, okay, mate?" a still-groggy Frank answered. He joined Stan in the living room, nursing his own cuppa. "Thanks for the meal last night, by the way. It was lovely to go out and have a right laugh without things gnawing away in the back of my mind," he said. "Oh, and Jessie was talking to me about something in bed later on that I wanted to mention," he added.

"That's what you call it?" said Stan, moving his cup to his lips and taking a tentative sip now his tea had chance to cool slightly. "I heard the moaning noises," he remarked cheekily. "So much moaning that I thought you had a ghost in there!"

Frank blushed. "It certainly wasn't that, you saucy bugger," he insisted. "Jessie stubbed her toe on the way back from the bathroom, I'll have you know, and turned the air blue. That's all that was."

Frank then took a dainty sip of his tea, extending his pinkie finger as he did so. Stan eyed him with suspicion but chose, in the end, to avoid further interrogation.

"You should put some trousers on, Stan," recommended Frank. "If a double-decker bus went past, they'd be able to look in and see you in your trollies," he advised, taking another sip of tea. "Anyway, about what Jessie and I were talking about..." he said, scratching his day-old stubble and uncertain as to how to begin.

"Out with it," said Stan. "No secrets, remember?"

Frank nodded. "Look, it's about this whole stag-do thing that the boys were on about last night. I'm just not so sure it's a great idea, what with the treatment and everything. Add to that the fact that I'm not a big drinker. And we know from previous experience, also, that strip clubs are not exactly my thing," Frank explained. "I mean, I know everyone's excited, and I really don't want to be a stick in the mud, honestly I don't. But I must remain practical, you understand. I'm not completely out of the woods yet, as it were, if you know what I'm saying?"

CHAPTER TEN

"You needn't worry, Frank," said Stan, moving a pace forward in Frank's direction, but, what with him being partially naked and all, Frank stepping back every time Stan took a step forward. It looked like they were practising a foxtrot, until Frank finally held out a firm hand to halt Stan's progress.

"Ah. Well the boys have told me what's in store, and it's nothing bad," Stan promised Frank. "Certainly not a boozy weekend. Well, okay, *some*. But you can get involved as far as that goes as much or as little as you want, if that makes sense?" Stan assured him. "Frank, I promise you that you'll completely love it, and if you trust me on this, you'll do it. I know Jessie's worried about you doing too much, but how about I have a word and give her an idea of what's in store. Put her mind at rest, yeah?"

"Sure," conceded Frank. "Just nothing crazy, though, all right?" he appealed. "Morning, my lovely," Frank said, turning to Jessie, who just appeared, bleary-eyed, in her dressing gown. "There's tea in the pot. Should be at the right temperature for you."

"I'm sorry. But why are you in your underpants, Stan?" asked Jessie of Stan, followed by a rubbing of her eyes.

"Pilates," replied Stan.

"Bless you," said Frank. It was one of his oldest jokes, but he would never tire of it even if those around him might have tired of it long, long ago.

"You should join me, Jessie," continued Stan, ignoring Frank.

"What, in my knickers and bra?" asked Jessie, having a yawny stretch, followed by another rubbing of her eyes.

Stan shrugged. "Whatever you want to wear. It's good exercise." He smiled a devious smile, flashing a quick glance at Frank, before turning back to Jessie. "I'm sorry to hear about your toe, Jessie, by the way," he told her. "There's nothing worse than stubbing your toe, and it doesn't half make you scream out in pain, does it?"

Jessie watched on, waiting for the rest of whatever it was that Stan was about to say, as it was obvious to her that something was missing. She was getting used to his rather unusual ways — which she now referred to as *Stanisms* — and waited patiently for some form of punchline. "But I didn't stub my toe...?" she said, when there was no follow-up forthcoming. She tut-tutted to herself,

FRANK 'N' STAN'S BUCKET LIST #4 – BRIDE OF FRANK 'N' STAN

heading for her tea, and assuming she just didn't get the joke that never really arrived in the first place.

Once Jessie was a couple of metres away, in the kitchen and out of earshot, Frank growled in a low whisper, *"You bastard,"* before conceding that he'd been beaten by the better man. "You can have that, very good," he told Stan.

"Frank, you've left your phone in the kitchen and it's about to vibrate off the table!" shouted Jessie from the other room.

"Ah. Set to vibrate," remarked Stan, with emphasis on the word *vibrate*. "Why am I not surprised?" he asked, frowning comically and raising his eyebrows knowingly.

Frank narrowed his eyes, pursed his lips, and shook his head from side to side. "Just stop, you," he whispered. Then he turned to the kitchen. "Grab it for me, please, princess?" he called into the other room. "Only I'm about to beat Stan around the head with my slipper just now!"

Jessie appeared a moment later. "Frank, it's some woman called Marlene asking for you," she offered with a shrug, handing his mobile out to him.

"Marlene?" asked Frank, wracking his brains, but with nothing presenting itself. He gave a shrug as well, and then accepted the phone into his hand. "Frank Cryer here," he said, after placing the mobile to his ear. He paced back and forth, as he often did when on the phone, and the confusion on his face clearly indicated he had no idea who this Marlene person was. Frank listened on, making occasional encouraging noises, as one does, for the benefit of Marlene, while he tried to work out precisely what the call was all about.

"If it's some salesperson, at this hour of the morning, no less, trying to sell you something, tell them to piss off!" whispered Stan.

But then Frank's face contorted, like he'd smelt a particularly nasty fart. He closed one eye for a moment, lowering the phone for a second or two, before placing it back up to his ear. He went to speak but then stopped, like he was attempting to qualify what he'd just heard. "I'm sorry. Did you just say... *Rodney Franks...?*" he asked down the phone after a long pause, and he said this in a tone

CHAPTER TEN

that indicated he was having a difficult time believing what he was hearing.

Jessie and Stan, at Frank's surprising utterance of the name of *he-who-must-not-be-named*, huddled closer.

"Well," said Frank, after a moment, "I don't mean to be rude, Marilyn, but... Sorry. *Marlene*... I don't mean to be rude, Marlene, but you can tell Rodney Franks that he's probably the last person on earth that I'd ever want to meet for lunch. And that's putting it quite charitably, as the guy is a complete... well, I won't say what I think, but if you know him, Marlene, then you must know what I mean."

Frank allowed Marlene to continue, shaking his head in a mixture of puzzlement and dismay. He resumed his pacing, moving through the living room, the hall, the kitchen, and then back again into the living room, where he eventually brought the call to its inevitable conclusion, saying, "Yes. Right. Thank you, Marlene." He lowered the phone, incredulous.

"Well?" said Stan.

"She was phoning on behalf of Rodney Franks," replied Frank vaguely, still trying to digest what he'd just heard.

"Yes, we got that bit," confirmed Jessie, gathering her dressing gown tightly about her.

Frank set his phone down. "Marilyn is Rodney's assistant, or his receptionist, or secretary, or something, and—"

"Marlene," interrupted Stan.

"Marlene. Sorry," said Frank. "And, as it should happen, Rodney is coming over to the Island tomorrow and wants to see the pair of us," explained Frank, pointing to Stan and then prodding his own chest in indication of who exactly Rodney wanted to see. "He's got something he needs to speak to us about, apparently, and Marlene said it would be in our best interests for us to meet with him. She emphasised that she was merely repeating Rodney's words, and to be fair she did sound perfectly pleasant herself, and even sounded a bit apologetic in the way that—"

"Frank!" snapped Stan, eager to get to the root of the mystery. "What on earth would that unctuous arsehole want to see us about??" he asked, placing his chin into his palm for exaggerated effect.

"Look, will you put some bloody trousers on?" said Frank. "I can't think clearly, what with that thing poking out in my peripheral vision!" he protested, pointing at the disconcertingly conspicuous bulge that was Little Stan. "Anyway, this Marlene didn't have a clue. But she sounded sincere about it being in our best interests in meeting him."

"It must be about the sale of the farm," gasped Stan, gripping onto Frank's arm like a lovestruck girl. "Maybe he's looked at the original sale documents when he first handed the farm over? Shit, what if he's trying to weasel out of something and get the farm back for himself?"

"Relax," Frank assured him, unhooking Stan's fingers from his arm. "Henk had his legal team pore over all documents concerned, and the contracts are as tight as, well, say, your undies. Anyway, we could spend all day guessing what he wants, or we could just wait until we meet him tomorrow, for lunch. I'll bet the miserable sod even makes us pay."

"Maybe you should phone Henk?" suggested Jessie. "You know, just to check in and make sure he's not heard anything that might explain the meeting? Forearmed being forewarned, and all that?"

Frank ruminated on this for a moment. "Yes, that's a good idea, Jessie," he agreed. "I think I'll ring him straight after breakfast."

Frank stood with his cuppa pulled tightly to his chest, the aroma of tea bathing his nostrils, positioning himself directly in front of the bay window and looking up Glencrutchery road towards the TT Grandstand. He took in the view — one of his favourites on the Island — but in truth he was wracking his brains. "Rodney Franks," he muttered to himself. "What the hell do you want with us?"

Chapter
ELEVEN

"It smells of piss in here," remarked Stan, sniffing intently. "Why does it smell of piss in here?"

"It's a bus shelter," replied Frank. "That's what they usually smell of, so just stop sniffing and you'll be fine."

The two of them had dived into a concrete bus shelter on Douglas Promenade, hiding from what was, they hoped, only a passing shower. "We look like bloody twins," observed Frank, casting his eyes up and down his companion. The two friends both sported beige knee-length trenchcoats, with their chins buried in the generous collars, and complemented by a black trilby hat apiece. "And what's with the hat, by the way? It's the same as mine as well, and ordinarily you never wear a hat, Stanley, because you hate covering up your hair."

Stan tugged down on the front of his hat with purpose, like a moody cowboy. "I saw you wearing yours last week and thought it looked splendid," he told Frank. "You should be pleased that you've inspired me! And besides, I thought it made me appear, I don't know... hard-bitten?"

"Hard-bitten?" said a not entirely convinced Frank, looking his friend over once more.

"Yes. Indeed," replied Stan. "And we don't know what this Franks devil might be up to. He could be spoiling for a fight!"

Frank laughed. "I don't think people say that since the nineteen-forties, Stan. And, besides, Rodney Franks may be many things, but I don't imagine being proficient at fisticuffs is one of them, so there's no worry there, I don't think. Keep in mind, he certainly wouldn't invite us to lunch if he was… *spoiling for a fight*, as you say," said Frank, raising his hands in Queensberry fashion. "Anyway, we should go," suggested Frank. "The restaurant is only two minutes away, and I think the worst of this rain has passed us by," he offered, confirming this with a skyward glance.

"We don't want to be early, though," advised Stan. "We want to arrive well after him and keep him waiting, as that will put him on edge and so give us the advantage."

Frank pondered Stan's point for a moment, but only for the very briefest of moments. "Don't be bloody daft. You've been watching too many cheesy American gangster films or something," Frank chided him gently, and then mused, "Hmm, we don't look entirely ridiculous, do we? Maybe I should have got changed when I saw you put your coat on? I'm starting to feel like I resemble Inspector Gadget or similar."

"Nonsense, man. We look professional, and like we bloody mean business," Stan insisted. "Anyway, come on, we should get going," he said, popping his hand outside the shelter, palm up, followed by his head poking out as well. "The rain's nearly stopped."

"Didn't I already say that?" Frank replied.

To Stan, the pair of them may have given the appearance of two professionals who bloody meant business. But, to the rest of the Island, it was more probable they appeared like two men of a certain age wearing suspicious-looking trenchcoats likely on a quest to find a back-alley sleaze pit which rented videos on an hourly rate. They danced around the puddles, eager to reach their destination with dry feet before the next passing shower arrived.

"I think this is it," said Stan, introducing the restaurant with a precise finger pointing up at the elegant signage.

"Looks very dear," suggested Frank, giving the building a once-over. "We just need to make sure that pompous arse is paying," he declared. And with that, hats were removed as they ventured inside, where they were greeted by a snappily dressed hostess with a menu tucked under her arm.

"Afternoon, gentlemen. Reservation?" she enquired, with a smile that was unwavering.

CHAPTER ELEVEN

"Franks," replied Stan, running his eyes around the restaurant. "Smarmy little so-and-so with a—"

"Right this way, sir," she replied. "Your host is already here."

Stan smiled. *"Host?"* he whispered to Frank, his voice dripping with sarcasm.

The young lady escorted them towards the rear of the restaurant, and then ushered them to a cosy alcove near to the fireplace. "Please," she said, introducing them to the table therein, and then left them to it.

The person sat at the table had their nose pressed into a menu, so Frank cleared his throat to attract their attention. There was no response or lowering of the menu and so Frank cleared his throat once more, only a little louder this time. A raised index finger emerged from behind the side of the menu, in indication that the person sat there was at the moment preoccupied. "Tell me the specials again," said the holder of the menu in an unmistakable nasally tone.

Rodney must have known who was stood waiting in front of him, of course, but in that moment of expressed indifference directed towards his guests, the control of the situation shifted from Inspector Gadget and his mate and over to the seated Rodney.

"Ah, forgive me," said Rodney, finally setting the menu down, and inviting his guests to join him at the table. "I did spot you coming over," he added. "But, as you both looked quite a bit older than I remembered, I thought you must have been someone else entirely. Please, do take a seat. I hope you gentlemen are hungry, as I understand the food here is most remarkable."

Frank and Stan had spoken in preparation earlier about doing their best to retain their composure, but Rodney Franks certainly did make such things difficult. He wore both a smarmy grin and his trademark cravat, as usual, and spoke to them like he was only feigning interest and with no genuine desire to hear anything they might have to say. Whatever they may have thought of him, however, they had to admit he was relatively successful in matters of business, and so perhaps these annoying mannerisms of his afforded him some kind of advantage in his business-related dealings. In any event, Rodney's frustratingly irritating manner was something with which Frank and Stan were sadly all too familiar.

"Yes, well, we nearly didn't make it," began Stan, looking down at his hand and giving his cuticles an inspection, like speaking with Rodney was a terrible inconvenience and that he had far, far better things to do. "We *are* exceptionally busy at the TT Farm, after all," he said, now casually looking the fingernails on his other hand over, hoping to get a reaction from Rodney.

"You're probably wondering why I asked to see you both," said Rodney, not taking the bait, and continuing on as if Stan hadn't spoken at all.

Frank shrugged his shoulders as if this were a point of only minor interest, or in fact any interest at all — though, the truth of it was, the two of them, he and Stan, had barely slept for wondering. "Not really," Frank replied nonchalantly. "But we thought we'd give you the courtesy of our time."

"Ah," said Rodney, at the waitress's arrival. "I ordered us a nice bottle of red," he told Stan and Frank. The waitress diligently filled their glasses with a polished smile, and Rodney waited for her to leave before continuing. "I didn't know too much about you, Stan, though I've done some research," said Rodney, addressing Frank.

"I'm Frank," said Frank. "That's Stan," said Frank. But Frank suspected Rodney knew this already.

"Apologies," said Rodney. "Anyway, I understand the both of you are successful businessmen, same as I am?" he asked, unable to resist giving himself a bit of self-praise in the process. "Largest taxi firm in Liverpool, from what I gather?" Rodney raised his glass, offering a mock toast toward that fact. "And," he continued, after taking a sip and swirling the wine around his gob, "I heard all about the work you did with the homeless shelters and soup kitchens in the UK. Outstanding. Truly outstanding."

Frank glanced over to Stan, unsure where this was going. "I'm certain you've not brought us here to discuss our charity work in general, Rodney. However, I'm sure it's our charity work on the Isle of Man, more specifically, that has?" he said, having another dig at Rodney's expense, as Stan had done, about their ownership of the TT Farm.

CHAPTER ELEVEN

"Oh?" said Rodney, motioning with his hand for Frank to continue.

Frank eased back in his chair. "We've gone over every inch of the paperwork for the sale of the TT Farm property, Rodney, and everything's above board," he said, prodding his finger down onto the crisp white tablecloth. "It's watertight."

Rodney lowered his jaw like he was either in shock or deeply offended at the insinuation. But then he smiled. "You're right," he said, which caught Frank and Stan both off guard. "Trust me, gentlemen, whatever work you've done about reviewing contracts, I've done ten-fold," he admitted. "Cost me a fortune in the process, as well. Bloody lawyers, am I right?" he said, with a crooked grin, suddenly switching tactics from smarmy to an apparent attempt to ingratiate himself with them, and raising his glass to them in a show of comradery that was not returned.

"*Weeelll,*" said Frank, slowly and deliberately, "If you're not here to discuss the TT Farm sale, then...?" Frank trailed off, raising his palms up, indicating he was fresh out of ideas.

Rodney cackled away to himself for a moment, and to those sat in the vicinity the trio must have appeared to have been old chums catching up over a nice lunch — although this was most certainly not the case. A nice lunch, yes, perhaps it would be. Old chums, however, not in the slightest.

"Please," said Rodney, pressing two menus in their direction. "I've been guilty of many things in my lifetime, but not being an impeccable host has never been one of them, I daresay." Rodney smiled warmly. Or had a go at trying to, at least, as smiling warmly did not come naturally to his face. "Now. I suppose I do owe you an explanation as to why I've brought you here," he offered. "After all, it's been rather cloak-and-dagger up to this point, hasn't it?"

"You could say that. Yes," replied Stan wearily, not at all amused.

"Right," began Rodney, placing his hand down onto the table and caressing it like a lover. "I must confess that you've all become somewhat bothersome to me of late, I'm sorry to say. Not so much you two, you understand, but in your association with the big Dutch oaf Henk van der Berg. So, guilty by association, if you will. You see, I don't really like being on the losing side of anything, gentlemen. It leaves a rather bitter taste in my mouth," he told them, smacking his lips together to illustrate the point.

"I'm crying inside for you," said Frank, pushing his chair back. "I'm not sure why we even bothered," he said, motioning to Stan. "Come on, Stan. I'm not sitting here and listening to veiled threats from this one."

Rodney sensed he was losing his audience, so reached down by his feet to retrieve his briefcase. "I've got something you may be interested in," he said, snapping the polished silver clasp open with a loud click. "Here," he said, taking out a brown envelope, which he then slid across the tablecloth.

Frank and Stan eyed the envelope suspiciously, like it was a ticking time bomb.

"You might want to open it?" said Rodney. "That's what you ordinarily do with an envelope?" he explained helpfully.

Stan rolled his eyes, tearing open the envelope. He peered inside, fully expecting some form of booby trap. But, when nothing blew up in his face, he emptied the contents cautiously onto the surface of the table.

"I don't understand," said Frank. "It's a photograph...?" He pulled his chair back up to the table, taking the photo up in his hand and holding it in front of Stan and himself like they were reading a postcard. "I don't understand," Frank said again.

"Look like anyone familiar?" asked Rodney, with a wry smile.

Stan moved in for a closer look. The image was rather grainy and appeared to be a photograph taken off a video. "It looks a bit like..." he said, straining his eyes... "Hang on, is that Lee?"

"Bingo!" said Rodney, patting the tabletop. "As I was saying a moment ago, I don't like being on the losing side of things. And so hence our meeting here today."

Frank stared vacantly at the image. "I still don't..."

"You still don't get it," replied Rodney impatiently, finishing Frank's thought for him. "Yes well *there's* a big surprise," he said sarcastically, with the smarmy old Rodney that Frank and Stan had come to know and loathe re-emerging. "Would you like me to paint a picture for you, then? What you're looking at is the head of

CHAPTER ELEVEN

your charity, Lee Watson. Turns out he's not such an upstanding member of the community after all."

"Are we ready to order?" asked the waitress politely, reappearing at their table. Her timing wasn't brilliant, to be fair, though of course she had no way of knowing this.

"*Ehm*, no," replied Stan, with as much courtesy as he could muster in the circumstance, before turning his attention back to the picture. "Is this not when he intervened when that security van was robbed?" asked Stan tentatively, putting his focus onto Rodney and leaving the waitress hovering, notepad at the ready.

"Five more minutes, if you wouldn't mind?" Rodney said to the young lady. "We're building quite the appetite over here." And, with her dispatched, at least for a moment or two, Rodney turned to address Stan and Frank. "Ah. You're nearly correct," he told Stan. "Except that's not *precisely* what happened. It's what was reported in the newspapers, yes, and the story he was more than happy to go along with at his little civic award ceremony. But not exactly true, no. You see, your friend Lee wasn't making his way over to that security van in order to prevent a robbery, like the good little citizen he made himself out to be," Rodney divulged. "*Oh, no, no, no,*" he sang happily, like it was the refrain to a nursery rhyme. "Your friend Lee, as it turns out, was actually *already* on his way over to that security van, you see, entirely intent on robbing its contents himself! And the only reason he didn't succeed, gentlemen, is because another band of thieves came along and interrupted him."

With this revelation, Rodney leaned back in his chair, took a sip of wine, and gave Stan and Frank a look of such smug satisfaction as might win the 'Most Punchable Face in Britain' award.

"Bullshit," said Frank. "I've had enough of this imbecile. Come on, Stan," he said, taking to his feet this time. "Four men went to prison for that robbery, Rodney. Are you aware of that little gem of information?"

As usual, Rodney had an answer for everything. "Please sit, Frank," he asked, now seemingly able to remember who was who out of the two of them. He adopted a more relaxed tone, and continued his interpretation of the events in question. "Frank, make no mistake, Lee Watson tore across the road to rob that security van. The only reason he didn't, as I said, is that he accidentally got tangled up with a group of armed robbers who also had the very same idea. As proof, in addition to that little still photograph in front of you, I've also taken possession of a videotape showing him bustling towards the van *before* he had any possible way of knowing an armed gang were pulling up in a car around the corner. I believe you made Lee's acquaintance not long after this, yes? And that you went on to employ him to work on your charity?"

Frank shook his head furiously. "Nonsense. Do you honestly think anybody will believe this?"

"Yes, I did doubt it myself, at first, when I was told," confessed Rodney. "So you can understand why I was so grateful, then, to have a witness come forward who was willing to sign a statement confirming that Lee Watson confessed to the entire affair. That is, to the fact that Lee's life is a complete sham, and that it should be *he* who's locked up for robbery, or attempted robbery, at the very least."

Frank sat back down, the gravity of the situation beginning to register.

"Ah, I've got your attention again?" asked Rodney, accompanied by his trademark smug grin. "Hmm, I take it you're not hungry?" he added, by way of nothing. "Only you've not even opened the menu, have you?" he said, and then, "But I think I already know what *I* want," he happily declared.

"What the hell *do* you want, Rodney?" asked Stan. "What exactly are you after? Is all this to get the farm back in your possession? Blackmail??"

Rodney appeared offended at the mere suggestion that he could be that devious. Though of course he was most definitely that devious. "The way I see it, we're all businessmen around this table," Rodney replied. "And I'm sure we can come to some kind of agreeable arrangement?"

"And what do we care if you've got a video of Lee?" asked Frank, playing it off like it didn't matter. "Take it up with Lee if it bothers you that much, why don't you?" he suggested, pretending he wasn't

CHAPTER ELEVEN

the slightest bit concerned, like it didn't affect Stan and himself in any way at all.

"Why, I thought I was doing the right thing by bringing it to your attention," offered Rodney, as if his motives were nothing but altruistic and beyond reproach. "You've all worked so hard on this charity of yours, after all. It would be a right shame for all of those food shelters and such that you've built up to come crashing down, is what I'm saying. I mean, how absolutely dreadful would it be if people were to find out that the man in charge of your charity was actually a ghastly thief, and ultimately, a fraud? My goodness, how dreadful indeed," he went on. "And I also understand that this Lee fellow is getting married to a friend of yours, yes?" he continued. "I forget the unfortunate woman's name. But she's a big old girl that looks a bit like a wrestler, I'm told? Yes, a bit of a pig in lipstick, by all accounts."

"You leave Stella out of this, Rodney, you horrid wretch!" seethed Frank, drawing the attention of those sat nearby.

Rodney pressed himself back in his chair. "Now, Frank. You shouldn't get too excited. I understand you're not a well man, and I'm concerned about you. I wouldn't want you taking a funny turn," Rodney advised, in faux concern. "All I'm saying is that this Lee fellow is getting married to your friend, Stella, yes? And I imagine she'd be quite upset if she were to suddenly find her new husband locked up for attempted robbery, yes?"

"What do you want, Rodney?" asked Stan. "And don't ask for the TT Farm, as that's not going to happen. There's a board of trustees in place that would block it, and that's even if we had any intention of giving it to you. Which we most certainly don't."

Rodney smiled. He always liked it when he appeared to have the upper hand. "It's good that we can talk, like the businessmen we are," he said, looking at each of them in turn. "I'd like nothing more than to make this entire sordid affair go away, and you don't need to worry about this so-called TT Farm of yours, gentlemen. I've moved on from that, as I know what you say is also correct about the trustees. But as I said earlier, that oversized Dutchman friend of yours has been a particular thorn in my side. And since you're mixed up with him, then you have, by default, become involved,

I'm afraid. And, unfortunately, all's fair in love and war, gentlemen," he told them, holding his palms up. "I've spent an absolute fortune to date, what with legal fees and planning fees on what was to be my TT Hotel, as well as that damnable racetrack I purchased up the north of your island. And what I'd very much like to do is recoup what I've spent on it all, and perhaps even have a little extra as well for the trouble. I'm sure you understand."

Rodney then produced a pen from the inside pocket of his blazer. "May I?" he said, reaching over for the photograph. Rodney turned it over and scribbled on the rear of it a series of digits, and then passed the picture back across the table, where Frank pressed his finger on it. "Oh, and you can keep the photograph," said Rodney agreeably. "I've got plenty more copies."

Frank glared, stony-faced, and then shared what Rodney had written for Stan's benefit.

"Ha-ha," said Stan, followed by an exaggerated sigh. "You've got to be kidding, right?"

"I can assure you, I don't kid on such matters, my dear fellow," came Rodney's reply.

"We can't pay that, Rodney, you absolutely incredible idiot," countered Stan. "You want us to give you that amount of money to keep schtum? Is that it?"

"No, gentlemen," Rodney answered. "That would be blackmail. You've completely misunderstood my intentions. I've come to you, as businessmen, on this wonderful island, to see if you'd like to buy my racetrack, and to buy it for the price I've indicated on the rear of that picture."

"That racetrack's not worth even close to that," Frank responded. "You're a crook, Rodney, and you're not getting a penny, not as long as I've got a hole in my—"

"We're good," said Stan, indicating to the returning waitress that her services were not yet required.

"Think about it, at least?" asked Rodney. "I understand the wedding isn't for a couple of weeks or so? And so I'm sure this friend of yours, Stella, will be perfectly fine with her current fiancé ending up in jail. Being the attractive looker that she is, I'm sure she's got men queuing around the block to put a ring on her overly

CHAPTER ELEVEN

plump finger? So it shouldn't be a problem?" he said, the sarcasm in his voice evident. "It'll be a shame for the charity, though. A real gut-wrencher. So sad."

"Rodney, we haven't got that sort of cash lying about," said Frank. "Your estimation of our wealth is vastly misjudged and inflated," he told him. "Rodney, I've got an ex-wife who has bled me dry, and a daughter that's just as expensive in her own way," he said, inexplicably cupping his breasts to indicate previous surgery that he'd subsidised.

"There is another option," said Rodney. "An alternative offer."

Frank smiled a pained smile to Stan, in a *what-kind-of-bollocks-is-up-next?* sort of manner. "Yes? And that would be...?" he asked Rodney.

Rodney grinned like a cat that'd just swallowed a mouse. If this were a game of poker, he'd presently be stroking an impressive stack of chips at the table with his fingertip such was the state of his confidence. "This taxi firm you own in Liverpool, this... Frank 'n' Stan's Cabs. I've done my due investigative diligence, and I have to say it's an impressive business you've got there. You should be proud! Anyway, I would consider buying a business as profitable as this from you... with which funds you would then purchase my racetrack, mind you. The amount I'd offer you is exactly the same as I've written on the back of that photo. And, naturally, all other photos and copies of the video, of course, would miraculously disappear once our transactions are complete."

"You can piss right off," said Stan, not mincing words. "That's our baby, mister, and there's not a hope in hell we'd sell it. And even if we did consider selling it, your valuation is light years away from what our business is actually worth."

Frank clenched his fist, and for a moment looked like he was about to launch it across the table towards Rodney's jaw. "Stella runs that for us, Rodney," he said through gritted teeth. "If we sell the business she'll be out of a job."

"Still. Better than having a husband in prison, perhaps?" suggested Rodney. "Well, assuming the wedding would actually go ahead in the first place. Heartbreaking, in either case. Though I'm sure she'd recover? Anyway, gentlemen, I've given you the options available,

FRANK 'N' STAN'S BUCKET LIST #4 – BRIDE OF FRANK 'N' STAN

and I'd recommend we attend to our dinner now? I'm sure you've worked up a splendid appetite, as have I. All this talk of business-business-business, don't you just love it?" Rodney, very satisfied with himself, set about arranging his cutlery in preparation for the upcoming meal.

"You can take your hospitality, Rodney, and cram it where the sun doesn't shine," Frank informed their so-called host. "And any appetite I did have has diminished. Rather like your hairline, you obnoxious pipsqueak."

"I hope you choke on your cravat!" added Stan, for good measure.

With that settled, Stan and Frank stomped through the restaurant towards the attendant near the front. She offered a sympathetic smile as she reached for their coats on the stand next to the door.

"We'll book in for another time," said Frank gently.

"Shit," said Stan.

"What's up?" asked Frank.

"I've only gone and left my hat on the table, and what with us storming away and everything, it might be a bit awkward if I go back to get it?"

"Just leave it, Stan. I was too nice to tell you it didn't suit you anyway," added Frank, pulling his own hat over his head. "Bloody Rodney Franks. What a complete cock!"

Chapter
TWELVE

Stella pressed her head back into the sofa, with only one eye on the television and not really watching it, and apparently not offering their new cat enough attention judging by its impassioned meowing. Regarding the cat, Stella had never really displayed any maternal instincts to speak of, and being a parent wasn't exactly top of the list of priorities for Lee, and so, as a sort of compromise, a new addition was brought into the fold in the form of a female tortoiseshell kitten that Stella had affectionately named Bovril. She'd considered the name Marmite, as the savoury spread was made as a by-product of the beer-making process and so very attractive in that respect. But she'd finally settled on Bovril as a name instead, because Bovril was a meat-based product. It was a close call, then, but with Bovril eventually winning out. Bovril the cat had shit on, pissed on, and scratched the hell out of pretty much everything in the place since her arrival. But once the initial teething issues were resolved, Bovril had endeared herself to both Lee and Stella, though possibly not to their furniture.

As for Lee, he was a new man of late. The job he adored was second only to his love for the woman he'd soon have the immense honour of calling his wife. He now had his own flat, and for a man who was sleeping in a discarded port-a-loo not all that long ago, his world had turned right around. The charity he was in charge of was moving from strength to strength, and he now headed up an effort that provided shelter and food — and, not to mention, hope — to hundreds of people across the country each week, and with those regular efforts only expanding. He could easily be forgiven for having a spring in his step, for he was a man who was certainly, at this junction, high on life.

"Everything okay, beautiful?" asked Lee, in his lilting Irish brogue. He smiled down on his two ladies, both of them curled up on the sofa. "Only you didn't eat all of your kebab last night, and there's at least two bottles of cider remaining in the fridge. That's not like you?"

"I'm fine," said Stella, rubbing Bovril's ear, but it was clear she wasn't. Stella didn't hide her emotions too well, and only really had a couple of expressions besides — one of which being pissed off, and the other being just slightly a little less pissed off. "When are you going?" she asked Lee.

"I've packed my bags, and I'll need to start the drive in about fifteen minutes or thereabouts so that I'll be there to meet the boys as they come over on the boat from the Isle of Man."

"Why don't you just meet them where you're going?" asked Stella, but Lee's slight eye roll indicated that they'd covered this ground previously.

"Well," he explained gently, "All I know is that Dave and Monty are coming over in their van with their sidecar in the back, and that Frank and Stan are coming over as foot passengers. Those two are going to jump in with me, and I'm going to give them a lift to wherever it is we're all going. Our final destination is all a bit of a surprise at this stage, at least to me, so I'm just following Dave and Monty in their van."

Stella only grunted in response.

"You don't mind me going?" asked Lee, busying himself collecting his wallet and keys. "Are you still upset about yesterday?" he said, dropping down to one knee in front of Stella, and running his fingers down Bovril's neck. "Is that why you've not been yourself and off your food?"

Stella lowered her head, offering the faintest hint of a nod.

"Stella, you need to get over this," replied Lee, firmly but not unkindly. He raised his hand from the cat and placed a finger under Stella's chin, pushing her head north so he could look into her impassive eyes. "Stella, I love you, okay? That woman at the

CHAPTER TWELVE

jewellery shop was just bloody stupid, and we certainly won't be going back there, all right?"

"She laughed when you said you were getting married to me," sighed Stella, in a rare glimpse of vulnerability. "She was lucky I didn't close the front door on her bloody head."

Lee ran his finger up her face, taking her cheek in his palm. "Stella, I don't care what anybody thinks about us. All you need to know is that I love you. You're perfect to me."

Stella cracked the flicker of a smile, but it was clear her anxiety wasn't entirely relieved. "I see people looking at us together, Lee. I can tell that they're looking at you and then wondering what the hell you're doing with me. It happens all of the time, I see it, but you probably don't notice."

"You seem upset, Stella," said Lee sympathetically. "If you need me to stay here, I can always cancel?" Lee proposed, and he really did mean it, his offer sincere.

"No, I'm fine, I think," Stella answered him. "I could do without you for the weekend, actually."

"Oh, is that right, is it?" laughed Lee, lightening the mood and coaxing a smile out of her. "Well if you get lonely without me, Idris Elba and Guy Martin are in the cabinet in the bathroom," he reminded her cheekily. "Just remember, Guy was a little sluggish on his last outing. So you may need to pop down the shop for new batteries," he told her, planting a tender kiss on her pencil-thin lips. "I'll phone you when I get there, all right? That is, wherever the hell *there* actually is."

It'd been a little over a week since Frank and Stan had their lunch with Rodney. Well, no food had ever been procured on their part, so 'meeting' would be a more apt description rather than lunch. Regardless, in the interim, Stan had considered purchasing a new hat, but on the constructive feedback from Frank that he looked like a plum when wearing it, he thought better of it. At least for the time being.

Aside from the matter of Stan's hat, the two of them had spoken at length about the situation in regard to Rodney both to each other and to their legal advisor as to the best course of action in the circumstance. With the weekend away with the lads to look forward to and the wedding approaching rapidly, they'd chosen to keep their meeting with Rodney to themselves, deciding not to mention it to Lee at this stage if indeed at all. As their expensive legal advisor had pointed out, even with a video and a witness statement, any case against Lee was still sketchy at best. This was the layman's summary that the two of them had taken away, at least, if not their advisor's precise words in legalese.

The problem the two of them had was that if they told Rodney to bugger off and called his bluff, it was a gamble as to what would actually happen next. It was a unique state of affairs, and there was no way to know how the police would handle the situation, or even what the press would make of it. But Frank and Stan, for their part, looked past the incident to the man Lee had since become. By some bizarre twist of destiny, fate had determined his path that day, and it wasn't to spend time locked up for attempted robbery, as far as Stan and Frank were concerned. Rather, Lee's destiny was to meet two dopey old plonkers and have a positive impact on the lives of hundreds if not thousands of people who were in a situation similar to where he had emerged from, which often involved living in a port-a-loo and eating from a bin. Frank and Stan's main fears, of course, which Rodney had been all too eager to instil, were that if Lee was prosecuted and possibly jailed or imprisoned, what would happen to the charity, and what would happen to Stella? In any case, they knew Rodney wouldn't wait for too long to receive a proper answer one way or the other as to his offers, so they knew they'd need to come up with a plan, and soon.

Presently, having safely arrived the previous evening at their hotel in Scotland that Dave and Monty had arranged as part of Frank's big weekend...

"Morning, boys!" announced Monty cheerily, with perhaps a little too much enthusiasm for Frank and Stan who, unlike Monty and Dave astonishingly enough, had indulged in a few libations the previous evening too many. "Did we sleep well?" Monty asked.

CHAPTER TWELVE

"All right, boys?" said Stan, nursing a glass of orange juice, and prodding an overcooked sausage that'd been sat under the hot lamp for that long that it was identifiable only from its dental records, so to speak. "I still can't believe the two of you, *Dave and Monty*," he said, pointing the aforementioned sausage at them in turn, "managed to spend the night in a hotel without one drop of alcohol passing your lips."

Dave nodded, accepting the accolade graciously. "I know, but I'd have gladly sacrificed the lot of you for a Guinness last night. But we needed to be fresh as a daisy, because, Frank..." he said, looking at Frank... "We've got a brilliant couple of days lined up for you."

"Last night was good fun, boys," said Monty. "Catching up over a few beers with you all was a wonderful start to the weekend, even if by a strange unprecedented twist of fate me and Dave weren't in on the drinking this time. And I'm glad that I was a little more disciplined where the alcohol consumption was concerned, for once in my life. It was... different, I'll give it that. I'm guessing the absence of Lee so far at the table means he's having a little lie-in after last night's festivities?"

Dave jumped in, reaching for another of the cremated sausages on Stan's plate he was currently helping himself to. "So, Frank," he said, fit to burst. "We've got a bit of a surprise for you today, what with it being your stag do and all."

"Oh?" said Frank.

"Right, so Monty and I have got a little surprise in the back of our van," Dave began, rattling his fingers on the table for a drum roll. Dave looked over to Monty, who was still standing, to build the tension. "Monty and I..." he said, looking Monty up and down to introduce him to the conversation. "Monty and I have a little..."

"Have a little what?" asked Frank.

But Dave had stopped his enthusiastic introduction, with his eyes now aimed directly towards Monty's feet. He looked carefully, screwing his eyes up, before lowering his fork. "Are those my bloody socks?" he asked, pointing at Monty's ankles. The socks in question were green with a pattern of little black reindeer all over them — a Crimbo gift from Becks and Tyler — and so rather unique and quite identifiable.

"Yeah?" said Monty, as if this were a stupid question Dave was asking of him. Monty hiked up his trousers a bit, to more fully show off the socks Dave had caught a glimpse of and recognised.

"What the hell are you doing wearing my socks?" demanded Dave.

"I forgot mine," said Monty simply.

"So you went into my bag and took out my only spare pair of socks and decided to wear them?" Dave asked.

"Yes, exactly," replied Monty, with his good eye impatiently searching for the breakfast bar, and then adding, "And it's a good thing I did. I quite like these."

"But they're my only socks for tomorrow, Monty!" explained an increasingly cross Dave. "I've had these socks here on for two days, and only brought one pair for tomorrow! So what am I meant to wear for tomorrow??"

"I'll give them back tomorrow...?" offered Monty, reasonably enough, it seemed to him.

"They'll be bloody dirty after you've had your trotters polluting them all day!" Dave told him, face reddening.

Frank tapped the side of his teacup with his teaspoon, in an act of diplomacy and an effort to restore order. "Boys, come on, now. I think I've got a spare pair of socks you can borrow, Dave, if you'd like?"

"Do you have undies for him as well?" asked Monty cheekily. "Only he might be looking for some of those later as well," he said, patting his bum, before wisely making a hasty exit in search of the scrambled egg tray.

Frank repeated the tapping on his cup. "The surprise?" he asked, pressing Dave for an answer.

Dave scowled at the retreating figure of Monty for a moment longer, before turning his attention back to the table. "Yes, young Frank," he said. "We've got a little surprise in the back of our van."

"Yes, the sidecar," replied Frank flatly, waiting for the actual surprise bit to be revealed, as he already well knew what was in the back of Dave's van.

Dave's face dropped. "How do you know?"

CHAPTER TWELVE

Frank was a tad confused as to the present line of questioning. "Well, we were following you up the M6 motorway for over three hours and I could see it through the rear window of the van."

"Oi! You were supposed to cover up the bloody rear windows, Monty! And, also, will you stop scratching your bum whilst you've got my underpants on!" Dave shouted over to Monty. "Sorry about that," he said, facing Frank once again. "Anyway, so you know how you love sidecar racing?"

"Yes. That I do," replied Frank. "We both do," he said, graciously including Stan in the conversation.

"Well, we've arranged a last-minute entry to a club day at the Melville Motor Club. It's a racing event at the East Fortune Race Circuit."

"Brilliant!" said Frank, beaming. "That's great news. I mean, I suspected it already, on account of spotting the sidecar and the direction we were heading, but Stan told me to look surprised. It doesn't matter, though, as it's going to be great to see the old blue boiled sweet back in action."

"Plus, it's a qualifying event, so we can hopefully get one of the signatures we need for the TT," added Monty, returning with his plate loaded up with his first very generous helping from the breakfast bar. "And it's a good day out, East Fortune, isn't it, Dave?" he asked. It seemed an innocent enough question to Frank and Stan, and Monty had only raised his left eyebrow by less than one millimetre, but this was somehow enough to set Dave off once again.

"I soddin' well knew you'd bring that up! There I am, good enough to lend you my own underwear, and you go and throw that in my face! You're supposed to be my friend, Monty," groused Dave. Now, I'm going to get some breakfast. And *you*," he said, prodding his hefty finger in Monty's direction. "Don't you be eating eggs, either. We both know what an impact they have on your bowels, God only knows why, and I want those underpants back intact!"

Dave stomped off towards the breakfast buffet, reciting a silent prayer for the fate his underpants would be subjected to throughout the remainder of the day.

"That escalated quickly?" said Stan, unsurprised as Dave and Monty were anything but conventional. He held his gaze, awaiting further explanation, but Monty was too occupied chuckling to himself to answer straight away.

"*Ahhh*," sighed Monty, rousing himself from fond recollection of past events, and then explaining to the others, "Let's just say the hospitality at East Fortune is *very* hospitable, at least where Dave is concerned." Monty leaned in closer, lowering his voice an octave. "After the awards ceremony last year," he added, tapping his nose knowingly.

"Yes?" pressed Stan. After all, he relished a spot of gossip.

"Dave apparently got a little friendly with the race secretary," Monty elaborated.

"A woman?" asked Frank, seeking to clarify what could be a very crucial point in understanding the unfolding of Monty's anecdote.

Monty confirmed by way of a nod, and then, explaining further, said, "Diana is most certainly a woman. She's lovely, mind, but seriously one of the scariest women you're ever likely to meet if you should have the misfortune of getting on her bad side. She's like Stella of the North, in that particular regard, though nowhere near as large," he said, holding his hands out like a fisherman illustrating the size of his latest catch. "Oh, though unlike Stella, she doesn't smoke..." he told them, pausing a beat to set up the forthcoming punchline. "Well, maybe in *bed* she does, as I'm sure Dave could happily confirm," Monty said, winking. "To be fair to him, though, if Diana asked you to drop your trousers, you'd do it without much hesitation."

Dave returned from the breakfast buffet, the modest-sized plate provided barely able to contain the contents heaped upon it. He glared at Monty. "You better not have said anything," he said. "You promised."

"I would never betray such a confidence. Especially not for such a loyal and dear friend as you," Monty told him, affecting a refined, almost noble bearing. His assurances might have been relatively convincing had he not then proceeded to hum the tune of "Dirty Diana," the Michael Jackson classic.

CHAPTER TWELVE

"Bastard," spat Dave, delving into the contents of his plate, and now clear that Monty had indeed confided in Stan and Frank despite promises to the contrary. "There was no proof that anything happened," he added, desperately shifting the goalposts from an *it-never-happened* argument to a *you-can't-prove-it-happened* defence.

"Oh? The cleaner found you both asleep on the pool table the next morning, Dave," Monty rejoined. "You had chalk all over your face, and I don't even want to think what that poor pool cue was subjected to."

"That doesn't prove anything," grumbled Dave unhappily, but his protest was minimal, unlike the offering on his plate.

Dave eased his white van — which was more rust than white these days, actually — into the gravel car park, offering a cheery wave to the marshal on sentry duty. East Fortune was a friendly little race circuit near Edinburgh. Race meetings at the event were organised by the Melville Motor Club, amongst others, and as was a similar story across the road racing spectrum, the success of these events was often down to an army of volunteers who provided their time and energy for the sport they adored. The track was a challenging circuit a little over one-point-five miles in length, and more than enough to test any newcomer or seasoned campaigner alike.

They'd been there before, of course, but this was Dave and Monty's first trip back since Dave had added the enviable accolade of TT winner to his already impressive road racing career. But it wasn't for that particular reason that people were eager to come and greet their old friend...

"Game of snooker later?" asked the entrance marshal, with impeccable wit.

"Up yours," replied Dave succinctly, before winding his window back up. He looked across the cab to Monty. "This is all your fault, Monty," he insisted, though with nothing to really back up his claim, and then remarking, "It's a good job Becks isn't here, as I'm sure she'd be just thrilled to hear about my alleged drunken shenanigans."

"*Alleged?*" repeated Monty, struggling to keep his laughter on the inside. "Anyway, don't worry about it, Dave," Monty assured him, "I'm sure nobody else knows about it," he said. However, the second they pulled into a parking spot, two fellow racers stopped their walk across the car park, turned, and in front of Dave's van, leaned over and simulated the cueing action in a game of pool.

"Wankers!" exclaimed Dave. "Monty, you're going to have to sort out the scrutineering and such. I'm hiding in the van till we go out on track," he moaned. "Ah. Wait. Here comes the rest of them," he said, in reference to Lee, Frank, and Stan, who'd followed in Lee's car behind them, and Dave's spirits raised slightly at the sight of them.

Stepping out of the other vehicle, Frank and Stan couldn't hide their delight. "I love this," said Frank, stretching like a cat after the long journey. He glanced around, soaking up the hustle and bustle of those arriving and those already there — the noises of revving engines, the smell of exhaust fumes, and the giddy excitement from those filling up the vantage spots to enjoy the day's racing. Small children followed the racers, eager to have their cap signed or perhaps merely to say hello to their heroes they watched and admired out on track. The racers were always delighted to oblige them either way, for they were, at one time in their lives, that small child wandering around as well, awe-struck.

Reluctantly, Dave emerged from the van, slower than a homesick snail, to assist in the sidecar removal.

"Aye, she's a thing of beauty," enthused Frank, watching as the big blue boiled sweet was released from the rear of the van and eased down the metal ramp.

"I missed her," added Stan, running his hands over the smooth lines like he was fondling a lover. "It's a great little set-up here, isn't it, Monty?" he said, now looking out around them. "Reminds me a bit of Jurby, back home?"

Monty took in the sights himself. "Yep. I love it up here as well. Proper Scottish hospitality, to be sure, and this lot can drink like you wouldn't believe. Oh, and you remember Dod Spence, from our Isle Le Mans TT?"

CHAPTER TWELVE

"Ah yes, the chap we named the Spirit of the TT award after?" asked Frank.

"That's the one. He should be about, somewhere. He's a proper legend around these parts. He volunteered his time and expertise to help them build that area over there," said Monty, pointing to the bar and café area. "In fact, this whole place survives by the work that the volunteers put into it, from building the tyre walls to the buildings all around the communal areas." But then, suddenly, Monty's cheery demeanour evaporated in an instant. "Oh, shit," he said, lowering his head.

"Is it Diana?" said Dave, immediately crouching down, which was rather pointless as they were stood in the middle of a car park with no available cover.

"No," replied Monty. "It's the McMullan brothers and Napier and Thomas. They must all be racing."

"Fuck! You're fucking kidding!" shouted Dave, bolting upright. "I thought they weren't all going to be bloody here!"

Lee leaned in close to Frank. "I thought this was a friendly affair?" he whispered.

"This is a bloody disaster!" added Dave, kicking his foot out at a discarded Coke tin.

"*Ehm*... why is it a disaster, exactly?" asked Stan, certain that he must have missed something completely obvious. "I know you and Monty are competitive. And that's fine, of course. But them lot are seasoned professionals, and with proper factory machinery. Surely, getting beaten by them is nothing to be embarrassed about...?"

Monty flicked through the race programme in desperation. His eyes were able to look at two pages at once, so it didn't take him too long. "Napier and Thomas are not listed as racing," he said, jabbing his finger at the starting line-up listed in the programme, then glancing over at the two figures hunched over their sidecar who looked, very suspiciously, exactly like Napier and Thomas. Monty swung his foot in the same direction of the Coke can as Dave did, but missed it hopelessly, before turning to answer Stan's original question and explain their abject annoyance. "We need signatures to apply for our Mountain Course licence, and the only way we can get them is to race in qualifying events."

"Like this?" asked Lee, confused, along with the rest of them.

"Yes, but it's not just a case of turning up, looking pretty, and getting the signature," Monty elaborated. "See, we need to finish within a certain percentage of the winner in our category, which is something like ninety-two and a half percent of their winning race average speed. So, for example, if the winner had an average speed of one hundred miles per hour, we'd have to get a race average speed of ninety-two and a half miles per hour to obtain a qualifying signature."

Lee nodded along, attempting to follow what Monty was telling him.

"Right, so ordinarily, the top guys know this," Monty went on. "And although it's not spoken out loud, if they were miles in front, they just may ease off a little to give the rest of us a chance, you understand? But unfortunately for us, the McMullan brothers' main rivals in the championships are Napier and Thomas, so we're going to end up with first and second place being stupidly quick, right? And so the chances of us getting within ninety-two and a half percent of the winning speed is as likely as..." he said, trailing off, in search of a proper comparison.

"Frank getting life insurance?" suggested Dave.

"Fuckin hell, Dave," said Monty. "I was going to go for something gentle, like a snowball in hell's chance, or something. But, shit."

Dave lowered his head like a naughty dog caught humping the leg of a chair. "Sorry Frank, no offence meant," he said. "Anyway, the Chuckle Brothers are going to be going full hell-for-leather against Tweedledee and Tweedledum, and our hopes of even getting close to them, I'd say, are slim to none. We may as well just pack up and go," he said, upset, though perhaps not quite as upset as he was making himself out to be.

"We're here now," admonished Monty. "So we're going racing, end of. And I know exactly why you want to turn on your heels and bugger off, mister."

"Oh?" said Dave.

"You're scared about seeing Diana!" Monty told him. "Now you man the hell up, fella, and get your leathers on. Team Frank-and-Stan are back in action!"

Chapter
THIRTEEN

Lee, Frank, and Stan watched the solo machines hurtling past, with the giddy enthusiasm of a dog with its head outside the window of a moving car. They didn't have a clue who the riders were, but that simply didn't matter — the visual spectacle of a dozen motorbikes jostling for position on a twisting stretch of tarmac was exhilarating. Throw in the toe-curling decibel level from race-tuned engines that produced a smell from the exhaust like catnip for race fans, and you had the ideal recipe for a splendid day out.

"I wouldn't want to be anywhere else," said Frank, taking a whiff of the smell of Castrol that hung in the air.

Circuit racing was a completely different proposition than the TT races. For instance, with the circuit being only a couple of miles long in total, unlike the TT's longer route, you'd see bikes flying past every minute or so on their way around. Throw in the fact that it was a mass start with all machines heading off at once — rather than a time trial — and you had the perfect ingredients to make one big and beautiful adrenalin-filled cake, iced with a generous application of exhilaration.

Busy preparing for their own race, Dave and Monty poked and prodded their machine. But, on the whole, they were happy with the set-up they'd prepared, so this didn't take too terribly long. Now, then, was a chance to have a sneaky peek at what the rest of the grid were up to, as well as an opportunity to catch up with old racing friends they hadn't had the pleasure of seeing for a few months. Some of the lads that Dave and Monty were catching up with today were the ones that'd be joining them in the paddock and start line at the Isle of Man TT later in the year. These lads and lasses were competitive on the track, but the comradery ran deeper than the potential for any possible result out on the tarmac. Ask any of these people for advice on a suspension set-up or the optimum gearing ratio, for example, and they'd be there for you in a millisecond. A collaborative family, this lot, and something that a lot of sports couldn't boast about but could well learn from.

"All right, boys?" bellowed a voice over the sound of revving engines. "Oi! Dave! Monty!" it sounded off, even louder this time. A rangy-looking chap wearing well-worn leathers, and with helmet tucked under his arm, flailed his free hand to get their attention. But, when that failed, he waded over, grinning widely to reveal a mouthful of crooked teeth in various states of decay and one tooth at the front missing entirely. By all appearances, if the Clampetts went into space, then this guy would be leading the mission. "All right, boys?" he said again, now that he was upon them. "TT winner, eh?" he said, looking down on Dave, his head being at a higher altitude to a fair degree relative to Dave's. Dave was tall but this fellow was even taller, although he did have far less meat on his bones as compared to Dave. "TT winner. *Noice*," he remarked, with something of a giggle-snort directly after. "Sign my leathers?" he pleaded, but then waved his hand like he was chasing away a fly. "Nah, I'm good, actually," he quickly declared, lest there be any confusion regarding the sincerity of his insincerity, followed by another of the giggle-snort thing he did.

"All right, Bert," replied Dave. But the greeting was delivered as a statement rather than a question, in such a way as to not intentionally invite further conversation. The fact that Dave half turned his back, also, would have been enough of a clue for most — though sadly not so much for Bert, who hovered regardless.

"Racing today?" asked Bert, undaunted.

Dave and Monty were stood next to a sidecar at a racetrack, dressed in leathers, with a helmet apiece resting by their feet

CHAPTER THIRTEEN

"Eh... no, Bert," replied Monty. "We're just passing through, as it turns out, but caught the smell of the burger van and so couldn't resist stopping by."

"Yeah," said Bert simply, Monty's sarcasm washing straight over him. Then he just stood there for a bit, offering nothing more than a vacant stare. "Oh," he added after an interminably long moment, his tone suddenly becoming urgent in a way that signalled he was leading to something important. And it was apparent this was the reason he'd ventured over in the first place, as well, judging by his giddy smile. "You know who's looking for you, don't you, Dave?" he asked. And, as he said this, he stretched his impossibly long neck towards Dave like a giraffe coming down from eating leaves in a tree, and pressing his face uncomfortably close.

"Simon Cowell?" suggested Dave dryly. "He heard me singing in the van on the way up?"

Bert narrowed one eye, not entirely sure what to do with that response, but choosing to ultimately ignore it. "*Diana*," he told Dave, offering a mischievous smile for Monty's benefit despite Monty having not much use for it.

"Oh," said Dave, shrugging his shoulders dispassionately as if this was news of little to no consequence, trying his best not to give Bert the satisfaction of any sort of real reaction.

"She's fucking fuming with you, she is!" added Bert, taking great delight.

"I'm not scared of Diana," said Dave, glancing over his shoulder. He gave the impression he wasn't bothered, but then... "She, eh... she didn't say what she wanted, Bert...?"

Bert shook his head, which was a long way up, as he'd risen to full height again. "Nope," he said, barely able to contain his glee. "But she's over by the medical centre, just there. You can't miss her, Dave. She's the one stood outside with a pram," he snorted, now unable to contain his excitement any longer. "*With a pram*," Bert said again, emphasising this particular point lest the implication should be lost.

"Bugger off, Bert!" snapped Dave. "And don't forget to tuck your head in when you're racing, mate, as you wouldn't want a passing tree branch to take it clean off."

Monty moved a few paces to the right — on the pretence of looking for some as-yet-identified discarded item or other on the tarmac — and, in so doing, affording himself a quick glance towards the medical centre. He jumped on the spot like he'd been electrocuted, shot, or a mixture of the two. Monty returned to the sidecar, using a clean cloth to remove a couple of spots of oil or dirt that didn't actually exist, saying nothing.

"Well?" asked Dave.

But Monty carried right on busying himself on things that didn't need busying over.

"Monty!" Dave shouted.

Monty dried his teeth on the breeze. "*Ehm*, she's over there, mate."

"Monty!" Dave shouted again.

"Bert's right. She's got a pram," Monty informed him.

Dave dropped to his knees, wailing, like a sack of potatoes. A very large sack of potatoes. A very large, wailing sack of potatoes. Then he lowered his head to the tarmac, placing his palms on the ground like he was praying to Mecca.

"Is he okay?" asked a concerned marshal passing by.

"Pre-race prayers," replied Monty.

Dave screamed like an animal in need of putting down. He glanced up at Monty with horror burnt into his very soul. "How's she had a baby?" he sobbed. "I mean, she must be at least... how old is she?"

Monty shrugged his shoulders, taking a cautionary step back, and then taking a further step back for good measure. "You can ask her yourself, mate, as she's coming over right now."

And with that, determining discretion to be the better part of valour, Monty retreated entirely, assuming a place of relative cover behind Bert's machine, though of course allowing himself a clear view so that he could keep one eye on the unfolding drama.

"Oi! Fatboy!" screeched a voice that'd bring fear to the bravest of warriors. "I've been looking for you!" added Diana, taking up a position on the nearby grass verge, safely away from any passing machinery, with pram in tow.

CHAPTER THIRTEEN

By the looks of things, half the paddock had been observing her progress, with her approach being followed with no small amount of eagerness, perhaps in expectation of some kind of impending altercation, or perhaps in anxious anticipation of the spectacle of seeing poor Dave shitting himself before their eyes.

"Get your carcass off my tarmac and over here!" commanded Diana, with steely intensity. She wasn't a big girl, like Stella, but she had an unwavering ferocity in her voice that would have been fine-tuned over the years by consistently taking control of a load of hairy-arsed bikers.

Dave complied without hesitation, bowing his head like he'd been castigated by his teacher for chewing gum in class and now heading to the front of the class to await his punishment.

"Look, Diana—" Dave began in earnest.

"What've you been saying??" barked Diana, cutting him off.

Diana then launched into a tirade the duration of which Dave was unable to determine, his attention, as it was, being elsewhere — with 'elsewhere' being the elegant Silver Cross pram that Diana continued to rock ever so gently whilst, simultaneously, ferociously berating him. Dave was only roused back to reality and snapped back into the room, so to speak, when Diana paused for breath, a brief interlude which allowed the race-prepared engines to have their chance to disturb the East Lothian countryside rather than her. "—And I swear to god I'll cut your bollocks off with a butter knife!" was her final statement. She glowered at Dave, who could feel himself collapsing like a wet cardboard box.

"I haven't got much money," Dave pleaded to her, turning out imaginary pockets in his leather racing suit. "But what I have got is yours, Diana, I swear," he assured her. "I'll sell the sidecar, I'll get another job," he promised gallantly. "Whatever you need is yours," he pledged.

And yet this, somehow, served only to get Diana's back up further, oddly enough. "What in Christ's name are you bloody on about?" she told him. "Honestly, Dave, if you're taking the piss out of me, I'll tear you a new one!"

Dave took a cautious step closer, in order to peer inside the pram and see just how much the wee one might resemble him.

"Ohhh, here's Daddy," Diana cooed soothingly into the pram. "What are you doing here? Do you not need to be getting ready for the race?" she enquired, looking up for a moment in Dave's general direction. "Yeeesss. Daaaddyyyy," she said, returning her attention to the pram once again and fussing to the little one inside.

"Yeah," confirmed Dave, "Monty's just giving the old girl the final touches before the race and..." he said, but he trailed off, as Diana was presently looking straight through him.

"How's my little queen?" asked Bert, creeping up from behind Dave. "Everything all right, Diana?" he asked.

"She's fine," replied Diana. "Only you'll need to get someone else to take over babysitting duties if your wife doesn't show up. I've other things to get on with, and with the first point of order being wiping the floor with this bellend right here," she added tartly, pointing squarely at a whimpering Dave.

"The baby is yours, then?" asked Dave, looking up to Bert with hope-filled eyes.

"Yeah," said Bert, who was now nearly crying with laughter. "It was Monty's idea! He said you'd see the funny side!"

"Bastard," said Dave under his breath, struggling to calm his shaking legs. "Bastards," he muttered, in reference to the lot of them this time (though not the baby, of course). But before he had chance to fully regain his composure, Diana was on him with another verbal assault.

"You told all of these oil-stained wankers that you'd defiled me last year?? There's a word for people just like you, David Quirk! Pretending you've slept with a woman to score points around the paddock, and then telling all and sundry? Pathetic!" she said, giving him a verbal lashing.

Dave had just taken on board and digested a fair amount of information, so he could be forgiven for appearing gormless. "I don't know what's going on...?" he said, looking for his wingman Monty for moral support, but Monty was too busy pissing himself with laughter, still hiding out behind Bert's machine.

"Diana, I didn't tell anyone we slept together!" Dave insisted. "Why would I want to go and advertise that fact? I wouldn't!" he

CHAPTER THIRTEEN

said. But, unfortunately, he knew as soon as the words left his lips that this last reassurance wasn't received as intended.

"You're a cheeky sod!" Diana yelled, before dropping it down a notch for the benefit of the now crying baby. "You think I'd let that thing of yours anywhere near me?" she said, more quietly this time so as not to upset the wee one, and pointing in the direction of Dave's crotch. "If you do, then you're even stupider than you look, and that's really saying something."

"So... we didn't, then?" asked an even more confused Dave. "But I thought... I mean... only we woke up on the pool table? We woke up on the pool table, I remember that much, and—"

"So what? I often wake up on the pool table after a good sesh," said Diana, not allowing him to finish. "Doesn't mean anything happened, you pervert! And the only balls I was playing with that night were billiard balls, you bloody tosser. Shame on you!"

Dave was happy to accept the insults this time. Only a few short moments ago, he was certain he'd fathered a child to Diana, and with Diana being the very last person he'd ever want to father a child with, actually. But the future was suddenly looking much brighter. "Look, Diana," he said, nervous yet relieved, "I swear to you by all that's holy, I never said anything, right? It must've been the cleaning person who walked in the next morning who spread it 'round, if I were to hazard a guess? But I never said a word."

"I don't care who said what. You just tell that bunch of grease monkeys..." she said, fanning her hand across the breadth of the racetrack... "that you didn't put that little peanut between your legs anywhere *near* me. *Capiche?*"

"Diana, in all honesty, it would be my considerable pleasure," Dave was happy to tell her. "Considerable."

It'd been some amount of time since Monty had been in what you'd call competitive action. Sure, he'd acquitted himself admirably at the Isle 'Le Mans' TT charity race, but that wasn't a balls-out competition with every man or woman on the track vying for the slightest competitive edge. And Monty's joints these days weren't as fluid as they'd once been, and with ageing reactions, plus injuries sustained over the years from being thrown about in what was essentially a tin can on wheels, Monty was in somewhat battered shape overall. Still, despite this, the big blue boiled sweet was well served in having Monty on board, as Monty's physical deficits were compensated for by an abundance of enthusiasm and passion.

Racing on a short circuit like East Fortune was mentally and physically challenging. Ten laps around this place required every single gram of concentration, for even the slightest lapse thereof meant you could easily miss the apex of a turn and run the corner too wide, losing valuable seconds in the process. Dave was an experienced TT winner now, but there was certainly no place for complacency — this he knew — for the standard of racing was exceptional, from newcomers in their orange bibs to seasoned campaigners eager to secure their place on the leaderboard. And so no quarter was given, nor was any expected.

"They look bloody good out there!" said Lee, for what must have been at least the third time.

Dave navigated their machine — with Monty's acrobatic support — through the corners with pinpoint accuracy, using every single ounce of his piloting experience. The machine underneath was sublime, though limited by the money they had to spend on it. The pure economics of racing meant that those with better machinery at their disposal would have a significant advantage due to the improved outfit beneath them, and this was never more evident than on the ever-so-brief straights where the more expensive outfits pulled away from Dave and Monty with little apparent effort. As expected, the two frontrunner teams — the McMullan brothers and Napier & Thomas — were in a league of their own. They were talented racers, of course, and of that there was no doubt. But their machinery was simply outrageously quick and, as a result of this, and as feared, both outfits took a lead over the field that was insurmountable, and one that was only to drastically increase over the course of the race.

For the spectators, the action on display was hypnotic, and you dared not blink for fear of missing anything. But all too soon, the

CHAPTER THIRTEEN

chequered flag welcomed home the McMullan brothers in first place, and with the Napier & Thomas duo bringing it home less than three seconds later.

The beaming smiles of Lee, Frank, and Stan — now spectating near to the start/finish line — were minimal comfort to Dave and Monty, who reappeared with faces like they'd been sucking the sourest of lemons.

"Good show, boys!" said Stan, offering up his hand for purposes of a hearty high-five, but it was a gesture not returned.

"Bloody waste of time, that was," offered Monty, wiping the sweat from his face.

Dave punched his fist into his chubby hand in frustration. "We couldn't have kept up with those top boys if we'd had a tow rope attached to them," he said.

"So no signature for your racing passport, then?" asked Frank, though, sadly, already suspecting the answer.

"Nope," moaned Dave. "Look, we need to get the van packed up and get out of here," he said, appearing thoroughly pissed off.

"You don't want to stay and perhaps watch at least a portion of the remainder of the racing?" offered Frank.

Dave nodded in the negative. "Nope," he answered. "No, I don't. Because *you*, Frank Cryer, are heading to the second part of your stag do!" he announced, smartly turning his frown upside down and seeming to forget all about racing results in an instant.

"I am?" said Frank. "But hang on, what about Lee? He's getting married too!" he reminded them, lest poor Lee be left out of the festivities.

"Ah, don't you worry about me, my lad," said Lee. "I'm just happy to be invited along and having a fantastic day out. That I am," he assured Frank.

"Come on, Frank," said Stan, looking at his watch. "This should be perfect timing, boys, actually, then," he said to Dave and Monty.

"You know," opined Monty, "It's not the end of the world, not getting a signature today," he offered, trying to look on the bright side of things.

FRANK 'N' STAN'S BUCKET LIST #4 – BRIDE OF FRANK 'N' STAN

"It is if we want to do the TT," Dave reminded him. "Or, at least, it's not ideal for our TT preparations, as getting one sure would have taken the pressure off."

"I know. But, there's several more qualifying races in the run-up to the TT," Monty reasoned. "And that just means that Team Frank-and-Stan will have other chances to go travelling again!"

Dave rubbed his thumb and forefinger together like he was counting cash he didn't have. And the reason he was doing this is that counting cash he didn't have is precisely what he was, in fact, doing.

"It's fine," said Monty. "I'll sell my appendix or something for medical science?"

"*Hmm,*" Dave responded, as if he was taking Monty's suggestion into genuine consideration.

"Don't worry, Monty, Dave wouldn't seriously let you sell your body parts," Stan laughed.

"Oh, he most definitely *would*," replied Monty.

"I most definitely would," Dave confirmed happily. And then, "Cheerio!" shouted Dave, in the direction of Diana over by the marshal's hut, now that they were gathering up to leave. And he was being completely sincere in his cheerful sentiments, rather than sarcastic. Possibly also very relieved, as well. Right, *definitely* very relieved as well.

"Up yours!" came Diana's concise response, followed by an extension of her middle finger for proper illustrative effect.

"I'm suitably intrigued," remarked Frank, as they followed closely behind Dave's van in their own vehicle. "No clues?" he asked, looking over to Lee, who was driving, and then to Stan in the rear of the car. But both were giving nothing away. "Well," continued Frank, "I must say I'm enjoying the weekend so far, at least."

Stan smiled away to himself, before sharing his thoughts with Frank. "I can't begin to tell you how much more I'm enjoying this weekend than I could have been, Frank."

"Oh?" asked Frank.

CHAPTER THIRTEEN

Stan rested his head against the car window, watching the countryside flying by in a blur. "This wasn't originally your stag do, Frank," he confided.

"It wasn't?" asked Frank.

"No. A few weeks ago we had to face the reality that you weren't going to be around much longer. As horrendous a thought as that was, we wanted to do something special for you. And so when the boys mentioned about East Fortune, and knowing how much you love racing, that was a no-brainer as we knew you'd enjoy that. Now, as far as the next thing we've got in store for you—"

"Yes...?" asked Frank, fit to burst.

"You'll just have to wait and see!" replied Stan. "But I've been thinking about this as I'm sat here— you know, how this could have been potentially our last weekend away. And I'm considering how I'm feeling right now, as compared to how I *could* have been feeling if things... if they'd turned out different," Stan went on. "Frank?" he said, leaning forward a touch and placing his hand on Frank's right shoulder. "Frank, this is the best weekend I could have wished for, when I think what might have been," Stan told his mate, his voice cracking.

"Leave it out, you two. I'm starting to mist up here, and as I'm driving, that's not good!" said Lee, smiling fondly at the pair.

Ahead of them, Dave activated the right indicator on his van, causing Lee to apply the brake pedal and follow suit, turning off the main road. "This must be us," remarked Lee, following Dave's lead, and with the road sign ahead soon providing Frank with his first clue as to what might be in store for him.

"An airstrip?" said Frank, in reference to the large blue sign that signalled they were indeed arriving at an airstrip. And if the sign hadn't served as enough of a clue in and of itself, the presence of several hangars and countless aircraft as they approached would have been a dead giveaway as well. "So... are we perhaps going away somewhere?" Frank asked, searching for some sort of explanation. But his fellow car passengers were remaining frustratingly tight-lipped, at least for the moment.

"Come on," said Stan, once they'd parked up next to Dave and Monty. "You're going to like this," he told Frank. They got out of the car, Stan first, and not a moment later, an excitable chap in blue overalls presented himself before them.

"I'm hoping you're Stan?" he asked of Stan, tapping his green clipboard and waiting expectantly for a response.

"That's us!" replied Stan, and with Frank trying to sneak a peek and catch a glimpse of the contents of the fellow's clipboard.

"I'm Jeremy," announced Jeremy, moving his clipboard slightly away in order to deflect Frank's attention. "Follow me, if you wouldn't mind?"

With that, Jeremey led the way, with Frank, Stan, Lee, Dave, and Monty tagging along like a row of ducklings behind their mum, following behind Jeremy with smart precision in order to avoid being blended by an errant aircraft propeller.

"If you'll wait here a moment?" said Jeremy, once they'd made their way near to a hangar. "I just need to make sure they're not filming."

"Filming?" said Frank to Stan. "Filming what?"

Jeremy then headed into the colossal grey aircraft hangar, disappearing from view, and leaving Frank to wonder just what the dickens was going on, particularly as Stan was now grinning like a Cheshire cat. Rather than Jeremy returning, however, another chap in blue overalls jogged back out from the hangar, covered in oil, with wild untamed hair and a pair of flourishing mutton chops.

"Is that not...?" began Frank to Stan, and with Frank even more confused now than before and struggling to reconcile in his head what his eyes were telling him.

"Now then, boys," said the new arrival.

"Guy bloody Martin!" said Frank, offering a firm handshake. But Guy was having absolutely none of that, and after accepting Frank's handshake took Frank in for a generous bear hug as well.

"Stan told me about the health," said Guy, taking a step back and looking Frank up and down. "Good news, boss," he said, flashing his teeth. "Good news, boss," he said once more. "Now, come on, I think you're going to like what we've got planned for you."

Guy escorted them to the front of the hangar, where the sliding shutter bay doors were then pulled ceremoniously to either side,

CHAPTER THIRTEEN

revealing the contents within. It took a moment for the group to adjust their eyes, due to the dazzling lighting inside the expansive structure.

"Oh, my word," said Frank, looking first inside, and then over to Stan. "They're Spitfires!" he exclaimed, placing his hand over his mouth. "They're completely bloody stunning," he remarked reverently. "How many are there?" he asked, but then counted them out himself, answering his own question. "Five of them," he concluded, looking over to Stan once more. Frank had an expression of pure joy on his face. He was like a nine-year-old boy who'd just been handed the keys to a sweetshop.

Guy moved in to explain further. "I'm presenting a documentary about the Spitfire," he said, which accounted, Frank realised, for the cameras, lighting, sound booms and, well, the presence of Guy Martin. "Stan got in touch when he read about the upcoming documentary, and he asked if you could come for a look around," Guy explained to Frank. "I understand your dad was a pilot in the war?"

"He was," said Frank softly. "In a Spitfire," he added, his chest swelling with pride. "I've adored these planes my entire life," he told Guy. "In fact, the first toy I can remember ever receiving was a model Spitfire. I've still got it, to this very day," Frank said, his eyes welling up.

"Come on," said Guy. "You can watch the filming for a bit, and then I'll introduce you to that chap over there. He's one of the Spitfire mechanics who keeps these beauties flying. He said he'll take you for a bit of a guided tour, and you might actually end up in the documentary, if you'd like?"

"If I'd like?" said Frank. "Too bloody right I would!"

Stan caught Guy's eye and offered him a wink. "Thanks for this," he said. "It means a lot, as you can see."

"Not a problem," said Guy. "And I'll be in touch when I'm next on the Isle of Man, by the way. I'm looking forward to catching up with all you crazy buggers again," Guy told Stan.

"Wonderful," replied Stan.

"Oh, and Frank?" Guy added, pivoting over to Frank again. Guy was grinning widely, as was Stan. Stan, as a matter of fact, looked like he was about to pee himself with excitement. He knew what Guy was about to say. "Frank, there's one more thing that we've arranged for you," Guy carried on. But Frank was too busy running a hand over the iconic paintwork on the magnificent plane nearest him.

"Frank!" shouted Guy, catching Frank's attention again. "There's something else," he told him.

"Oh?" said Frank, although still somewhat distracted.

"I hope you're not afraid of heights, Frank," Guy advised.

"What's that? Heights?" said Frank, suddenly very interested.

Guy sidled up to Frank, placing his arm around him. "You see that one there?" said Guy, pointing over to the Spitfire closest to the hangar entrance. "What's different, do you reckon, about that one as compared to the others?" Guy asked him.

"It's... a two-seater...?" replied Frank slowly, in a kind of astonished anticipation, daring to dream about the next words coming out of Guy's mouth.

"It is," replied Guy. "And guess what? You're about to see me climb into the back seat," he told Frank. "That's exciting, isn't it?" he asked, clapping Frank's shoulder and giving it a little squeeze.

"Oh," responded Frank, and Guy could feel Frank's shoulders sag as Frank said it.

"I'm only kidding, Frank!" said Guy, to Frank's immense relief. "We need some aerial footage of this beautiful creature, actually, and I thought you might like to take up position in that back seat there when this lovely goes up?"

"You're not pulling my leg?" asked Frank, now gently taking a grip on the front of Guy's overalls and resisting the urge to plant a sloppy kiss on his face.

"Not at all," replied Guy. "You're really going up in that!" he told him.

"I'm going to fly in a Spitfire?" asked Frank.

"You're going to fly in a Spitfire," confirmed Stan, taking his camera out of his pocket to record the moment.

"You're going to fly in a Spitfire," repeated Guy, very happily confirming that which Stan had already very happily confirmed.

CHAPTER THIRTEEN

Frank was dressed up for his trip into the great blue yonder in short order, with his friends eagerly awaiting his departure into the sky. As the Rolls-Royce engine of the Spitfire burst into life, the glorious sound brought a sense of fond sweeping grand nostalgia to those watching on, paired with serene smiles all around.

"I can see him!" shouted Stan, pointing towards the rear seat of the plane once Frank was situated in the cockpit. And in return, he received from Frank a raised thumb pressed up against the canopy, followed by an enthusiastic wave. Stan sobbed as the plane eased away from the apron and toward the runway, continuing to clap his hands long after the plane had risen majestically into the sky. "Go on, Frank!" he said, punching the air, as the tears ran freely. Stan had envisioned this moment, originally, as being Frank's swansong. But now, God willing, it was just the beginning of the next chapter in Frank's life, and in Frank and Stan's friendship.

"I always wanted to be a fighter pilot," said Monty wistfully, staring up in wonderment, and then back to Dave stood next to him. "They said it was pointless, on account of these," he explained, twirling the tip of his finger around his eyes. Monty sighed at the memory, as the rejection was one that caused him pain, by all appearances, to this very day.

"Nonsense! You'd have made a wonderful fighter pilot!" offered Dave, full of encouragement.

"You think?" said Monty.

"Sure," Dave answered. "You could see two planes coming at you from two different directions, all at the same time! Am I right or am I right?" Dave told him. "If anything, you'd be the perfect role model for any aspiring fighter pilot. In fact, I might start calling you Douglas Bader!"

"A role model," said Monty, repeating Dave's words agreeingly and with no apparent idea who this Bader chap was. "I like that, Dave. Thanks, mate, that means a lot," Monty added. *"Ohhh,"* he uttered in wonderment, his attention now returned to the Spitfire, "They've just done a barrel roll! Go on, Frank!" he called out.

"Wow!" said Lee, watching on. "Did you see that??"

But of course they all saw it, none of them being able to take their eyes off of the marvellous machine.

"After that aerial manoeuvre, I do hope Frank's packed a spare pair of underpants," remarked Monty. "You wouldn't want to go anywhere without a spare pair of underpants, after all, now would you?" he said thoughtfully.

Chapter FOURTEEN

"You ready, you come!" shouted a female voice, followed by the firm tapping of a finger on the door of the changing room, a changing room which consisted of little more than a rickety bench inside what was likely once a broom cupboard.

"You come!" demanded the assertive voice once more.

Frank removed his assigned dressing gown in preparation for this current stage of the day's proceedings, placing it tentatively on a metal hook on the back of the door.

"I'm not sure about all this," confided Frank. He glanced down at his nether regions and gave a bit of a start, not entirely comfortable with what he saw there.

"It's fine," said Stan, appearing a little too at ease in Frank's opinion for their current attire — or, rather, the lack of it.

Frank exhaled deeply. "I don't think I've ever worn paper knickers like this before, Stan," he admitted, running a finger around under the elastic waistband uncertainly. "I'm just a bit worried about how transparent they are, and if something might possibly drop out of them that perhaps shouldn't?"

"Frank, relax. You were worried for no reason when Mrs Kay was waxing areas that hadn't seen the light of day in years, and if it didn't fall out then unprompted, it's not going to fall out now," said Stan, automatically lowering his eyes to the area referenced. "You're nice and smooth down there now, and your shoulders are as smooth as a baby's bum as well. And, besides, a nice fake tan will make you look healthier, and will also nicely highlight your teeth whitening. Trust me, Frank, it's a winning formula, and it's how I look this fabulous all throughout the year!"

Frank appeared to still need some convincing in regard to continuing on and entering the next phase of his beautification process. "You're probably right, but if I think about what we've just gone through, well, I just don't think it's natural to be pulling hairs out of... well, down *there*," he said, lowering his voice in case anyone should have wandered into their broom cupboard in the last ten seconds or so without them knowing. "And now you're inflicting this next bit on me."

"Nonsense," declared Stan. "You're going on your honeymoon in a few days, and you'll be speedo-ready after today, among other things," he told Frank. "And it's not unnatural to have a little cultivating done down there, either," Stan informed him. "In fact, Jessie had her own intimate areas attended to yesterday."

"Honeymoon?" laughed Frank. "I hardly think a few days in the Lake District necessarily constitutes a... Wait, hang on, what did you say just then? How the hell would you even know about Jessie's, *erm*, 'cultivating,' as you put it?"

"Girl talk," said Stan simply, like this should have been obvious. "Now come on, let's do this thing. And, seriously, Frank, Mrs Kay has seen it all, body types of all shapes and varieties, so you do not need to suck your stomach in like you were doing before, okay?" he told him. "Oh," he added, "You may want to make sure that Junior is safely tucked in, though," he advised, pointing in the direction of Frank's paper knickers. "That's one thing she doesn't appreciate."

"What? But she's bloody seen everything already!" Frank rightly protested.

"Ah. I mean she doesn't like unexpected appearances, I suppose you could say," Stan clarified.

Mrs Kay was a Thai lady who worked wonders with massage, beauty, and removing hair from places that hair had no proper place being. Frank had been plucked, shaved, waxed, and had instruments shoved up his nose, into his ears, and into his... well, everywhere. And the result of this was that, for the first time in about twenty years, he could finally boast that he had more hair on his head than everywhere else.

CHAPTER FOURTEEN

Once Frank had come out of the closet, so to speak, with Stan, he was directed to stand in a tent-like structure which was open at the front. It was designed to allow the person inside to be sprayed but the residual to be caught and fall harmlessly to the floor rather than coating the wall behind.

"You bend!" commanded Mrs Kay, repositioning Frank, and worryingly — at least from Frank's point of view — disappearing from his peripheral vision. But she dispatched the contents of her spray gun with the precision of Annie Oakley. "You turn now!" she demanded. There was no time for small talk, as this was a woman on a mission.

Frank felt the gentle caress of fake tan being applied to areas of his body that he'd long since forgotten about. "The spray is a bit... dark...?" said Frank, laughing nervously, but Mrs Kay provided no immediate reply.

"She doesn't really speak English," Stan told him. "Or, at least, only just enough of it to shout out orders," he explained.

"Oh. *Ohhh*, my," said Frank, clenching his cheeks as the cold spray encroached upon the delicate skin of his inner thighs near to his knicker-covered nether regions. He looked down to his arms and then down to his legs where the disparity of his still white feet was a stark contrast to the rest of him. "Stanley?" he said, his voice panicked as Mrs Kay continued her spray application. "Stan, does this not look a little bit too dark?" he asked. "Oh, I don't know about this, Stanley," Frank moaned, beginning to regret his decision to agree to the procedure at hand. But every time he moved an inch to look at himself some more, and then moan again some more, he received a sharp reprimand from Mrs Kay.

"No move, silly!" she yelled, before setting back to work.

"Stan, I don't like this," Frank whinged. "And it feels like my knickers are starting to come down..."

Frank moved to adjust them, but was then promptly hit with a slap of the hand and a further reprimand from Mrs Kay. "No move, silly!" she said again.

"I can't believe I let you talk me into this, Stan. I'm starting to look like Donald bloody Trump!" complained Frank. "And I don't *want* to look like Donald bloody Trump!"

"No one does. He's an orange shitgibbon," said Stan, very sensibly. "But don't worry, mate, I'd say it's more brownish than it is orange," Stan offered. "So no worries there."

"I look like I've fallen into a vat of gravy browning, then!" cried Frank, correcting himself. "Has she taken up the wrong spray or something??"

Stan stepped forward, sneaking a peek over Mrs Kay's shoulder and to the spray gun in her hand and the bottle loaded into it. "It's labelled as nine-out-of-ten on the darkness scale," said Stan, straining his eyes. "There's a picture of George Hamilton on the bottle, even. That's a bold choice for you, Frank."

"But I didn't choose it! Please tell me you're joking!" said Frank, the strain now evident in his voice. "I'm getting married at the weekend, and I'm going to look like a bloody Mars bar up at the altar!" he protested. "How long does this stuff last for, anyway? Maybe it'll wear off by the time of the wedding...?" he asked hopefully.

Stan shrugged his shoulders, taking a moment to adjust his own knickers. "It'll last a few days," he answered. "Also, keep in mind that it takes a little while to soak in, too, so it'll actually get a bit darker still than it is right now. Sorry," he told Frank. Though, to Frank, it didn't sound like Stan was really all that sorry at all, or at least not as sorry as he ought to have been.

"Darker??" squeaked Frank. "Jessie's going to kill me! This is all your fault, Stan! *Oh, come with me and I'll make you look dashing for your big day*, he says. Load of bollocks, Stan!"

"No move, silly!" said Mrs Kay.

Frank wanted nothing more than to put a fair amount of distance between himself and this woman, but with her being in an awkward crouching position at present, he was worried about knocking her off balance and her tumbling over. But as soon as she moved to one side, however, giving Frank a glimpse of freedom, he made a break for it... or tried to, at least.

"No move!" shouted Mrs Kay, instinctively reaching out and grabbing at Frank. And, unfortunately — for both parties involved — this grabbing involved her taking a grip on Frank's flimsy knickers, which offered no resistance whatsoever, coming away in

CHAPTER FOURTEEN

her hand, and leaving poor Frank starkers. Alas, his new darkened sprayed-on skin tone was even more apparent now that it showed in sharp relief against the *very* white areas now suddenly on proud display.

"Frank, calm down!" advised Stan. "Frank, I'm only winding you up about the tan getting darker, okay? Relax. The fake tan drops down a shade after you've had a shower in the morning, all right? There's no need to panic, mate. Trust me, you'll look wonderful," Stan told him.

"I spray bum!" said Mrs Kay, giggling. She didn't actually spray people's bums, and was only having him on, though Frank had no way of knowing this. "Hold still!"

But Frank removed himself from Mrs Kay's nefarious clutches, making a beeline towards the dressing room door, using one hand to cup and one to cover — though it was relatively hopeless in that regard, as there really wasn't much dignity left to recoup at this point. "I'm good, thanks," he said to Mrs Kay, and then, to Stan, "I think we're done here?"

But despite Frank's wishes, they weren't done. Far from it, in fact. There was a scalp massage, an exfoliating facial, some sort of meditation exercise, and the final part of their indulgence day was a manicure which Stan promised would do wonders for Frank's cuticles.

By the time his manicure came around, Frank had accepted his fate. These other procedures, at least, were much less invasive, and the comfortable leather chair he was sat in for the manicure also doubled as a back massager. So that was nice. As a colleague of Mrs Kay applied the finishing touches to Frank's nails, he couldn't stop staring at them, and could kind of understand why Jessie would often spend so long perfecting her own. "Don't you be telling Dave and Monty that I've been and had all this done," he said to Stan, who sat in the adjacent chair, relaxing back like a cat in front of the fire. "They'll think I've gone all... all..."

"Gay?" suggested Stan. And after all, he could certainly joke in such a fashion.

"I was going to say soft, Stanley," Frank answered him.

"I don't need to tell them two big lummoxes anything, because they were down with me last month themselves," Stan told Frank. "And let me tell you, Monty getting waxed was a two-man job. Well, two-*woman* job, that is, and Mrs Kay had to place her foot on his back in order to get enough leverage to get the bloody wax strip off! They nicknamed him Sasquatch."

"They actually called him Sasquatch?" Frank said. "I thought her English wasn't that good...?"

"Hmm, she could have said Yeti, now I think on it," answered Stan. "Either way, in their line of work, they know what such hairy beasts are called!"

"Ah. Fair point," replied Frank. "Anyway, was that for the hair on his back, the applied foot action? Or was it for the hair around his... you know..." asked Frank, denoting the unspoken tail-end portion of his query with a well-timed whistle.

"His back, I'm hoping," said Stan. "Though either way, I suppose it explains why the drain plug in the shower is constantly getting backed up. I mean, if he's that hirsute."

"Hair suit?" asked Frank, unable to resist the opportunity for a pun.

"Indeed," replied Stan. "Anyway, I can't believe my best friend is getting married at the weekend!" said Stan, deftly steering the conversation away from the subject of Monty's excess body hair.

Frank had a faraway look for a moment as he drifted off to a happy place. "Married again, eh, Stan? I must be mad," he said, but with a grin.

"Jessie's special. Very special," Stan told him. "You've done well there, my old mate. I've said it before, but fate is an amazing thing."

"Oh? How so?" asked Frank.

"Just the whole coming to the Isle of Man thing," answered Stan. "Here we are with new friends, a new business, new relationships, and now we even own a racetrack as well! And all this from getting on the boat. Imagine if we hadn't sat down by the Liverpool docks that day and decided to come over here in the first place. I wonder what we'd be doing right now?"

"I'd probably be wondering who my now- ex-wife was out sleeping with!" replied Frank. "It's all fate, though, as you say," he

CHAPTER FOURTEEN

went on. "I must admit I didn't see the whole racetrack thing on the horizon, however. That was a bit of a curveball. Rodney Franks is one crafty bastard, I must say."

"Crafty bastard, is right," agreed Stan.

Rodney Franks, as the two friends had experienced, had indeed been a crafty bastard. Frank and Stan had precisely zero intention of selling their taxi business to him no matter what the price. This did leave them with a dilemma, however. The gravity of the situation with Lee was not lost on them. And particularly so, as Lee himself had confirmed to them that his original intentions regarding the armoured van had indeed been fuelled by financial gain, or, as he told them, the allure of a warm cell, mainly.

Lee had broken down in tears when presented with Rodney's allegations, as it turned out, it having brought him back to a time in his life where he had nothing to live for. He felt worthless back then, he'd told them. But Frank and Stan had witnessed how far Lee had come. And not only had he merely turned his own life around, but he was now changing the lives of others as well. In fact Lee was tireless in his efforts for the charity, and Stan and Frank's current reflections on the subject of fate applied equally to the situation with Lee, they felt. Had he not been dragged so far down in his life, for instance, then perhaps he would never have become the man he now was. And the man he was now, in fact, was not just an employee, he was a friend. A very dear friend. And they weren't about to go and throw him to the wolves.

Lee was part of Team Frank & Stan, and the boys protected their friends. They did run the situation past a solicitor for the sake of good order. There was a chance that Lee could find himself in a spot of bother, particularly with the statement from Rodney's mystery witness. That was bad enough in itself, but the greater victim would potentially be the charity. One whiff of a scandal and all Stan and Frank's hard work in that regard, and all that they'd achieved, could be undone in an instant. The other option, aside from throwing Lee under the bus, was for Frank and Stan to pay Rodney a boatload of cash in one form or another. Rodney wasn't stupid, however, which is why he suggested any payment would be in the form of purchasing the Jurby Racetrack — where Isle Le

Mans TT had been hosted — as any demand strictly for cash would amount to bribery and extortion and would potentially land Rodney behind bars.

Once again, fate had a hand to play in their ultimate decision to pay Rodney off, and by so doing, purchase the Jurby racetrack. Lining the pockets of Rodney Franks was the last thing they wanted, certainly. But, if they didn't, they ran the risk of Lee ending up in prison, as well as the charity being subjected to mountains of unwarranted adverse media attention. And as it turned out, interestingly enough, Rodney had no real interest in the racetrack — having purchased it mainly for purposes of leverage against Henk — and so it'd likely fall to rack and ruin if left in his care. And it was on this point where the subject of fate entered into Frank and Stan's thought processes...

Because motorsport, and in particular road racing, was now in the boys' blood. They simply adored it. They admired the back-of-the-van mentality, the comradery, the atmosphere, and, well, pretty much everything associated with it, really — the whole kit and caboodle. If Frank and Stan hadn't had the pleasure of going to East Fortune, they wouldn't have truly understood the sacrifice that Isle of Man racers went to in securing their Mountain Course racing licence. If the Jurby racetrack closed, then the local people that contributed so much to the sport they loved would have even less opportunity to gather their signatures and would need to travel even more at even greater expense.

Of course they didn't tell Rodney that they had any interest in the racetrack or else the price would have risen dramatically. But they *did* have an interest in it. True, not at first. They'd told him to take his offer and shove it, initially. But, after having a think on it, and then going to East Fortune in particular, they'd had a change of heart. By purchasing the track, as expensive a proposition as that may have been, not only would they ensure Lee's videotape would disappear but they would also be helping local motorsport at the same time as well. They rationalised it further by reasoning the charity could use the track for future motorised fundraising events, as could the local community — they'd no idea for what, but such details didn't normally stop them. Plus, their charity

CHAPTER FOURTEEN

fundraiser, Isle 'Le Mans' TT, would hopefully become an annual event, so there was that also. And so they grudgingly agreed to settle with the cravat-wearing cretin that was Rodney Franks. Stan did have one unnegotiable condition, which was the safe return of the hat he'd become so fond of but had forgotten on Rodney's table at the restaurant that day. Fortunately, Rodney had retained the hat. And, thus, Team Frank & Stan became the owners of their own racetrack. They also knew two eager petrolheads, as it should happen, who'd be happy to step up as assistant track managers, in addition to their farming-related duties... none other than Dave and Monty. And so it all worked out in the end.

Still in his manicure chair, Frank stretched, contented, as the soothing pulses in the backrest caressed his grateful muscles. And then a thought struck him, which he was happy to share. "Thinking back, Stan. Do you remember when Monty was walking around the farm all gingerly and bow-legged like he'd just climbed off a horse?" he asked. "He said he'd been attacked by a chicken, if I recall, though that never did make much sense as an explanation. Was his peculiar gait that day anything to do with him being here, by any chance?"

"Yup. He went the whole hog and had his bollocks waxed," Stan answered.

"Ah, that explains it. That Mrs Kay really does deserve a medal," replied Frank. Frank held his fingers out in front of him like he was playing an imaginary piano, admiring his manicure. "I must say, Stan. My nails do look lovely. I'm not sure about this bloody tan, though!"

Chapter
FIFTEEN

The day before the wedding was organised chaos. Then again, it wasn't organised... so, basically, just chaos. The early wedding plans of a rather modest affair had morphed into something akin to a state occasion. Distant relatives on all sides, invited as little more than a courtesy, had quite unexpectedly ended up RSVPing in force. However, while one would like to think this was solely due to the desire to witness the joining of two couples in love or to celebrate Frank's temporary reprieve from his death sentence, the truth of it was more likely that Frank's kind offer of assistance with airfares and hotel accommodation had swung people's decisions to the positive side. Getting people to the Isle of Man wasn't necessarily cheap, depending upon where folks were coming from. Of course the pay-off once arrived in terms of awe-inspiring natural beauty was entirely sufficient to warrant any expense, was Frank's opinion, though he never expected as many folks to actually take him up on his generous offer as did happen. Still, it wasn't something he was going to do every day — getting married, that is — so what the hell, thought Frank, it was only money.

And so, presently, Dave was behind the wheel, and with Monty in the passenger seat...

"Oi, check that notepad, will you, Monty, me old son?" requested Dave. "What time's the next plane in? How we doing for time?"

"Twenty minutes, Dave. Plenty of wiggle room," Monty replied reassuringly. "This is the last batch, yeah?" he asked.

"Should be, yes," Dave answered him.

Dave needn't have worried about the time. By this point, he could have completed the drive to the airport with his eyes closed. It was the fifth or sixth return trip he'd done that day in the span of several hours in their rented minibus. They'd already dispatched Lee, Stella, Molly, Susie, and a further litany of assorted relatives eager to have availed themselves of Frank's generosity. The boys didn't have a clue, picking up the various and sundry relatives, as to who was who or which side of the wedding party they belonged to. But, in all cases, Dave and Monty made sure to extend a cordial welcome to the Isle of Man to everyone.

"Afternoon, Fairies!" said Monty and Dave in unison as they drove over the Fairy Bridge on the way to the airport for this last pick-up. Greeting the fairies was engrained in local culture, and failing to do so could result in serious misfortune and strife, or so it was believed.

"Me and you managing a farm and helping out at a racetrack," Monty sighed dreamily, a little further on.

"I know, mate. It's brilliant, isn't it?" Dave answered.

"We can really help local motorsport, you know," Monty continued. He had clearly been giving the matter some deal of thought.

"I know, mate. It's going to be great," agreed Dave.

"And to think, when I was younger, they said I was that stupid that I'd be lucky to get a job shovelling horse manure at a stable. And yet here we are now," Monty remarked.

"I know, mate," replied Dave again, pretty much on autopilot at this point, but then, after what Monty just told him had registered, said, "Wait, hang on. That was a bit harsh, I reckon, no?" Dave then thought a moment, and added, "Bullies, eh? What do they know, Monty? Screw 'em, I say."

"Right up the pooper with a pineapple," Monty declared.

"That's rather... specific, isn't it?" Dave considered.

"It was my parents," was Monty's solemn response.

"How's that?" asked Dave, a little confused now by Monty's train of thought, as it appeared to have switched tracks.

"The ones that said it," Monty clarified.

CHAPTER FIFTEEN

"About the pineapple?" asked Dave, attempting to work out what Monty was telling him.

"About mucking stalls," explained Monty.

"Ah. Right. Well, you showed them, then, didn't you, buddy?" replied Dave supportively. "So they must have maybe said it for motivational purposes, yeah?" Dave added, trying his best to put a positive spin on it somehow or other.

"Yeah," said Monty flatly. "That must have been what it was."

They were both silent for a bit, and then Dave spoke up again. "*Erm...* Monty?" he said.

"Yes, Dave?" answered Monty.

"Well," said Dave, "I just realised... I mean, well, you *do* shovel horse manure in a stable now. We *both* do, actually, amongst other duties."

Monty considered this for a moment or two before replying, reflectively, "Yes, but it's because we *want* to, Dave. Not because we *have* to."

"Fair enough, Monty. Good point," Dave happily agreed.

In not too terribly long a time, Dave pulled into the parking bay outside the airport entrance. "Right-ho, Monty. Grab your sign and let's get the rest of them off to their hotel," Dave instructed. "Then, me and you can go for a well-deserved pint or two!"

And at this, Monty took hold of his greeting sign reading CRYER/WATSON WEDDING and headed into the airport arrivals lounge. He hadn't ventured more than two meters inside when a gaggle of old folk waved enthusiastically in his direction.

"We're here for the wedding!" one of them shouted.

"Are you here to give us a ride, handsome??" shouted another, who'd clearly made good use of the drinks trolley on the short flight to the Island.

"Come on, young ladies," replied Monty, laying on the charm. He skipped over to them, grabbing some of their bags, at which point one of them took their frilly wedding hat from its box and plonked it on Monty's head, offering him a cheeky slap on the backside for good measure.

"Saucy old buggers," mumbled Monty under his breath.

It was fortunate they'd hired a sixteen-seat minibus, as Dave and Monty had clearly got their calculations wrong, there being a bit more of them than expected. And two of the blue-rinsed mob, in fact, were rather more reserved than the rest, it seemed, and hung at the back of the group.

"Nothing to be afraid of, ladies!" said Monty encouragingly. "I'm Monty. And your names are...?" he shouted over the noise of a plane taking to the sky above them. "I'm here on behalf of the wedding party, ladies. Nothing to worry about with me, ladies. Completely trustworthy, I can assure you," he prattled on, giving them his most assured smile. "Just head over to the minibus on the other side of the road," Monty indicated as they made their way out of the arrivals lounge, giving the two rather more cautious ladies in the group special attention and herding them along, and pointing to where Dave stood offering them as well as the others a friendly wave.

"I'm Nancy, and this is Mabel," said Nancy, shuffling behind Monty.

"I hope the flight over wasn't too bumpy?" offered Monty, but received nothing but vacant smiles in return as the sound of yet another aeroplane taking off actively competed against the sound of his voice. "I said..." he began, but Monty knew he was fighting a losing battle, and so settled for, "Come on, ladies. I'll get you to the hotel and you can have a nice cup of tea."

On the drive back, the inane chatter of old folk was difficult to talk over and interrupt, and so trying to get them to say hello to the fairies on the return leg to their hotel in Douglas was a bit of a challenge. Nevertheless, "They seem a right old laugh," confided Dave to Monty. "We'll need to catch up with them for a drink at the wedding reception, yeah? I reckon they'll tell a story or two. No idea who's related to who, mind, but they're mad as a box of frogs, and I like that about them."

In Douglas, a twenty-minute-or-so drive from the airport, Dave pulled up outside the Claremont Hotel, where the remaining guests were to be booked into. He turned the radio down and swivelled around in his seat in order to address his audience in the back. "Okay, ladies," he said, slapping the side of his captain's chair to attract their collective attention... to no avail. *Anyone's* attention would have been nice, actually, thought Dave, but no one was

CHAPTER FIFTEEN

biting. Dave turned to Monty. "No wonder they're lively, they're getting stuck into a bottle of prosecco," he whispered.

"They're a spirited bunch, I'll give them that," Monty agreed.

"Okay, ladies!" Dave said, spinning 'round and trying again, this time with increased volume, and this time with at least a modicum of success as he managed to get the fleeting attention of a few of them. "Right, you," he said playfully, to the nearest of those few, "You look the soberest out of this lot, so I'll tell you what the plan is. That there is your hotel," he explained, slowly. And he explained it slowly because, despite being one of the more sober of the group, she was still relatively sauced. Monty handed her a wad of cards with phone numbers printed on them. "These are the numbers of everybody in the wedding party. A coach will pick you up at eleven-forty a.m. and take you to the wedding, which starts at twelve-thirty. So, plenty of time when you get there to have a glass or two of something, okay?"

The elderly lady nodded, but she had one eye looking for the prosecco.

"Are you two the strippers?" shouted a voice from near the rear of the bus.

"Let's get them out of here before they bloody violate us," said Dave to Monty, confidentially.

The two boys were like bouncers at a nightclub trying their level best to get the remaining punters out of the club at closing time, and one by one they managed to coax the old birds out of the bus, watching on as they all made their tipsy way safely into the hotel.

"Where's all the husbands?" asked Monty, in reference to the fact there were precisely no men.

Dave shrugged his shoulders. "Dunno. Maybe this lot finished them off?"

"Whoa," said Monty, stopping Dave slamming the bus door shut. "There's two more on the back row, Dave, hang on."

"The ones asking if we were the strippers?" asked Dave nervously.

"No, I think it's different ones," Monty answered him. "Come on ladies!" Monty said, firmly but ever-so-politely, to the bus's last remaining occupants. "We're at the hotel, and they've got a nice cup of tea waiting for you!"

The two passengers didn't move.

"Are they pissed?" asked Dave. "Or maybe asleep?" he suggested. "Here. Go and round them up, Monty," Dave advised.

Monty went white. "They don't seem to be moving, Dave. What if they're... if they're...?"

"They're *not*... are they?" asked a very worried Dave. "Well go and see, mate," he urged. "What are you waiting for?"

"Why me?" protested Monty.

"Because you're closest!" said Dave, ever the voice of reason.

Monty climbed back inside the bus and then twisted his neck around like an owl. "It's the two old dears I was talking to at the airport!" he called back to Dave. "Hello, girls," Monty said in as least threating a manner as he could muster, addressing the ladies now. "Nancy. Mabel. It's Monty, do you remember? We need to get you off the bus now."

Nancy and Mabel were, fortunately, still amongst the land of the living. But they were also still not moving from their seats. Nancy looked at Mabel, then out of the bus window, and then over to Monty with a look of bewilderment.

"We're at the hotel," repeated Monty, pointing to the building. "This is your hotel, ladies. The rest of your group are inside. Over there. Just there."

Mabel answered, though spoke as quiet as a church mouse. "We need to get to her grandson's wedding," she told Monty, while receiving a nod of agreement from Nancy as she did so.

"My grandson's wedding," confirmed Nancy. "We need to get to the plane," she said, and with that, held out her printed ticket for inspection.

Monty took the ticket, and for a brief moment his eyes were unified. "Thank you," he said, handing the ticket back. Then he clambered back out of the minibus to an awaiting, and increasingly impatient, Dave, who'd a mind for a pint of something cold. And Monty knew this was so, because Dave had in fact just told him, '*Monty, what's the holdup, because I've a mind for a pint of something cold.*'

Monty leaned in close. "We might have a small problem," he told Dave.

CHAPTER FIFTEEN

"What, like me not having a pint in my hand?" replied Dave, quite reasonably, he felt.

Monty gulped, hard and repeatedly. "Those two on the bus..." said Monty.

"Yeah?" said Dave.

"They need to get to a wedding," said Monty.

"Yeah," said Dave, not understanding the problem. "Well we've brought them to a wedding, haven't we, so...?"

"I think it's, *ehm*, the wrong wedding we've brought them to, actually...?" offered Monty, then wisely stepping back a few paces for safety's sake.

"Monty, what the hell are you on about?" Dave asked.

"Those two still in the back have a flight ticket to London Luton airport," explained Monty. "They were milling about, earlier, with that lot that've just gone inside. I just assumed they were part of the group, but... apparently not. Oh, shit."

Dave wasn't having it, unable to believe anyone would just follow Monty blindly like that, and wondering if Monty were perhaps just making an ill-timed joke and taking the piss. "Don't be stupid. And come with me," he said, dragging Monty back onto the bus. "Excuse me, ladies. Are you on the Island for the Cryer-Watson wedding tomorrow?" he asked of them.

"No," replied Mabel. "We're *leaving* the Island for a wedding. That man had a sign for a wedding party and was quite insistent that we follow him, and then brought us on here. I thought this coach was bringing us to our plane?"

"Where's the plane?" Nancy chimed in. "I don't see the plane. It was an awfully long trip to get here to the plane. But I don't see the plane anywhere about at all," she said, thoroughly disoriented and confused.

"There's no plane," agreed Mabel. "Where's the plane gone?"

Dave smiled, offered reassuring hand gestures, and then returned once again to his position outside the bus. He clenched his fist as Monty joined him. "One bastard job, Monty. One bastard job!"

"But..." Monty began to say.

"You went not fifteen yards into the airport, and you've only gone and managed to kidnap two oldies!" Dave whispered ferociously.

"But..." said Monty.

"For the love of all that's holy!" Dave went on. But then he sighed. "Right. What time's their plane leave?" he said. "In fact, it doesn't matter, let's just get them back to the airport before someone puts us on a 'Most Wanted' list."

"But... Okay," said Monty.

"All right, ladies, we'll have you back at the airport in no time at all!" Dave shouted through the open bus door. "No need to panic!"

Hosting the reception on the farm as well as the wedding service was a generous romantic notion and a super idea in principle. In practice, however, it was a different matter entirely because it was a logistical nightmare that could have placed even the calmest of men under unbearable strain. Yet while lesser men might well crumple under the pressure, Frank was fortunate enough to have his wingman Stan — the very *epitome* of calm under pressure — at his side to oversee and ensure everything went both smoothly and perfectly according to plan...

"Why the hell are there bloody chickens running around on my fucking red carpet!" screamed Stan, out past the courtyard and tearing out his proverbial hair. "There's cocks everywhere! Is this some kind of joke??"

Ordinarily, Stan was fairly good with cocks. But, right now, the more he chased them around, the more they remained just out of reach. Exhausted, he decided to take a short break and rest his bum in one of the chairs he'd set up for the service. Only the chairs weren't there, because he hadn't set them up yet. "Where's the seats for the service?" he mumbled to himself, confused. "Where's the bloody bastard chairs!" he said, now shouting again, and at nobody in particular. And it's not like anyone could have given him much of an answer anyway. What would they have said, except for, *'The chairs aren't there, Stan, because you haven't set them up yet'* or similar?

Stan was on the verge of tears. He was a broken man, and the trouble had started early. He'd taken to wearing a Bluetooth headset, for instance, because he'd seen a programme on the TV about

CHAPTER FIFTEEN

wedding planners in the United States and that's what they all wore. The problem came in the form of the headset he'd gotten not being compatible with his phone, a phone which probably didn't even have Bluetooth capability to begin with. What this meant, then, was that every time his phone rang, he had to take the darned headset off and answer his phone the traditional way anyway. This, of course, did not escape the notice of Dave and Monty, unfortunately, and the pair had spent the entire morning prank calling him, taking great delight in observing Stan's ensuing headset shenanigans.

Becks approached Stan from the front so as not to startle him, armed with a cup of tea and a cordial smile. "I've got this, Stan," she said in her most soothing tone. "You need to calm down or else we're going to be having two weddings *and* a funeral, and I think there's already been a film made of something or other to that effect, yes?" she told him. "Look, I'll sort out all the cocks, as well as the chairs, all right? And there's a phrase I never thought I'd say. But right now, you go and join Frank in the kitchen and leave this to me, alrighty? You just relax, I've got this," she said, pressing the tea into his hand. "A nice cuppa will sort you out, yes?"

"A nice cuppa will sort me out. Yes, a nice cuppa will sort me out," Stan muttered to himself, repeating the mantra.

"Oh," Becks added, very mildly, so as not to upset him, "Do you know where Dave and Monty are? Only I thought they'd be back here by now."

Stan was trying his best to regulate his breathing, aided by the aromatherapy the warm tea in his hands was providing. "One last airport run," he told Becks. "They mentioned something about a kidnapping they were involved in, but I just hung up on them, as they've been winding me up all bloody day on this blasted thing," he said, taking hold of the headset, plucking it from his head, and throwing it in the direction of the nearest chicken.

Becks was a marvel. Calm under pressure, thoughtful, considerate, and just an all-around spectacular person to be around. "Stan, you have to remember we're on a working farm," she gently reminded him. "Who cares if there's chicken poop on the carpet or the donkeys have eaten some of the flowers, right? It's all part of the charm."

"What? The donkeys have eaten the flowers??" said Stan, his blood pressure rising again.

"Relax, Stan. *Reelaaaax*," she intoned softly, like she was placing a hypnotic suggestion. "Spend some time with Frank and enjoy your tea. I've got this."

"Relax," Stan told himself. "*Relaaaax*," he said, Becks' mesmerisation technique appearing to take hold once again.

Becks had sacrificed a day of shopping with the rest of the girls to help out with the planning, as she'd seen the vein in Stan's head getting progressively enlarged the closer it got to the wedding day, and so decided to lend a helping hand. And that helping hand was now pressed gently on Stan's back, guiding him back towards the farmhouse. "And just so you know, Stan, all of the wedding guests travelling over to the Island have arrived safely, and are all settled in at their hotel, from what Dave told me earlier, before the, ah... well, *erm*, just before," she said, not wishing to repeat the word 'kidnapping' at this stage. "We're nearly ready here, and it's really just a few minor details left to do, which I've got and will sort out for you," she told him reassuringly, ushering him inside.

But then Stan dug his heels in. "Wait. I just remembered, one of the lamas has taken a shit over by the chocolate fountain!" he protested. "I need to go and—"

"Already sorted," Becks assured him. "And the lamas are back in their enclosure thanks to the heroic efforts of my very able young assistant Tyler. Now go!" she told him. "Shoo!"

"But I—" Stan began to complain.

"Shoo!" Becks said once more.

Inside the farmhouse, hunched over the desk in the office he and Stan shared, Frank held his pen like a paintbrush, staring blankly through the window like a tortured artist desperately seeking inspiration — in this case, from the Manx countryside on view. Fortunately, unrelated, but affording him some small peace of mind, the spray tan he'd gotten just recently had lessened in its intensity, just as Stan had assured him it would, leaving him sporting what was at least the appearance of a rather healthy glow. Nobody had warned him, however, of the after-effects on his bedsheets, which resulted in him receiving quite the fright the

CHAPTER FIFTEEN

morning after the application, worried he might have had a little accident in the night.

"You look deep in thought?" offered Stan, placing a bum cheek on the corner of Frank's desk.

Frank lowered his pen, placing it down onto the surface of the desk. "Lee asked if I'd help him with his speech for tomorrow. Which I accomplished earlier. So I suppose that might help explain why my creative juices are now depleted, and why my own speech is still just a blank piece of paper at present," he said. Frank held the paper up for inspection to illustrate this very point. "So did Becks throw you out of the way?" he asked of Stan, although he already suspected the answer.

"Eh, no, not at all," replied Stan, casting a glance out the window and towards the marquee. "She and Tyler have got it all under control, so, you know, I thought I'd simply leave them to it. That is, knowing I can trust them, I've delegated the few remaining tasks to them, is what I mean to say." Stan coughed. "As a professional wedding planner should," he added, and then coughed again.

"So she's thrown you out of the way," said Frank, laughing.

"She's thrown me out of the way," Stan reluctantly concurred, taking a sip of his tea.

"I've been watching on, and everything looks magnificent, by the way," Frank told him. "Truly it does. And I'm glad we decided, in the end, to have the wedding here. It just feels right, if you know what I mean? Oh, and I'm grateful for your help in pulling this all together. You're a friend in a million, Stan, honestly you are."

"*Pshaw*," said Stan, waving away the compliment, though very obviously deeply appreciating it. "Anyway, about tomorrow and Stella. I was thinking..." he went on.

"Yes?" replied Frank.

"Well, I know you're getting married as well, of course..." Stan told him, finger poised... "But I think we should both walk her down the aisle? I've spoken to the vicar, and he said it's fine if you come down with Jessie first, and then—"

"I think it's a beautiful idea, Stan," Frank answered him. He didn't even need Stan to finish, as it had always been his dream to walk Stella down the aisle. "I didn't think it would ever happen, her getting married, if I'm being honest," Frank admitted. "But here we are, aren't we? Thank you, Stan. Yes, we're all going to have a fantastic day, and hopefully the good weather that we ordered will put in an appearance, yeah?" he said, then adding, "Oh, and how's your own speech coming along, by the way?"

"Ah," said Stan. "Well I started writing my best man's speech, sure enough, but then ended up deciding to just leave it."

"Oh?" said Frank.

"I decided to wing it, actually, and just shoot from the hip, as it were," Stan told him.

"Should I be worried?" enquired Frank.

"That you should, yes," Stan answered him, a mischievous grin forming.

Frank pondered this for a moment. Stan, after all, was the man who'd known him for pretty much his entire life. He'd shared the laughs, sorrow, pain, previous conquests, and all the rest. But, as such, and above all, Stan thus had the ability to rip him a right new one via his speech. Frank gave Stan a playful punch in the arm. "You wouldn't throw me under a bus, would you, old buddy?" he asked his best chum.

But before Stan had chance to confirm or deny his intentions one way or the other — whether they be nefarious or perfectly innocent — Jessie appeared, stood in the doorframe of the office, cheeks flushed. Her sudden, unexpected appearance caused Frank to grab for his paper, in case his future wife should somehow be able to see and read a wedding speech he hadn't even started yet much less finished.

Tucking the blank paper into the top drawer of the desk, Frank then leapt to his feet, rising like a salmon at spawning time jumping up out of the water against the current. "Hello, my darling! How was the day shopping?" he said, extending his arms and puckering up his lips invitingly.

Jessie went in for a quick cuddle and a peck on the lips, but then pulled back. "It was wonderful," she said. "Well, it *was* wonderful, at least, until..."

"Until?" asked Frank.

CHAPTER FIFTEEN

Jessie appeared to be running several competing thoughts around in her head, unsure which one to begin with in answer to Frank. "Until..." she began... "Well, until Stella got into a fight with two rugby players in the pub," she said, settling on a starting point.

"Blimey," said Stan. "Are the rugby players okay?"

"They took quite a beating, from what I'm told, but suffered only superficial cuts and bruises in the end, thank goodness," Jessie told them. "And it doesn't look like they want to press charges, either, which is a positive result, thankfully," she went on. "Wait, hang on. Why do you two not look overly surprised about this?" asked Jessie, in relation to the rather relaxed expressions staring back. "And why aren't you asking me if *Stella* is okay?"

"It's Stella," said Frank with a shrug, as if this in itself should be explanation enough.

"It's Stella," said Stan, nodding in concurrence.

"Wait, but I thought Stella was going shopping with you and Susie?" asked Frank. "How'd she end up at the pub, anyway?"

"Well she's not too keen on the whole shopping thing, as you know, so we had to bribe her into going with us by promising her a pint while we were out and about, if you recall," Jessie answered.

"Ah. Right," said Frank.

"Yes, but she couldn't wait, and then went off on her own," Jessie told them. She lowered her shopping bags and fell back into a chair. "She seemed a bit solemn all day, if I'm being honest," Jessie went on. "I put it down to pre-wedding jitters, and didn't think too much about it beyond that. We arranged to meet her a bit later at the pub, and I was looking forward, myself, to enjoying a half-pint. But when we turned up, she was getting turfed out of the pub. The barman said she'd had about ten pints of cider, and she was arm-wrestling with the rugby players, as it happened, when it got a little nasty."

"Where is she now?" enquired Frank.

"Susie took her up to bed early, as I think she was a little upset," said Jessie. "Not to mention blitzkrieged on the ten pints, mind."

"She'll be okay," ventured Frank. "A little sleep and she'll be fine. Stan, will you see if we've got any steak in the fridge to place on her knuckles or any facial injuries? Oh, or look for frozen peas, yeah? I recall that helped when she had the spat with the Navy boys."

"What's she like, eh?" said Stan, chuckling. He was about to go to the kitchen to carry out Frank's request, but Jessie wasn't quite done yet.

"That's not all," said Jessie, lowering her head. A day out with Stella was a new experience for Jessie and had taken its toll on her both physically and emotionally. But it was more than that. "Guys, I'm not sure how to tell you this," she said, shaking her head sadly. "Guys. Stella has said her wedding with Lee is off."

"What??" said Stan and Frank, both at once.

Jessie looked back up at them with tired eyes. "I'm afraid she said she doesn't have any feelings for Lee anymore," she told them.

"Oh, bugger," replied Frank, not entirely sure what to make of this news. "Surely it's the cider talking...?"

Jessie shook her head in the negative. "No, we've been talking to her about it the whole drive back. She's completely adamant that she doesn't love him anymore and that the wedding is off."

"Oh, shit," Stan replied.

"And there's absolutely no convincing her otherwise?" offered Frank desperately.

"We already tried," answered Jessie. "Believe me, we tried. But no luck."

"Oh, shit," Stan said again. "Does Lee know?" he asked.

"No, not yet," Jessie admitted.

Frank bit the back of his hand, pacing, weighing up what to do next. "Lee's off having a few beers right now, as we speak, and looking forward to the most important day of his life. What the hell are we supposed to do with this information? Fucking hell, how are we going to tell him that Stella doesn't love him anymore? How are we going to tell him that his bloody wedding is off??"

Chapter

SIXTEEN

Stella didn't snore like anybody else. Stella didn't snore like anything on earth, or possibly even in the entire universe. It was even worse when she'd been drinking.

"Go and wake her up, will you?" suggested Stan of Frank. "I've not had a wink of sleep all night for worrying, and she's in there making a noise like she's brought the entire Royal Philharmonic brass section home with her. Honestly, Frank, our pampering facial the other day will mean nothing if we've got bags under our eyes today."

Frank tentatively pressed his ear up against Stella's door, even though this wasn't entirely necessary as the noise already emanating quite clearly from within indicated she was still in there and still fast asleep. "I don't want to go in and startle her," said Frank. "I did that years ago and she ended up throttling me whilst still half-asleep, and I don't really want red finger marks around my neck on my wedding day."

"No Jessie with you, by the way?" asked Stan on a different subject, noticing Jessie's absence, as she'd been there the previous evening.

"No, she wanted to stay over, but I didn't think it was the done thing to see her on the morning of the wedding," Frank answered. "Anyway, we should have tried harder to wake Stella up last night and see what she was playing at."

"We'd have gotten no sense, Frank," Stan told him. "She was well-oiled, so we did the right thing letting her sleep it off."

FRANK 'N' STAN'S BUCKET LIST #4 – BRIDE OF FRANK 'N' STAN

Frank jumped back from the door. "I think she's awake!" he whispered, deducing this from both the creaking floorboards and the sudden absence of snoring.

The two of them didn't want her to come out and then have a conversation with her, of the type they were about to have, taking place stood there in the hallway, and so they retreated to the kitchen. They heard her heading to the bathroom upstairs, and prepared themselves for her imminent arrival by sitting together at the kitchen table like job interviewers awaiting their next candidate.

"Wait, if she's gone to the toilet, we could be waiting all bloody morning," Frank rightly pointed out. "We may as well put the kettle back on."

Fifteen minutes or so and a second morning cup of tea apiece later, Stella emerged from down the stairs. She offered the two of them an indifferent glare. "That flusher's broken in the toilet," she said, walking straight past the pair of them to bury her head inside the pantry. "I'd call a plumber or something, if I were you, because it's not pretty."

Frank looked at Stan, and then over to the rear of Stella. "Stella, *ehm*, your nightshirt is tucked into your knickers?" he offered, as delicately as he could.

She turned towards them, unconcerned, and with no apparent intention of sorting out her wardrobe mishap. "Why are you lot sat there like a pair of bloody bookends?" she grunted, before ripping open a twin packet of frosted strawberry & cheesecake Pop-Tarts.

Stan bit his lip for a moment, composing himself. "Stella, you do have a recollection of yesterday's events?" he asked. But he then continued on, without waiting for a response, "Well, in case you don't, I'll remind you. Apparently, you sank ten pints or thereabouts of Guinness, and—"

"Cider!" Stella interrupted.

"Cider, then. Yes," said Stan, correcting himself. "And do you, perchance, remember the very small matter of you deciding not to get married to Lee today?"

Stella polished off the Pop-Tarts in short order, without even bothering to toast them, and returned to the cupboards in search of more. She then shrugged her shoulders, as if that should be

CHAPTER SIXTEEN

confirmation enough of any life-changing decisions made the day previous.

"Stella," said Frank, in his sternest, most headmaster-like voice. "Stella, this isn't good enough. Are you seriously telling us you're not getting married to Lee?"

Stella walked over and picked up a teaspoon from the kitchen table, using the handle to scratch her right bum cheek. "Correct," she said, placing the spoon back on the table.

Frank was temporarily lost for words. First, because that was the spoon he'd been using to stir his tea. And, second, of course, was what Stella was saying, and the nonchalant manner in which she was saying it. "Oh, is that right?" he said eventually. "And I suppose you've told Lee of this epiphany you've had?"

"Of course I have. *Duh*," replied Stella, scowling at the very notion of such a stupid question being asked of her. "I left him a message while I was on the bog."

Stan couldn't help but laugh. It wasn't a funny laugh, either. "Stella!" he snapped, before lowering his voice and evening his tone. "Stella. You've told the man you're due to marry today that you've changed your mind, by sending him a text message, while just sat on the toilet? Honestly?"

"Don't be soddin' stupid, Stan. How crass do you think I am, for fucksake?" Stella answered, finally liberating the t-shirt from her knickers. "I left him a bloody voicemail *yesterday*, last night, when I'd gotten up late in the evening and was sitting on the bog, not *today*, the day *of* the wedding," she scolded him. "This morning, just now, I was only checking for messages. And of which there were none, by the way. Which only confirms my suspicions that he doesn't bloody care."

Stan placed his hands down on the kitchen tabletop, unable for a moment to even look at Stella as he spoke. "Stella, you're making this sound so trivial. Like you're cancelling the milk order before you go on holiday, or something. Stella, you're walking out on a man who *loves* you," he said, trying to impress upon her the gravity of her decision.

"Where's all this coming from, Stella?" asked Frank. "It just doesn't make any sense."

Stella retrieved a packet of cigarettes from the front of her knickers, and then produced a lighter from a location very much less clear. She lit her ciggy, and then plunked herself down at the kitchen table. "The whole thing is a bloody joke to begin with," she announced, sucking furiously on her fag. "Lee doesn't even want to be with me, now does he?"

Frank and Stan shared a confused exchange of befuddled glances to each other. "What are you on about?" asked Frank.

"You've seen how people look when they spot us out together. They look at him, and then they look at me. You can tell they're thinking to themselves, *what's he doing with that fat freakshow?* It's obvious," Stella told them. "Let's face it, I was kidding myself thinking this would ever work. I mean come on," she remarked, looking down at herself. "It's only a matter of time before he buggers off with someone else, I know it is, and so I'm just speeding up the process and making the decision for him, is how I see it. I mean, I've caught him looking at other women when we've gone out, now haven't I? I'm not bloody stupid."

"Lee *adores* you," said Frank, shaking his head in disbelief. "This is ludicrous. Stella, I hate to tell you this, but all men will have a sneaky peek at other women from time to time. It's just our nature, okay? It doesn't mean anything in itself."

"Ahem," said Stan, noting his objection to Frank's claim.

"Not *all* men, of course. Fair enough, Stan," said Frank, conceding this one small point to Stan, before turning back to Stella. "But you take my meaning, Stella. Lee *loves* you, Stella, and of that there can be no doubt. Now, it's okay to be afraid once in a while, and we're all vulnerable at times in our life, but please, Stella," he told her, looking straight into her eyes, "I've seen how happy Lee makes you, and you, him." Frank reached out, patting Stella's hand. "Stella," he said softly, "Stella, the man loves you."

Stella wasn't having it, and drew her hand back, out of Frank's reach. "He's going to sod off the first time some pretty tart looks at him twice!" she insisted. "I don't need him in my life! I've been happy without a man for this long, and as long as I've got Idris and Guy in my bedside drawer, then that's all I need!"

CHAPTER SIXTEEN

Frank slapped the flat of his hand down on the table in a rarely seen outburst. "Right. This is rubbish, and you know it!" he said. "You want to know how much he loves you, Stella? Well I'll bloody show you, then." Frank stood, reaching into his pocket, where he retrieved a piece of folded lined paper. "I sat with Lee for over two hours helping him with his wedding speech, Stella. He's been working on it for weeks, he said, but wanted to get it just right. He told me he wanted it to be perfect for you and asked for my help, as he wasn't sure his English skills were up to the task. Here it is," he told her, waving the paper. "I made a copy for you to see this, Stella. I shouldn't really be showing it to you, but as you're not getting married, then I suppose it doesn't matter at this stage, now does it? *This*, Stella," he said, staring intently at her, and snapping the folded paper open, "This is Lee's speech he was meant to give, and in his own handwriting, no less."

Frank laid it down on the tabletop for her to read:

My Wedding Speech

Note to self: Thank everyone for coming and remember to tell Stella that she looks beautiful. Make sure trousers fly is all the way up.

Blow her a kiss

I'm not very good with words or particularly good at writing them down. I joked with my good friend Frank that I can just about manage the alphabet. So, that's exactly what I'm going to do today. These are some of the reasons I want to spend the rest of my life with you.

Blow her another kiss

Here we go, then...

A – Adventurous. I don't need to dwell on this one as it's self-explanatory. (Wait for laughter to subside)

221

B – Beautiful. Beautiful, inside and out. Seeing your lovely face warms the cockles of my heart. (Wait for laughter – I hope - to subside at mention of word 'cockles')

C – Caring. I love that you care about me. You smile when I do something well. That means a lot to me.

D – Don't. As in don't you take shit. You say it how it is. It's funny, liberating, and I know you'll always be truthful.

E – Enjoy. Enjoying each other's company. Even if we're sat at home doing two different things, I always know you're there. I'm never lonely with you in my life.

F – Friend. Because you're that.

G – Grateful. You're always genuinely pleased when I do something nice for you. It's lovely to be appreciated.

H – Honest. See letter D.

I – I love you.

J – Just. You're just perfect the way you are.

K – Keep. You always keep me on an even keel.

L – Light. You light up my life like a lighthouse on the shore - you're a beacon of safety, hope, and security.

M – My. You're my one true love, and I'm ever so glad I found you.

The rest of the speech continued onto the back of the paper. Frank picked it up and then read aloud for Stella's benefit the remainder of Lee's work-thru of the alphabet. "Zombie tits," he declared, once reaching the last letter of the alphabet, and then he neatly folded the paper back up. "Hmm, we may have to amend that zed listing," he considered aloud.

CHAPTER SIXTEEN

But when Frank looked up, he saw Stella sobbing uncontrollably. He gave a contented sigh, knowing the paper had done its job, as hoped for.

"Zombie tits is what he called me on our first date!" wailed Stella, unable to control her emotions. "What the fuck have I done?" she moaned. "What have I done??"

"I guess we don't need to amend that last bit, then?" asked Frank, more to himself than to Stella, really, as the answer was evident. He moved in for a consoling cuddle. Never did he imagine that 'zombie tits' would be the one particular line that would serve to convince Stella of the error of her rash decision and set her off in tears.

"So can we safely assume you want to marry Lee once again?" asked Stan, moving in for a bit of cuddle action as well.

"Of course I bloody do!" wailed Stella.

Stan snapped his arm forward. "Right. It's still early yet," he said, glancing at his watch. "Can we assume he didn't hear the voicemail yet, otherwise we'd have heard from him by now?" he asked, looking to Frank. "What do you reckon, Frank?"

"Seems like a safe assumption," Frank agreed.

"Well, then, Stella," he declared, "You need to get on the phone to him right now, I should think, and tell him that you were simply having him on, and taking the piss, as it were. He knows your sense of humour can be a bit... peculiar, at times, yes? So it's not too late to sort things out, is it?"

"No. No it's not," Stella agreed, dabbing at her eyes.

"Then what are you doing still sitting here?" he told her. "Go!" he said, with a quick clap of his hands to emphasise the point. "Go!"

"Oh. And Stella," added Frank, when Stella was just at the foot of the stairs. "You know when Lee reads his speech at the wedding, you have to make out like you've never heard it before, right? I want to see genuine tears from you when you hear it, as if you're only hearing it for the very first time!"

Stella smiled. "I promise," she promised. "And thank you, Frank, and thank you, Stan... you pair of great bloody wazzocks!" she told them, before disappearing up the stairs.

Chapter
SEVENTEEN

Jessie paced the living room, struggling to keep the nerves at bay. To keep herself busy, she'd dusted the TV several times already, and the hoover had been used that much it was in danger of overheating. It wasn't her first time down the wedding aisle, of course, but she felt like she was doing it all over again for the very first time. She felt like a young girl again, who'd met her Prince Charming. She'd never been looking for a new romance, reasoning that one marriage was more than enough, and was quite happy to remain single, with perhaps a role as a grandma should Dave find someone special. That, for a long while, had seemed unlikely to happen — though with Becks now on the scene, there was at least some hope at present in that regard.

Jessie was getting married in less than two hours, and she'd not done any makeup, her hair was tied back, and she was wearing an old pair of jeans and one of Frank's t-shirts she'd borrowed that she was particularly fond of. She couldn't sit at peace, and for a fleeting moment considered cracking open the bottle of whiskey that she kept in the glass cabinet by the door.

Meanwhile, Dave knew how important this day was for his mum. And, in Frank, he was welcoming in the most perfect stepdad that he could have possibly hoped for. Sure, the thought of his mum and Frank together — *together*, together, that is — wasn't one that he dwelled on overly much as it tended to make him a little queasy (and, as such, was something that Monty was very, very eager to bring up whenever the opportunity arose). Still,

Dave was happy if his mum was happy, and for her special day Dave had insisted on personally escorting his mum to the wedding at the TT farm, about a twenty-minute drive from her house, in a vehicle which he was to provide.

What Dave hadn't exactly clarified to his mum was why he'd instructed her not to get dressed or apply makeup in advance of arriving at the TT Farm. Dave had given his assurances that she'd have plenty of time to make herself look beautiful, but as the clock kept ticking away and with no Dave in sight, she was beginning to regret the decision to entirely trust her son to fulfil his promise.

... And so the lure of the whiskey bottle, at present, was proving to be too tempting to resist. "Just a nip," Jessie promised herself, twisting the key in the aged cabinet lock. But before she could liberate any of the amber liquid, however, a dull rumbling noise caused the crystal glasses on the cabinet shelf to vibrate and gently clink against one another. Curious as to what might be going on outside, Jessie glanced out the window as the intensity of the rumbling increased dramatically to an extent that she thought the Isle of Man had been subjected to a minor earthquake. "What in the world?" she muttered, pressing her nose up against the window. And then, once the source of the rumbling came clearly into view, "What in the world?" she repeated, but this time with more emphasis. "You've *got* to be bloody joking."

Jessie marched over to the door and swung it open. "David Quirk, you've got to be taking the piss!" she said.

Dave was stood there in her driveway, and he flipped up the visor on his helmet to address her. "Not at all. Your chariot awaits, m'lady," he replied, adopting his poshest voice and offering an awkward curtsy that nearly toppled him over. He took a step back, and with an introductory wave introduced the road-legal sidecar he'd been preparing with Monty in the lead-up to the wedding.

"You're serious?" asked Jessie, placing her hand over her mouth.

Dave nodded in the affirmative. "You always said you wanted to be a passenger one day, did you not?"

"Not on my bloody *wedding* day, Dave!" she cried. By this point, many of the neighbours were peering through their windows, presumably wondering if there'd been an earthquake as well.

CHAPTER SEVENTEEN

Dave patted the seat of his mechanic beast affectionately. "I was going to use our sidecar, mine and Monty's, at first, but what with all the qualifying races we're doing and such, we couldn't afford to have it tied up for too long in non-race-ready condition. Fortunately, however, me old pal Mikey came through and offered me the use of his lovely machine for the occasion. I've rigged up indicators, a horn, the racing slicks have been replaced by road-legal tyres, etcetera, and it's even taxed and insured, so I'm fairly certain we won't have any problems from the police."

"*Fairly* certain?" said Jessie, and then, "Heaven help me, where's that whiskey?" she muttered to herself under her breath.

"Aw, hell's bells," said Dave, "I'm a TT winner, and that ought to give me the right to ride a sidecar on the roads. It'll be fine!" he told her. Dave moved over to the passenger portion of the machine, fussing over his creation like Dr Frankenstein admiring his latest work of cobbled-together bits. "And this is why you need to get dressed when we get to the farm, if it's not obvious by this point," explained Dave. He leaned over to highlight where the handgrips were for her, and even the padded seat he'd installed. "But don't worry, it's very comfortable, Mum," he assured her, in reference to the seat. "I've had Monty test it out, and if it supports his lardy arse then it can handle yours very easily."

"Don't be daft, Dave," Jessie protested, "I've not got any leathers or a helmet!"

At this, Dave raised his hand, swirling his fingers like a cheap hypnotist attempting to conjure something from the air. It didn't conjure anything from the air, necessarily, but what this clearly rehearsed signal did achieve was to prompt a neighbour to open their door and appear outside.

"On my way, Dave!" said a rather excitable voice. Barry from next door made his way down the garden path, with leather suit, gloves, and helmet tucked under his arm. A white material hung down from the rear of the helmet, where it was affixed with Velcro, and wafted in the breeze with every step Barry took. "Here you go!" he said once he'd reached them.

"It's a wedding veil, of sorts," said Dave, as Jessie accepted the goods from Barry and ran the fabric through one of her hands.

"Thanks, Barry," Dave said to Barry. "I asked him to keep these next door so that you didn't see them and the surprise given away," he explained to his mum. "I just hope the leathers fit you."

Barry looked Jessie up and down. "They'll be fine," he offered. "I've seen your mum sunbathing in the garden, and I'm sure these will fit her."

Jessie took a cautionary step away from Barry. "I bloody told you he'd been watching me!" Jessie whispered loudly to Dave out of the side of her mouth, unconcerned if Barry could actually hear her.

"*Ehm*, right-ho, Barry. Thanks for looking after them for us," said Dave, politely indicating to Barry that it might in fact be a good time for him to piss off.

"I tried the leathers on," added Barry, for no particular reason, and without invitation. He rubbed his left breast. "They felt nice," he said, giving his nipple a gentle squeeze through his clothing.

Dave stepped in front of his mum. "Yeah, thanks again, Barry. We've got to get going now, so thanks and all."

While Dave's words were again polite, his tone made it eminently clear that it would well and truly indeed be a really, really good time for Barry to piss off right about now, and Barry finally got the message.

"Mum, we are absolutely going to get you a bloody CCTV system installed," said Dave, once Barry had headed up his garden path and back into his house.

Not long after, and with her leathers on and now a well-served whiskey on her breath, Jessie pulled the helmet over her head and slipped into her gloves. The improvised wedding veil flapped gently in the breeze like a flag. It was an impressive display. And on the back of her leathers, Dave had affixed a sign that read *GETTING MARRIED*. And, to additionally bring the point home, he'd secured a row of tin cans from the rear of the machine by string, to trail behind them and to further attract passing eyes to both Jessie's arse hanging out and a little further up to the sign.

"All aboard!" said Dave, clapping his hands together, after Jessie was all suited up. He took his mum's hand and supported her descent into the machine, but progress was laboured. The leathers were a perfect fit — as predicted by Barry in his own unfortunate

CHAPTER SEVENTEEN

way — but Jessie's flexibility had apparently reduced with age. She placed her bum on the padded seat from the open back of the passenger compartment, but then struggled to swing her legs inside. Dave dropped to one knee to render assistance, but it was proving to be a challenge to get her inside.

"I can't get my leg over," said Jessie, with strain in her voice. She tried again, without success. "It's no use. I just can't seem to get my leg over," she told Dave.

"You better be saying that to Frank tonight, also," Dave put forth. But his brilliant wordplay went straight over Jessie's head, and probably for the best that it did, actually.

"Sorry, I just can't work out how to..." Jessie said distractedly.

"Here," said Dave. "It's just a matter of positioning yourself correctly, lining everything up properly, before you... Ah, there you go, Mum," he said, as the appropriate body parts were finally slid in as they were meant to slide in. "Just remember to hold tight, and let me know if you fall off, yeah?" he joked, in innuendo-laden fashion. But, again, his world-famous humour washed over her, and it was perhaps just as well.

Once underway, Jessie's initial apprehension and reservations were allayed not only by the generous slug of whiskey she'd necked, but also by the fact she was soon having a whale of a time. Dave glanced over, periodically, to make sure she was not fallen off and bouncing down the road like a bowling ball— he was a good son like that. It was a surreal experience for Dave, riding a sidecar on regular open roads and navigating at a more sedate pace than that to which he was accustomed. His mum was, in fact, as it should happen, a pretty decent passenger, and he pondered trading her in for Monty on their next racing outing. She was certainly much lighter than Monty, and so that had to be worth a couple of extra seconds per lap.

Now, the Manx public are generally a benevolent breed, and this was amply demonstrated along Dave and Jessie's way by folk stopping on their travels to offer a friendly wave or those in cars offering an encouraging toot on the horn to what they could be forgiven to believe was the happy couple. (Though perhaps slightly misleading in presentation, Jessie and Dave *were* a happy couple, of course, albeit just not in the respect that most people were likely to expect based on appearance alone.) Dave even passed a couple of police cars travelling in the opposite direction, with the officers giving quizzical stares and perhaps uncertain if they should be arresting Dave or applauding him. Either way, Dave and Jessie eventually made it to the bottom of the Ballahutchin Hill, a long straight road leading down to the infamous and challenging Ballagarey Corner. Dave didn't go crazy, but as soon as they were in the unrestricted speed limit section, he opened the throttle for a brief moment, taking care to ensure Mum was still attached, which fortunately she was. Ordinarily, in a race, Dave would have the throttle pinned as he flew through the Crosby section, past the famous pub on the right and then over the Crosby Leap where the suspension softened, with some of the quicker outfits — and most of the solo machines — having their wheels clean off the ground. But not today, as this was a rather more leisurely affair. Still, he gave the throttle just enough juice as he dared, enough to give his mum a thrilling ride. And finally, at the end of it, Dave indicated left and, pleased that his wiring worked perfectly, took the turn that led down the driveway and to the TT Farm.

Once parked, Dave jumped off, offering a hand to Jessie, who rose gingerly, looking herself over to make sure she was still intact. She popped off her helmet, revealing a most enthusiastic grin plastered widely across her face.

"You enjoy that?" asked Dave, unsure if he was going to get a slap on the chops or a warm hug, but encouraged by his mum's expression, at least.

Jessie didn't often swear and when she did Dave was usually a contributory factor, but, today, it was with a positive intention. She jumped up and down on her toes like a sugar-fuelled child on Christmas morning. "That..." she began, and then shook her head, looking down on the sidecar, and then back to Dave... "That was bloody, bastardly brilliant!" she exclaimed, grabbing Dave for a generous embrace. "I now know why you spend all of your time, money, and effort on these things," she said, in reference to the three-wheeled rocketship next to her. "What a rush that was!"

CHAPTER SEVENTEEN

"This is it, mate," said Stan, brushing Frank's shoulder for any uninvited detritus that may have appeared there. The two of them looked resplendent in matching grey three-piece suits, with floral buttonhole providing colourful contrast, and with Stan deciding to leave the kilt he'd purchased back at the wedding fayre for another occasion. This wasn't really due to Frank's insistence at there being nothing too ostentatious, mind you. Rather, Stan had simply come to the conclusion that having his newly waxed bollocks exposed to the elements in the brisk Manx March air was perhaps not the wisest of choices, on reflection.

"You really have done a splendid job pulling this place together for the wedding, Stan," said Frank, stepping out from the kitchen door and onto the courtyard terrace, which afforded a splendid view over much of the farm.

A portion of the field immediately to the rear of the courtyard had been transformed over the previous few days. Fortunately, the Isle of Man weather had taken heed of the prayers offered up and had provided a cool but dry day the afternoon of the occasion, which meant the wedding ceremony could take place on the raised platform at the head of the marquee that held the onlookers. A dozen or so rows of blue velvet chairs were separated up the middle by a vibrant red carpet which led the way through the marquee area and onward, up to the temporary altar. The cheery vicar stood under a lovely wooden latticework arch — which had been covered generously in white, yellow, and red roses — engaging in good-natured small talk with those seated nearest to him. What had originally been conceived as a small gathering of close family and friends had most definitely grown legs, and in the literal sense as well, with the seats all being filled now with expectant guests.

"Stan, have you seen Stella?" asked Frank. "Do you know if she's okay?"

"Stella and Jessie are both fine," Stan assured Frank. "I stuck my nose in earlier and they were getting their hair done and makeup on. There was one minor complication, in that Stella had either forgotten or simply not bothered to shave her legs. But Becks and

Susie were on hand to take a leg each, so it got sorted out easily enough, I imagine, though I didn't hang about to watch."

"And Stella's not changed her mind again?" Frank enquired.

"No need to worry there, Frank. You can put your mind at ease, right enough," Stan told him. "She now knows that she was being completely stupid before, and showing her the wedding speech turned out to be a stroke of genius, I have to say." Stan paused, noticing a couple of elderly relatives who'd turned around to look admiringly in his and Frank's direction, and he offered them a friendly wave. "You do look very smart," he said, looking back to Frank. "In fact, I'm actually feeling a little bit proud and emotional as I look at you stood there. Any chance of a cuddle, you think?"

Frank smiled. "You don't need to ask, Stan," he said, collecting Stan in his arms and bringing Stan in. "Hang on, are you wearing my aftershave?" asked Frank, pulling away at the conclusion of their quick cuddle.

"Sharing is caring, Frank," declared Stan sagely, before swiftly moving the conversation along. "Dave looks very smart, also, by the way," he went on, deftly changing the subject. "Not an oil mark in sight, either on his clothing or his hands. He's all ready to escort his mum down the aisle."

"I'm a bit confused actually as to who's walking who down the aisle, now you mention it," replied Frank, squeezing one eye closed as he tried to work it out in his head. "I mean, if we're walking Stella down, the both of us, but we're supposed to be at the front with the vicar waiting for Jessie, then I'm not sure we can—"

"No, what you need to do is stand at the front with me, and then we'll run back to get Stella," explained Stan, jumping in. "No, wait, hold on," said Stan, getting a little confused himself at this point, "I suppose there's no point in us standing down the front in the first place...?"

Frank nodded. "Exactly," he said. "What say we all simply walk down the aisle together, you know? Down the aisle all at once?" he suggested. "After all, we're one big happy family anyway, aren't we?"

"Can we do that?" asked Stan.

CHAPTER SEVENTEEN

"We're adults, we can do whatever we want," Frank rightly pointed out. "And we're the ones paying for this shindig, after all. So why not?"

"Hmm, fair point," Stan admitted. "Only, wait, hold on, you're not supposed to see the bride-to-be beforehand, are you? Or are you? Aww, hell, I don't know how it's all supposed to work, these things, exactly."

"It's fine, Stan. I'm sure we can break precedent on this one occasion." Frank looked over his shoulder, back in the direction of the farmhouse. "So, we're certain Stella and Lee have kissed and made up at this point?" he asked.

"Must have. I didn't press the point with Stella. Figured I didn't want to open that wound up again. She seems happy enough, though," replied Stan. "Right. Anyway. I'll go and tell the guys it's time to make this happen," he added with a giddy grin. "I'll also tell them that we're all going to walk down the aisle together, yeah?"

"I wouldn't want it any other way," Frank confirmed.

"Looking good, Dave," remarked Stan as they passed each other on the cobblestone courtyard, Dave arriving in advance of his mum. "Five minutes or so and we're good to go. I'm just going to tell the ladies," Stan informed him, talking over his shoulder as he walked past.

Dave took up position next to Frank, towering over him, bulging bulk of a man that he was. Dave adopted a pose, crossing his arms, stroking his chin, frowning, and looking, overall, rather dour and severe.

"Looking sharp, Dave?" offered Frank, wondering what the whole deep pensive brooding schtick was all of a sudden, but Dave didn't break his steely demeanour.

"What are your intentions for my mum, exactly?" asked Dave suddenly and without preamble. "She's not knocked up, is she? Because, if you've gone and knocked her up, you bastard, I've got a shotgun in the back of my car."

Frank smiled a toothy smile, but then his lips straightened out and came together again when he saw Dave wasn't smiling back. "You, eh... you okay, Dave?" asked Frank worriedly.

Dave turned to face Frank directly, and he moved forward so that there was very little space between them. He looked down on Frank, looming over him, and, maintaining his icy gaze, said, "Are you using this wedding to muscle in on my territory? 'Cause let me tell you, fella, if you think you can weasel your way into my turf…"

Dave trailed off dramatically, leaving the rest of his threat implied by a menacing narrowing of the eyes.

Frank was dumbstruck. "Weasel my way into your *turf*? Dave, I don't even know what you're talking about. *What* turf?" Despite the fake tan Frank had received only a few days prior, the colour was draining from his face.

"If you think you can weasel your way into my turf…" warned Dave gravely… "Then you've got another thing coming, bud." And he narrowed his eyes even more than they were already narrowed.

Frank looked around for Stan. Or for anybody, for that matter. "Have you been sniffing petrol?" he asked Dave.

"I'm not sure you've convinced me," answered Dave, shaking his head in disappointment. He removed his hand from his chin and snapped his fingers smartly. "Boys, throw this no-good shyster into the back of the van!" he ordered. "His kneecaps have got an appointment with my cricket bat!"

Frank's face was now a ghostly white, and he looked about frantically in search of who these boys of Dave's might be and from which direction they might be coming. "B-but, I-I…" he stammered, unsure what precisely to say or to do.

But just as Frank was about to make a run for it and head for the hills, Dave started to grin, which grew to a very wide smile, followed by a belly laugh, followed by a slapping of his thighs.

"Relax, Frank," Dave told him merrily, chuckling away. "I was watching some dodgy gangster movie where someone was getting married to the boss's daughter. The guy shit himself in the film, so I thought I'd use the same lines with you. And it worked a treat!"

"Ah-ha-ha," laughed Frank, though it sounded rather more like he was choking and in need of the Heimlich manoeuvre than an actual laugh. And it was more relief for the continued safety of his kneecaps than appreciation of Dave's comic genius, really. "Very good, Dave," he offered half-heartedly.

CHAPTER SEVENTEEN

"I've given the girls a three-minute warning," Stan informed Frank and Dave as he joined them. Stan held out three fingers for the benefit of the vicar waiting patiently at the head of the red carpet, and also for the harpist — seated near to the vicar — who began caressing the strings of her magnificent instrument, to the immediate appreciation and delight of the waiting congregation.

Frank glanced around, looking suddenly lost and distracted.

"What's wrong? Everything okay?" asked Stan.

Frank patted his pockets, like one does when leaving the house, looking for phone, wallet, or what have you. "I feel like I've lost something, though I'm not sure what," he said, patting his chest. "Did I give you the ring? Have you got the ring?" Frank asked, in reference to Stan's best man duties.

Like every best man, ever, Stan returned a blank stare and then, open-mouthed, checked his own pockets in a faux panic-stricken state. "Don't worry, of course I've got the ring, Frank," admitted Stan eventually, after drawing out the tension for as long as he dared.

Frank continued to wrack his brain, checking his pockets once more, trying to work out what it was exactly he could possibly have lost, misplaced, or forgotten. And then in a moment of realisation that a young Kevin McCallister would have been proud of, it struck him like a thunderbolt the thing he finally realised was missing. "Where the hell is Lee?" he asked, darting his eyes between Dave and Stan, but receiving nothing but genuinely blank expressions this time in return. "Shit," Frank said, looking at the rear door to the farmhouse. "It looks like Stella is coming out now. So where the bloody hell is Lee?"

Stella's imminent arrival up the red-carpeted aisle to the altar hadn't gone unnoticed by the harpist, who now changed tempo, launching into her angelic stringed rendition of Mendelssohn's "Wedding March" to welcome the blushing brides-to-be, assuming the other bride, Jessie, to be not far behind.

"Tell the harpist to stop!" said Frank, looking to Stan, and then offering a reassuring smile to the entire congregation who'd now turned to greet the wedding party.

Stan jumped forward, hand in the air. "Just a short delay, folks!" he shouted, with the harpist rightly taking this as a hint to stop playing the wedding march, at which point she deftly switched back to a non-wedding-march type of arrangement.

"So where *is* Lee?" asked Stan once re-joining the others. "Does anybody know?"

"Monty was supposed to have picked him up, like, well, ages ago, I think," Dave offered.

"Ah," said Frank, relieved. "And where would Monty be at the present moment, then?"

Dave shrugged his shoulders. "With Lee?"

"Not helping, Dave?" remarked Stan, casting him a look. Then, to Frank, he observed, "So. We're currently none the wiser as to where Monty or Lee might..." But he trailed off as a car pulling in from the main road caught his attention from the periphery of his vision. "Wait, hang on," Stan said. "Is that him now?"

"That's Monty's car, all right," Dave was happy to confirm. "He certainly left that a bit late?"

Sure enough it was Monty, and Monty was hastily grabbing his jacket from the rear of the car as his passenger jumped out once they'd parked.

"What the hell is Lee wearing?" asked Stan, straining his eyes. "A green velvet suit, it looks like? What an odd choice. He looks a much skinnier version of the Hulk?"

"More like the Green Goblin than The Incredible Hulk, I'd wager," ventured Dave, showing off his impressive knowledge of comic-book superhero lore.

"Green Goblin?" asked Frank.

"Spider-Man villain Norman Osborn, and later Harry Osborn," replied Dave, grinning proudly.

Frank just shook his head.

"Well whatever he looks like," said Stan, "It's a peculiar choice of outfits, I think we can all agree."

Monty sprinted over from the patch of grass which was serving as a temporary carpark, followed a ways behind by his passenger, who appeared, for some inexplicable reason, to not trust the grip on his shoes and was staring down at the ground and moving at a much slower rate — the result of which being that no one could immediately see this fellow's face, though they of course assumed

CHAPTER SEVENTEEN

at first, fairly reasonably, that it must have been Lee. "I found him!" announced Monty, pleased as punch.

"Good work, Monty!" said Frank, slapping him on the shoulder. "Although I didn't know Lee was *lost*, necessarily, in the first place," he went on. "Only... Monty?" he added, before glancing briefly and nervously over to Stella, who was proceeding to their position and flanked on one side by Susie as her maid of honour. "Aww, doesn't she look stunning," Frank offered, and then, turning his attention back to Monty once more, "But, Monty? As I was about to say, who the hell is that? Because it's not Lee. I thought it was our Lee. But now I can see that it's not our Lee at all, is it?"

Monty looked at his velvet- green-suited companion, who'd just now managed to catch up. "It's the wedding singer," he replied, as if this should have been completely obvious.

"Dwayne Lovestruck," announced Dwayne Lovestruck. "At your service," he said, extending a hand.

Dwayne was roundly ignored, his cordially offered hand left in the wind, and with all attention promptly returning to Monty. "Where the hell is Lee?" asked Dave, in hushed tones, so as not to alert Stella. "Please tell me you've got Lee somewhere in your car? Where is he? I don't see him," he said, looking past Monty and over to the car. "Please tell me he's hiding in the boot...?"

"Do you not check your messages?" asked Monty, appearing bewildered by this line of questioning. "I've been phoning and texting all of you," he said, looking to each of them.

"We were getting dressed for the wedding and such. So I'd say we were otherwise pretty much engaged, yes?" replied Dave. "Monty," Dave went on, still in a whisper, but his tone ever more urgent, "Monty, where is Lee? Because I really don't want to have to go and tell Stella that we've lost him. Now, I understand you may have already outlined the answer to my question in texts earlier, texts which I haven't read. But, Monty, I ask again, *where is Lee?*"

"And since when do we have a wedding singer?" Frank added in.

"I booked him, don't you remember?" Stan reminded him. "Did Stella not tell you at the time? I'll tell you later if you don't recall," he said, before then homing in on Monty. "About Lee...?" asked Stan, taking a gentle grip on the lapels of Monty's suit jacket.

Poor Monty could feel the sweat running down the arch of his back and into the crack of his arse. "He wasn't there at the hotel like he was supposed to be," he said, holding his hands out in submission. "I went to pick him up on my way here, just as I was told. But he wasn't there." Sensing that further clarification would be immediately sought, Monty continued with his explanation, and was now surrounded like a referee in a particularly contentious football match. "Look, he wasn't in the reception area when I went to pick him up," he went on. "Right, so I went up to his room and knocked, but there was no answer. So I went back downstairs to the receptionist and had her call the room. But, again, no answer. So, in view of him getting married, she agreed to go up to his room with the key."

"*And...?*" pressed the three onlookers in unison, in shouted whispers.

"He wasn't there. Like I said. So I just assumed he must have ended up spending the night up here, with you lot," Monty told them. "And that's when I went downstairs and found this guy," he added, motioning a thumb over at Dwayne Lovestruck.

"Dwayne Lovestruck," offered Dwayne Lovestruck yet again, though wisely, this time, deciding to keep his hand unextended. "At your service."

"He told me he was the wedding singer, but that he'd missed the coach with the rest of them headed here. So... you're *welcome?*" said Monty, a little peeved that there was little appreciation to be had for him delivering up the wedding entertainment.

Unfortunately, the congregation were starting to fidget by this time. After all, it was March in the Isle of Man, with a cool sea breeze blowing through. There was, at least, a moment of interest for them as Jessie appeared, and this was accompanied by an audible cooing from the crowd as they finally caught a glimpse of both the brides. And the brides were a sight to behold, the both of them oozing a fair amount of sophisticated elegance, even with, and despite, Stella's patent leather hobnail boots on full display.

"You look radiant," said Frank, placing a gentle kiss on Jessie's cheek as she joined him. "As do you, Stella," he added happily to her.

"Where the fuck's Lee?" barked Stella in response, stepping over the compliment she'd just been given. She wasn't stupid, and would

CHAPTER SEVENTEEN

have obviously been expecting Lee to be standing next to her by this point. Also, as she was standing right bloody next to the others, she could make out bits of what they were saying even though they'd been whispering.

Like synchronised swimmers, Dave, Monty, Frank and Stan all stepped several paces away to a safe distance at precisely the same time and with military precision. Dwayne, who didn't move, was left isolated in the process, remaining the only one stood directly in front of Stella. Feeling the need to present himself to her now he was alone, Dwayne extended a cordial hand. "Dwayne Lovestruck," he said, introducing himself for the third time. But then a look of horror swept over his face as he recognised this as the woman who'd assaulted him previously at the wedding fayre. "I'll just, *ehm...*" he offered, pointing over to the location he was about to hurriedly carry himself — which was, not coincidentally, far away from within Stella's fist-swinging distance.

Frank raised his hand slightly. "Stella, can I just ask...?" he said, venturing forward a pace. "You did actually speak to Lee about the initial voicemail, didn't you?"

"You did explain to him how you weren't being serious in that first message?" added Stan. "Please tell me you did?"

Stella shook her head at precisely the same time as her bottom lip started to quiver. "His phone just went straight to voicemail," she said, struggling to maintain her composure. "I left him three messages and texted him. I just thought that... that..."

But, at this point, she wasn't able to contain it any longer, and salty water erupted from Stella's tear ducts as she simultaneously let out a pained groan — which served to drown out the harpist, and attracted all eyes from the congregation in her direction.

"Hang on," said Stan. "If Lee's bed hadn't been slept in then that means he didn't sleep in his bed last night, surely?"

"Way to go, Poirot," whispered Dave.

But Stan felt the need to continue with this line of reasoning. "Stella, you told him last night you didn't want to get married."

"What? Did she??" asked Dave, incredulous.

"Yes, but let's not get into that now, Dave," replied Stan, and then, to Stella, "Stella, if you told him last night that you didn't

239

want to marry him, and he then didn't sleep in his bed... well, it sounds like he's buggered off, last night. I hate to say it, but maybe he's not picked your messages up from today where you said it was all a mistake, or joke? And so perhaps, as far as he's aware, you still don't want to marry him?"

"I think the fact he's not here confirms that, Stan," suggested Dave sadly. "And I could have maybe gotten to that conclusion a lot quicker than you, no offence," he added. "Anyway. So then what are we going to tell *that* lot?" he said, motioning over to the guests.

Stella was getting herself worked up into hysterics, and Susie was left with no other option than escorting her back to the privacy of the farmhouse. With that done, "I don't mean to be insensitive to the situation," said Stan. "And I fully realise we're missing one of the intended grooms. *But...*" he continued, looking at both Jessie and Frank indicatively.

Frank took Jessie's hand. "We can't get married without Stella," he said. He took Jessie's other hand, and now looking directly into her eyes, added, "I'm so sorry, my love. But I just couldn't... in the circumstance... I hope you understand?"

Jessie nodded. "We couldn't celebrate our lives knowing what pain Stella was going through," she agreed. "Frank, I'm just happy to be with you, and if we need to postpone our wedding, then I completely understand. Now go," she said. "You should be with Stella. Dave, Monty, and I will speak with the guests and the vicar. To be fair, I'm sure they'll have a general idea of what's going on after hearing and seeing Stella anyway."

Dave's arms were crossed once more, with him deep in thought. "It just leaves us with the question of where the hell Lee is, now doesn't it?" he pondered aloud.

Dwayne Lovestruck stepped forward, like he had something valuable to contribute to the conversation, though, alas, he did not. "I presume I'm still getting paid?" he asked. "Only I turned down a gig in Harrogate to come over here, and I've bought this new suit," he said, fingering a velvet green lapel.

Chapter
EIGHTEEN

Patience and optimism were in plentiful supply at the TT Farm. The last thing anybody wanted to do was pull the plug on the day when there was, at least, the faintest glimmer of hope. Sadly, and reluctantly, Oliver the portly vicar with a ruddy face eventually had to make the decision for them all for he had a christening to attend to in the north of the Island. Plus, it was too cold for folk to sit much longer in the great outdoors. With the wedding off, Frank had suggested the guests at least make use of the marquee and the free bar, and whilst a number did, just to be sociable, nobody was really in a partying spirit after witnessing one of the brides-to-be being jilted before even reaching the altar. This wasn't something people were eager to celebrate, necessarily, and so coaches were called and people shipped en masse back to their hotels where they could eventually warm up and perhaps have a few drinks there without worrying about feelings of guilt for celebrating that which was not celebratory (as they might have had they remained at the farm). Frank wasn't entirely sure some of the older guests knew what was happening, as some attempted to throw confetti as they boarded the coach — and at least one was whistling the tune to the wedding march — but at least these few attendees were happy, if perhaps dementia-addled. Unfortunate for most of the guests, more generally, however, was that if the wedding didn't happen on this particular day, but possibly at a later date, then they wouldn't see it as they were all on the early flights home the next morning.

It'd been a pretty crappy day all considered, but Frank, Stan and the gang tried to retain a positive outlook if only for the sake of Stella, who was now holed up in her bedroom.

"How is she, Susie?" asked Jessie, nursing yet another cup of tea, as Susie entered the room and joined them now in the kitchen.

"Mmm, not so good, I'm afraid," Susie told them. "She's torn her dress to pieces," she revealed sadly.

"Should we... maybe call the police?" offered Monty tentatively.

"I'm not sure that destroying a wedding dress would amount to a jailable offence, Monty," said Stan, casting Monty a look.

"That's not what I meant," Monty answered, lowering his head, reluctant to say what he really had in mind. "Look..." he began, almost apologetic for what he was about to say. "Look, sorry, but the hotel is next to the promenade, is what I'm thinking. I don't even want to suggest anything dreadful should have happened, but... there's the big old Irish Sea in front of it."

"Shit," said Dave, entering in. "He wouldn't, would he? I mean, we *are* talking about him jumping into the sea, right? Rather than sailing away on it?"

There was a hushed silence around the kitchen table. "I'm sorry for bringing it up, and all," said Monty. "It's just if he thought the love of his life had binned him off the night before his wedding, you just don't know what he'd do."

Frank, who'd been in the other room, wandered into the kitchen to join them, phone pressed up against his nose, oblivious to the previous discussion. "I've just checked on my phone and I've got twenty-three missed calls," he said, as he sat down.

Dave leaned in to help, as he knew how utterly rubbish Frank was with his phone — in fact, he'd caught Frank trying to change the Sky TV station with it only the day before. "Anything from Lee?" he asked Frank, but then decided to just take the phone and have a look for himself, knowing it would be quicker that way.

Dave made murmuring noises as he scrolled down the list of missed calls. "*Ohhh*," he said, when apparently he'd reached one of great interest, capturing the attention of the others, but then he went flat. "Ah. Sorry," he admitted. "I was going to pretend Frank had gotten a text from a 'Slutty Susan,' asking if he was free for a

CHAPTER EIGHTEEN

bit of fun, but then I reconsidered, figuring it wasn't perhaps the correct time for it."

"You're maturing, I think," Monty replied, nodding in a sort of proud approval. "That shows great restraint, mate."

"I know, right?" said Dave happily, before settling back into the task at hand. "They're all missed calls from private numbers," he reported, scrolling through.

"And who owns the private numbers?" asked Frank, with naïve sincerity.

"*Ehm*, you don't know who owns them, Frank. That's why they're private numbers, after all," replied Dave. "Wait, hang on," he said. "There's one message here, a text, from someone called Bollock Chops."

Frank smiled, assuming a punchline to be forthcoming.

"No, I'm actually being serious this time," Dave told him. "See?" he said, holding the phone screen out for inspection:

> Frank, or was it Stan? I forget which of you is which. I told a little fib, so, sorry and all that. You two and your oafish Dutch friend have really been a thorn in my side. I said I'd just let it go and I meant it. That's what made doing it so hard.

Frank read the text aloud, and then rolled it over again in his head. "Who the hell is 'Bollock Chops,' and what the hell are they on about?" he asked, at something of a loss.

Stan pressed his hands on the kitchen table, as if preventing himself falling over. "Frank," he said cautiously, "Frank, you assigned that name to it last TT when you realised what a Grade-A arsehole the owner of that number actually was. I mean, is if there was ever any doubt in the first place as to what an arsehole he was, yeah? Remember?"

Frank closed his eyes, wincing. "Aww, no, that's bloody Rodney Franks. What's he gone and done?"

"Has he kidnapped Lee?" asked Monty, punching the palm of his hand angrily, and ready for any sort of action required, definitely the more violent the better where Rodney Franks was concerned.

Frank resisted the urge to throw his phone to the floor. "No, Monty, I don't think so," he answered him. "But I've got a sinking suspicion I know what Rodney was talking about, now," he said, sharing a knowing exchange of raised, concerned eyebrows with Stan, who appeared to have a good idea himself as to what Rodney was unfortunately on about as well.

Monty and the others looked to Frank expectantly, waiting for some kind of explanation. But then Frank's phone vibrated in his hand. "Sorry," Frank said, raising his finger to ask for a moment and to indicate he should take the call. "Another private number," he said, reluctantly placing the phone to his ear. "Yes. This is Frank," Frank said softly into the phone, afraid of what the caller was about to say. Because, whatever that might be, whatever Frank was about to hear, Frank suspected it would not be good.

Frank sat, dejected, listening with a pained expression over his face. "I have no comment," he said eventually, before ending the call and placing his phone on the table. Frank allowed his eyes to wander over to Stan. "I now know who the private calls were from."

"Who?" asked Stan.

"That was a journalist. And only one out of many who'd been trying to reach me for comment, if I were to guess. Rodney Franks has released the video of Lee to the press," Frank told him, confirming their worst fears had been realised. "That man is a spiteful, horrible, cockwombling bloody *bastard!*" he spat. "I'm sorry. Excuse my language," he said, looking around the table. But no one sat there in the kitchen, save Stan, had any idea what Frank was talking about, much less why it was something that would provoke such anger from him.

"Please tell me Lee and Stella haven't released a sex tape?" pleaded Dave, swallowing what could have been a little bit of sick in his mouth.

"No," said Stan, gravely, and then turned to Frank. "Frank, if Lee thinks he's been jilted, and the press have been in touch with him

CHAPTER EIGHTEEN

about this video... Shit, Frank, what if he really *has* walked off the end of a pier? This is not good. This is really, really not good."

Frank's twenty-three missed calls, as it turned out, were bettered only by Stan, who'd had at least fifty. It must have been a slow news day on Fleet Street as it appeared that every newspaper had column inches to fill and were only too eager, unfortunately, to sink their journalistic teeth straight into the neck of an entirely well-meaning charity that had done nothing but good for the community. And the scale and success of the charity meant to the papers that they were only that much more ripe to be torn down — something the British press were most accomplished at doing and in which they took great delight.

All thoughts of the wedding were thus put to one side, at present, and replaced now by collective concern for their colleague and friend. Their mobile phones continued to ring incessantly, and the temptation, of course, was to throw them in a drawer. But they needed to remain available and kept close at hand should Lee finally make contact. Stella, for her part, exhausted her contact list for people to call to see if they'd heard from him, while Stan phoned around to the area hospital and clinics. Dave and Monty, meanwhile, were dispatched to walk around Douglas to see if Lee was, perhaps — they hoped — merely drowning his sorrows at a local watering hole.

After a great deal of worry, anxiety, distress, and pacing of the floor, Frank, with great relief, raised his hand and motioned to the others. "You've got him...?" Frank asked, phone pressed to his ear, and collapsing into a chair. "It's the police," Frank mouthed to the others as they gathered around him. "Is he..." asked Frank, into the phone, with voice breaking, struggling to ask the question... "Is he all right...?"

Stella's hands were shaking as she retrieved another fag from her packet, ready to put the cigarette up to her mouth even though her lips held one already. "*Well?*" she asked, as Frank concluded his call.

Frank took a moment to try and compose himself. "Stella. Stella, he's fine," said Frank, to a collective sigh of relief. "He's been arrested and spent the night in the cells, but he's come to no harm," he told her. "At least he's alive," he said, taking a few deep breaths to sort out his rattled nerves, and saying out loud what everyone was thinking: "Thank goodness he's alive."

Very shortly thereafter, Frank, Stan, and Stella spent three hours in a sterile waiting room at police HQ, ironically, a few yards down the road from their house on the Island and a stone's throw from the TT course start/finish line. The police, for their part, were brilliant, for they knew how much great work the charity had done, both in the Isle of Man and the UK. And then eventually, the arresting officer — who'd been so compassionate to Frank & co — reappeared, stood in the doorway to the reception area of the station with a caring smile on his face. "Right. I've got someone looking for a lift home," he announced, before stepping to one side.

"Lee!" screamed Stella, lunging forward and nearly taking the officer off his feet in the process. "I thought I'd lost you!" she sobbed to Lee, squeezing the life out of him like a boa constrictor, and joined a short moment later by Stan and Frank.

"I can go?" asked Lee to the officer.

"You can," the kind officer was happy to confirm. "You've been released on bail, so you just need to abide by the terms of your bail conditions."

Lee offered a grateful smile, before turning his attention back to Stella. "I don't understand," said Lee. "I thought you didn't love me anymore...?"

"You didn't get my voicemail?" Stella asked.

"Yes, of course," Lee answered her. "That's why I'm a fair bit confused? Not that I'm complaining at the moment, mind."

"No, not the first, rubbish, one," explained Stella. "The second one I sent this morning, telling you to disregard the first one."

"Ah. Sadly, I was locked up here. So I didn't get that particular one, you see," said Lee.

Stella cradled Lee's face in her hands. "You didn't answer your phone. I left you a message saying I'd just made a stupid joke. But that's not really the truth," Stella admitted. "I only said what I said

CHAPTER EIGHTEEN

because I thought I was too fat and horrible for you. Can you ever forgive me?"

Lee's eyes welled up. "So you don't want to leave me, then?"

Stella shook her head emphatically, from side to side. "No. I want to spend my life with you!" she answered.

"I sat in that holding cell thinking about how I'd lost my job and my reputation," Lee told her. "But that was nothing compared to the hurt I felt at the thought that I'd lost *you*, Stella. I love you so much, my little Zombie Tits."

Frank and Stan gave them both a few moments together to sort themselves out. "Come on, let's get you out of here," said Frank, once he felt they were ready. "Oh, and Lee," he added, "For what it's worth, you've not lost your job. *You* are the reason the charity is what it is, yeah?"

"So you can get that crazy notion of losing your job right out of your head," Stan entered in, continuing Frank's expressed sentiments. "You're with us for the long haul, boyo, so there's no getting rid of us that easily!"

"Boyo?" said Frank, raising one eyebrow slightly.

"What, isn't that how the Irish talk?" protested Stan mildly. "I'm just trying to speak his language, is all."

"So it is, auld fella," Lee said, laughing. "So it is."

"You two great tosspots!" wailed a grateful Stella to Stan and Frank, overcome with emotion all over again. And at this point, they all made their exit, with Frank and Stan gently ushering the reunited pair out of the police station to avoid further distraction — a further distraction to the police officers at hand, that is, as Stella's keening was causing some worry and upset.

That same day, later on, when Stella had once again regained her composure and Lee felt it safe to leave her side for a moment, he released a statement to the press which broadly represented what he'd said to the police. He certainly wasn't hiding from his actions, but he wanted people to understand them...

> At a relatively young age, I found myself surrounded by violence, alcoholism, and isolation. I wanted to carve out a life for myself, so I moved to a new country to escape my

past. Unfortunately, my demons followed me, and I ended up homeless, penniless, and without hope. One day I snapped. I'd had enough of life on the streets and the prospect of a warm cell became appealing. I intended to rob the security van, not for financial gain, and certainly with no intention to harm anybody. As strange as it may seem, I didn't want the money, truth be told. That wasn't my goal, that's not what I was thinking, if thinking is what you could even call what I was doing. Rather, I just wanted to be safe and away from the streets. In a bizarre twist of fate, though, crazily enough my actions rather unexpectedly ended up preventing an armed robbery. And, thus, my life flipped over to the path I now find myself on. I have found purpose, I have hope, I've found love, and I have a desire to make the world a better place for others, others who may find themselves in a position similar to that which I'd once been in.

I've made missteps to be sure, make no mistake, but oddly enough I wouldn't change it for anything. For, you see, if I did, I may not have turned my life around in the process, and I would not have become involved in Frank Cryer and Stanley Sidcup's lovely charity. And it is through this charity that I've had the great honour and privilege of helping hundreds if not thousands of people, and will, by the grace of God, continue to do so.

I'm deeply sorry to those I've hurt by my previous actions, but in no way should they reflect on the fine, exemplary work that the charity undertakes. The integrity and good standing of the charity is without question. My previous actions should in no way undermine this.

Frank, Stan, and Jessie eventually retired back to Stan and Frank's house on Glencrutchery Road after what had been, it could certainly be said, a particularly challenging and emotionally charged day.

CHAPTER EIGHTEEN

"I'm sorry you're not Mrs Jessie Cryer," said Frank, raising his glass of wine in Jessie's direction by way of consolation. They were all sat around a fire, by the hearth, to warm their bones.

"Oh, I'm not worried," Jessie assured him. "There's time enough for that another day, soon enough," she said kindly.

"Ta, luv," Frank answered. "And, Stan?" Frank continued, "For what it's worth, you're the greatest best man that never was! Ever!"

"I was, wasn't I?" said Stan in reply, adding, "Indeed I was," to happily answer his own question.

"Cheers, mate," said Frank, raising his glass. But then, "Holy shitsticks!" he quickly added, slapping his forehead with his free hand.

"What is it?" asked Jessie.

Frank set his wine glass down onto the coffee table in front of them and reached into his pocket for his phone. "I forgot to tell Dave and Monty that we've found Lee! Those two poor buggers will have been searching around Douglas the better part of the day by now!"

"Hmm. The exercise will do them both some good, I think?" considered Stan, a crooked smile forming across his face. "Anyway. Cheers!" he said, having no intention of letting a good toast, or good wine, go to waste.

"Cheers?" said Jessie with a shrug, going with the flow, and raising her own glass in preparation of applying it to her lips.

"I suppose, what's a few more minutes going to matter?" agreed Frank, placing his phone down and taking his wine glass back up. "I'll leave the lads to their exercise, then," he declared with a chuckle.

Chapter
NINETEEN

The press continued to hound them for the rest of the day and well into the next. Today's news is tomorrow's chip wrappers, as they say, but it remained to be seen what the fallout of Rodney Franks' double-cross would truly be. Early sentiments on social media were generally sympathetic to Lee on account of the charitable efforts Lee had put in since the incident, demonstrating how someone can, given the right support, turn their life around 180 degrees and better themselves. One good thing to come out of the whole sordid affair, at least, was that Frank and Stan now owned the Jurby racetrack and had grand plans for it, ably supported by their new assistant management team of Dave and Monty — who were champing at the bit to get going. It remained to be seen if Rodney would have caused the trouble he no doubt wanted to generate, or to the extent he wished to, or even if the police would end up pressing charges of some sort or another at the conclusion of it all.

But, today, it was decided, was not a day for worrying about such matters. And so it was that the group found themselves enjoying a leisurely stroll along the old Douglas-to-Peel railway line.

Frank kicked out a loose stone, sending it tumbling merrily along the path in front of them. "Do you remember when we first walked along here?" he asked of Stan, who ambled along beside him.

Stan swung his foot at the stone when they'd caught up to it, missing it miserably by a wide margin. "Aw, bollocks. I never was much good at footy," he lamented.

"But you're good with balls in general. So there's that," Frank was quick to point out, not unreasonably.

"So there's that," Stan happily agreed, laughing, the chugging of his expelled breath, in doing so, leaving puffs of smoke-like vapour held in the chilly air — appropriately enough, given their present location. "Anyway, to answer your question, I remember it like it was yesterday, Frank," Stan continued, addressing Frank's original query. "And what a rush that was seeing the Isle of Man TT races stood less than three feet away! I remember seeing Dave and Monty rocketing past and feeling like a bloody proud parent," he said. "If not a nervous-as-hell proud parent," he added. "We've come a long way since then, haven't we, my old friend?" Stan asked. But it was the sort of a question that was in no need of an answer.

Frank and Stan were like mum and dad on a family day out, with the rest of the family way out in front, desperate to explore what lay beyond the next corner. "Wait for us!" shouted Frank, throwing out a firm wave, which was promptly ignored.

In the near distance, Lee skipped along with his arm around Stella, and with her trying her best to mirror his feet and failing miserably, causing her to stumble, but always rescued at the last minute, every time, by Lee pulling her upright again. The rest of the gang were further up, and almost disappearing from view around a bend.

"They look happy. All of them," Stan observed contentedly.

Frank nodded, and then glanced down at his feet. "I'm not sure wellies go with the suits we're wearing?" he remarked. "But it is a bit muddy, so I suppose they were a good idea."

"We could have taken the car all the way, but I just wanted us to have a walk there, you know?" answered Stan. "It's daft, but just nice to see everyone together on the railway line where our TT journey began. Is it daft, Frank?"

"It's not daft, Stan, not at all," Frank told him. "It's nice, I agree. And Edgar's going to be waiting for us there?"

CHAPTER NINETEEN

"Sure is. He's providing his chauffeur services," said Stan. "Do you like him, Frank?"

"I can't say I fancy him, no. He's not my cup of tea, I'm afraid," Frank replied, trying his best to repress a cheeky grin but not entirely succeeding.

"You know what I mean!" said Stan, with a playful slap.

Frank placed his arm around Stan. "I think he's a complete gentleman, Stanley, in all seriousness," Frank assured him. "And I'm genuinely pleased that you've found someone who cares as much about you as we all, the rest of us, do. I know you'll be happy together."

"Turn right!" Stan suddenly shouted, indicating where the rest of the gang should turn, calling up to them before they disappeared from view completely.

"Just after the gate!" added Frank, pointing furiously.

"To think we'll likely be back out here in a few short weeks, with the sun glaring down, watching the boys in the TT races," Stan went on, continuing their own conversation. "That's where we can dish out revenge on old Bollock Chops."

Frank's eyes widened. "You know, the TT almost slipped my mind, what with the wedding organising and everything! Oh, Stan, you know, that's really made my day thinking about that," he told him. "Come on," he said, picking up the pace, "Them lot are certainly not going to wait for two old buggers like us. Oh, and I'm not sure we're cut out for revenge, Stan. It's not really our thing. We'll get Henk on the case, though. He's certainly built for matters of revenge more than us, more well-suited to the task, I'd say. Oh, or Stella, of course."

"Not sure anyone deserves to be set upon by Stella?" suggested Stan. "Not even our worst enemy?"

"Fair point, yeah," Frank conceded, laughing. "That might well be considered cruel and unusual punishment."

Soon caught up and reunited, the group converged at the top of the lane. This was the exact spot that Frank and Stan had first experienced the adrenalin-fuelled spectacle of seeing a sidecar racing mere inches away from their faces at maximum velocity. As there was no racing action to see today, however, the rope that sectioned off the lane where they stood from the main Douglas-to-Peel road was absent. The traffic on the road today was rather more sedate, of course, with the occupants of passing cars witness to one of the more unusual spectacles they might be likely to see on this particular day.

"Give me a hand, Frank," asked Jessie, leaning on his shoulder, now they were all together again, as she removed her wellies. Once this was done, she took out her high heels from her handbag and grew what seemed to be at least a foot in height instantly once they were placed on her feet and she'd straightened up again.

"You look beautiful, my love," said Frank. "You too, Stella."

Lee took Stella's hand, proud as punch, giving her fingers a gentle squeeze. "Love you," he mouthed.

The two girls, Jessie and Stella, stood next to each other, with Frank and Lee taking their place on either side of their respective ladies.

"Ladies and gentlemen!" boomed the jovial voice of the vicar, raising his hand to bring the small crowd to attention. "I'm delighted to be here today and with the kind permission of the registrar, in what has to be one of the more unique venues for which I've ever had the pleasure of conducting a wedding. We're a day later than expected, as it should happen. But I'm overjoyed that we managed to get there in the end!"

Cars slowed to a crawl, their drivers bewildered by the sight of Jessie in her wedding dress, and with the rest of the wedding party in their various finery as well, all stood next to the main road in the middle of the countryside. Those passing by wouldn't have known the significance of this spot and the importance that this very location had played in the evolution of Frank and Stan's relationship with the Isle of Man.

Unfortunately, Stella's dress wasn't salvageable after being torn to bits in a fit of pique. Fortunately, a last-minute white dress was secured from a local boutique. And, once again, Stella's dress was complemented with her trademark hobnail boots.

Molly wiped a tear as the vicar continued with the service, followed only a short moment later by Stan's cheeks encountering some moisture on them as well. He always cried at weddings, did

CHAPTER NINETEEN

Stan, only this time he had Edgar to offer him an arm for support and a monogrammed handkerchief with which to dab at his eyes.

"You okay, Monty?" asked Dave, nudging his pal.

"Won... der... ful..." replied Monty, sobbing gently.

Tyler was as good as gold, stood with his mum. And Susie, well, Susie was just a quivering mess watching her best friend marry the man she, Stella, was destined to be with.

The owners of the little white house overlooking the lane peered down from their window, quite unsure who the crackpots were getting married in the lane next to their house. Perhaps they thought it was some sort of film production taking place. Either way, they eventually ventured outside and offered warm applause, along with the rest of the group already present, when the vicar proudly announced...

"And with that... I now pronounce you husband and wife," he said to Lee and Stella. And then, turning a couple of degrees to port, "And you also, as husband and wife," to Jessie and Frank. And then, addressing all four of them, "You may kiss your brides!"

Happy to oblige, Frank leaned in for a gentle, yet tender, kiss. Whereas, by comparison, Stella and Lee were all about the tongue action — much to the marked non-delight of Tyler, who didn't bother attempting to contain his feelings on the matter, and producing an audible *"eeerrrhh!"* to the amusement of all gathered.

Seconds after the vicar concluded the proceedings, Edgar had produced a picnic basket and, like the most accomplished host, champagne glasses were soon dispatched and topped up.

"You're not bothered that it was just us?" asked Jessie of Frank, taking a sip as the bubbles nipped her nose.

"Not at all, replied Frank." He looked around at those closest to him. "In fact," he said, raising his glass, "I wouldn't have changed today for the world." Then, addressing everyone, and glass in hand, he shouted, "Here's to love, happiness and memories!"

"Love, happiness, and memories!" came the collective reply.

"Oh, one more thing," said Edgar, raising his finger. He offered Monty a knowing wink, before dashing back to the farmer's yard where he'd graciously been allowed to park his car.

Monty stepped forward to offer an explanation. "When I went down to the hotel to pick Lee up, you see, all the other guests had gone home as scheduled. But there was still one person left. He looked a bit lost, to be honest, and I didn't think I could leave him there."

"Who the hell is that?" asked Jessie, straining her eyes, as Edgar made his way back with the lost soul in question. "He looks... he looks like an elf?"

Stan started to laugh. "Cheers, Monty," he said, raising his glass to acknowledge Monty's first-class effort. "That, my good people," Stan then told everyone assembled, "*That* would be the wedding singer we booked, a one Mister Dwayne Lovestruck."

And without further invitation, Dwayne, coming upon them in his green velvet suit, had burst into song in the middle of the Manx countryside, next to a bunch of crackpots getting married in a muddy lane, next to the most famous racing track on earth.

"Brilliant!" said Frank, tapping his foot along to what sounded more like the bleating of a hungry calf from the nearby field that'd somehow wandered away from its mum than it did to any type of wedding song Frank had ever heard, but with Frank loving it just the same and without even the slightest of complaints. "Absolutely wonderful! Cheers, everyone!"

The End

If you've enjoyed this book, the author would be very grateful if you would be so kind as to leave feedback on Amazon. You can subscribe for author updates and news on new releases at:

www.authorjcwilliams.com

J C Williams
Author

authorjcwilliams@gmail.com
@jcwilliamsbooks
@jcwilliamsauthor

And if you've enjoyed this book,
make sure to check out the other volumes in the series (so far!):

And more...

The Lonely Heart Attack Club series!

And *The Seaside Detective Agency*, and *The Flip of a Coin*.

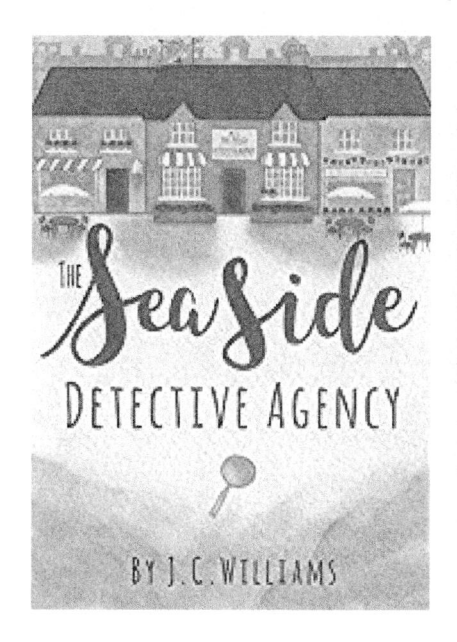

You may also wish to check out my other books aimed at a younger audience...

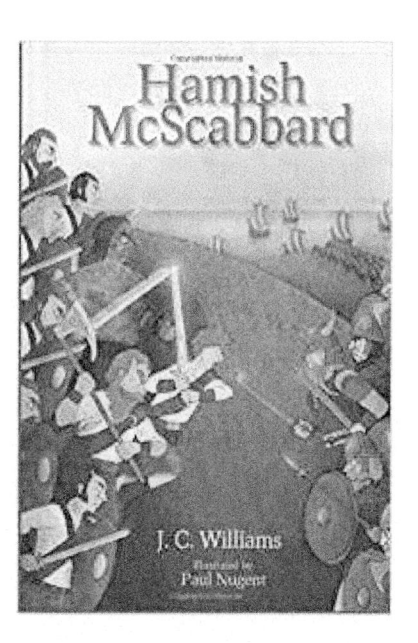

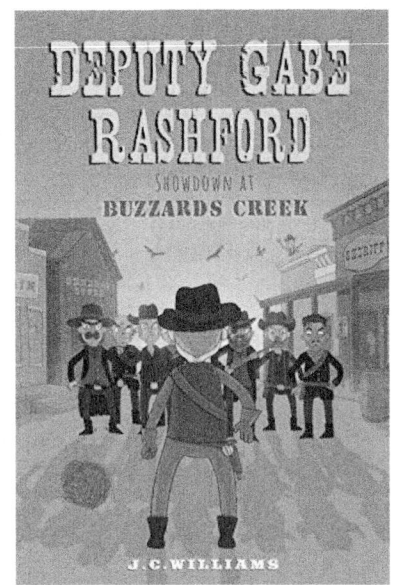

All jolly good fun!

And also...

For the *very* adventurous among you, you may wish to give my hardworking editor's most peculiar book a butcher's. Lavishly illustrated by award-winning artist Tony Millionaire of *Maakies* and *Sock Monkey* fame.

Recommended for readers age 14 and up.

Printed in Great Britain
by Amazon